Other Published Work by the Author

Parthian Stranger 1 The Order

Parthian Stranger 2 Conspiracy

STEWART N. JOHNSON

Order this book online at www.trafford.com
or email orders@trafford.com

Most Trafford titles are also available at major online book retailers.

Printed in the United States of America.

ISBN: 978-1-4907-1925-2 (sc)
ISBN: 978-1-4907-1927-6 (hc)
ISBN: 978-1-4907-1926-9 (e)

Trafford rev. 02/06/2014

 www.trafford.com

North America & international
toll-free: 1 888 232 4444 (USA & Canada)
fax: 812 355 4082

I want to thank Breanna B. Gibson for allowing me to continue to produce my work, and for publishing my work for this I thank you.

CONTENTS

CH 1

Isabella and the Colonel

Deep underground, in the city of Washington, in the District of Columbia, just outside of Andrew's Air force base, sits an old abandoned bunker network. Within this system, is the oldest continuous spy program. It was set up by the CIG director of operation, Walter Breem, AKA Walker, who then appointed, the Colonel. He would be in charge of foreign affairs. It used to be Davio, who was accidentally killed awhile back. Word had leaked that a former East German Agent was found, hidden away in the United States Prison system and was going to surface. Within the secret branch of the Oval office, a newly founded group was created to head up anti-terrorism, and in doing so, this East German Agent was its primary operative. However, it did interfere with what plans the current organization was doing in covert operations. In turn, the Colonel contacted a former CIG operative, named Isabella, to get involved and take control of this group. This group soon discovered the two were competing for the same person.

A bit of a quandary was occurring; the current spy network that was in place was failing at every turn. Their well-trained agents were dying at an alarming rate, and all by one man, that man, who carries the signature gun, only one of its kind in the world, in the hands of the most powerful person on the planet. Jack Cash lays in the middle of one of the largest, most complex conspiracies ever known in the United States; for they, the group is known as the Spy Game. It was conceived over thirty years ago. It was to keep an eye on those that needed to be watched, some were set free, some were tortured beyond belief, others were simply killed. This organization, did it all, with little regard to human life. Within this organization, is a hit team called the Exterminators. A group of well-trained killers, who were summoned to Washington DC to take on their new foe, Jack Cash.

A special meeting between Isabella and the Colonel, is taking place, as the balance of power sits in the corner of whomever has Jack Cash and right now, they do.

"Were in the middle of a crisis here, and I thought we were the only spy game in town, let alone the US. Walker assured me that we had the Presidental's seal of approval, however, the Speaker of the house was getting anxious over Walker's potential nomination to the highest office in the land, especially with our botched Presidential assassination attempt." Said the Colonel.

"Then it was the Vice President's turn, and we got him, and now the President turned around and appointed the wrong person. It was supposed to be Walker, but he was turned down, in favor of a woman, her name is Senator Linda Jackson, and why is she important, well she is the one who enlisted, Jack Cash."

The Colonel points to a bag being pulled in by two men in purple suits, marked by Haz Mat and placed on the table, in the decontamination room.

"So what is our plan now?" asked Isabella.

"Well first off, we need to send team number one down to watch over the new VP Linda Jackson," said the Colonel.

"Are you saying, we need to follow her around, with the Exterminators? I don't think that's a great idea."

"If I asked you to think, I'd ask you for something, maybe I should send you down there, I may promote Kimberly."

"Kimberly, she is your assistant."

"Precisely, and so were you, oh about five years ago."

"Yeah, but she does have Miss Harrison in her pocket?"

"True, true, you got me there, I guess I will look for another candidate. Make yourself useful, get our prisoner out of that bag, and let's begin the questioning."

"I got my own problems." Said Isabella.

Isabella walked through the door to see the two men still in suits, she said, "You guys can take off those fake suits."

"We can't, the contents is radioactive."

"What do you mean?" inquired Isabella.

"Touch him and you'll get the shock of your life."

"What are you saying, you mean literally electrified, how is that possible?"

"Well, Isabella, it was just like this, we got to the warehouse, Ox let us in, and showed us to the package, we went to grab his shoulders and ankles, and an electrical shock overcame us."

"So how did you get him in the bag?"

"Ox picked him up and placed him in the bag."

"So where is Ox at, and when will we let him take Jack out of the bag?"

"Well, he suggested, we'll keep him in the bag."

"Why's that," she was defiant, she crossed over and went to the bag and began to unzipped the bag, just then a stench came over the room, she placed her hand to her mouth, and began to dry heave, as she tore out of there.

"Hey Harold, what if we use the Haz Mat hose, and electrocute the package."

"Yeah, let's try and see what will happen, said Henry, as he pulls off a hose, from the wall, and adjusted the nozzle and as Harold turned on the foam, a quick second. They were both on the floor as the powerful hose, spun out of control, the two were slipping and sliding, not able to get up. The room began to fill with foam, the table was empty. Henry hit his head and was knocked out. Harold, held on as long as he could, then he went down in a thud. With both men down, and the hose was still out of control.

Isabella, came out of the restroom, only to see Ox, the 6-9 foot giant, who had been with her, the group's number one hit women, Protima, who was heavily armed, and dressed in all black, with a cape, and a mask.

Isabella said to them, "Hey you, we need your help pulling the package out of the bag."

"I wouldn't if I were you." spoke the giant.

"Why?" inquired Isabella.

"He is being watched, and he has some hardware that allows others to track him."

"Really, how do you know that?" asked Isabella, as the two were walking together.

"I threw a lead blanket on him, and I noticed his wristwatch, it was similar to the one we used in special forces." said Ox.

They both stopped in their tracks to see the room filled with foam, Ox said "He must have got out."

"Great, it will be my turn to kill him." spoke a loud Protima.

"No Protima, stay back, we need to see if he is still with us." said Isabella firmly.

"Very unlikely", said Ox.

"What are you saying?" asked Isabella.

"Simple, while you guys live down below here, you have no idea, what's going on up top side."

"What are you saying?", repeated Isabella, now on the phone telling someone to turn off the foam in the Haz Mat room. The giant waited with Protima, she was eager to get her hands on something.

"Tell me what's going on?" inquired Isabella, who said she had a team scrambling to get the foam off, while still talking with Ox and Protima.

"Well from what I can tell, a cleanup of agents is occurring, since after the Vice President was killed, some have said there is a conspiracy at hand, and the real target was the President, who by the way, is off in Air Force One. The buzz I got is that a new spy is on the scene, and every agent is on the lookout for him, even in town is Ben Hiltz, the west coast handyman, and now there is a newly created organization, formed up by the Vice president, Miss Linda Jackson. She has appointed, him, (as Ox pointed to the bag), as her first agent, so while you play kidnapper, and hold him down here, I'd say less than four hours from now . . ." Then they all heard a very loud "Beep, Beep, Beep" noise.

Just then, the bunker was rocked with an explosion, sending everyone diving for cover.

"Beep, Beep, Beep . . .

"Oh my God, we're under siege," yelled Isabella frantically.

"See what I told you."

"Shut up Ox, go in there and get our leverage," screamed Isabella. Isabella sees the Colonel, who yells at her, "Have you seen my assistant?"

With her guns drawn, Protima, holds her position, and said, "Go on, get in there, I will hold them back."

Ox went into the slippery room, to see that the bag was on the floor and open, he looked inside to smell the foul odor, and to see it was empty, and on the floor was the wristwatch, as Isabella joins him, and said, "Where is he at?"

They both look at one another, they begin to search, as the Colonel comes to the door, and said,

"We have been breached, by Black Ops, and its Colonel Jeremy Wright, we gotta to go, where is the package?"

"Not here sir" said Ox.

"Try the laundry chute" said the Colonel pointing at it. "Send Protima down it, you're not going to fit through there. Besides you come with us Ox. Isabella let's go." The Colonel, Ox and Isabella left the Haz Mat room. Ox told Protima to hop into the laundry chute. Protima comes into the room, holsters her guns and helps the two guys in the Haz Mat suits up. The others in her team were coming around as well, as they all watch Protima, go head first down the chute.

Jack was conscious and on the move, literaly. His right hand was all over the bleached blonde woman's breasts, as he was trying to hold on. She was helplessly dragging Jack along, she stopped to allow Jack to rest. She cracked open a capsule of smelling salts, he was still droggy. He was clearing up, as she then inserted a needle into his neck, to whisper, "Trust me, I'm on your side, I'm with spy club, and work for Lisa, this is an antidote, for what ails you. Above us is a highly trained force coming to free you from the enemy."

"What" said Jack, trying to grab at her chest, as she didn't put up much resistance, to his advances, his mind was clearing up, as was his strength. They heard a huge thud, then someone began to

5

curse, beyond belief, they kept quiet, only to hear a walkie talkie conversation,

"Yeah this is Protima, nothing yet, I really hit my head pretty good, but, our package is down here, I need a team, do you have one?"

"Meet us at exit 27 for a helio lift off, to section 2, over."

"Roger, when I wait one."

Protima turned her head around a corner to see several wet spots of residual foam, to yell,

"I'm on the scent."

Jack was on the move with his new companion, opposite the way Protima was going. The blonde led as if she knew the bunker system well.

She stopped to allow him to reach her. And said, "We can rest here, it's not long now, before we hit the river. Let me introduce myself, my name is Kimberly and you are Jack Cash, right?"

"Yep, thanks for rescuing me, now it's time I rescue you and get you out of harm's way."

Jack turned to see she was holding a gun on him and said, "Hands up, I know you spies can be tricky, but you see, I wanted you all to myself."

Jack stood up, to see her now in the light and said, "Sure, what were you thinking?"

"Well, for starters, that you will shut up. I got the gun here, and I want you to tell me how you killed my father?"

"Who is that?' asked Jack honestly.

"You know him as Davio Hernandez."

Jack shrugs his shoulders and said, "Well I don't know really."

"Bullshit, he went down to Cuba, to find you and now you're here, and they say you killed him, don't move or I will shoot."

Jack was thinking either to rush her or.

"I'll take it from here, Kimberly, lower your weapon" said a mean and ugly looking girl, dressed in all black, with two guns held out."

"No," Kimberly yelled and the other girl shot at Jack, Jack took the bullet in the heart, and went down, and rolled on his side, only to hear the two of them argue, as he began to unzip his light windbreaker, only to hear, "But he killed my father."

"What's going on here?" said a deeper voice.

"Protima shot, the package," screamed Kimberly.

"Excellent, now go over and confirm his death Protima, said the Colonel. To add, "Hurry up; I believe we have been breached."

Now fully awake Jack, Jack grasped at her, he held his hand at her throat, to pull her close to him, as she was bent over him, she could not say either way, but to hear "Alright catch up, we gotta go." from the Colonel, who held Kimberly by the arm forcing her along, allowing Protima to have her fun with Jack.

Jack held firmly onto her throat with his very large hands, as he was choking off her air and blood supply, enough to subdue her. She fell over him, to the ground. Jack saw the others scurry away; he rolled over on top of her; only to hear,

"We have located the target," yelled a man.

Moments later up walks a woman of distinction, Lisa; her red hair indicated her strength and command power, to yell, "Help Mister Cash."

Two assault Marines, went to Jack to see that he still had her firmly by the throat, they helped Jack up off Protima and pulled her away from him, while the other two helped Jack along. He was wobbly, to see his savior Lisa, for her and said, "Help Mister Cash to the helio, and take the other one with us as well."

Meanwhile, the Colonel and Isabella were scurrying out of the bunker maze, to a hidden helio, as their team was losing men by the minute, for her to grab his arm and said, "Who would of ever thought to use the Armed forces, I'd say were doomed."

"Come on, I'll show you how this is done" with that the Colonel pulls his 45. Caliber pistol, and makes a break for it, with Isabella he held her wrapped up with one arm, as his prisoner.

The newly formed Black Ops Marines watched, waiting for word, they watched the Colonel and Isabella get in the Helio, and it took off.

A Marine reported to HQ what happen and was told to assemble the bodies and head back to transport for their team, all other teams continue the search, as a Captain appeared to this group to announce, "We have the target in our control, continue the search for every person not connected with us."

"Yo Captain, what was this all about?"

"Sergeant, it is need to know basis, but I can tell you this, our platoons are going to make up a new division, were going to be called the First Division, and our new home is Quantico."

The Sergeant, sees the Captain hurry over to a stunningly beautiful woman, for which he said, "I'd hit that."

The Captain caught up with Lisa and said, "The Colonel and Isabella got away by helio."

"That is unacceptable, from this day forward, I want complete background, info on every man in this division, including yourself, stay here and secure this place, and all captured prisoners will be taken back to Quantico. I want a small detachment to guard Jack Cash," said Lisa, pointing to him. Two burly Marines, helped Jack out. Lisa noticed him stare at her, and said, "What are you looking at Captain?"

"Nothing Ma'am."

"It's Misses Curtis to you, and all the men, you are in command. Over, do you understand this?"

"Yes Ma'am." said the Captain, at attention.

Jack looked up to see it was Lisa, as a Doctor followed the group out to the helio, to hear, "So doctor, what's the prognosis?"

"He can travel to Quantico."

"Perfect, that's what I want to hear, instead of Andrews Air Base, where they are waiting for us."

The doctor approaches her to add, "We have given him a sedative and a toxic fighter, but we need to go now."

"Hold on, my Helio will be here shortly, ahhh there it is."

In the distance over their view was a huge warship, fully armed, quickly came to a landing on the grass, they all duck their heads. As they got in, Lisa helped Jack up , as the two fell back into a seat together. Jack was passed out, helped up by a Sergeant, newly arrived, to help Jack sit up. Then he sat across from them as Jack had his head fall onto Lisa's lap. The doctor went to Jack's knee, reached up to feel for a pulse and said, "It's shallow, let's get him to the hospital now, I'd say the Toxic fighters are kicking in."

Lisa slipped on the headphones and said, "Let's go to Quantico and step on it."

She lifted off her headphones and said, "How is he doing Doc?"

"This one is a tough one, he should be fine, heart rate is stable, and I can hold his head, if you want to move over."

"I'm fine, just monitor his breathing." the doctor looked at Lisa, to see he needed to back away.

"Yes Ma'am" he said looking at her, to give her respect, said the Doctor.

Jack felt comfortable and safe, as he smiled. Lisa's phone was buzzing, as she said, "Yes, we have him, but the Colonel and Isabella escaped. Place the base on lockdown, I shall be there, and hold on." She paused to speak to the pilot, and said, "What is our flight time?"

"Ten minutes tops Ma'am", spoke the pilot.

"Ten minutes, I want a gurney on the roof, with the best you have, and a perimeter set."

Lisa closed up the phone, as she placed her hand on Jack's head, to begin to stroke his face, thinking, "Yes, we need to get you support, if we're going to make this work, then we need to find out who the Colonel is connected to, before I report to Walter."

The helio slowed its descent to the approach, as it touched down on the largest building on the base, the helio was immediately turned off. Jack was hoisted quickly up by four husky Marines, placed on the gurney, and whisked away. Lisa saw the Sergeant and said, "From this point forward, you will stand guard at his room, monitor who goes in and out, and report to me, anything," she hands him a secondary phone.

Lisa's phone rings, she answers and hears, "The helio was blown up over the Hudson, recovery teams are on their way."

She slid the phone shut, feeling like she was getting a handle on this whole thing.

Meanwhile, the Colonel and Isabella, safe in their helio, was above the action on the ground, monitoring the action , as their own hit squads had survived the raid, and escape, arrived. The Colonel said, "Looks like the reinforcements are here."

Men in all black were mowing down existing Marines.

Isabella said, "Yeah, but they have the package."

The Colonel said "True, true but I have the serum, should they try it, and it will resist any information extracted from him. Until we get the right people to Jack, besides, we already have a team in that hospital, I just received word, he is at Quantico, General Hospital. Tonight we too will be there as well."

"Too bad for Kimberly, and Jarod, for them to get blown up, they were very loyal" said Isabella.

"Don't fret, there safe, over the Hudson, they jumped out, as we blew up the helio to fake their own death's, there on their way to Quantico, along with Ox. Once the team finds Protima, we're all going down there to finish this before we go to Vienna," said the Colonel.

An excited Isabella, exclaimed, "Looks like Ox has made contact with Jerod and Kimberly, and the three are on the move, along with the strike team." while looking at her SAT-NAV camera.

"Good lets land" said the Colonel talking to the pilot who took them to a rendezvous location, for which the Colonel led Isabella out and down on the makeshift landing spot. The dirt levels to the white limousines, with secret service looking men waiting, as the pair ran across the marshy lands, up to the road, a door open, and the two slid in, to see the CIG head chief, and said, "Sit across from me, you too," said Walker.

The Colonel spoke first," We got our staff intact."

"Good, we shall wait for the other three?" said Walker.

"How did she know about our secret place?" asked the Colonel.

"She, as your referring to Miss Lisa Curtis, is a friend of our new Vice president, Linda Jackson, who has asked the current President to take this program from me and give it to her."

"What about all the work we have done?" asked the Colonel.

"It's over, the whole cloak and dagger, is done, we at Langley will continue to monitor agents, and from now on, you're on your own, now get out."

"Wait, what about our current plan?" asked the Colonel.

"Oh you mean killing the package?"

"Yeah that one," asked the Colonel.

"Well the offer is still on the table. You kill him, rather than trying to extract information, then I'd say yes, you'll have your ten million dollars, plus a ride to Vienna, to live out the rest of your lives."

"Thank you, we won't let you down."

"I think you already have, now get out!" said Walker, as the two stepped out to see Ox and a white van coming towards them, the Limos sped off.

"Back up plan, Ox and the others, got out to hear, "Find some transportation, were going to finish this once and for all." said the Colonel. Then says to Isabella, "Let's go." As they took the van and left the three standing and watching them leave.

Back at Quantico, a team of specialist were looking over the nearly naked Jack. Jim and Brian, removed the gun, holster and wallet, the bullet stuck to the wallet. A guy with a box arrived to put on a new wristwatch on Jack's left wrist. Brian and Jim left the room, went up a set of stairs, to see Lisa. Jim said "Jack is ready for them to help him."

"Good, nice job, take his stuff to the armory, and Jim I want you to go to Jack's room, get it ready, with surveillance. I have two of our most trusted, Mitzi and Trixie, waiting in the room for him."

"Yes Ma'am."

Lisa watches the best doctors on the base work over her new project.

Ox drove another white van, he stopped as they got to the base. The base entrance was by the rifle ranges, Marines were all over the place. There was no line to get in to this side of the base, except a single gate guard.

The huge van was a perfect fit for Ox with his massive arms. The gate guard allowed him through. Ox drove the back ways, along well established back roads, to the north end of the rifle range, Ox stopped at the gate to the actual base, where several guards were waiting. There were four Marines in view, as one made a call. One

Marine got the Ok and waived Ox on, as another placed a tracking device in the wheel well. Ox drove off with the other 3, Jerod, Kimberly, and Henry who just flew in, down the main road to a stop sign, they cruised through that, not a single person was about, as they past'd the parade grounds, for Ox said, "Past these building get out, and scatter."

Just then a rocket was coming their way, all the doors opened, they leaped out as the rocket came in and erupted in a huge explosion and a fiery destruction. On the move was Kimberly towards the hospital and Jerod, and Ox went the other way, the gunfire came raining down on him, a maintenance truck stopped, a bearded man slid the side door open, for Henry, inside was the Colonel and Isabella.

"Take us to the hospital," said the Colonel smiling at the driver, who waited for the other, Jerod.

"How was the swim?"

"Oh you know, it was alright, Kimberly complained the whole time, you know about her hair and all that."

"Where is she at now?"

"She is heading to the hospital, then pose as a nurse, she will report when she is close to the target."

"Good, that means once we get up there, the package will be all alone, and then he will be ours." Said the Colonel proudly.

The van accelerated faster as bullets peppered their new vehicle, as it was going as fast as it could, up a hill, to the back of the hospital.

Jack laid back against the pillows; his eyes were closed as Lisa entered the room, the door closed, as she stood beside his bed, and said, "How are you feeling?"

"Better," said Jack opening his eyes.

"Do you need anything?"

"Nah, I'm fine."

"Let me explain how all this is going to work, from this point forward, you work with me, not for me, and not for some agency. You are free do whatever you want to do, in exchange for your work, and capture of a single person, I will pay you a million dollars in cash."

"You mean gold," asked Jack.

"If you like, do you want to work with me?"

"What does that entail?"

"What you're doing now, you know going out and getting yourself into trouble."

"I need a little more direction than that," asked Jack.

"Oh I see, so if I say, I'd like for you to take a look at the top 500 most wanted."

"I'd say let me see that list."

"So we are on the same page."

"Sure, would that mean I'd see more of you?" asked Jack with a smile.

"Yes you will, I think this will be a good relationship, I've decided to have some of my best agents near you, to support you", she went to the door, and let the door open, just as two girls came in. Jack recognized them as Michelle and Magdalena. Both girls stood at the end of his bed, for Lisa and said, "Here is your support team."

"How does all this work, are they here for the night, do they work with me, or do they relay your messages" asked Jack.

"Let's say, they are at your disposal, to use as you see fit. Yes I will relay messages to you, as you need them, but I won't tell you what to do, how you do it, and when you do it. But when you do, do it, do it well. Then you will have all the resources as you need."

"What now, do I, get to, get up, and go after those who took me."

"Nah, they are already here on the base, and I imagine, they will be coming to see you, trying to convince you to join them, however, they can't offer you what I can. See you only have one person above you, and that is the President of our United States. As for me, I'm only your partner, so to speak, listen, we will talk later, I will leave the three of you, plus you have your nurses."

"Before you go, I'd like to have my weapon back."

"I'll have Brian bring it back to you, along with your phone."

"See ya later, girls take good care of our VIP." said Lisa smiling back at Jack.

"Yes Ma'am", they said in unison, Lisa left the room. Moments later, mysteriously, a man walked in, as the two girls watched as he looked at Jack's wrists, then placed a new watch on his left, pulled the pin, as the watch face began to spin, extracting the current venom, coursing through his body, till the spinning stopped, using a syringe, he inserted into the side of the watch, and extracted 77 units of venom. He put it away, smiled and left.

Jack watches as both girls work their way around each side of the bed, to grasp each hand of Jack's, to look at him and said, "Here is your chance Jack, to see her breasts", teased Magdalena, as Jack felt tired and went to sleep.

Sometime later, Jack awoke from a weird dream, only to see a dynamite looking blonde. He was getting a focus on his eyes and realized it was the girl who had saved him, Kimberly. He then began to feel a fluid being streamed into his arm, he yanked it out. He lunged for her, it caught her off guard, his hands at her chest, he ripped open her white blouse as he landed on top of her, they were on the floor. Next to him was Magdalena, her eyes glazed over. Jack had his hand clinched at Kimberly's chest, as he used his free left hand to connect with her head, she was fighting back, as she began to yell, then scream. Jack used his left fist to pound her nose. A direct hit splattered her nose, as she went into a panic mode, as he threw one more punch, she went limp.

Jack got up, and grabbed Kimberly's hair, and pulled her along into the bathroom. As her lifeless body was pulled up next to the toilet. Jack left the bathroom and then knelt and listens to see if Magdalena was still breathing, Kimberly opened the door, Jack turned to see her with gun in hand, she began to shoot, one glazed his leg, as he dove over Magdalena's body and used it as a shield and as Kimberly emptied the magazine all the rest of the rounds found Magdalena's body. Jack lunged at Kimberly, he used his fist and drove it into her nose again, as bones crunched, only to see that Kimberly was now in fact dead, as she slumped forward, with her gun at her side. Jack went to Michelle she too was in a coma like state, he lifted her body up, and set her on the bed. With her head on the pillow, then he covered her up.

Jack was on the move, quickly thinking, then thought "Aah the girl" he went back, into the bathroom, to pull the small gun from Kimberly's hand, and found a couple of clips under her skirt.

Jack reloaded, and he went out of the room to the stairwell, dressed only in his gown. Taking two steps at a time, with gun in his hand, he went down to the lobby and tried the door, but it was locked. He used his fist and banged but not a sound could be hear. Jack went back up the stairs to the first floor and tried that door, same thing, it was locked. Same with the second, third, and fourth floor, he climbed up to the top of on the tenth floor. When he tried that door, it opened. Up a set of stairs, up to a landing sat a helio, Jack went to it, slid in, and looked at the controls. He had no idea, what to do, he looked around, realizing he was trapped, so he slipped back out. He went down the stairs to the elevator, hit the down button and the doors opened, he hit four, the door closed, and went down. Arriving on the fourth floor, the doors opened, and Jack got off, went down the hallway to his room, pulled the sheet back to reveal a sleeping Michelle, then got an idea, and went around, and picked her up, and then carried her to the next room. He opened the door, to see it was empty, and laid her on the bed, and took a blanket to cover her up. Jack left the room, eased back into his bed, and rested. A little time later, he opened his eyes to hear his door open and to see it was Brian, with a box, and his holster, for which Jack said, "Brian, can you help me out?"

"Yes what do you need?"

"There are two girls in the bathroom, can you take them out?"

"Sure hold on" said Brian, he went into the bathroom, thinking one thing, then coming up with something else, as he looked on, then looked back at Jack. Brian gagged, then he began to vomit, his face was white and he left the room quickly.

Jack was exhausted, and laid back in his bed and was out. He felt a mask over his mouth, his eyes opened to see a host of people, a team of doctors who said, "He is awake and out of the coma, call Miss Curtis immediately."

Jack's eyes were going a mile a minute, back and forth, the more he realized it was all a dream. Jack calmed down, enough to stabilize his breathing, then he calmed down.

Outside, the base was under attack, men and women were running all about. A single lone figure stood beside the entrance of the hospital, watching as though it was a scene right out of Iraq, gunfire was all around, just as a van drove up, stopped, as the door slid open, a silvered hair man stepped out, along with a black woman. Damien didn't hesitate and sprang into action. He pulled his 9mm and lunged out and knocked the Colonel down, turned and punched Isabella squarely in the jaw.

Damien yelled, "Get out of the van and come around here, you two over there."

Military police swarmed them taking the Colonel and Isabella into custody, as the Colonel asked, "Who are you?"

"Just a driver", said Damien.

"But how did you know who we are?"

"Intel", as he pulls out a four square picture, showing his picture and who he was, to add, "It was courtesy of Walter Breem, Chief CIG."

"It figures," said the Colonel, on his way inside. Damien followed them to insure their arrest, and to stand guard.

In walked the new spy chief, Lisa Curtis, her blazon red hair was evident, as she waved everyone out. Jack had his mask taken away, the doctors took a step back to allow her room.

She came to him, took his hand in hers and said, "Thank God you're alright, your healing fast, how are you, do you need anything?"

"Company."

"Of course, that is why I'm here, as we speak, do you remember Linda Jackson?"

"Yes, I guess" said Jack, feeling the softness of her hands, and thinking of what it would be like to go even further, she was talking and he was day dreaming.

"Do you want to do that?" she asked honestly.

"Sure why not?" said Jack trying to focus on what she was saying, he began to feel his hands warm up, as the passion was increasing for him to hear her say, "Alright tomorrow morning."

With that, she gets up, she bends over and kisses Jack on the cheek, and said, "You didn't hear a word I said did you?"

"Nah, I was just."

"If that is what you really want, I'll give it to you, but I want you to have a clear and rational mind when that occurs."

"Alright" said Jack as if the doctors could not wait any longer, they passed by Lisa to reattach the oxygen mask, as Jack fell fast asleep.

Lisa went out in the hall to see her two trusted support friends and asked," What is the status?"

"Well great news, Damien caught the Colonel and Isabella, and a guy named Jerod." said Trixie.

"We do know from Walker, the Intel was right on, and that two hit teams are headed this way. In addition to the Colonel and Isabella, there should be more" said Mitzi.

"I have a new assignment for both of you" said Lisa.

"Sure, fire away" said Mitzi.

"From this list, I want the top twenty of our best recruits to fly in tonight, so that I may present one to Jack as his new assistant."

"What about us? Her and I, would like that job" asked Mitzi.

"Where did that come from? You both are my finest support agents."

"We were talking about it, and thought it would be a nice change of pace, working to support a spy, especially as good looking as him, you know I'm a RN, and that if he gets shot I can care for him." Said Mitzi.

"I don't know, I'll have to think about that one, what about my liaisons at the pentagon?"

"I know an attorney who would love that position?"

"Who is that, do I know them?"

"It's Erica Meyers, she is well qualified, and may be our best connections when Jack starts violating other people rights," said a confident Mitzi.

"Yeah maybe your right, having you close by and out in the field could be to our advantage, especially with both of your knowledge's, and keep a leash on Jim, who seems as anxious as you both."

"Any ideas on who else?" spoke up Trixie.

"That's just it, there is no one else, and I don't know if Jack is even receptive to you both."

"Are you letting him decide or did you just assign?" asked Mitzi.

"Listen girls, there is no guidebook here, I can't say if four or ten, will be his support agents, I don't even know what roles they or you will play, let alone travel, this is all totally up to Jack. There are so many variables here, what if he wants to sleep with you, both?"

"Ah he won't sleep with us," both girls said giggly.

"That's just it, that's what he was thinking with me" said Lisa coyly.

"No, no, you got us all wrong, we will let him sleep, but we will take care of any of his needs and fulfill every dream or fantasy he ever had."

"Oh."

"Don't forget, we were with Ben for an awhile, till we took over operations."

"Is that what he wanted?"

"Isn't that what all men want, besides he wanted to marry us both, if you get my drift", said Mitzi.

"I think I do, alright consider you two on the support team."

"You won't be disappointed," said Mitzi. Both girls had a smile on their faces.

"But, I want you two, to get those other girls out here for an interview" said Lisa, as she was walking away from Mitzi, to hear, "Are you coming?"

"Nah, I'd rather stay here and guard him through the night." said Mitzi.

"Really, I thought I told you to start tomorrow?" said Lisa who stopped, to decide if she was making the right decision or not.

"And who will watch over him tonight?" asked Mitzi.

"Why the doctors and nurses."

"And who are watching over them?"

"I guess you are."

"Thank you", said Mitzi.

The two waited for the elevator, when Trixie said, "What about a pilot, a driver, and personal bodyguard?"

The doors open, to see a heavily armed Marine exit, and stand guard as they got on, for Lisa to say, "Do you have someone in mind?"

"Sure how about Damien?"

"You're not suggesting, my driver Damien are you?" asked Lisa looking at her.

"Yes matter of fact I am, he is a certified pilot, and personal bodyguard."

"I know I handpicked that one, what is your angle?"

"None, but you know that he was the one who took out the threat, so I thought he would be a good candidate, to help out." asked Trixie.

"Alright, I'll consider it, make sure all those girls are here tomorrow morning."

"Yes Ma'am" said a smiling Trixie, who waved at Damien, as he got into the large SUV, to take his seat next to Lisa, and said, "Where too?"

"General's quarters, I'll be there, nice job, you know", she said closing up her phone, only to look at Damien, and said, "Were you trying to get my attention?"

"No Ma'am, just eliminating a possible threat."

"Someone brought it to my attention, that you wanted to go work for our new spy, is that true?"

"Nah, I don't know what you're talking about?"

"Alright I will allow it under one condition", she looks at him, while he drives with a smile on his face, it faded, as he heard, "That you have no physical or emotional contact with any of those girls assigned to him, do you understand this?"

His frown signaled his displeasure with that ultimatum, then said, "Sure, I don't know anyone on his team."

"You do know that I know of your affair with Trixie, the late nights and after hours get together."

"Oh her, is she part of this team?"

"Yeah, you know who I'm talking about, Trixie, you know my assistant who goes by the name of Trixie."

"Honest it wasn't my idea."

"Please don't patronize me, you could just as fast be back in the program where I found you." said Lisa.

"I'm sorry, you're right, from this day forward, it will be over."

"How serious are you?"

"Oh just casual, here and there, you know working close by and all that."

"You know it's not that I don't accept you too together, it's just the fallout after it's over, between you too." said Lisa.

"You don't have to worry about that, I remember what you said when you first hired me." I take that very seriously, it was that my role is that of supporter for you, I'd take a bullet for you, or defend you to the very end, as I told Trixie. Her and I are just friends and that's it" he said biting his lip, hiding his true feelings.

The SUV came to her new quarters, she said, "Tomorrow morning 0800, tell her that I want all those girls to be ready."

"Will do, Ma'am." said Damien with a smile.

Damien watched her shut the door, he saw secret service all over the place, as he was waved on, he knew that their era was over, and now he had someone new to defend. As he drove to his girlfriend's place, he parked the SUV, he got out and sensed something in the shadows. He didn't hesitate pulled his weapon, and ran towards the shadow, it moved, as did Damien, he was on a full run, in between the buildings. Out from the shadows stood a giant man, Damien dived as rounds peppered his current position, he rolled and fired, the man was gone. He followed, he pulled his phone to call, Lisa, and she answered and said, "Yes Damien."

"I'm facing something by the barracks, heavily armed, shots fired" as rounds buzzed his position, then all of a sudden he was lifted up, and thrown, he lost his phone and gun, as he hit face first on the chain link fence, he laid back, he was out.

Ox was running towards the hospital.

Trixie, opened the front door to see the black SUV, but was wondering where was Damien?"

She called out his name, looked around, and then went back inside to her desk.

Lisa stood in the hallway of the marine barracks and said "I need a driver, choose your best to take over."

"How about Ramon, he will be back, soon."

"Yes, that will be fine."

Moments later Ramon appeared, and said, "Ready Miss Curtis."

"Take several men to the hospital, and double, triple the security, I feel the attack may happen tonight." said Lisa.

"The Delta force commander is in the waiting bay, shall I let them go after them." said the Officer of the day.

"Yes, but I want prisoners, no shoot to kill, you hear me," said Lisa.

"Yes Ma'am."

The taller man assigned his most trusted to go inside, then dispatched his others, as he went down a corridor. He then went down some steps to a tunnel system. Along a walkway were heavily armed men, dressed in heavy camouflage. He saw the Captain, simply known as Danger, who turned with a gnarl on his face, he waited until the Major said, "Danger, it is all yours, aim to wound, capture, zip tie, and capture.

"How many?"

"Our Intel says, The Colonel and Isabella are being held in the basement of the hospital, there are four strike teams of five, and two on their own."

"Thanks, we will neutralize the insurgents."

The Captain hands Danger a cell phone, and said "Hit and hold down two, it goes to Miss Curtis, notify her when the base is secure."

The two shook hands, as Danger barked out orders, the men stood then filed down a dark passage way, he turned and went back up stairs. As he entered into the control room, he took his seat next to his two officers, multiple screens showed the entire grounds.

"Zoom the camera on the black SUV."

The Captain stood and looked at the monitor to see a figure on the ground and said, "Is that agent Damien? Can you get face recognition?"

"Yes sir, your right, its agent Damien, he is down and out."

"How did he get over that ten foot fence, can you roll back the tape?"

"Sorry, it's not fixed and were at a live feed."

"Can you send the MP's to pick him up?"

"Yes sir."

The Captain watched as the forty plus Delta force, went building to building, flushing out the enemy, one by one, those in black were going down, as quick as it occurred it was ending. As night turned into morning, the Delta force was still in sweep mode, collecting twenty three prisoners, with two still at large. As the sun broke Delta force retreated into hiding and holding their positions.

CH 2

The New Team

Day broke, the sun blazed through the partly opened drapes. Jack awoke, to see a hot brunette reading, her plunging neckline was showing off her assets, she had a cute smile, nice complexion, she was cute. Jack felt the urge, so he moved, enough to alarm Mitzi, to get up and said, "Hold on, Jack, my name is Mitzi, I'm here to help you out."

She met him at the side of the bed, as he slid off, for her and said, "Put your arm around my neck, I'll help you up."

She helped him up. As he slid his hand across her super soft neck, his hand rested on her right breast, and cupped it, as the two walked to the bathroom, she helped him to sit down and said "When you're done just call me", she left, slightly leaving the door open, as she stood guard, only to see a new nurse, enter, a blonde with a long oblong face and bleached blonde hair, immediately a red flag over came her and said, "Who are you?"

"Shift change, my name is Elle, said Kimberly. She wore a huge smile.

"You're early; the shift usually occurs at ten o'clock, what did you need?"

"To give Mister Cash a shot?" said Kimberly.

"Of what?" inquired Mitzi?

"And you are?"

"His personal nurse, so what are you giving him?"

23

Kimberly, hid, a syringe behind her back and said, "A vitamin B booster."

"He doesn't need it, as Mitzi pulled out her pistol to point it at her, she added, "Set the syringe down, and place your hands behind your back, Kimberly surrendered the syringe, as she realized Mitzi wasn't going to play around. She did as she was told, as Mitzi zip tied her small wrists, in the front, Mitzi then led her to her chair to sit down. She knelt and tied her ankles, cinching them tight, while Jack flushed, he tried to get up, using the rail, and he looked up to see Mitzi face to face. She helped him up, this time he was on her right side as he slid his hand across her neck and onto her other breast, the two walked back to his bed, he flexed his foot, then noticed a hot blonde in a nurses outfit and said, "Hi, how are you", as Jack stood at the railing.

Mitzi backed out and said, "Allow me to change your bed, talk with Elle, she came up early to visit you."

Jack smiled at her, while Mitzi, stripped the bed, she adjusted the pad and pulled out new sheets and a blanket. She quickly changed the two pillow cases, as Kimberly watched the nurse work.

Kimberly was no nurse, as she looked at the target, her intense makeup hid her face, she knew he was in good hands. And knew that she would have killed her, so she sat in silence, while Jack stared at her, to see the bed was sharply made. Mitzi came around, to unfold the sheet, and lowered the rail for Jack. She helped him in, then covered him up, and propped up the pillow for him, she asked, "Is everything alright?"

Jack put his arm over his eyes to block out the light.

Mitzi went to the light switch to dim the above lights, and then went over to the sofa to sit. She then got on the phone to get someone there to get her prisoner, all the while watching Kimberly.

Line of taxi cabs and private cars lined the entrance to the base. As the large gates closed and MP's were still stationed at the large gates, a woman in a lead cab got out and said, "Do you know when the base will be open?"

"As soon as the all clear is given, hold on."

The guard went in, to announce over the speaker, the base is now secure, we will be opening the gates shortly."

The gates opened, and the passes were shown, ID's were checked, and two men with mirrors were there to check for devices Each cab took off to go on to the base. The line thinned of the cabs, as all twelve girls, were directed to a lone building. Next to the lone building sat a sleek black SUV. Each of the cabs opened up, the girl exited, each having a light luggage. Instantly names were flowing around as a Sergeant called out the names. Some were extremely young, but it was evident they all have one thing in common. Each of them had extreme beauty, which was evident.

Behind that building, the dew on the morning was all over Damien as he awoke, realizing he got knocked out, he sat up to clear his head. He got up and looked at the secure fencing, he climbed over the fence carefully, missing the heavy barbs. He saw his phone and then his gun, he checked his watch to see it was fifteen to eight Now Damien was on the move to his job, and to the SUV, he got in, and backed it up, and then drove it to his boss and waited, he was on time. Lisa was at the door at her building waiting for the doors to be unlocked, then a sergeant held the door open for her. She waited, then went out. The passenger door was open, as she saw it was her normal driver, waiting for her. She said "Ramon, take the driver's seat, and relieve Damien, he can sit in the back."

Trixie, awoke and dressed then grabbed her clipboard, with the directory of girls, then a thought occurred to her, maybe, Damien was over there last night with the girls."

Trixie stepped out to see the black SUV and Lisa, was saying something, as she met up with Trixie for her and said, "All here and accounted for?'

"Perhaps," said Trixie, in a dejected tone.

"Cheer up, didn't you have fun with your man last night?"

Trixie just watched her pass by, then followed her in, as Lisa held onto a small notebook. She then rang the doorbell, the door opened to screams, then silence, as Lisa stepped in, and said, "All right ladies gather around, when I call your name, line up. Number one, Esmeralda, Joana, Erin, Jen, Lianna, Manicka, Freya, Andrea,

Darlene, Halyn, Monroe, Carrie, Dylan, Jill, Allison, Erica, Morgan, Lysandra, Kosta and Audris, fine your all here. Now bend the line around, each of you were selected by those who feel you have what it takes, to become part of our team. Your mission, if you're chosen, is to be close in, and provide services to the one you're helping. You will report, assist and defend, who you're helping, this is a two way street, if you don't like the one we selected for you to help, on your way out, just say so."

A girl raised her hand, and said, "What do you mean, personal services?"

"I'm sure you can figure that out."

"Then you can count me out."

"Fine, your Jen, anyone else?" she looked them over, to see her grab her stuff, she paused and said, "May I at least have a chance to visit this guy? It is a guy, isn't it?"

"Yeah, it's a guy, who is married, he is a family man," said Lisa, as others changed their tune, for her and said, "I'll be honest with all of you, this job is going to be dangerous, yet a good payday, however, you will be working 24-7 for the next two years or so. You will be his constant companion, are we ready to go over there." as they all watched Jen leave.

The girls nodded, as Lisa went out to the parade grounds where Delta force had the enemy assembled. Some of the girls shield their eyes, whereas others were outright staring as they walked and made it to the hospital, Ramon, brought the black SUV over into position, as Damien got out to hear Trixie say, "What is going on here?"

"Don't you know?"

"Nah, I spent the night on my back."

Trixie went by rapidly, as the girls filed in, Lisa took the first five and Trixie with her up, as Damien was in the lobby with the other girls, he was gawking at them, much too a few stares of contempt, and disgust.

Lisa got out first to and said, "Line up along the wall, as I call in the first person."

Lisa and Trixie went in to see Mitzi sitting on a chair, Jack was watching TV, and had just finished breakfast., Lisa went to Jack and asked, "how do you feel?'

"Better, my strength is returning and my head is clearer."

"Well remember what we talked about yesterday?"

"Maybe, why?"

"Well you agreed to have a personal assistant, do you remember that?"

"Yeah, thanks."

"What do you mean?"

Jack points over to Mitzi, and said, "I'll take her, and she has agreed to do it."

"That's nice Jack, but she has other duties, but if you are sure?, I do have a whole list of the top candidates that were flown in from all over the country, and can you at least wait to make a decision?"

"Sure", said Jack looking over at Mitzi, who saw Lisa, noticing Trixie wasn't happy either.

"Trixie will you take over, while Mitzi and I have a little talk."

"Next", said Trixie to announce, "This one is Esmeralda," in walked a stunning Latin woman, with a beautiful complexion, Jack just stared at her to see that her hands were cold as she touched his, she smiled as Trixie said, "She speaks 5 different languages and is our top translator, do you have any questions Jack?" he just stared at her and didn't say a word. But "No."

A frustrated and confused, Trixie, was already over all of this as she called out, "Next."

Esmeralda left, for Trixie to see a stunning brunette, wearing a huge smile, and a white dress; she leaned over and hugged Jack and said, "Hi, nice to meet you."

The two were engaged in a long conversation, as Lisa directed Mitzi to another empty room, and said, "I allowed you to be on his support team, not be his personal assistant."

"My understanding was that whatever it took to defend and protect him."

"What do you mean?" said Lisa.

"Just that, the enemy came in, posed as a nurse, and tried to inject him, I'm just doing my job, and another thing, and I wouldn't need to be here if we had some help."

"Fair enough, you have Damien and Jim."

"No I mean, a police officer, like someone already working to watch over him at night."

"Good idea, how about you and I coordinate on all actions and we will play it by ear. I'm sorry, let's go back and see how Jack is getting along."

Lisa and Mitzi came in as Erin was leaving, Lisa asked "How are we doing?"

Mitzi takes her chair and moves it by Jack, to see Jen walk in, a cute brunette, similar to Mitzi, in build, a strong woman with her own ideals. As she stood a bit, Jack smiled at her as she spoke for most of it, then left, for Jack and said, "I like that one." Lisa chimes in," she was the one who was ready to leave."

Jen heard them and said" That's because you were a little vague on what all of this entailed."

"So how has that all changed for you now?" asked Lisa, who had her arms crossed.

"Now that I met him, you can count me in", said Jen.

Next in was a blonde, with a ferocious smile, and gleaming white teeth. The two hit it off, as she left she kissed him good bye, as Jack said, "That one too."

"Wait there is more," said Lisa.

"Can you just have all of them come in at once, let's get this over with," said Jack.

Lisa stood at the door, to lead all of them in, the first one was a stunner, a beauty queen, Jack shook his head "No", she left, then it was the red head, Jack shook his head "Yes", then a long haired brunette, named Darlene, Jack shook his head "No". The two left standing, were evident friends of both Trixie and Mitzi, both received "No's". The next group in, was the hottest of all. All girls were stunning to look at, especially Monroe, a big tough blonde bombshell. Quickly Lisa was onto what her two assistants were doing, they could have their own beauty pageant right there,

She had to break up Monroe and Jack who were talking about other things, that made her even blush. This prompted Carrie, a former CIA agent, to walk out. At the foot of his bed was Dylan, a tall brunette, who was actually rubbing Jack's feet, while the other two just stood awaiting their fate, both girls received "yes's", as the last group came in. Instantly, two very hot Amazonian woman stoled the whole show, Jack said "No." The last three, each had something different to offer, Lysandra was a trainer, a strong Greek woman with blazon green eyes, and Kosta, a Latin fast talking woman, and lastly there was Audris, a former Super spy sex thing that came as a gift from Ben. Like himself who was now a super spy thought he should present him with a gift to Jack, what could he say, as she left, Lisa said "who will it be?"

Jack points to the one still rubbing his feet, for which she answered "yes I will be his new assistant, my name is Dylan."

"You and I need to talk", said Lisa.

"Alright can you wait until I finish?"

She finished, and then covered his feet, and said, "I'll be back soon."

The hallway was crowded, as Lisa said, "Go back to your barracks; I have another plan for the rest of you, your training will start later, as she led Dylan into the private room, to shut the door and said, "Had you ever met, Jack before?"

"No, I'm from Washington State."

"I know all that, do you have a boyfriend?"

"Does that matter?" said Dylan.

"It is to national security."

"O' Kay no, I'm single, I like to work out!"

"What about sex?"

"I like guys if that is what you're asking?"

"No, I just want you to be safe."

"Don't worry you can count on me, you know I was the compliance officer."

"Alright, you have the job, you're on a thirty day probation period, and Mitzi is your direct supervisor, as she hands her a phone. That phone is your life line to Jack and me, you'll be in constant contact.

You will be given two credit cards, one is the expense account and the other is a per diem, let me take you back in, so you and Jack can get acquainted."

Lisa led her out to an empty hallway, and back into Jack's room to hear Trixie say, "Trixie and Mitzi, come with me", as Dylan walked in, Jack had laid back, Dylan went up to him, her smile was infectious, as she said, "Hi, my name is Dylan, but you can call me anything you like, what would you like me to do first?"

Jack looked at her distinguished frame and said, "Do you work out?"

"Yeah, two or three times a day, do you?"

"No, not really, I just seem to run a lot."

"Running is fun, I like to swim as well", she noticed he was staring at her chest. She said

"I can't help notice you're staring at my boobs, do you want to see them?"

Jack just looked at her, to turn his head away, for her and said, "I'm not shy, nor am I a girlie girl, I'm a tomboy, and if you want I could strip naked right here, right now."

"Enough", said Mitzi, as she came back in with authority, to add, "Dylan, it's time for you to take some tests, say your goodbye's to Jack. Trixie will show you the when's and where's, Jack do you want and say anything to Dylan before she goes?"

"Good luck."

Dylan waved goodbye, as she left the room, led by the now focused Trixie, who did all the speaking and said, "Says here, you're a captain, do all Captains go around positioning their superiors?"

"No, that would be unethical."

"Exactly, Mister Jack Cash, rank is that of a general?"

"Did you say General?" asked Dylan.

"Yes." said Trixie.

"Oh, I'm sorry, it will never happen again."

"I know, because, like you, and all the others are going through a battery of tests and the top one will get the job, but because, Jack chose you, you will get a preference, over everyone else."

"Just tell me what I have to do."

"Simple, what is asked of you."

The pair walked together, as Trixie, spoke candidly, to say, "Look around, and see everyone and everybody is a potential bad guy. Last night a band of former spy teams tried to assault the man you were coming onto so strongly, in this business, were the ones who get used, were not the ones who are allowed any form of happiness or pleasure, can I ask you a question?"

"Sure"

"Why did you volunteer for this assignment?"

"I didn't, I was chosen as the one likely to survive, you see I was the one nobody liked, I could kick ass, and take down most boys, so when I got the call, well naturally I flew down here."

"Do you always strip for your superiors?"

"Nah, he was the first, besides he is totally different than any other guy I have ever met, he has a scent that made me quiver."

The two went out onto the parade grounds, to see it was empty then they walked over to the building they were staying at to see a tall magnificent woman.

"Come in girls, class is in session, my name is Miss Margaret, I'm the Spy trainer, for the Government, take a seat."

"Oh I'm not with you all" said Trixie.

"This may pertain to you as well, unless you have something else more pressing?"

"Well, no," said Trixie as she took a seat, to hear" Listen up girls, you have all been chosen, to become the founding members of a newly sanctioned organization, as erected by our new Vice President of the United States, Miss Linda Jackson, she has asked Miss Curtis, to find the very best potential agents, to become simply known as Spy Club, this secret organization, sole mission, is to support our Super Spies, for which they will never know. That's right, we take the motto from Forced Recon; Swiftly, Silently, Secretly and Deadly, simply put, is that you will all be trained to use whatever means available to stop, assist and ensure that the Spy that you are guarding, is safe, at all times. As a founding member you will have a territory to cover, as the Spy works, you will provide Intel, communication and support, using and recruiting others along the way to assist you, any questions?"

One of the No's stood up and said "I thought that this was over?"

"On the contrary, upon a battery of tests, mental, emotional and physical, those that make it will assume the role, from that one will be selected to assist, the Spy."

"What does this training involve?" asked Darlene.

"A simple cut and dry approach, to guarding someone, able to keep your distance, then when necessary, strike."

"Sounds like you're a stalker" said Lisa, who quietly walked in, everyone looked at her, then laughed.

"Here is your boss, please stand up for Miss Curtis, the head of the Spy program."

"Thank you, Miss Margaret. Girls I want and say, currently Jack has chosen, one to serve him, but in the meantime, I encourage each of you to excel in all the challenges that Miss Margaret has for you. In the event, at a later time, if you're needed, you may all be called to serve, if for some of you that this is not what you want, then I strongly urge you to sign this paper stating you want out, and from this day forward, you will keep it a secret till your put in the ground, understand?"

"Yes Ma'am" in unison.

"I need Trixie, everyone else carry on."

"Yes Miss Curtis, well I guess you do need to be somewhere Miss" said Miss Margaret.

Trixie gets up, to meet up with Lisa, as the two exit, for Lisa and said to her, "What's wrong?"

"Oh nothing really."

"Come on I know you, you're my friend."

"Alright, Damien, was supposed to come over last night."

"Get in", the two got into the black SUV, to continue the conversation, as Lisa tells her, "Your in way too deep with Damien, regardless of what he does, if you're going to continue, you must set aside your feeling; besides he spent last night on a threat."

"Oh I didn't know."

"Maybe I might have made a mistake to promote you, because if it weren't for Mitzi's recommendation, well I don't know, you act and seem so young sometimes."

"Your right, I will listen more to Mitzi."

"No you won't, you're on your own now, and for that very reason you're on the team. You're the best air traffic controller we have, your good at what you do, you just need to work on your communication and social skills, which everyone lacks, so come on, I want you to prep my new choice for Jack's assistant."

Jack was resting as Mitzi continued to monitor his progress and challenge all those that came in, even her life has changed, from assistant to Lisa, to becoming a spy in her own right, and to who lay in that bed, was her ticket to ride.

She began to compose notes on protocols and procedures. On her phone, which was her life line to this world, a secret phone was exclusively hers, tamper proof, unlike Jack's arsenal of tools, it was her only device, she got up to review all of his tools. She carefully laid out some tools on baskets made of wood and lined with magnetic material that she knew no one could touch. This included his signature gun, in its white box and clear top, she felt a hand on her butt, she turned to see Jack was awake, she smiled at him, and now he was touching her front, she moved closer, as she heard voices, receiving a little pleasure, but for only a brief moment, she stepped away when she saw Lisa and Trixie and heard "How is our patient doing today?"

"He seems fine."

"I want you both to know, I thought about how all this will work, I want you Mitzi to be in charge of all ground movements and actions; however it will be away from Jack, to allow him to do his thing. As for you Trixie, anything in the air, to include transportation, and air support."

"Yes Ma'am" said Trixie, falling away in the background.

"Then there is the case for a personal assistant, after thinking about it, I've decided to choose Jill Thomas, any objections?"

Neither said anything, for her to continue, "To round out the team, Damien will be the bodyguard, driver, and pilot, and lastly I know a young Detective, who is light on his feet. He will give us a data base to work with, his name is Greg Davis, that rounds out your team, the team leader is Mitzi, she also will hand out your checks, as I must go, I will allow you both to attend Miss Margaret's classes, that is until Jack goes back to Montgomery, then the whole team will go down there."

Lisa left the room. Jack was looking up at the two girls who he thought was going to get into to it, only to calm, to see Jack was staring at them, when all of a sudden, a striking blonde with short hair walked in, with a phone of her own, and said, "Hi, I guess I'm the one who made it."

"Are you carrying?" asked Mitzi.

"Yep, I always have my .38 pistol on me at all times, so where do we go from here?"

"Well I imagine, you and Jack should get acquainted, we will leave you to that", said Mitzi with a smile on her face, as the door closes, Jill goes to Jack's bed and said, "Hi I'm Jill Thomas" she extends her hand.

Jack just looks at the baby, on her first big adventure and says "Yes I know your name."

"What can I do for you?" she said innocently.

Jack thought about that one, thinking, what she would look like without her clothes on, but thought about it and said, "I'd like a paper, current if you can find it, then maybe a protein drink, shake or slurry, and then some carb loaded foods, like steak, potato, with all the fixings, and lobster, with a butter sauce, and then finally, that girl who was here earlier, what's her name?"

"You mean Dylan?"

"Yeah, that's it, have her wear as little as possible, like shorts and a tank top."

"Anything else?"

"Now that you mentioned it, some clothes I want to get out of here."

"Where do you want to go?"

"Mobile, of course."

"Is that it?"

"Yeah that is it, now run along, and send Mitzi back in."

She left the room, to see Jill Thomas. Mitzi asked "Hey, can you help me out a bit?"

"What do you need" said Mitzi giving her a stern look.

"Well he wants a paper, some food and a girl, and definitely not me."

"Listen" said Mitzi getting in her face and said "That's what your job is, is a gopher, you get whatever he wants, desires and needs, anyway possible, what does he want?"

"Well a paper?"

"That is down in the lobby, what's next?"

"A heavy carb load lunch, steak, potato and lobster."

"That's easy, go to the hospital kitchen and place that order, and give them twenty minutes tops, what else?"

"He wants Dylan, for his companion, well; he asked she wear little as possible."

"Like what lingerie?"

"No, shorts and a tank top."

"He wants to work out, so get her and I'll have some clothing for him to wear, when you get back, anything else?"

"Besides the clothes, he wants to go to Mobile, is that in Alabama?"

"Yes, it is, I should tell you he is from Mobile, Alabama."

"But, I thought he lived here."

"Does it matter where he lives, he is a traveler, and you better get used to it?"

"I just didn't know, I don't think I like the idea of moving to Mobile."

"Are we having a problem here?" asks Mitzi.

"Well, no, but I'm not moving to Mobile."

"So go tell Miss Curtis, you want out, there are nineteen others ready to step up."

"No, you're right, I need to get focused, I'll just have to tell my boyfriend, I'll be moving."

"Whoa, wait a minute; you have a boyfriend, you're going to have to end that even before you begin."

"Ops, I didn't mean and said that" said Jill, only to see Mitzi was on the phone, she connected with Lisa and said, "We have a problem here, can you meet with us."

"I'll be there in five minutes."

Mitzi slid the phone shut and said, "Don't worry, you're out, stay here and watch over Jack, I'll get what he needs", Mitzi was on the move, and into the elevator, as the doors shut.

The stairwell door opened, in walked a huge giant, all six foot and nine inches tall, led as his backup, entered weapons drawn, carefully they checked the two empty rooms, to the last one, the giant slowly opened the door, his huge hands engulfed the handle. Both of them moved in.

Jill was talking to Jack about how sorry she was, only to be caught off guard, as both guns were held on the two of them, which froze Jill. Ox, the giant saw the white box, he went to it, opened it up, saw the pearl handled gun, whereas the giant reached in, he grabbed the gun, turned and aimed it at Jack and fired three tight shots. Jack was vulnerable, but all three shots missed, as Jack scrambled off the bed. The newly escaped Protima knelt down to get off a couple of shots, as the giant shook then short circuited and died as the gun burned his hand, he fell forward and fell with a thud.

All the while Jill was crumbled up in the corner, weeping, as Jack lunged at Protima, catching her off guard, seeing her friend was dead, for her and said, "What the hell."

Jack had his hands on her as the two were rolling around, as Jack got in a couple of elbows, Jack knocked the gun out of her right hand, which she reached for, and then began to punch back.

All of a sudden a single shot rang out, as the bullet went through Protima shoulder, both Jack and Protima stopped fighting long enough to see Jill Thomas in a FBI standard shooting position. Jack felt Protima, as he was wrestling around with her, to aim and squeeze off all the rounds in her gun, only to see Jill up against the wall, she slid down, blood covering her white dress.

Protima pushed off Jack, as he reached out for the closest weapon, as Protima was on the run, Jack scrambled over to the giant, and pried his weapon from his hand and was up. Jack was hot on her tail.

Meanwhile in the basement, there were two holding cells, both padded, in walked two men, in intervals wearing Haz Mat suits, and said, "Clear out, this area is under a chemical alert?"

The MP's cleared out as the two pulled off their hoods, to show it was Jerod the fat man, and Harold, the skinny guy. They unlocked the two doors, both of the Colonel and Isabella emerged.

The fat man hands them pistols, and Colonel said "Call in our backup, now, were going upstairs to end this now."

Protima was in the lead, but Jack was gaining, as they were heading down. Lisa and Damien rode the elevator up to the sixth floor, got out, as Lisa was in the lead, she opened Jack's door, to see her friend had bled out, her eyes were still open holding her gun in her hands. Lisa walked over the dead mass of the giant, his hand was burned, she screamed, "Get on the phone and call in the Calvary".

Protima hit the lobby, just as the rest of her team, on one side, on the other was the MP's, guns drawn, it was at a standstill, till Jack pushed his way through, at the door stood a man with his badge out saying he was the FBI and your all under arrest.

Jack shot Isabella in the leg, as she let out a yelp, the MP saw the agent pull his weapon, as the MP's in unison fired at the black man all below the belt, he went down in agony. Jack rolled to drill the Colonel in the knee, it shattered. Jack was on the move, while holding the Colonel arms. All was quiet as Jack held the Colonel, the other FBI agent, surrendered their weapons, as their boss lay in agony.

Both Lisa and Damien, stepped out of the elevator, they had their guns drawn. Mitzi came from the kitchen, with a platter of fresh hot food, Jack was suffocating the air from the Colonel.

"Men get up, take those two for medical assistance, Lisa went over to Jack to see him release his prisoner. The Colonel fell forward. Jack was covered in blood, he made his way up from the floor. FBI swarmed and those against were taken into custody, both Isabella and the Colonel were wheeled off to ER. Jack stood, his arms down, as Jack shook out the cob webs and said, "Where is she at?"

"Who Jill", asked Lisa.

"Nah, the black suited girl, was hit with one shot", said Jack looking around, to realize she was gone. Lisa came to him and said,

"We need to get you out of here, staying in one place too long is unwise."

"Where do you suggest?"

"How about Montgomery, the base has been cleared of enemy agents and replaced with more secure agents."

"Sure, what about Mobile?"

"If you like I can get you on a hop tonight" said Lisa, as Jack was motioning for Mitzi to come over to him.

"What are you doing?", asked Mitzi.

"Eating, all this violence has given me an appetite" says Jack as he sits down, and begins to cut into the steak, Lisa looks over Mitzi and said, "Why are you doing that?"

"The whole idea of a personal assistant, was she would run the errands."

"She chose a boyfriend over Jack, so she stayed with him while I did her job."

"So, that is why you called me back?"

In between bites Jack said, "Oh is she my new assistant."

Lisa looked at her senior aide and said, "Is that it, you want to do that?"

Mitzi looked at her and said, "Jill wanted to get to know Jack a little better, so I took it upon myself, to speed up the process, you did put me in charge of the team."

"Yes I did, your right, were all here to help him out. I have bad news for you both, Jill is gone."

"I know", said Jack, enjoying the lobster tail, as the two talked while in the middle of the calm chaos. Lisa said "You're right, you're their overall boss, besides if it weren't her up there it would have been you."

"What do you mean?"

"Jill was shot and killed."

"Oh, I'm sorry, I had no idea, that could have been me."

"That's what I like about you, you're honest and sincere."

"It's the nurse inside of me, so what are your plans with him?"

"He wants to go back to Mobile, what do you think?" asked Lisa to Mitzi.

"Maybe we should let him go; actually trying to control a monster is virtually impossible."

"I like you're thinking, you must have some experience."

"Just a little, when your with Ben, as his aide, things are totally different. Actually there is no playbook on what they do, how they do it or let alone think, for Ben he bedded everything he saw, and including those that support him, whereas, Jack is more like a family man who finds himself in trouble. I will tell you each of them creates a huge wave wherever they go, and pray you're not in their wake."

"Your right, I'll let you lead us, so go talk to your man" said Lisa smiling at the women who was now in charge.

"Will do boss" said a smiling Mitzi, as Lisa gathered the troops and began the cleanup, as Mitzi came to the table. Jack was still eating, and asked "Is there anything else you would like?"

"Nah, I'm fine", with one hand still on his gun, and eating with his left hand to hear,

"Hi, my name is Mitzi, and I'm your handler, if you need anything I will provide it to you, so Lisa was saying you were thinking of going back to Mobile?"

"Yeah, can you make that happen?"

"Absolutely, whatever you want."

"You're the one that was in my room, earlier, you're nice. You didn't mind that I grasped your breasts?"

"No, actually, it was nice someone even noticed."

"So what is your role with me?" asked Jack, staring at her boobs.

"Well let me tell you how our relationship could work, I've worked Intel with other spies, in the past, some like me close, while others at a distance, so what do you want?"

"I don't know, I don't have a clue what you want me to do next."

"Well let me tell you, trouble will find you, then it's how you deal with it, using the skills you learn becomes your tools, then a reputation develops. Before I came aboard I researched you to find out how you are more of a humanitarian than a killer, thus ensures a single life is saved, than killed. We have already had other agencies contact us about possible cases for you to work on, interested?"

"So that is what I do now, be a government detective?"

"No, actually your role is simple, you are the direct link to the President of the United States, he is your only boss. You're his instrument for dealing with trouble on face to face needs."

"When do I get started with that?"

"Well that is the tricky part, he is on his way out of office this year so you have the rest of this year to train, and build up a reputation, then when the Commander in Chief calls upon you , you will be ready, but realistically, we will all know when you're ready. You know, I think I would like you to talk with Miss Margaret, she is the government's liaison and protocol officer and she can give you a better insight of the do's and don'ts, about being a spy. Most important, some of your resources are available to you, but from this day forward, I am yours to call upon for anything." she said as she touched his hand and smiled."

"Really, in that way", he said with a smile, back at her smile."

"Yeah, really" she said.

"Oh by the way, do you know my name?"

"Yeah, it's Jack Cash, Spy."

"Good", said Jack, still eating, as she went back over to Lisa who was ordering people around, and said, "Were going to be leaving tonight for Mobile. Jack, would like to have his assistant join us."

"Is that you?"

"No silly, I believe her name is Dylan?"

"I don't think she is ready."

"Does it matter?, my experience says there are those that do and there are those who pretend, it's like what occurred here, I strongly feel if Jack chooses someone, then I'm Okay with it, unless of course if you want me to, then I'll take on that responsibility."

"Wait, I agree, but I have one more candidate."

"So who is that, do I know her?"

"She is from Montgomery and I will send her down to meet up with your team, in Mobile."

"Oh before I forget, when do you think you'll start paying Jack, from my count, he is credited with all of this , so with all of these and what he did in Cuba?"

"I get the point, next time I see him will be in Mobile with his payments."

"It's still a million per"

"What are you saying?"

"I'm not saying a thing, I work for him and report to you, but in turn, I want him to get caught up, and with me in charge, I just want it to be even, after each job he does. In turn, if other agencies want his services, then they will all know the price."

"It doesn't work like that, whomever Jack gets, regardless, that he brings them in dead or alive he will get the million." said Lisa.

"That's not how it reads, as ordered by the President."

"What are you saying?" said Lisa.

"According to Jack's attorney, Miss Erica Meyers, she sent me a copy of the declarations page, and I quote, "In accordance with the spies on the national level, they will be paid one million dollars, for the following conditions, known of, but not actually, arresting them, or shooting them, and accessory to the crime and caught. Lastly, a known target, like the two he just wounded and not killed, to include that FBI agent who interfered, unlike you, who oversees the grand scheme, here is my orders, signed by the President, George White, the third."

"So it was you" said Lisa, astonished by the new revelations.

"Yes, I was the one who vaulted you in your position" said Mitzi.

"Why didn't you take it?"

"Because I'm the behind the scenes type of girl, who likes to mix it up from time to time, and you're the one who seeks the glory, my glory is behind the scenes. Knowing the job, we'll get it done the right way, but most importantly our man is covered."

"So what does that make us?" asked Lisa.

"In my book, equals, just playing a part as to what the President needs, and were here to see that the job can be done and executed."

"Great, I just wished you had told me earlier of your plans and we could work together."

"I really couldn't, things would have been different, and things just have a way of working themselves out. You get what you want and then so do I."

"Alright so what do you need?"

"I want a C-130 outfitted for Jack to travel around in, complete with a galley, and a master suite, a car, and a gadgets or tech guy available. Joining our team, will of course be Trixie and Damien, if that's alright. We also need a military officer as a liaison, someone you can trust, and someone who can take orders from a woman."

"You got it, I'll give you Jim, the best gadgets guy I know. As for a military man, I'll have someone on that flight down to Mobile and we will have Dylan ready to serve. What are your plans later?"

What did you have in mind?" said Mitzi, strong and confident.

"Just a sit down, so we can get each other in line with the other."

"We can, but I'll still take your lead, all I care about is Jack's welfare, and the rest will work itself out."

"That's refreshing to hear, I was about to worry about another power struggle."

"Not from me you're not, I'm your biggest supporter, always will be, I just wanted to let you know where I stood."

The two embraced in front of all the men, but as they broke, they turned away, as Jack walked past them and said, "I'll be up in the room, when you're finished, can you send her up there?"

"Yeah, sure will" said Mitzi.

"Is that for Dylan and a booty call?", asked Lisa.

"Nah, I thought it would serve Jack well if Miss Margaret and he talked."

"That is good thinking, yes my friend we need to talk, you're right on."

"Later I gotta go, my man is awaiting", said Mitzi, on the phone.

Lisa got into the elevator with Jack; she looked at him Jack asked her "What did you think of Jill?"

"She was brave; she stood up for herself, too bad, she wanted out."

"Wait what?" inquired Lisa.

"Yeah, Mitzi told her some of her suppose duties and she freaked out, and that was why Mitzi is here and Jill is up there dead. She was like a deer caught in the headlights, not to mention when she saw the giant."

"I have to admit, he was a pretty large man."

They got off the elevator as Jack walked slowly, Lisa wanted to help him, but didn't know where to start. She realized her friend was right, she was the compassionate one, she was not, as she held the door open, for Jack to hear, "This is a crime scene, you can't come", the guy stopped in mid-sentence, to see it was Lisa Curtis, and in walked Jack Cash, as she told the others to move out of the way. Jack pulled out the drawer and pulled out a t-shirt.

Just then a commanding voice spoke, everyone turned to hear her, say, "All of you get out of this room, Jack Cash wishes to have some privacy", said Mitzi. With paper in hand, ushering the crime scene's people out, including Lisa. Mitzi shut and locked the door and said, "Come let's get you cleaned up."

"I'm a bit tired can you help me?" asked Jack.

"Yes, that is why I'm here for you."

Class session was over as Trixie approached Dylan and said, "Jack wants you to join the team, will you accept?"

"Yes, and get away from all this boring stuff. Sure, where do I report?"

"Be at hanger number 2, at 1800 hours; be packed and ready to go."

"Will do", said an excited Dylan. Then Trixie went to Miss Margaret and said, "Mitzi would like to know if you could come to the hospital and speak with Jack Cash on being a spy."

She looked at her and said "You can tell him it would be an honor." As she gathered her stuff up, the two walked together as Miss Margaret asked her," How long have you been with the spy?"

"I haven't, I was just chosen, and it's really my boss, who has the experience."

"What do you think I should say?" asked Miss Margaret inquisitively.

"What do you mean?" Responds, Trixie.

"Well I really have never sat down with a spy before, it's like a personal visit to the White House and spending a one on one moment with the President, except he has the authority to kill me for no reason, and get paid a million dollars doing it."

"Really, he can kill anyone he likes?" said Trixie with a smile on her face.

Miss Margaret just looked at her, as they approached the hospital. An MP stood at the door and said, "ID's and state your business."

"It's a hospital" says Miss Margaret.

"Not at this time, it is a secure place, by order of the President. All rooms are on lockdown. I see you're a clinical doctor, Miss Margaret Jones, you may come in You will be escorted up to see Mister Cash, he is waiting for you, ah, and Miss West, they have been expecting you, in through there."

The guard stood by Miss Margaret, who stepped away from him when they got in the elevator. The guard said "Don't be afraid, we're here to protect you."

"Not me you're not, I've seen this before, you guys only mission is to protect one person."

"Your right Ma'am, our VIP needs all the care possible."

The door opened at his floor, as a crowd of people waited in the hallway, looking very uncomfortable, they passed by them, as the guard knocked and said, "This is guard 14524, I have Miss Margaret Jones, to see Mister Jack Cash, please."

The door opened, there standing freshly dressed was the honorable Jack Cash, as he zipped up his windbreaker, he turned to see Mitzi, who escorted her in, and whispered to her, "Could you do me a favor? We have about two & a half hours before we fly out, and could you explain what it means to being a spy, maybe some responsibilities, and maybe some expectations, alright?"

"Yes" said Miss Margaret.

"Jack I need to go out and finish off the arrangements, do you need anything?"

"No thanks", said Jack.

"Don't worry I'm a call away and sooner". He watched her leave He sat on the bed, as Miss Margaret found a chair and position it in front of him.

CH 3

The Big Secret

Miss Margaret looked at Jack as he looked back at her, she was undecided as what and said. As for fear, it might be disrespectful, until Jack spoke, "So what do you do?"

"I'm the government's special liaison and protocol officer."

"What does that entail?" asked Jack sincerely.

"Well I instruct those unfamiliar with the military and government agents, like you."

"Really on what subjects?"

"Well not really any one subject, but mainly on mannerisms and conduct. Take for instance, you and don't think I'm disrespecting you at all."

"Nah, if Mitzi thought it was important, then by all means let me have it."

"Really," said Miss Margaret, as she took a deep breath, then let it out. She began and said, "You're what they call an enigma, you are as powerful as our Commander in Chief, and don't have to worry about re-election every four years, if you live that long. The average life span of a Spy is two years tops, so most spies accumulate lots of wives, just look at Utah, anyway, you live hard, play hard and live within the confines of the hospitals, for all this they pay you a suppose million dollars a head, which from my experience you will probably not ever see. You know the Government is cheap, now on to you, you have all the power any man could ever want, but you need to find a balance, ground yourself on ideals true to yourself, and never let anyone ever tell you what, when or how to do something. When you're at a scene, you are the ultimate person in charge, no one else. Handlers will come and go, chose those you can trust, if you have a gut feeling about someone, add them to your support team. A good support team has a core of about four members, each has a specialty. Take for instance the blonde, not so pretty, but a good companion while your off. Then a brunette, a smart one running the show. Always two women and two men.

The first one should be a pilot, driver, etc., maybe they could even double as a bodyguard. This is highly unlikely with your status, same as a reputation, and lastly a Mister fix it, a do all problem solver. That is your team, some spies have assistants and there usually their wives, who can really be loyal and trusted beyond a reasonable doubt, once your position or Intel fails, look to your assistant to be at fault. This type of woman needs to be strong yet gentle in the bed, an extension of yourself, taking care of all your needs. In your life twenty four seven, even sleeping in your bed, you must know her every secret to totally trust her. Now on to you, you have the power unlike before, where there was limitation to where you could go and who you see, but with the enactment of the Edison act, named after another great spy Thomas Edison, 76 countries adopted this act, which allows you complete access to their countries. Then to work freely, and your one and the other is Ben. From the great Mississippi river, which is the line, to the east coast of America, is your suppose territory." She paused and took a breath to add, "Let's look at you as the supreme leader, you travel state by state cleaning up the streets. By your presents and programs you implement, once you capture them and then turn them over to Miss Curtis, you will get your reward. In addition, you may get accolades from the President himself or even cities or states, then maybe even other countries depending on what you do, there are so many hostile situations here and abroad that it would take hundred thousand agents to clean them up For you, you need to choose which ones suit you, it's like a cause, and if you believe in it enough, then you will have no problem doing it no questions asked. As I can tell from your body language, you're a humble man, which for this is good trait. With so many power hungry individuals out there, that's why you're an enigma."

She looked up at him and he was just looking at her. She said "Do you have any questions?"

"That sounds like a lot of responsibility where do I go from here?"

"That's simple, go where your heart takes you, trouble will find you. As an example, young girls are taken every day across America, and no one knows where they go, or what happens to them, that could be where you go."

Jack looked at her, and said, "Has that happen to you?"

With tears streaming down her face, Jack slid off the bed, and comforted her saying, "Who was it? Allow me to hunt them down and exact revenge on them for your behalf."

In between sobs, she pulled out a photo, and handed it to him, he looked at her and saw her name was Annabell Ryan and asked,

"So this is my next job?, I'll find out where she went and let you know, there now, stop crying."

She wiped away her tears, and calmed down and said, "Thank you."

"Had you notified the local police?"

"Yes, State Patrol and any agency who would listen, that's how I became an advocate for bringing back the Spy program. You know it ended at the end of the cold war, as the US flexed its muscles and said, no to the program, but here you are now, right in front of me and now I've taken up the fight to train the next spies."

"Well don't fear, Jack is on the case, can you tell me a little about her?"

"Well she decided to attend college at the University of Memphis, and study human behavior sciences. Up to last week we texted back and forth, it ended, her phone was found in a lake.

"She has a different last name, was she married?"

"No, she has my maiden name of Ryan; we thought she would be safe."

"Who are we?"

"My Ex-Husband and I, he still lives in Oklahoma, and I travel the world."

"Alright, what is your phone number?"

She told him as he programmed it, and sent out a blast e-mail to every agency, he added a President seal to the E-Mail. As Jack scanned the photo he asked "And her measurements are?"

She looked at him weirdly, then answered,"36-22-30, she is 5-6in one half, 105pounds, blonde, green eyes, 19 yrs. old, and a birth mark on her right triceps."

He sent it to one million agencies and told her "There I sent it, I guess we're off to Memphis."

"Again, thank you", she rushed him, as he sat on the edge she was trying to embrace him. Just then Mitzi came in and said, "How did the session go?", she went over to the dresser, & clicked off the audio recorder, and placed it in her pocket. She watched as Jack comforted her as she said, "What can I do to make it up to you?"

"Nothing, maybe at some later time another lesson."

"Anytime."

"Alright, Jack needs to go; you'll continue working with our prospects?"

"Yes of course, anything for Mister Cash."

She picked up her bag, and waved goodbye, as a guard escorted her out.

"So how was the session?" asked Mitzi.

"You'll get the highlights on you recorder, it was fine, a little more awareness. Hey had you ever experienced or known someone who was kidnapped or stalked?"

"No, but Trixie has, it happen to her, she escaped but the guy was still on the loose."

"When did that happen?" asked Jack.

"Oh it happens all the time, every college across the country has girls go missing without a trace, some are beaten, raped or even killed, too many for local authorities to handle. Why, you have a job?"

"Yeah, looks like I got several hits on this woman, as Jack hands the photo to her.

"She is pretty, who is she?"

"Miss Margaret's long lost daughter."

"Oh my God, really, what do you plan on doing?"

"Take a detour to Memphis, is the team assembled?"

"All except Damien, I guess his Mom was ill, and he had to go home."

"Any backups for him?" asked Jack.

"Why what do you have in mind?" asked Mitzi.

"Oh I need some feet on the ground.," replied Jack.

"We could probably get a squad of the Delta force team to do that."

"Make it happen, I think I like where this is heading."

"So do I" said Mitzi as she opened the door to see Trixie. Trixie said "Keep Jack Company, I know."

Jack had a smile on his face when he saw her, she looked different in his eyes, all he was thinking, "Ah a play thing."

She stood by the door, with a smile on her face yet. She was still not moving but said "What is going on here?"

"Just waiting for the show to begin." exclaimed Jack from his bed.

"What show?"

"It's all coming from you, so they say."

"I still don't follow you, I'm one of your assistants."

"Yes, so what do you do for me, come closer."

The door opened it was Lisa and a well-dressed man, as she asked "Are we interrupting something?"

"Not yet, what do you have."

"Well we just got word, you have a job, we would like to help out where ever we can", said Lisa.

"Well I heard Damien was gone, so I need somebody to fill that role," said Jack, watching Trixie back her way out of the room.

"I took care of that, there is a man in the hanger, also John here would like to volunteer."

"Fine, but I need bodies to help me search. How about all those girls you recruited for the assistant's position?"

"Perhaps, I hadn't thought of that, alright it will give you a chance to get to know them."

Lisa leaves, leaving the smartly dressed man alone with Jack, and said, "If you don't mind I'd like to go as well"

"Why, what are your motives?" said Jack as he typed his name in his database and asked, "Is it for your advancement or is this real intention?"

The guy was frigidly and said "both, to be honest. How many men would love to be in your position, twenty beautiful women at your fingertips, to do", Mitzi blew back in, interrupting him and announced. "The plane is ready, and at the last minute they enacted a place for you to rest and lie down. Also a team of Delta's volunteer, with their Commander. A guy named Danger, he seems somewhat respectful for a man. Who is this?"

"A new recruit, meet Major John Lincoln", said Jack, who was getting up to address her. Jack asked "Is there an in-flight movie and dinner aboard this flight?"

"Possibly" said Mitzi, adding, "We're ready whenever you are", as she said, "Have you seen Trixie?"

"I guess I scarred her off."

"Doubtful, why's that?" asks Mitzi.

"I asked her role was on this team, and her answer was that she was way too cold for me to trust", said Jack with regained strength. As the two began to walk together, they pushed three on the elevator, Jack whispered in Mitzi ear, it made her giggle, and she replied

"Don't worry, after this trip you'll be able to trust her."

They hit the lobby to some cheers from the MP group, applauding Jack and wishing him well, as he exited to an open door on the SUV. Lisa was at her passenger side door, as Jack slid in and went along to be behind the driver. Mitzi was next to him, with Trixie. In the back was the Major.

The doors shut, the SUV sped off, as Lisa turned and said, "Sorry Jack, we couldn't locate a separate room, but next time."

"I already worked it out", said Mitzi, to add, "Besides when you have twenty base craftsman at our disposal, they just called to tell me it was finished, not air tight, but enough for our man to sleep the next four hours."

"Well done, I'm impressed", said Lisa. Jack placed his head by the side of the window, his hands in his pocket, a warm hand was on his thin trousers, it was Mitzi's, warming up his leg. Her other hand was on her phone, texting and organizing the trip. They hit the tarmac, and drove down to the open third bay where the SUV came to a stop. All the doors opened, Jack got out, he then helped Mitzi out, to see all the military men had assembled, they came to attention, as the Major said,

"At ease."

They still stood at attention, until Jack Cash faced them and said, "Thank you men for helping me out. I will need each of you to pair off with a woman, change into normal clothes, and blend in, that is all."

"At ease ", yelled the Captain, as he stepped forward to see his friend. As Jack was ushered into the other hanger he asked "What brings you out to the fight?"

"Oh you know where the boss goes, so do I."

Danger just looked at him, to shake his head, he turned to yell, "At-Ten—Shun, now listen up, before you is what we fight for, he was equivalent to the President of our United States. You will treat him and the women on this mission as if they were the President's own first wife. This mission is utmost importance to national security and will be held in the highest esteem, do you understand?"

"Yes Captain" the soldiers all said in unison.

"Dismissed, fall out, make a single file line."

Jack stood at the door listening, then waited for the ramp to drop. On it was an older looking man past his prime with a scruffy beard, who spoke up and said," Welcome Mister Cash, my name is Jim." Standing at the controls was a familiar face, it was Brian, the armorer, who said," Hi."

As a crew of men, walked past them, carrying their tools in hand, they were leaving fast enough for Jack to turn and see a cover came off of a car, it was silver looking. The car fired up and Jim drove it up the ramp, as Brian waved him up, he parked it. The two worked feverously to secure it into position.

Then Jim motioned for Jack to follow. He walked with Mitzi's help, till he went past the car, to a freshly built room. Jim opened the door, to feel the warmth, as Jack stepped in to see a large king size bed. Jim said,

"A Modern King size bed, complete with a bathroom, a sofa and lights all around, a meeting table. In here is the assistants bed, here is the intercom system, our flight time is about four hours, give or take, but if you need anything press that, I'll leave you to rest."

Jack stuck out his hand as the two shook , Jack said "Thanks, how was Cuba?"

"Oh just about finished. Since you left another division came in and relieved us."

"Again thanks." said Jack still trying to get his bearings. Jack went to his bed. As the covers were turned back, he slid in, still dressed and all, Jim and Mitzi covered him up.

"You're welcome, now get some rest." said Jim, not to press the ordeal.

Jack heard some noises, as Brian pulled out Jack's gun with a glove of his own and placed it in the white box, then plugged the box in. He then left.

Jim stood at the edge of the ramp and said, "The Delta teams along the starboard side, and at no time will you touch the tarp." simply meaning the car.

One by one they found a cot to sit on. Dressed in hoodies, twenty women boarded to silence, and found a cot, last to enter was Lisa, the Captain, the Major, and his support staff, a blonde British looking guy, named Greg, and his newest assistant Dylan. Mitzi saw that Brian was holding the door for her, Trixie got on last to see Jim, as he raised the ramp, turned on the running lights, and said, "Can you two play hostess while Jack is resting and were ready to go?"

Mitzi looked over the make shift gallery to decide it was nicely laid out, with seats and a small serving table, two portable coffee makers, and two boxes of MRE's, with a toaster oven.

Lisa took a seat by the two men, to hear them bicker, while Dylan took a seat kitty corner to her As Jim past her and closed a curtain, then fired up the plane. As evening set in Jack was fast asleep.

Trixie exclaimed, "This is a nice set up."

"So" said Mitzi, and added, "This isn't for you, nor the coffee, or the food."

"What do you mean?" as she shows her mean side.

"You don't get it do you? Do you remember when I brought you along to assist me and I told you that we do things we don't have to do, but we put on a smile and grin and bear it, even if it tears you up inside."

"What do you mean, I did everything you told me to do."

"This is all about Jack, everything, even her."

"What, his assistant, so" said Trixie.

"They will all do it for their country , and enjoy it."

"What are you talking about?"

"About you and Jack earlier, I heard you refused his advances, is this true?"

"Oh, well I have a boyfriend, it is Damien, and I would never cheat on him with no one."

"Had you even listen to a thing I said, you don't get it, I bet I could walk back in the back and ask any of the eighteen other girls if they would like to spend a little one on one time with our boss. What do you think they would say?"

"Probably yes" said Brian, who said, "Got any coffee?"

She looked at him, hesitate to move, so he said, "You don't need to get up, I'll do it, if that is alright with you."

"Sure go ahead, as Mitzi got up to look back at her friend in disgust, and said, "I'll have it ready and bring both of us a cup, sorry."

Mitzi worked a bit, then over the intercom, she heard Jim's voice say, "Were taking off in two minutes hold on."

Mitzi sat back down, to feel Trixie's hand on her arm and said "Are you saying that Jack wants me off the team?"

"No, he hasn't said a thing to me, why, what is your concern?"

"Well I thought about what you said, and maybe your right, I should be warmer to him, I just need a little time."

"Take as much as you like honey."

Midway through the flight, while others slept, an army soldier got up and used one of the Heads. As he opened the door a tall blonde revealed her face to him, as she pushed him into the very large room, in an instant she was down to her bra and panties and between his legs. She was on fire, as she got him off. He did everything from not screaming, as she kicked him out, and closed the door.

The turbulence was hell to pay while trying to sleep through it, Jack awoke to see Mitzi sitting on the new sofa, and said "Here's a cup of coffee for you, black." Jack sat up and turned to face her, he was groggy. He showed her he was happy to see her too, from his waist below. She nearly dropped the coffee, as she handed it to him and looked down at him. Jack said "Do you see something you like?"

"Yes of course, I just didn't think it would be that big."

"Nah, I'm half risen, but if you take off your top it could probably go all the way."

For her it had been a while, she hesitated, long enough to throw caution to the wind, as she got up and went to the door, locked it. She pulled off her top, her faded white bra had seen better days, in one motion she popped it off to allow it to fall away, for Jack to see how perfect they were, she came to him. He was nearly out of his clothes in a flash, he embraced her, the passion was turned up a notch as it had been a while for Jack as well. As Mitzi unbuttoned, and wiggled out of her pants, then stood up to pull her panties down, her thick bush was wet, as she climbed on top of him and inserted him in. He was huge compared to others she had in the past, she did all the work. Jack played with her breasts, she lowered herself to him to kiss him on the lips, their tongues met, Jack felt her sleek arms, all the while, she was on fire, then exploded, to saturate him. She just kept on going, as Jack had his hands at her hips, she was taken all of him to her hilt. When it was closing in on another, over the intercom was, "Listen up, prepare for landing, as Mitzi let out a scream barely heard over the loudspeaker and the sound of the plane. She collapsed on his chest, then instinct began to kiss his mouth and hold his face in her hands and said, "I think this is a start to something good, I feel full. Hey and don't worry I have my tubes tied."

She slowly extracted herself off of Jack, to see he was lying in her pool of goodness. She threw back the covers as he curled up on a pillow as she dressed. She checked herself in the mirror, this time she had a smile on her face. As she unlocked the door, she stepped out to see a girl who was going back to her seat, then Mitzi closed his door. The plane came in for a landing, taxied, and the plane came to a stop in a private rented hanger, the ramp went down. Ten new cars lined the one side, as the troops were out first, each were a driver. They waited as the girls exited.

Mitzi opened Jack's room with Lisa and Dylan, and Trixie.

Lisa said, "Get up sleepy head, pulling the covers off of him." Lisa still held onto the covers as all four women just simply stared at his oversized manhood, fully erect, and still bobbing. Even Mitzi, it took her breath away by its size. Dylan said, "Shall we help him off, I mean up."

"No wait," said Lisa, still watching it sway, as Jack touched himself, then awoke to see all four girls scatter, while Mitzi was left to explain.

Jack just looked up at her and asked, "Can you hand me my clothes?"

Jim stood at the edge of the ramp, as Brian lowered it to show it was lighted, the troops exited, as Danger instructed them, to one side as the girls exited. Jack stood next to Jim, then walked down the ramp with Mitzi and Trixie, he said "Listen up, I just checked all my E-mails to confirm there are five colleges that have the highest abduction rate, with that we have four per car. In number one car I want Major Lincoln, with Miss Margaret, and Trixie and Mitzi. Take off now, and go to the University of Memphis."

"Now onto the helpers. Will the men line up on one side, along with the remaining girls, except you, you're with me," he said to Dylan.

"The next car is heading to central Arkansas at Little Rock. It will staff, the first man"

"Lieutenant Casey Sir."

"Casey, Audris, and the last man with Allison"

"Corporal Rogers, Sir"

"Car three", Jack stepped off the ramp to get closer to the men in uniform. He called out as the car on the end left" Lt, O'donald, Lysandra, Sgt Lawrence and Freya. You're all going to Mississippi University in Jackson, Mississippi."

"Car four, SSgt Sinclair, Lianna, Sgt Morris, and Erica", they all took off together. Off to Jack's right was Lisa, Danger, and Greg, the new member of the team.

"Car five, will have the following, Sgt Gallegos, Esmeralda, Cpl Mills, and Halyn".

"Next we need support teams, and going to Nashville, I'd like Lieutenant Abraham, Darlene, Sgt Wagner, Joana, and Sgt Grant".

"The next car number seven will be Lieutenant Clark, Carrie, Jackson, Kosta, and Manicka, you're on the outskirts of Birmingham."

Lieutenant Casey accelerated the Mercedes to the border of Tennessee and Arkansas. Next to him, he keep looking over at Audris, who sat facing him. Her long blonde was flowing as she was reading her e-mail from Jack. Allison and Cpl Brian Rogers sat back as Allison was playing with his leg. They then heard "Alright listen up, here are our orders from Jack. He wants us to hit the University in the morning and begin to track down the friends of those that were taken. In the glove boxes are ear pieces. Place them in your ear and you may communicate with each other. Jack also says he wants each of us to work independently, once we uncover somebody directly involved, wait for him to arrive. Under no condition will we engage with the enemy, all we do is report. As for money inside, there is an envelope of four thousand dollars, one thousand each, but he would like for us to live in the dorms, and scourge for handouts, the cash is the last measure. One of the two girls is assigned the phone to text & do check in's. The length of this mission depends on what we uncover."

"Then that will be you Audris, you hold onto the phone", said Casey.

In the back Rogers was fighting off Allison, as Audris, knew what this was. She lifted up her phone and clicked a picture of the two in an embrace and sent it to Jack.

Jack stood back on the ramp and said, "Alright, Danger, Spancer, Greg and Erin, take the last car into the city, you will be my back up. I guess you're coming with me, he said to Dylan, who was ready. Lisa said, "What about me?"

"I thought you already got some action." smiling, as Jack looked at her.

"That was an unforeseen viewing."

"What's fair for you, should be the same for me."

"You'll have to get a rain check, I want to go" said Lisa.

Jack looked at Dylan, then to her and said, "Alright get in, one in the back, as the two girls went to the car, but the doors didn't open. Jack was talking with Jim and said "I made a mess, can you clean it up, sorry, will you be here?"

"Well from this day forward, this is your plane, so where ever you go I'll be in the air, or on the ground. While your away, we can be finishing the room."

"Looks good to me.," said Jack.

"Nah, when we get it done there will be an escape pod up front, and your room will be air and sound proof."

"Well do what you have to, looks like I have a couple of girls wanting a ride", as Jack looked at his confirmation E-mails from all eight cars.

"Well boss you take it easy, call me if you need me, but we should be about thirteen hours down."

"Alright, I'm going to find a place to eat, hey do we have a working galley?"

"Not yet but it's in the works, as this one will go into service fleet, and our other plane will be ready in a month or two."

Jim watched as Jack jumped off the ramp, and to the waiting car and said "Open, start, heat to 72 degrees, stealth mode. The doors opened, Dylan got into the back, she climbed over a bulky bag which Jack went to pick up. Dylan said, "You don't need to move it, it's fine, it's your car."

Jack released it to slide in, the doors shut, and the car eased off. He looked at Lisa and said, "Jim did a nice job for you, this is a nice car, you're not driving?"

"Yeah it likes to drive itself, like auto pilot, as Jack opens his arm console. It lifted up a huge lap top that slid off the screen and attached to the front press. Uncovering the radio and air controls, as he said, "list out all incoming E-mails, as he plug into his phone. Lisa sat in amazement as Dylan propped up against his duffle bag, Lisa saw the bag and asked, "Is that the bag from Cuba?"

"I imagine, I don't know, Jim didn't say a thing to me."

"He doesn't have to, everything in this vehicle is accounted for, even what is yours. It's listed on your phone, it's an E-mail from me."

Jack said, "Display all files from Lisa", it was up there before he was finished speaking. With his hand on the wheel, both of them looked at all of them, she said "Do you even read what I send you?"

"No not really, that's why I need an assistant" he looked at Dylan in the rear view mirror."

"Well I guess I could, but that really isn't my forte, I like to fight", she said from the back.

Jack looks at Lisa and said "From now on, let's find out if anyone knows new technology."

"Don't get me wrong, I'd love to learn, can you send me to school." asked Dylan.

Jack told Lisa, "Don't worry about this, I'd rather, you were able to kick ass, than worrying about my E-Mails." As Jack went to touch the screen, Lisa touched his arm.

"Close" said Jack, as he looked at her. Looking at the speed, he ordered it to "Slow down, abide by the law, find a place to eat, what do you girls like?"

They were both quiet, for Jack said "Pancakes, eggs and steak."

The car took a sharp turn and went through a residential area. It popped out at a-all-night diner at a truck stop, right next to an interstate. As the car came to a stop, it idled, Jack closed the window, he ordered the car to, "Off, shut down, unlock and open." He pulled his phone out, as he got out first.

Jack stood helping Dylan out to stretch her legs. He looked in his duffle bag, just as he thought, from pesos, to dollars. He went in and pulled out a wad, then zipped it up, he closed the door. They went in.

In a another car was Danger, was driving sat on the street, while Erin sat up front on her phone, as Spancer said, "Let's go in and join them."

"Hush up, it does work like that, I'll let you sneak out and hit that fast food place but don't get close to him." Jack and his party was shown a booth, Jack allowed Dylan in, as Jack had his back to a wall.

Across from him was Lisa, he pulled out his phone, as he placed it on secret mode, then the waitress walked up.

Jack looked over the single page menu and said, "Take their orders first."

"Cup of coffee, black, and no sugar ", said Lisa.

"And you miss?' the waitress asked.

"I'll have a Danish and an orange juice."

Jack handed her the menu and said "I'd like the steak and eggs, can I get a side of pancakes, with strawberry syrup please? And were in kind of a hurry."

"Anything to drink sir?"

"Yeah, I'll take a tall orange juice", said Jack as he was texting back to car six, and said, "Dylan by chance did you document who was in what car?"

"No, you didn't ask me to?"

Lisa looks at Jack then and said "Your job as his assistant is to record and document what he needs. Have you learned anything yet?"

"Not really, you will tell me what to do, won't you, like, if you want sex?"

Both Jack and Lisa looked at her as the waitress brought the food. Dylan scarf the Danish even before she left and said, "On second thought, can I have two eggs and hash browns please."

"Sure anything else?"

"No I'm fine."

"For you Mister, we cooked the steak Medium, was that alright?"

"Fine, thanks", as Jack ate, he text back and forth to his teams and said, "Mitzi is at the University and made contact with a girl who was approached. I guess they went dorm to dorm. Trixie choose the sorority row, it's not uncommon that outside girls would try to recruit them.," said Jack while he ate.

Thirty miles outside of Memphis, Darlene announced, "Jack wants us to go to the sorority house and begin questioning, so step on it Lieutenant John.

Danger had a good view of Jack and Lisa while he watched Dylan's head bob up and down. He said "Is she doing what I think she is doing?" a bit laughing.

"Nah that's the way she eats, you know like an ostrich" said Erin, still on her phone, only to look up to see Spancer was running back with a load of food in bags. Greg reached over and opened up the door for him, he slid in and shut the door. One by one he handed out breakfast sandwiches, a drink and hash potatoes bars.

"Thanks bro", said the Captain.

All four ate and watched Dylan's head bob up and down.

"What's in the other bag?" asked the Captain.

"Oh lunch, who knows from the looks of it, we may be going anywhere.," said Spancer.

"Hush boys, we got an E-Mail, Jack wants us to come and pick up Dylan."

"I guess the way she eats didn't help her out any?", said Danger, as he pulled the car out and along the front.

Jack said, "Dylan, you need to go with the support team, Lisa and I need to talk privately, thanks." She got up and excused herself, then walked through both doors. As Greg held the door open for her, she slides in, Greg got in and the car sped off. There was silence as Erin said,

"Jack wants us to provide additional help and interview sorority girls, step on it," Danger slowed and waited.

Jack hands a hundred dollar bill to the waitress, and said, "Keep the change, the meal was marvelous." He held the door open for Lisa, the two went to the car, the doors opened and they both got in. Jack said "Start and drive to sorority house row", as he plugged his cell phone in, and said "Display?"

"This is harder than I even expected", said Lisa.

"What are you talking about?" asked Jack looking at the road, and the gauges, and his display screen.

"You know, finding you a personal assistant."

"You don't have to, from now on I will choose them. I will tell them exactly what I want and what I expect it. Jill was nice, but lack something, as for Dylan, well she was too butch. I need to find a super smart girl that can handle herself in a fight. It may end up being Audris, you know she was a gift from Ben, and having been exposed to the whole spy thing, but one thing does bother me."

"What's that?"

"She is a tattle tailer, and I don't need one of them."

The car slowed, as Jack looked at his rear camera to see a tail, he said "Ignore, friendly", the car sped back up.

"How about I let you decide who you want from now on. I'll just throw people at you and you decide.," said Lisa.

"Sure, all I want are people who are like me. Someone who wants to get the job done and done right and are willing to go the extra mile, no game players, certainly not ones who bob their heads when they eat."

"That's what I like about you. Oh and one more thing, would you consider a partner?"

"Just as long as she is pretty like you and can defend herself."

"You, and that whole thing in Cuba got me to thinking. A skilled partner might be the ticket to saving your life."

"Any ideas?"

"Yep, I have several candidates, now all I have to do is convince them to be your partner."

"That shouldn't be that hard, look at me I'm a nice guy."

"It's not that, it's that you like to bed anything that moves."

"Hey, I'm changing my ways."

"Just like what you said to me, I know you want me, hell half the base wants the boss, but I got to uphold a reputation. Maybe in six month's when there isn't a threat of exposure and those around us, we can really trust."

"Like Mitzi, and Trixie."

"Mitzi wholeheartedly, but I don' know about Trixie, you know she is seeing Damien?"

"So what, as long as it doesn't interfere with the mission, I don't care." said Jack.

The car slowed, as Jack took hold of the wheel and parked behind the another Mercedes.

He pulled out his phone, and got out. Jack waved to Danger to come forward, they did, as Lisa went inside. Their car came to a stop, they all got out, Jack said, "Dylan come here, I got a mission for you. Go to each of these sororities and find out if anyone else has been recruited, make sure you have pen and paper, and take your team. Then Jack approached Danger and said, "What I need is the support team to do is track down leads, uncover existing problems, following me doesn't help anyone. See that car over there? It has the state of the art detection and counterterrorism defenses, if I need you I will call Erin, you got me?"

"Yes sir" as he tried to salute, for Jack, who held his arm down, he added, "Do you know why I choose you, you have a bad reputation, but I believe your compassionate at what you do and who you believe in. So tell me who you think is your most dangerous solider, other than yourself."

"Well, actually you decided that when you assigned Cpl Spancer, with me."

"I have no idea, but I like the name. I want you two to hit every fraternity and when Lieutenant John Abrahams gets here, I'll direct him to you guys. Do you understand what I want?"

"Yes Jack."

Jack texted to Darlene, what he wanted and where to go. As he walked up to the huge house, Mitzi had all the girls in the living room as Jack entered. Jack asked "What do you have?"

"Well this is what I know so far, all the girls had been asked by a pretty blonde, who doesn't even go to the school. However; just yesterday a transfer student just arrived, and that is their pattern. A student will visit, and then you never hear from them again."

"This could be a case by case basis" said Jack, looking over at Miss Margaret, trying to console them. Then he heard "That's not the worst part, one of the girls, her name is Cami, she said that Jessica said that there was a professor who could help her pass easier. And that, will let me have you talk with her. She is in here", as Mitzi leads Jack down a hallway, Jack pauses and said, "If I had kept you behind would you have written down who was in each car?"

"I already know, does your assistant need to know?"

"How?" said Jack in amazement.

"She didn't do anything did she? Look, I had place explicated instructions for everyone to call me and tell me who was on each team. Like it or not, I'm really your true assistant."

"That's nice to know.," said Jack.

Mitzi knocks for Jack as the door opens, standing in just her lingerie was Cami. She had been crying. She looked up to see Jack and she rushed him and gave him a hug. He comforted her, saying, "It's alright, your safe, have a seat, let's talk about what happen", as Mitzi closed the door. Jack turned and said, "Mitzi could you come over here, you don't mind do you? She's my assistant."

"No, as I told her, what is your name?"

"My name is Jack Cash, I'm here to find a girl named Annabell Ryan, when we found out that you had been approached, what did they promise you?"

"Oh, 50,000 cash, but my family has money, and I have a fund I live off of."

"Did you tell her about that?"

"Yes, to get her to leave me alone."

"That was a mistake, now you are in trouble. Can you remember who this Jessica said that they could help you?"

"No, not really, all she said was he was a professor."

Jack looks over at Mitzi and said, "Have Lisa go talk with the President of the University, while you check male and female professors, probably someone in philosophy field. As you were saying, how did she get in touch with you?"

"By visit."

"Never by phone?"

"No."

"Do you know what she drove?"

"No, I was always inside."

"Jack," said a voice, it was Darlene.

"Back here". In walked Darlene as Cami's eyes lit up. She said "She is sure pretty."

"Indeed she is, as Jack gets up and added "Can you have whoever rode in with you stay with Cami, while I need you to follow me", Jack goes to the entrance to see Joana. He said

"She will do just fine, what's her name?"

"It's Joana", said Darlene.

"Very nice"

Jack gets close to her and said," I'd like you to do me a favor"

"Yes, how can I help you?"

"Actually I need for you to spend the next few days with our subject, go to her classes. I'll have Mitzi enroll you, you too will be the best of friends. In addition, I need you to get out all the information necessary, write it all down and text it to me or Mitzi, she is in the back room."

Jack sees Mitzi , and asked her to come over. She takes her time, with all the girls hanging all over her and says "How can I help you?"

"We have a problem. We need to get everyone out of here, I think I might have made a huge mistake. From now on, can you screen all the girls that I ask to join us, and also, let's take our two teams we have and make them a permanent two platoons of spies."

"I'm way ahead of you, funny that was what Lisa told me too."

Jack thought a moment, then said, "Can you give me that list and hand it to Darlene, as a text was coming in as unidentified. He read it, and said, "We got some action, and everyone needs a phone, and now", said Jack running, looking at his gaps, he was on the move in between houses and down a hill. He saw men with guns. The shotguns were cocked as shots were fired. Jack pulled his weapon. On the porch was Greg, apparently knocked out. Jack went In the house, to see nude women everywhere. Jack went to the back where several men stood in a line. A couple of men were hand tied to a pole, with dogs at their feet, the semi nude men were laughing. Jack thought about what and said, when a scream was heard and a girl called out "Jeb, watch out". As they turned to see Jack, in that moment he choose to spare their lives, and shot them in the thigh. All four of them were shot before they could react. He zip tied their hands behind their back, kicking their shotguns away, he heard "Aw that hurts mister, who are you, you ain't the sheriff?"

"What are you saying? The sheriff is dirty?"

"Hush up Jeb, he is probably a new deputy who doesn't know it yet."

"Know what yet?"

"That around here I'm the law," said a guy behind Jack, he added, "Drop your weapons."

Jack turned slowly to toss his gun at the sheriff's feet, to hear, "Now you put your hands on top of your head and kneel down." He looked down to see the pearl handed gun, as the sheriff knelt down and said, "In these parts, outside of North Memphis is my territory."

"Hold it right there", said a command voice, then added "Don't you dare touch that weapon, you are under arrest. As Jack got up to see, it was Danger, with a smile to and said "like that?'

"Yeah like that", as Jack picks up his gun, holsters it, and shows the sheriff his badge, and then puts it away. Jack said "Now you were saying sheriff, it's your way which is?"

"I want my attorney." said the sheriff.

Danger cinched down the hands of the sheriff and whispered in his ear, "Your under arrest, as if you held the gun on the President of our United States of America, that constitutes a traitor, and under the homeland act, you are considered an alien. I will personally take you and your friends to a secret place that you can scream your lungs out, then after I torture you to that point, I will get behind exactly what you meant when you told my boss, it is your area and you could do as you see fit."

The guy peed his pants, and began to shake as Danger whispered,

"Oh and by the way, you placed a gun on my boss and his name is Jack Cash, International Bounty Hunter, with a license to kill you, but his motto is spare a life, so that they are found not guilty, where as I shoot to kill and never ask question, now get up you maggot."

Jack finished cutting down his two men, Jack turned to hear a gunshot, and Wagner went down, there standing on the porch nude, was a woman with her hand outstretched firing another round, as Lieutenant John, ended her life.

Jack made it back up the hill and said, "Get everyone outside", as he sees the other guy check his friend, and said, "He is dead."

"Come on up here and zip tie everyone. Greg was helping everyone outside, most of them still nude, for a lineup. While Jack said "Lieutenant John, find Capt. Danger, and bring him here."

John searched and heard the screaming and found who he was looking for and said, "Jack wants you two to help him out."

"Spancer keep it up we'll get this pig to talk."

Jeff and John made it back upstairs to see Greg and Sgt Grant securing the prisoners, then Jack said "Listen up, tonight there was an attack on my men who were asking questions about a girl who was missing, and for this, two people are dead. With the power vested to me, I'm allow to kill all of you, although I'm a nice guy and believe in justice. All I want from you are the names of those that you know that are missing, and if anyone knows who a Jessica with blonde hair is, probably not a student, but is on the campus. I also want to know what ties you have with the sheriff and whatever illegal activity he was in to. Now who's first, speak up, cause in a hour or so you'll have more visitors than you can ever imagine.

Spancer broke through the screen door to announce, "I broke the sheriff, he said there is a little house off Eldridge road where this Jessica lives. Before he died he said there was a woman involved, her name was Alexis Roberts. Then all of sudden they all began to talk.

Jack pulled out his phone and texted Mitzi and brings whom she had. Jack said, "Danger and John you come with me, Spancer you and Billy stay here with Greg and write down info and have Erin send it to me, come on guys."

Jack, John and Jeff ran back up the hill, past the houses to his car, one in the back, and one in the front."

"Seniority out ranks you", said Danger.

"Open trunk, and doors, Jack opened his door, and pulled out his bag, and placed it in the trunk.

The trunk closed, as Jack slid behind the wheel, Jack set his phone in the dash, as the car came to life, he backed up and then sped off.

"This is really nice, "said Danger, but as Jack looked at him, he shut his mouth.

CH 4

The Rescue-Little Rock Ark

J ack positioned the car beside a low growing hedge, while both Jeff and John Abraham wanted out to surround the suppose missing girl house. Jack knew he found his two new assistants that were going to join his team, he thought. While he was processing data on his lap top, the two men swept the area, with wearing the infrared goggles. Then a thought occurred to him, he pulled up his steering wheel control and a heads up display, he chose to send off his bird, seconds later, it was shot off, he used a joystick to control its flight, up around, with a camera under it, in front of it, and to the rear, the pigeon was of a like size, it went up and then down the chimney, to hover. It then landed on a pile of logs, next to the chimney, for a quick view, then back in the air as it was at quarter speed. Evidence was there of someone, who was now gone, just as the bird saw Capt. Jeff Danger was looking in. At the front door and as the bird flew around, saw John Abraham in the rear, as the bird found a chandelier to land on, only to go blank as the house blew the doors out and exploded, the screen went dead.

The house burned a bit, but the rest of the house still stood. A claymore mine at head level took off both of their heads clean off, as the remnants was swinging.

"It was on", thought Jack, moving, with gun out upon realizing the men needed assistance, to see the reminisces of Danger at the front door, he said to himself "who goes out of their way to rig a house to blow, not to mention, at head level, how did they get out?"

Jack pulled up his phone to text to Mitzi, that the two men were down, suggest a clean-up crew, then made his way through the house. In the back door he saw the other man, turned, and went back, gun drawn, he went to the kitchen. He found a bar card that said Cuba, Tennessee, how ironic, as he picked up his blown up mechanical bird, minus the feathers, as he looked around and saw the remnants of the mines dangling at head level, he noticed a door to the garage. He tried it, it opened, he realized this was their way out. Basement popped in his mind, he turned around and tried the door, then went down the stairs, to see it was a sleeping pad, it smelled of urine and other fluids. No sign of anyone, he went back up, only to stop. In between the wall was a card, the same one up stairs, he pulled it out to see what it said,

"Help me, they are taking me to Eudora, Ark, A R, 4-6-08."

"Interesting", thought Jack, he was going back up the stairs when he heard a couple of voices, outside, to hear "Hold it Javier, there might be more, take the girls to the south location. Jack moved, with gun ready, to see two guys get into a van and peel out. Jack missed them, but went outside, with bird in hand, to his car. The trunk opened, as he tossed the dead bird in.

Jack slid behind the wheel and the car fired up. He was on the move and on pace as he turned to follow the van, as he thought, "a front and rear telescope would come in handy." They passed through the city, to find 61 south interstate. Jack kept a slow pace, but couldn't see if there was anyone in there, he was texting to all other cars, and passed on the news. Mitzi took over car 8, with Spancer driving, Greg in the back with Erin, with car six driven by Lisa, who has Darlene and Dylan.

Jack noticed the van turn off, Jack slowed, then turned. He slowed as a train came, he knew he had lost them, but as he noticed a red beeping dot at the bottom of the screen, he scrolled to show the map. The car had it fixed as the target, so everything was fine, the train passed, he drove on, he paced the car to do the speed limit. He noticed quickly that he was out of place with the beat-up trucks, not another newer car anywhere. All of a sudden over a hill, it opened up to a bar, where a hundred plus cars were at, Jack slowed his car. He then decided to park on the north side of the building, he zipped up his Jacket, and got out and said "Lock and secure."

Jack pushed the bar door open, and stepped in. In that moment he knew he was out of place, people close to the door stared at him, even the server snubbed him. He went in. His being there was creating quite a stir, as he took a seat at the bar, a very large man came over to him, placed his huge hand on his shoulders and said "Mister, this is a private club, we would like you to leave."

Jack looked up at the giant and said, "I'd advise you to take your hand off of me, before I canoe your head."

"Ha, Ha, Ha, laughed the man, until he felt the barrel of Jack's gun. The guy stopped laughing, then turned serious, as Jack motioned for him to bend down, he did as Jack pulled his badge. He said "I'm an International Bounty Hunter, my name is Jack Cash, and I want some information, there's a white long van outside, tell me who they are", said Jack looking up at the guy to show he was serious.

There was a pause; the ultimatum was there, while others around them cleared out.

"They're in the back, follow me."

Jack was hot on his tail as a door opened, they went in, moments later, six shots could be heard. Jack opened the door, and screamed at the top of his lungs, "From this moment forward, this place is closed, so leave at your own free will."

Some people rushed Jack. He took his time, as he canoed several men's heads. He had his gun out and declared, "Why don't you all come at me."

That stopped them dead in their tracks as Jack dialed up the reinforcements. Trixie texted back she was five minutes away, in a transport plane with Jim, ready to land. She rounded them up, then text to Jack "your troops are jumping now." Jack now realized he needs some help. He turned when he heard a loud voice say, "Everyone on the floor, this is the FBI my name is Rick Teal, and my partner is Emily Webster," Jack saw the two FBI officers, as everyone was silent, he added, "Now put your hands on top of your head, I believe a federal officer commanded you to assist him, who is first to answer him?"

A hand was in the air, "speak" said Rick.

"The mister was inquiring about those girls in the white van, well, they have a place in the back, and that's where they should be at." said one guy; all were on the ground covering their heads.

"You heard that Jack", yelled Rick. Siding up with him.

Jack stepped out from the shadows, so that they could see him. Jack said, "Yeah, I heard that", as he moved towards them, his gun still out and ready. He turned the corner, the door opened, it was Spancer and Billy with semi—automatic weapons ready to rock and roll. Just then the voice of reason said, "I'm Mitzi with the President of our United States, GOA, office, who are you?"

"We're with the FBI office out of Helena."

She looked at Jack as he said "Were sorry to hear about Jeff and John."

"What can I say, this game is tough."

"Well what do you need?"

"Besides these two, who else do you have?"

"We have Erin?"

"Can she E-mail or is she a fighter?"

"Both, she is tough."

"Alight, I'll take her with me. Do you have access to troops?"

"Yes", they both said, as Rick allowed Mitzi to go first, and said, "What do you need?"

"A small force to secure all of this and on stand by for a fight down in Eudora."

"Eudora, what do you know about that?" asked Rick.

"Well I found a bar card at one of those houses, why, what's so special about Eudora?" asked Jack.

"Well it's where the State's national orchestra is and there a touring group" said Rick.

"What's states do they go to?" asked Jack.

"Oh I don't know, here in Arkansas, maybe Tennessee, Mississippi, Alabama" said Rick.

Jack looked at Mitzi who looked back at Jack and said, "You better get going, we will clean this up."

Jack came closer to them, as Rick said, "We need to talk with you."

"Come on out here, let's talk", said Jack. As he was in the parking lot, he noticed the white van was gone, and asked Rick Teal

"What do you have?"

"Well we received a text message from you, and we responded, did you not get our text?"

Jack shrugged his shoulder, and said," No."

"Well anyway, Emily and I have been tracking the Professor."

"What's his name?" asked Jack.

"It's Alistair Richards, head of psychiatrics, I think he hypnotizes the young women, then kidnaps them, then forces them into some sort of slave trade. Up and down these two states and along the Mighty Mississippi River, we pull out young dead girls who have been raped and battered. I was just wishing someone like you would have come to help us. I will tell you, I can mobilize three separate National Guard units to help, what do you say?"

"What is your phone number?" asked Jack.

Rick Teal gave him his number, plus the Commander of all three units, then Jack said,

"Can you pass these numbers onto Mitzi, she is my assistant."

"Will do, can we go with you?"

"Sure, or I can just meet you to regroup."

"Greenville, there is an airfield, small, but a C-130 can land there."

Jack passes him, and then turns to holster his weapon and asked,

"How did you know I was in there?"

"We saw you pull up as we got here."

"Alright I see", said Jack, as he saw a long haired brunette, in the back seat of the Mercedes. He tapped on the window, she opened the door as Jack said, "Do you want to go with me?"

She looked at him, and then said, "Sure, should I tell Mitzi?"

"Nah, she already knows, come along."

Jack helped her out, as he went to his car and said "Unlock, start, eighty degrees, warm feet and chest". Jack opened the door for her as she slid in and shut it. Jack went around the car, got in and said,

"Systems check, continue coordinates on target. The car took off, and they were heading west, north, night was setting, as the van was one hour ahead, projection was Little Rock.

"Really", thought Jack, as he had his hands on the wheel. Erin sat back, she seemed uncomfortable being in his presence, he knew he should of left her behind. He commanded stealth mode, and auto pilot, he plugged his phone in, and opened the four hundred plus e-mails, as he said, "Private screen."

Erin said "You're not driving? How can the car go that fast? We're going like two hundred miles per hour, but it doesn't feel like it."

"This car is a person, she is called Sara, if you want something you ask Sara to slow down. How fast do you want to go?"

"Well the speed limit, for starters."

"Who are you? Do you know why you're here?"

"Yeah, to be your assistant", asked Erin.

"Do you know what that means?" asked Jack.

"Yeah, you talk with people and sometimes meet with some people."

"No, I don't really think you grasp what I do, do you?"

"Yeah, you work for the President of our United States."

"And what does that mean?, really."

"I don't know, really, but I'm willing to learn."

"I kill people for a living" said Jack, looking over at her. She was speechless and in a bit of a daze she said "Well that makes sense now."

"What does, well when Miss Margaret said there would be times of violence, and I thought I could handle that?"

"And now?" asked Jack, wanting to strike a conversation with her to take his mind off of Jeff and John.

"I don't think so, I want out." she said defiantly. She tried for the door handle only to see that there was none.

"Right here, right now, out in the middle of the Arkansas back country, I don't think so. When we get to Little Rock, I'll send you home. Do you still have that phone? Call car 2, and get Audris on the line."

She did as she was told. The car slowed, as it got onto I-40 west, then instantly the car was in top gear, and doing 200 miles per hour. With sixty miles to go, twenty minutes clicked off, he went out to the Central Arkansas University main campus. He slowed, as the beep was close, but so was the gas gauge. Jack pulled into a gas station, he got out and looked in the car at her and said "I think you need to go to the bathroom."

"Alright", she said as she now could push the door open and got out.

Jack watched her leave, as he swiped his per diem card, and pumped the tank full 200 dollars, filling his eighty gallon tank. He then went to his trunk, to find a bottle of special additives, he opened one up and put it in the tank. Then Jack called Jim, as Brian answered and said, "Yes sir?"

"Where's Jim?" asked Jack, isn't this his phone?"

"Yes, I'm holding to correspond to where you are going, Jim is flying the plane, we're on the descent into Little Rock AFB, we'll be on the ground in a minute, need support?"

"I need a pickup."

"How say you? For you?"

"Nah, one of the girls wants to quit."

The phone was silent for awhile, so Jack slid his phone shut. He saw a blonde haired girl appear who looked like Audris. Everything about her was different. She got into the car and the door shut.

Jack finished pumping, he closed and locked the lid, took his receipt and put it in his pocket. He watched Erin walk past him to the waiting car. Jack got in to see a sweet smiling face. Audris, who said, "So, why the switch? "I thought she was a good choice for you."

The car fired and off it went, as it drove towards the white van, it slowed, Jack told Audris, "She quit."

"Really, nobody does that, that will be the last time you see her."

"What do you mean?" asked Jack honestly.

"Well when we all joined the program, we had to sign an execution order, if we quit or fail you while in the field. Did she do that?"

"Well, I guess she did." said Jack shrugging his shoulders.

"That's crazy, she must of forgotten about that order, or maybe she's just plain stupid, anyway, I'm next up so don't worry I'm all yours, there will be nothing that will cause me to quit."

"If I let you out, can you find your way into that house?"

"Absolutely, I'll do whatever it takes."

"Do you have a phone?"

"Yes, the one you gave us."

"Great, take it and don't for any reason use it unless it's a dire need, understand?" said Jack, he added," For your back up, I'll call car number two."

Car two was behind Jack. He let out Audris, car two watched as Jack went around the corner. Lieutenant Casey said, "What is going on?"

They all watched as Audris knocked on the door, and she went in."

Casey grabbed the phone from Erin, to scroll down the texts and said, "You bitch, what have you done, the phone is shut off?"

Casey turned on the phone, to dial up Jack, it went on ringing, then Jack answered, "Rogers, you got those zip ties, Casey puts the car in park and lunged at Erin, who opened the door, as she slipped out.

"Ah let her go" ,said Allison.

Casey was cussing and said "Look, Audris just went into a house, and we can't help, Christ all mighty, what are you two doing, shit."

Casey got out of the car, and ran towards the house with his gun drawn, he came up to the front window and saw Audris screaming at two people. He became distracted when another car pulled up and three guys got out, he didn't recognize any of them. Casey stood still and watched as the 3 men storm the house. They past him, with guns drawn. Lieutenant Casey follows them in, he was stopped at the door by one of the men, who showed a badge, to say, "Were undercover, back off, were here to difuse this situation." Audris was let out, and was comforting a older man.

Meanwhile, Jack parked his car across the alley on the next street over, at the other house. He sees a white van. Jack used his phone for confirmation, it was his target. He reloaded his weapon, his phone was ringing, but he turned it off. Jack moved out of his car, to the white van, where a guy sat in the driver's seat, waiting. Jack turned the knob, opened the door, and placed his gun to the guy's head. He said,

"Hold it where you're at, you move and your dead."

Just then a loud siren started up and in that moment, the guy moved, knocking Jack back and down, as the guy dove away scrambling to get out of the passenger's seat, and frantically trying to get out. The guy saw Jack get up, so he pulled a gun and fired at Jack. Jack swung away, and returned a shot of his own, His shot was true. Jack pulled away and turned to see another guy, coming down the stairs on the outside of the house, Jack asked "where are the girls?'

The guy scrambled, as Jack shot him in the leg, went over to him, and Jack, zip tied him. Jack went to the house and down the stairs, he saw a sea of women. One of the girls said "Hey you're not the handler."

Jack cold cocked her on the cheek, as she went down, the other women all cheered as they came towards him. Jack said, "Whoa, stay where you're at, I'm calling in reinforcements, so sit still it's almost over. Jack was texting Mitzi to tell her what he uncovered, but, need some girls to take their places. Jack asked the girls "How many are here?"

"Twelve Sir."

"Has anyone told you what is going on here?" asked Jack.

"Yeah, they said we're going to see the Mistro in Eudora, on our way to Europe."

"Where are you all from?" asked Jack.

"Some of us were from Memphis, Nashville, Alabama and Mississippi."

"Who took care of you?"

"Well that one girl you knocked out, and three others who are with the handler tonight."

Jack was back on his phone to see all the missed calls. Jack called up Jim who answered and said "I'm sorry."

"Don't worry about it, can you meet me, at this location with Brian, I need some more ammo, and bring as many Air Force personnel women, at least twenty, and a bus."

"Will do" said Jim, who waited for Jack to hang up.

Jack turned and said, "Girls I need someone who wants to help me out?"

"I will, "said a girl similar to Erin.

"Alright, what is your name?"

"My name is Desiree Johnson, what is yours?"

"Jack Cash, International Bounty Hunter."

"Cool, what do you want me to do, Jack?"

"Go up to the window, and watch out for anyone returning?"

She went past him, up the stairs, while Jack zip tied Marissa (the girl that got cold cocked)and as the others told him what her name was. Jack called out to the other girls and said "Lay down and rest, you'll be out of here soon."

"What if we don't want to be out of this situation?"

"Tough, shut up and sit down."

Jack went upstairs. He saw Desiree at the window of the front door she said, "Something is sure going on across the street."

Jack went over to the window, to see it was the house he remembered sending Audris in, now cops were all over that place. "Good", he thought, the diversion would buy us some time so they could get the girls out, and keep the other girls from coming back."

Jack looked how stunningly beautiful Desiree was, she was similar to Erin, except much more mature, she turned to look at him and said,

"Are we in trouble?"

"No, do you have any idea why you're here?'

"Yeah, for fame and fortune."

"What do you mean?" asked Jack, motioning for her to help him out.

"Well they said we would get 50,000 dollars to do this, and live a life of comfort."

"What about next year, or the years after that, let alone twenty or thirty years from now?", asked Jack.

"I don't know, I hadn't thought about that."

"How about, where will you spend that money, had you even seen it, let alone, why be in a basement and not a classy hotel. No, you have been duped into believing 50,000 dollars is a lot of money, plus they want you for your body." said Jack. Looking at her realizing the huge mistake she had made. Desiree began to cry, she quickly wiped away her tears, and said, "Jack here they come."

Jack motioned for her to come towards him, then switch places. Jack stood behind the door, as the door opened, and three girls came in laughing. They saw Desiree and asked her, "What are you doing up here sweetie?"

Jack slammed the door shut and said "Hands up." he was motioning with his gun.

"Who are you mister?"

Jack said, "Doesn't matter, shut your mouth. Desiree, come here and place this on their wrists."

"What do you think you're doing?" said the blonde one.

"Making a citizen's arrest."

"On what charge?"

"Treason to the national security."

"What does that mean?" said the blonde.

"Anything I deem necessary" said Jack. He added "Desiree, zip tie their hands". Just then, the blonde rushed him Jack shot her in the head, she fell face first dead. The other girls were stunned and said, "Mister we don't want trouble, are you a hit man?"

"No, I'm a federal agent, and anyone who gets in my way is going to die, so put your hands behind your backs."

"Listen Mister we can show you who our contacts are."

"I'm looking forward to that, have a seat. Desiree, can you watch the door, Thank you."

Then Jack looked at the two short haired brunettes and said, "Begin, who's first?"

"You're not going to kill us, are you?"

"Give me a good reason, tell me how all this works and I will let you go, or should I say, how about the promise you made to these girls."

"Alright, how will I know you won't do what you did to Beth?"

"It's all about trust. If I feel your trustworthy enough, then you will be allowed to go. So tell me how it all works."

"Well about two years ago I was approached, while I was in college, from another girl who has since retired. This is our last year, we thought it was legitimate, we were paid $50,000 for the year, each of the girls are paid that, so what is wrong with that?"

"Why are they staying in a basement?" asked Jack.

"I don't know, that's what was chosen."

"Where does all the girls go for the 50,000 dollars?"

"I don't know."

"That is not a good enough answer for me. I was thinking, how about overseas? Into a slave trade?"

"What no, that's not right, just last month I got my girlfriend into this?"

"Really, have you heard from her?"

"No, they said for the first six month, they are in training."

"Is that what they call it? So who is supposed to come next?"

"Well, we make the final trip down to Eudora, where we wait for a photographer to take their pictures, and then we leave them behind, that is the last I know."

"Has any of you ever heard of Annabell Ryan?"

"I have, said the other girl, she was the all-American soccer player, prized by the handler."

"Who is that?" asked Jack.

"He was more known as a skunk, for all those nasty cigars he smoked. All we know is that his name is Mister Roberts, but he isn't the real devil, you have to watch out for his wife Alexis, she likes girls."

"Where are all these people?" Jack asked.

"Well, they're in Eudora, it's a gated and private exclusive community."

As the other girl said, "Yeah, everyone knows everyone, you're going to have to know someone to get in."

"Oh I do know someone, I think I have the solution, it's called the National Guard."

"You have access to the military?"

"Yep, I'm with the military." Jack said proudly.

"So, you're quite powerful?"

"Jack, there is a bus outside" said Desiree.

"Open up the door, let them in, can you go down stairs and get the girls together, and bring them up."

In walked Jim, he said, "We got what you needed, here are some rounds," as he hands Jack an ammo vest that holds 30 clips, which are loaded. Jack slides in on with Jim's help, as Jack reloaded his gun and then holstered it.

Jim said, "Alright, let's get these girls on the bus, and make the transfer."

Jack said, "Change of plans, I need you to take the car, also the bird's in the trunk and was blown up, and can you replace that?"

"Yes of course, you're probably low on fuel?"

"No, I filled it up"

"Really, what did you put in?"

"I don't know 91 or supreme."

"That's alright", said Jim, "But in the trunk is the boost, for every 20 gallons, you put a can of octane boost in."

"So take the car back to the plane, and oh by the way, do you have any more zip ties?" said Jack.

"What are you going to use for transportation?"

"I'll take the van." Jack said.

"No worries, I will take the recharge gun box out of your trunk and put it in the van, so what about those two girls?" Jim asked.

"No, I will take them with me. Your names are?"

"I'm Susan and this is Amber. We pledge to get you in, and stop this horror."

"Fine, keep seated," as the girls from the basement left, the women from the Air Force came in, not as pretty but pretty physical.

"That's it" said Brian, carrying a zip tied man.

"Two down and one captured", what about this one?"

"Desiree, you're not leaving?" asked Jack.

"I'd like to stay, if you don't mind."

"Well, it's up to you, I can't say no or yes, either you want to participate or not." said Jack motioning for them to go.

"I'd like to participate, if you don't mind", asked Desiree.

"Alright Jim, do you have a manifest for all those women?"

"Yes, here you go."

"Thanks we will see you in Greenville?" said Jack.

"Or where ever you're at, I've activated your tracking device."

Jack sees them out, and then closes the door. Then Jack heard,

"Mister are you going to let us go?"

"No, you have to earn my trust; Jack sees the keys in the dish bowl and says, "Are these the keys to the van?"

"Yeah", said Amber.

"This is a step in the right direction. Desiree can you watch the door."

"Yes Jack", she said. Jack went outside and looked over the van, he opened the passenger side door, to see the fallen guy gone, and the blood cleaned up. In the back, the seats were taken out in place of a mattress. He saw the set-up, girls in the back seat, the prisoners in the very back. He will drive, thinks Jack. "And have Desiree in the passenger seat, Definately." Jack went back into the house and past the two prisoners as Susan said, "Mister I need to go to the bathroom."

"Do it where you're at", said Jack as he past them, he went down stairs and said, "Listen up ladies, my name is Jack Cash and I want to thank you for your participation, I hope this is all volunteers?"

"Yes sir, but some were getting hungry."

"What do you want?" asked Jack.

"Were not picky, you choose", said one of the stand out girls.

Jack came up the stairs and asked, "Desiree can you escort our two prisoners to the bathroom, do you mind?"

"No, not at all."

"What, how will I wipe", complained Susan.

"I'm sure you'll figure it out", said Desiree, standing back.

"Come on at least put my hands up front." showing them from behind her,

'I'll cut you free, if only I watch you" said Jack "and Desiree is in the other room."

"Fine, I told you before, you can trust us." said Susan.

"As I said, you need to prove it to me, as Jack cut off the zip tie; she turned and gave him a kiss on the cheek as she said "If you let me, I will really prove it."

"Get going", said Jack as he pushed her along, as Desiree led Susan in first, she did her business, then it was Amber's turn, both were very open, and revealing. Jack said, "Come on let's go, let's see your wrists. Jack cinched up her wrists up front, then said,

"Go take a seat on the couch, he did the same thing to Amber. He saw Desiree next as the door was open, he lingered a bit. He saw her undo her pants, and she pulled them down, and then her panties, he then left, as Desiree had a smile on her face.

Jack hit the kitchen to see if they had any take-out menus. He found an Italian menu, he pulled up his phone to call the number, he heard someone say, "Can I have twelve meals with meat lasagna, and twelve without, ranch dressing on the side for all, and miscellaneous pop, and twenty four waters. You can you put silver ware and napkins in with that and how much will that be for pick up?"

"$300 dollars with tax and it will be ready, in twenty minutes."

"Great, thanks." Said Jack.

"Are you going out to get some food?" asked Amber.

"Nah, I'll send Desiree." As she looked over at Amber, then Susan, then to Jack.

"I heard my name?"

"Yeah, would you mind going out and getting our food, here is, $ 300 dollars, and the address is on that brochure."

"Sure, no problem" she said in a loving way. Jack tosses her the keys, she went out and starts the van, and pulls it out. She went down to the corner, turns left, past car 9, both girls duck down. Then Monroe slides over the seat, starts up the Mercedes, and slides in behind the van. Monroe says, "Text Jack and tell him us ladies are on the road, as they followed her past car 2, as Rogers said, "Hey isn't that the van?"

"Nah come back here and give me some more loving", said Allison.

Desiree, pulled out her phone that she had in her sock. She dialed up a number and said, "Yeah, you were right, I have the spy in my sights, I'm out getting food for the group, a lot of changes, he is with me He is connected to at least four National Guard bases, he had support coming, they took his car away, but he has enough rounds to stop an army."

"You want me to what, poison him?"

"I can't, if he asks me to taste all the food, and drink", and , He'll know it's me, fine."

"Rat poison, soaked in water then dip in some aspirin, it won't kill him, just knock him off his edge." said the voice on the speaker phone as Desiree was swerving trying to drive the van.

"Alright, oh before I forget, the women all have been traded out with some Air Force girls."

"No worries, we'll hit the van before the destination."

"Alright, I need to take 65 south to Dumas, and that is where you hit us, should I jump out?"

"Yeah, I'll beep you, just before it happens."

Meanwhile Andrea was texting all this action to Jack, Jack looked at his incoming texts, as he was watching his two prisoners. He said "When did Desiree get picked up?"

"In Nashville."

"Who recruited her?"

"I did", said Susan. She wore a huge smile on her face.

"How did you meet her?"

"Well actually, I was at Tennessee State University and she met me, and we hit it off."

"Really", said Jack, as Jack tapped into the Tennessee State University data base, to see a roll that showed they had a Desiree, however, the two pictures don't match, nor the I D numbers. So Jack then texted back to car 9 to follow her, and pick him up a meatball sub, and a soda. He started to think about his next move, thinking he has a mole, he pulled up his map to Greenville, he sees where an ambush would be good. So instead of taking 278 south, out of Pine Bluff, looks like He'll take 425 south to Monticello, over the hills.

An urgent text came in from Lisa, stated they had no leads and the professor is on a two week emergency leave, without his wife, should we pick her up?"

"yes", texted, Jack to include, "Know any photographer's?", linked to all these, currently have plan in works to take Eudora.

Car 9 reported that the van stopped at a convenience store, came out with a sack, then on to the restaurant."

Jack heard a voice that said, "Some of the girls need to use the bathroom."

"Yeah, go ahead, you don't need permission," said Jack looking up to see a brightly smiled girl. Jack stood at the place in front of the door to the bathroom.

"Alright, my name is Deborah, please to meet you, she said coyly."

"Will you two stop it" said Amber.

Jack smiled at her as she left and went back down the stairs. Jack went back to his receiving text messages, Morgan got your sandwich, and saw that the girl looked anxious, as she got closer to Desiree, and said she has a satellite phone.

Jack erased that one, to text, "car's 3, 4, 7 and 8; to assemble at Greenville airport, ASAP, leave two behind for each college."

The texts came back from car 4, Lianna and Sgt Morris will stay at UAB. SSgt Sinclair and Erica Adams will head west. Jack responded by texting, "Pick up a disposable cell phone, and send a text to a specific number he gave them."

The next text that came in was from car 3, Lysandra and Sgt Lawrence, will stay at Mississippi University at Jackson, and Lieutenant O' Donald and Freya are heading this way.

Jack texted back, saying, "Pick up a disposable phone and text back at a new number."

Car's 7 and 8 turned around and as Jack texted, "State who was who, in which car?"

Car 7 was first to respond, Lieutenant Clark, Kosta, Sgt Jackson, Carrie and Manicka.

Car 8 was SSgt O' Brien, Jen, Monroe, Sgt Bauer, and Brooks.

Jack typed in, "Meet at the airport and text me when you're in position to cars, 3, 4, 7 and 8, out."

The van came back, as he received a text that Morgan will place the food on the driver's seat.

Desiree came in, with two big bags, and then set the keys in the bowl, for Jack and said, "Can you set up a plate for Susan and Amber."

"What about you?" asked Desiree.

"Oh, I'm not hungry." Said Jack.

"Oh, alright" said Desiree, in the kitchen, pulling out the food. Jack to call out and said, "Debby, can you get food for all the girls in the basement please."

"Debby, huh, sounds like you're getting cozy with your charges." said Amber.

Debby showed up, with a smile as she heard that and said, "Yeah, while you were gone, we had an orgy, and you weren't invited."

Jack finished his text to Jim and said, "Can you send out a recon plane over the Eudora area?"

Jack put his phone away, to announce, "I'll be outside for a moment."

"Sure go ahead", said Desiree. Jack went outside and opened the unlocked door, to see the hot sandwich, and soda, he got in, and quickly downed half the sandwich and half of the soda, he looked up several times as he finished it off quickly along with the soda, he then placed the remnants in the bag, and he stuffed it under the seat. He opens the driver's door to see the door at the house open, and at the door was Desiree who said, "Is there anything I can do for you Jack?"

"Well now that you say that, I do have a bit of a headache, can you find me an aspirin?"

"Yeah, sure hold on", said Desiree, she said with an excitement to her voice. As she went back in., then came back out, and handed them to Jack. He popped them in his mouth, and drank some tap water and said "Thanks I need that."

Desiree went in, as Jack followed, he spit out the two pills, as he went in he said, "That was awful", he saw Debby at the table, with some of her friends. Jack saw a unopened soda, and he popped it open, and took a drink. He bent down and whispered and said, "Debby, I don't feel so good, can you and your friends watch over me downstairs and keep an eye on Desiree?"

"Yes, we will, that's what Jim told us to do?"

"Good for him, now I need to go rest" said Jack.

"Hold up, I will go with you" said Debby.

"Where are you two going?" asked Desiree.

Jack stopped to see the three girls and said "I'm not feeling too well, when their done eating can you zip tie their hands please", Jack turned and went down stairs. Jack chose an empty bed, hopped on it and took a pillow to prop himself up.

Debby looked around and said, "Alright ladies go upstairs and get some chow." Desiree said, "He left me in charge."

"Don't test me miss, I'll have you put down", said Amber. The Air force women all stood in a line waiting, with arms crossed, waiting. For Desiree to get her food, she seemed anxious, then went downstairs looking for Jack. She sees Debby, for which she says," Are you going to stand there all night?"

"If I have too, Jack was tired, so he went to bed."

"Can I at least see him?' asked Desiree.

"What for, you don't have anything to offer him, so don't push it sister?"

Night turned into morning as all ten air force girls stood proud, while Desiree slept on her chair. Susan and Amber, slept on the sofa. While Jack slept with one eye open, and the other shut, maybe six hours of sleep, he was recharged, he awoke, got up, and up the stairs he went. Jack said, "Excuse me, thank you girls for the security. Can you get the other girls up, we will be ready to go shortly."

Jack did his business, then, washed his hands, he stepped out to see the line had formed for the only bathroom. The Air Force girls took care of Susan and Amber, while Jack grabbed the keys, to take them out side. He got behind the wheel, he fired up the van, turned on the heat, he let the van warm up. He waited as girls started to come out, as Jack went around to open the side doors, the two prisoners were taken to the side, and set in. Then all nineteen girls got in, Jack slid the door shut. He saw Desiree, take the passenger side door. Jack saw Debby and asked

"Do you have any experience in driving vans this size."

'Yeah, sure, I can drive a dump truck."

"Nice to know that, go ahead and get in, and sit behind Desiree."

"Yes sir", said Debby.

Jack got in, backed out the van, as Car number 9 was ready. As Jack turned the corner, so was car 9, driven by Morgan. The van went left and so did car number 9. As Morgan looked to see who was in the back seat, she crossed over the lane. She stopped, down went the window, as did theirs, and said, "Get in, were following Jack hurry up."

Cpl Rogers, got out and got into the back with Allison. Both looked pretty messed up, as Morgan stepped on it and asked "Where's the rest of your team?"

"Well lieutenant Casey went into that house with the white van, and was arrested."

"So what were you two doing last night?'

"Oh nothing, mind your own business" said Allison.

'Don't you remember what you signed at your entrance?'

"What are you talking about? There were some forms?" asked Allison.

"They were much more than that, you're not suppose to fraternize with the opposite sex, unless directed by Jack himself."

"What, who wrote that bull shit, he can't tell me what I do with my body."

"Oh yes he can" said Andrea texting to Jack and added "It's like your cheating on the President."

"What President?"

"You know of the United States, what you have done is treason to our boss, our body, mind and everything is the possession of

Jack's to do as he sees fit, not for you to decide you want to have sex with him."

"I'll give him sex too, if that's what he wants."

"You don't get it do you, that form you signed asked if you were a virgin?"

"What, you're not all virgins?"

"I know I am, and proud of it" said Morgan.

"Me as well, I was recruited when I was fifteen, and I'm proud of that, our faith lies in our leader", said Andrea.

"You both are crazy, I'll do who I want" said Allison.

Meanwhile, Jack drove slower until car 9 caught up, as they went through the city, and onto 65 south. Jack looked around, the hills and all the trees was a good sign. The next big sign read, Pine Bluff. Then Jack asked "Does anyone need to stretch their legs?"

"Yeah", said a couple of women.

Jack saw the exit, and saw he needed gas anyway, so he pulled off. He went to the nearest gas station and parked.

"I'll go pay for it", said Desiree. Volunteering.

"Alright, go watch her", said Jack as he pumped the gas. Half the girls went in. They saw Desiree pay with credit card, and took the key to the bathroom. Two women followed her, they listen through the door and heard, she was talking on the phone to someone. As she finished, the two girls came out and around front, to see Jack and say, "She has a phone."

"Thanks", said Jack as he got in, in his rear view mirror he see's car 9, everyone got in the van. They waited for Desiree, as she was hurrying over and into the passenger's seat to ask Jack, "You weren't thinking of leaving me behind, were you?"

"Nah, it never crossed my mind", said Jack.

They drove out of Pine Bluff, to hear, "Are we still on course on this road?" asked Desiree.

"I didn't think I had one, said Jack, as he turned off the road and slammed on the brakes. Jack pulled out his gun and said, "Hands behind your back", as Desiree hit her head on the dash and recoiled back into her seat, Jack pulls a zip tie, and secures her wrists and said.

"Where is your phone?"

"You're not going to touch me, I'm an FBI agent."

"So, Debby will you search her, strip her if you have too."

Debby reached into her pants and pulled out her phone to show Jack."

"You know what you're called." said Jack.

"Am just doing my job?" said Desiree.

"Really, by who's order, my background check shows you're a renegade agent."

Jack showed her what it said, "Kill her, Desiree is bad", by order of the FBI chief.

"Now let's see, if I'm not mistaken, all agents fall under him, or shall I say you, either or, your dead. And now on to you, who you were talking too and what is their plan? She sat in silence and waited.

"Either way it won't save you, we're going this way. Debby hold onto that phone but don't touch anything it could be bugged. You poisoned me once, and the next time I'll kill you myself."

Desiree sat in silence, as she wept. Behind her was twenty two angry women ready to kill her themselves.

"Debby can you drive, I'll be back here." said Jack.

"Yes sir."

Jack got in the back, as the other girls got in, Debby drove.

Jack was communicating via text messaging, he knows Car 9 was behind them, and car 8 was close to rendezvous point. With car 3 with them. A new message it was from Lisa, she said she was cleaning up the house, how are you?"

Jack wrote fine, and kept it up. Then he saw a rocket heading their way he yelled "Stop".

A rocket whizzed in front of them, and crashed in the trees. A huge explosion erupted.

Jack said, "Hop out I'll drive", Jack jumped in the seat and waited till Debby got in. Jack said "Shove that phone of hers in her pants," so that is just what Debby did. Desiree's crying was annoying everyone so Jack said, "Open up her door and kick her out."

Debby did that, as Desiree flew out, she rolled a bit. She got up just as another missile came in right for her, she exploded.

Jack stopped the van, to text the AFB. He instructed air support and minutes later two Hornets flew over and another explosion could be heard. Jack said "It should be smooth sailing from now on."

CH 5

The Mistro-Missile

J ack slowed the van, the sign said "Greenville". He turned towards the airport, as those that saw him waved him on. The airport had a small field, he drove to a huge hanger. All the teams that he requested, to include those from Memphis, who were flown in by charter were there waiting. Jack parked next to the aircraft, he got out and said, "We don't have much time, you got any food?"

"A hot meal inside" said one man beside the plane. Jack opened the rear doors and said," There is food inside, go get it girls."

Jack walked up the ramp to his room, he opened the door to see Lisa holding court. She was dishing out punishment and told everyone to clear out, Jack smiled at Mitzi and Dylan as the door shut.

Jack looked through his drawers and pulled out some clothes and stepped into the bathroom. He stripped down and heard "You have been busy, I like when you're in the offensive mode, people either stand or fall." Lisa watched him step in and take a quick hot shower. Jack stepped out and said, "It isn't fair, you get to see me and you're still dressed."

"Again, I told you when there aren't forty people around, besides you have your pick of twenty plus girls," said Lisa.

"Doubtful, everyone has a role to play." said Jack, finishing drying off.

"What do you think about dividing the remaining Delta force teams in to two distinct teams, one as a direct support to you and the other for cleanup for me?"

"Only if you hire someone, I think that could help out."

"Well sure, you can hire whoever you want."

"Sure but will they get paid?" asked Jack honestly, as he dressed right in front of her.

"Absolutely, who do you have in mind?"

"Her name is Master Sergeant Snyder, I call her Debby."

"What is your plan later?" said Lisa, smiling at him as he finished dressing.

"Well after I eat something, I'm going after the Mistro, he is some suppose conductor. But first I need to drive Susan and Amber to the process house in Eudora, and I want no support till I get the Mistro under arrest."

"You got it. What are your plans with the girls?"

A knock on the door, Lisa opened the door to see Mitzi, who had a platter of spaghetti she said, "The AFB gave us a galley and stocked it with food exclusively for Jack, this is what Jim told me to tell you."

"Fine set it down, as Jack slid his wallet in and then his holster, he picked up his newly loaded gun and two clips. He was putting his older jacket on when Jim came in to show Jack a new Jacket. Jim said, "Along the liner is a roll of plastique explosives and blasting caps, then on the inside pocket, is a special explosion proof bag. Inside the jacket are over one hundred zip ties. In addition, there are four protein bars and finally a hydration system that holds two quarts of pure R/O water, this tube pulls out."

Jim walked around to point out how the water was evenly distributed, and said, "See the grooves, it is to allow anyone who shoots at you to be diverted to the magnet in the middle of your back, see how the water feels?"

"Yeah, it's like having a cool jacket on, and there doesn't seem to be much sloshing going around." Said Jack pretty amazed.

"Finally, the water works two ways, its cool now, but do you see this tab, pull it out and the jacket gets really warm, but it's a one and done deal, were working on trying to make this jacket electrified, to protect you when you're down and out." said Jim honestly concerned, as Jack and Lisa could witness.

"In addition there is ten thousand dollars cash, in two bundles of one thousand dollar bills."

"What do I do with that?"

"What do you mean?" asked Jim honestly.

"Well you should know that these thousand dollar bills are hard to make change for and second, there for special transactions only, wouldn't that look to suspicious?" Jack hands them back.

A smile came over Jim's face, and stuffs them in his coat pocket and pulled out two large bundles of one hundreds in two bundles, and hands them to Jack, and said, "This is what I thought you could use, the other was someone else's idea, not to mention who, they both looked at Lisa who smiled and said,

"Well I didn't know."

"Do I have to sign that out?"

"Nah, that is you're to keep, do whatever you want with it."

Jim helped Jack put the money in specialty-designed pockets, so it was evening him out, in between bites, Jack said, "I want to add a person to your team."

"I usually work alone," said Jim, looking over at Lisa, who shook her head and said, "Whatever Jack wants."

"Fine, I guess I have a partner now, what about Brian, is this who it is?"

"No, her name is Debby; I guess she can drive anything."

"I could use that", he said in a condescending way, under his breath, he said, "A woman, it's not like we already have enough of them."

"Great, I will let her know, she is out in the van," said Jack, "Now I want as many girls as we have to do this, if Lisa won't then let them all go?"

"What do you mean, quit?, they don't quit under any circumstance."

Jack pulls out his phone to pull up the e-mail from Audris, to show Lisa.

An infuriated Lisa said, "This whole idea, was that these girls were for you, exclusively."

Mitzi began to scream at Lisa, and said, "Leave Jack alone so that he can finish his meal."

Mitzi's entrance, caused quite a stir. Jack was still eating. and Mitzi said, "What's wrong, is the food alright?"

"No, it's not about that, can you ask Allison and Cpl Rogers to come here and have them sitting out in the chairs, and then I need all the girls inside that van, including yourself, send in the two lieutenants please." said Lisa. Jack was nearing the end of his meal. Jack finished his meal, and drank down two cartons of chocolate milk. Jim announced, "Alright I'm off, if you have a need for me I'm a call away."

Allison and Cpl Rogers appeared, looking innocently, waiting.

Mitzi stood by the door, aligning everyone into specific places, she opened Jack's door, and said," They are ready are you?".

"Yes, send in Miss Wylie?" said Jack, as Lisa exited, and said," I'll be in flight control. Will you be long?"

"Nope, just long enough to see.", Jack stopped in mid-sentence to see a real beauty stroll in. A dynamitic smile and a killer body Jack said," So, it says here you're a IT specialist, is that true?"

"Yes", she said biting her lower lip.

"Well then we need to get you upstairs in the flight cabin and help them out up there. Why don't you report to Jim, he could sure use your help."

"Alright, if you insist, but are you sure you can't find something I can do just for you?"

"Nah, not right now, but maybe later." said Jack watching her go, and said, "Send in Corporal Rogers." He stepped and saw Jack. Corporal Rogers started out by saying," look I'm sorry I didn't know?"

"Know what?" asked Jack, and , "I called you in here to go over the plan at the forward position, I want you and a few of your soldiers to stay with me as I advance. Then when we need an outside parameter's set. You'll be in charge of that. Is that alright with you?"

"Yes, but can I ask you something?" said Rogers.

"Sure, what is it?" asked Jack.

"This sounds like punishment, is it?"

"You're getting warmer, get out or I will have you arrested." Jack followed Corporal Rogers out, as he saw the women had assembled and said,

"This is how this is all going to work, as he explained what he wanted to do. Then Jack said, "Thank you for you service in helping us out." Jack then announced, "Are all the squads ready for me? Corporal Rogers and this group will position themselves on the outskirts, I'll see you soon."

"How do you know the Mistro is even here?", said Lisa.

"A text message told me so.," said Jack.

Mitzi stuck her head in at the ramp, and said, "Were off, they are waiting for you."

Lisa watched as Jack stepped off the ramp and down to see all the waiting girls and said, "Divide into two groups, I want the FBI officers to head up one group and Dylan the other. Now let's get in", as Jack opened the door to see Amber and Susan smiling he said "here let me cut off those bindings."

"Thank you Jack. What took you so long?"

I need time to get use to you both", as Jack closed the door, he turned to see Debby who said, "No you don't, you're not doing this without me."

"Alright get in."

Jack got in to hear, "Once this is over, if I decide to work with you guys, it better be exclusively for you?"

"It will" said Jack.

"Then count me in", said the Delta force commander, Colonel Tim Nelson.

Jack started the van, pulled it out, and off it went.

Meanwhile Lisa called the two lieutenants in first, they entered at attention, she said "Please close the door. How do each of you feel about working with Jack and my organization?"

"Fine Ma'am", said Paul Clark.

"What about you, Mister O'donald?"

"I don't know Ma'am, saw some action and others not so, it wasn't our finest moment."

"Well how would you like to transfer and work for me?" asked Lisa.

"Sure that is fine with me I know I can get my squad on board."

"Congratulations, Paul Clark, assemble your team, your new rank is Captain and you're in charge of Ground Ops. Set out your men on paper, all will receive promotions. Then there is an Officer, Rick Teal, allow him to join your team."

"Yes Ma'am."

Paul leaves, and shuts the door, to see Luke O'donald just looking at Paul, and said, "Just what happened?, then he added, "I didn't say I didn't want to go."

"No, but I'm in the speed game, you snooze and you lose. Does that mean you want to transfer?"

"Yes, I do?"

"Well that's great, alright I need you to account for your men, then Captain, you're promoted to cleanup and evaluation team."

"Alright, what, I have been promoted and with a new title, are you sure?"

"Yep, signed, sealed and delivered by me to you. Come on buddy, let's break it to our teams."

One lone man stood outside the door, waiting for their word. He was being held by force, as the other members weren't so happy with him, even though Jack himself let him off the hook. Delta did not."

"That man is a traitor, and must face punishment", screamed one Delta.

"No, you need to go outside and ask all your men if they want to transfer? Now go, then come back and I want you to sit in the meetings.," said Captain Paul Clark.

"Yes Sir."

Luke leaves, only to pass his new rival, Paul, who goes out to talk with his men. Meanwhile Paul takes it upon himself to report to Lisa. He knocked on the door and heard, "Come on in".

Paul looks at Allison, then sees Jim, the pilot, and then Lisa and heard "Come on in and join us. This is Jim. What do you have for me, Paul?"

"Luke and all the other men have agreed to transfer, beginning with Sgt Tony O'Brien, Sgt Craig Bauer, Sgt Art Jackson, and Cpl Spancer.

"Excellent, now Jim show the Captain what you have."

"Well Captain, you have all your weapons, so you and your team needs to change back into your Black Ops gear. Then I have this tracking device which indicates where Jack is at. Then each of your team will have this ear piece to talk among each other, in addition, in this ear piece you will hear my voice, I can tell you to abort. Lastly, I need to know who is your sniper?'"

"That would be Sgt Art Jackson," said Paul.

"We're on a first named basis, you can drop the ranks Paul."

"Yes Jim."

"Now get your team together, change and be ready to roll, in twenty", then he said, "Dismissed."

Jim looked over at Lisa to acknowledge that order. She smiled and said "Yes."

Paul left to see Luke was at the door. "Come in Captain", as Luke stepped in and shut the door.

"Now did everyone agree?"

"Yes Ma'am."

"From this time forward, you may address me as your boss, or Miss Curtis, and drop the military titles and forget the Ma'am."

"Thank you Jim", said Lisa, motioning him out. She saw him leave, then she said "Now Luke, name off your transfers."

"Myself, Luke O' Donald, Rodney Sinclair, Javier Gallegos, Jimmy Mills, Steve Brooks, and Billy Grant"

"Excellent, now open the door and go get your charges and line them up and then bring in Brian Rogers."

Luke went out the door and Jim went back in to hear "Do you think I made the right choice?"

"Only time will tell, although he seemed a bit hesitant for this job."

"Alright, what about your new assistant,"

"I think it was nice of Jack to do, however she is off with him now."

"That's what we need, more hard chargers like her."

A knock on the door, and in walked Luke, with Brian in hand, and said, "Stand where you're at", as Luke closed the door.

"Now Mister Rogers you're charged with treason as it pertains to corruption of national property, how do you plead?"

He raised his head he looked ashamed and said, "Guilty, but I thought Jack lessen my punishment?"

"Do you understand the charges and the penalty?"

"No I guess not Ma'am."

"On the charges of treason, with respect to the corruption of national property (Jack Cash). This is the fraternization of women that are out there in support of Jack Cash. This crime carries a penalty of being sent back to your former unit and a mark in your record as to having done such an act. How do you feel about that?"

"I'm fine with that, then send me back."

"That was a test, Mister Rogers, and you failed. I know Jack likes you, but I don't know. What do you think, Jim?, Do you all agree?"

Jim spoke up and said "It's one thing to steal, especially from the President of the United States, but it was just like you had an affair with his wife? How can you feel fine with that? If I knew there was a man out there who defiled one of the President's own, what do you think they would do?"

"I understand now that you put it that way, I feel bad," said Brian, now realizing what he had done.

"Well Brian, I haven't known you very long, but I remember what Jim said when you boarded this plane, the women are off limits. Now nothing has changed, and I didn't know about the Presidents own. I'd have shot you on the spot when you and her came out of the head, that might have been overlooked, but you two in the back of that car, that's twice as we know about. You're a disgrace to us and that uniform you so wear, I will request a general court marital, what do you say about that?"

"I'm sorry?"

A confused and very upset Lisa, said "Sorry to who? Are you going to get a special invite to the white house and tell the president oops you slipped and stuck your dick in one of his women? Are you? I don't think so, besides, if that's what Jim said, then it must be true. Get out of my face you maggot, your time here is over."

Next to walk in was Allison, who thought she was off the hook earlier. She stood in a slumping fashion. Lisa said, "Will you please close the door."

She shut the door and smiled at her. Lisa said, "Wipe that smile off your face, this is an inquiry into your actions while on this plane and in the field." Lisa slides the paper over to her and said, "Conduct unbecoming a privileged lady and guardian to Jack Cash, how do you plead?"

"Not guilty."

Lisa pulls out the big contract she signed and turned to the pages that affected her. Lisa said, "You pleaded not guilty to that charge. Is it true you kissed Mister Rogers?"

"He kissed me, he was the one who fondled me while I was on the plane. I was in the Head and he forced his way in."

"Had you ever met adds Rogers before?"

"No."

"Is it true that you and him are from the same small town?"

"No, I don't know where he came from."

"Is it true, you're the same age?" asked Lisa.

"No, I don't know, is he?"

"Is it true you went to the same High School?"

All right, I do know Brian. We met in college at USC. He went into the army and I was here. When I saw him I just knew we had to do it again. What's wrong with that?, it's my body."

"Not according to this document, your body belongs to the government, especially to that of Jack Cash. It is appalling that you would lose composure for a little pleasure. In the end, you are a disgrace, my vote is to put her out. You are a liar and a traitor and are not taking this job seriously."

"I was never given a chance to do my job, all I've been doing is following people around, it's kind of boring.", she said in a whim.

"That was nice, why didn't you speak up or voice your concerns? Said Lisa. She adds, "What I'm about to say to you, pains me because as time went by, you would have been my choice to be in operations control with me. But now I don't know. Can you be trusted? You're the girl with the honors and a business degree, you were the very best in your class, with in impeccable record. I'm just disgusted by you. What do you think Jim?"

"I want you out as well" said the older Jim.

"However, Jack said he really liked you and I can see why, that is why I may give you another chance." If I bring you back into the fold do you promise to actually ready and truthfully sign this document? It states; I work for one person only, it's my job to uphold this document to the best of my abilities and in the end I would even give my life for him, which is Jack Cash, International Bounty Hunter."

"Yes, I will affirm that and I do promise to follow and obey, from this day forward." Said a sincere Allison Wylie.

"What were you looking for?" Lisa moved in closer and said, "This is no game. My first strike for you was at the school, by Miss Margaret, who told me that you slept through the ethics part of the class, the part you're in trouble for. The second strike was the sex. I have you on video tape from the plane. The third strike was your inability to get out of the back seat of car number two, which your fluids destroyed a 3,000 dollar seat."

"Wow, you did all that for what? We are here to support one man, Jack Cash. From what I hear, you're a disgrace, but if Lisa will work with me, I think you could be an asset to the team, unlike some others who found themselves in jail. What do you say? Do you want to continue or do you want out?"

Lisa looked over at Jim who winked.

"I guess I will stay, for now." Said a somber Allison.

"You need to show us that you really mean what you say, not what you mean." said Lisa.

"I will, thanks," she said as she walked out.

"What are you thinking? She is a liar" said Lisa.

"Yes, but look at her, what if it were known that it was Mister Rogers the whole time that manipulated her, like she said? Some women cannot resist the charms of a man, nor his scent. I heard she is a phenomenal IT person who writes software, we could use an asset on this team. If we get the two of them apart, and like you said, if Jack Cash approves it, then she does stay?" asked Jim.

"You have a point" said Lisa, then added, "That is why we hired her in the first place, it's for what she could do with a computer."

Jim left as Luke entered and saw Lisa. Lisa said "You handled yourself well, now I need you to drive back to Little Rock and pick up Erin, she quit in the middle of the mission on Jack and now she is missing. Pick her up and get those that are in jail out, and come back here. I'll be waiting."

"Yes, Miss Curtis", said Luke, with orders in hand.

Jim address the Black Ops team and said "Commander Paul Clark is in charge, as he probably has already told you, you're our new support team for one, Jack Cash. There are no other targets, each of you is vested with the knowledge of one thing and one thing only, to protect Jack at all costs, but only when asked to? Understand?"

"Yes Jim", they all said in unison.

"Off you go", said Jim.

Jack pulled into the valley of this exclusive community to a set of gates where Jack stopped. Amber got out and punched the code, the gate opened, Jack drove through. Jack said, "Alright this next part keep your heads down till we get there."

On the left and on the right were pristine lakes, it was the afternoon, the sun was hot and the dew off the grass indicated it had rained, there was patchy fog.

"Up on the right is a service road, take that" said Amber.

Jack came to a stop then turned to the right, up a small hill, then plunge down into a valley. There were huge box like structures with a sorted amount of cars in and around the structures. The road then opened up to a huge warehouse type of building. Amber said, "Park on the very end by that other van."

Jack slowed the van and went around the back to find a spot, and then parked it.

Amber told Jack, "Now this is the tricky part, usually there are ten to fifteen women in processing, but today it looks empty", she was still talking as Jack jumped out, and closed the door of the van. He went in the huge open warehouse that looked like an empty lounge. On a bulletin board was a flyer that read "Special incarnation for this month's class, all are welcome at the concert hall."

Jack turned to see Amber, and some of the girls had made their way in from the van, Jack said, "Everyone back on the van, were going to the concert hall."

Jack held Amber back, by holding her arm, and said, "Wait Amber, do you know where there is a fashion place."

"What do you have in mind?" she asks.

"A little knock out, drag down old fight."

"Sure, let me show you the way." she looks at him weirdly.

They all got back in the van, as Jack drove back onto the road. He looked in his rear view mirror and a truck was coming at them full speed, he said, "Hold on girls".

Jack turned the wheel sharply as the truck hit the rear quarter of the van stopping both them. Jack was out, with gun in hand. Before the two hillbillies could react from the truck, Jack shot them both in the head. He turned to see that the van was un-drivable. He saw Amber and said, "Some of you must take that truck, while other group comes with me."

Team one with Debby and Dylan occupied the long bench seat, of the truck. Jack just yanked out the men from the truck and the six other girls hopped in the back.

Team 2 Had Susan driving, with Emily and Amber up front, and six girls in the back. Jack drove the long handled stick shift. The truck was bumping and Jack was dumping it. It was erratic until he got the hang of it.

Jack drove up the hill turned right and then back on the main road. They drove past a huge lake. Shops were plentiful, he was on Main Street, he saw a photographers shop. He parked at an angle and he went to the door, he went in. He saw a picture, the caption said her the name was Helen Carr.

He could hear voices and a little giggling. Jack turned the corner to see a tall voluptuous woman with red hair taking pictures of two young girls half clothed. She paused to look at him, and said, "Are you next?"

"Are you Helen Carr?" asked Jack, as takes a picture of her with his phone.

"Yep" she said.

You're under arrest Helen Carr?" said Jack as he pulled his weapon to motion her to the back.

He zip tied her up and behind him was Dylan who said, "Help them out, and have the other teams spread out. As Jack opened the door, she turned and said "How did you find out?"

"Well it was quite easy, someone needed to get the pictures out, I imagine once we check your computer we will find out the truth."

"You need a warrant."

"Who says that?" asked Jack, as he pulled up her mainframe. He broke out a screwdriver, he yanked off the case to see the mainframe. Jen held his arm, to unplug the unit.

Jack pulled the board out, and handed it to her; you will need this too."

"Well my rights." said Helen.

"Your rights were revoked once you committed a crime. There is a new law in town, by order of the President of the United States declaring you a traitor and I am the instrument that carries out that power, I have three choices?"

"What are they?" she asked.

"First one you cooperate with me, and we give you a somewhat fair treatment, the next one is that I maim you"

"And the last one" she asked.

"Well, I shoot you in the head." said Jack.

"Alright what do you want to know?"

"Tell me everything, the whole operation," said Jack and added "Is this going to be long?"

"Yes, it is local, regional and national to international."

"Good, let's have local," said Jack clearly threatening her with his gun out, he puts it away, as he has his phone, for her to begin, she spoke, "On the local level is the Mistro, the conductor of the Eudora orchestra. He is having a big event tonight, the whole town will be there, the Mistro then travels regionally. That's where they traffic young girls, at his compound. It's a hotbed of over a hundred girls, from ages 13 to 24, the rest are working in each of the shops. Next is the wagering operation, which covers all fifty states. It includes all college sports, especially football. Then in Panama, we have the drug operation, where I had been once on a vacation."

"The next phase is the biggest money maker, it is on every college campus, the influence of young girls to be sent overseas."

"All right, hold that thought", as Jack pulls up his phone to dial up Lisa and said, "I have someone who can expose everything, names and numbers, can you pick her up?"

"Yeah, I think so," said Lisa.

"Immediately, I mean literally, by air."

"Well we have your immediate back up plan?"

"Let's use it, she has the most valuable importance." Jack said.

"Have her ready?, were five minutes away" said Lisa.

Jack slides his phone shut and said, "Dylan I'm taking this one away, come on with me." Jack took Helen's wrist, then her arm, past the girls and said, "I'll be right back, find some dresses for the girls, were going to a party, and I'll be back soon."

Jack led Helen, according to the name and picture, to the truck. Jack lifted her up, and into the passenger seat. He started up the truck and backed out then, out onto the main road. The roads were still empty and said, "It's sure a slow town?"

"Yeah the population, oh about 2500, give or take on who stays." Helen said.

"Tell me how did all this start?" Jack asked.

"Well the Mistro was looking for a place to set up shop, he guaranteed young workers in exchange for his palaces he wanted to build. Look around, this would have gone on forever had you not come along to stop all of this. How did you even get in here? Local police and state and even federal officials were paid to keep everyone away." said Helen.

"I'm not everyone, I work for the President exclusively, I do what I want."

"That's evident. Where are you going, and where are you taking me?"

"What do you mean?" asks Jack driving frantically.

"Well the process center is back on that road", she was pointing to it as they passed. Jack slowed, backed up, then saw another gate and said "Who is in there?"

"That's the processing center for all incoming girls."

"Heavily guarded?" Asked Jack.

"Not necessary, its set up like a prison, it has an electrified fence and outside guard dogs, all I know it's a dangerous place, they're in an uproar?"

"How's that?" asked Jack.

"Well there was suppose to be a van early this morning, you know I was secretly laughing thinking someone has finally caught on."

"Why didn't you notify authorities?" inquired Jack.

"What and get killed, I love this town, except for all of the criminal elements."

"Don't worry it will be over soon" said Jack as he drove on. He turned left, went down the road for Helen and said, "This is the security force and it's workers."

"Really, then tell me where is this party."

Jack stopped the truck, as he saw a crate with a parachute on it float down with some speed. He got out and popped open the box, and pulled out a large bag, he used two hands to lift it up and put it in the truck bed, Jack got back in, and said, "Now is there an open field?"

"Yeah the way you came in, is an open pasture" said Helen, looking at him with some confusion.

Jack steered the truck back on the main road and saw the road open up to a short cut out. He stopped on the gravel road. Jack said, Get out", she came over to him and he said, "Get up here."

Jack pulled his phone out for a quick text; "need support in complex, circle around to pick up package".

Jack put his phone away. He jumped up in the back, he unzipped the bag. First he pulled out a body harness and he helped her into it, he zipped it up. Then he said "turn around" and Jack clipped her with a huge horseshoe clamp. She said, "What are you doing back there?"

"Getting you ready for a plane trip to Washington." in the background they both could see the welcoming committee, the trucks were closing in on them.

"I hope you have another plan cause in a minute or so they will be here.," said a freighted Helen beginning to panic.

"You won't be", said Jack as he twisted the weather balloon base, and instantly in soared upward. Pulling out the cable, above them was a plane on approach, from its rear troops jumped out. They were on their path to the ground to intercept the committee. Jack grinned and said, "Bye, Bye Helen".

In an instant, she was lifted off.

Jack hopped back down, as he made his way back to the truck, he backed the truck up. Jack plowed into the first vehicle, as the gunfire was loud. Jack slipped out and saw five parachutes in the air, as the plane flew off, with Helen trailing in the wind. Four trucks were ahead of him now, the men were armed and were shooting at Jack, they themselves were taking fire from above as Black Ops was engaging, and coming to Jack's rescue, as they hit their targets. Jack went around the other side, he knew he needed prisoners, so instead of head shots he was aiming for the thigh. The troops were on the ground firing from the east to the west. Jack traveled south, taking and wounding as he went. He put all eight men down from the trucks. He yelled "Cease fire, everyone down", Jack stood and said, "Get together" to his prisoners. One of the prisoners said, "Who are you, your trespassing."

"I'm trespassing, on who's land?" to add, "This is United States Land, you pay taxes to them, and I work for the government, no you're all under arrest."

"By who's authority?"

"By the order of the President of the United States, my name is Jack Cash.

Turning the corner was the crew from the diversion, for Jack and said "Thanks for helping me out in Little Rock, let's get these trucks off the road, I'll take Audris with me in the last truck. See if you can get any information from these guys, here are some zip ties. For you others your next order is to break into the holding facility, just over that hill."

The fence is electrified, so be careful, and thanks for coming back."

Jack and Audris got into the last truck. Audris threw her empty parachute frame, harness and pack in the back and jumped in. Jack easily drove the automatic truck, he whipped it around and was back into town. The girls were gone from the streets, along with the other vehicle. Jack drove by the smaller building to see the road open up to a lake. He saw the house and people gathering along the edge of the lake. The drive turned into a one way road, as cars lined up on both sides of the parkway. The road on the right was a parking garage structure, he drove in. First he drove to the top then he came back down, as he found a place by the door, he parked. They both got out and saw a door to the house. Jack was looking at the stairs, and took it down two flights to a locked door.

Jack said, "Go back up and be a look out while I get this door open."

Audris went back up as Jack unzipped the lowest lining. He took a piece of plastique explosive, placed it along the handle under the silver plate, then out of a bag he put a blasting cap in.

He went up one flight of stairs, pulled out his phone, aligned the frequency's and hit send, the plastique blew.

Jack went back down to see that the plate was blown back. He thought "Not enough Plastique."

Before he put on more plastique, he took out his all-purpose tool, used the flat tip part and released the hatch and opened the door. He thought about Audris, who was still up there, thinking if he should scream at her wait or just roll. Jack went through the door, inside felt nice, slightly warm. On the right was the wine cellar, he stepped in, grabbed a bottle and set it in the door. He then pulled his gun and down the hallway he went, past the wine cellar number one, there was windows on the left to see the lake. Then he went down one more floor, thinking "that was nice, underground rooms, and then he hit a dead-end. The door he came through closed behind him, instantly the room began to fill with water, it was cold, probably from the lake. Just above him, it looked like a vent, but it had to be twenty feet away at best. Jack knew either he would freeze before he made it to the top or he would need to find another way out. The water was up to his waist, he thought about his gun. He was caught off guard as his feet went in a circular motion with the water, as it continued to pour in. As the water got about ten feet deep, it stopped. The cold water was debilitating. Jack went into survival mode and pulled the tab for the cool water, it becamed charged, and instantly he was warm, then spun the ring on his watch, he aimed it and hit the button on the side, the ring shot up and wrapped around the metal grate. It instantly reeled in the ten foot cable, as it retracted it back he was out of the water. Now he was stuck under the grate, with his free hand he unzipped the lower pocket and wadded up a ball of Plastique. He swung over, and set it on the hatch lock, then inserted the blasting cap.

He pulled out his phone, as he wiggled back as far as he could, he took off his jacket and wrapped it around his hand, then pressed go, a delay then an explosion. Jack swung up with his feet and unlatched the grate. Then with all his mite, he swung back over and did a chest press. While holding onto the ledge, he pulled his feet up and in one motion lifted the grate to flip over on the grass. He unlatched the watch line, as it zipped back into place. Jack adjusted his jacket, it was waterproof.

Jack walked up to the front of the house, knocked on the door, the door open and a porter said , "Sir, this is a black tie event, are you even on the guest list."

"Where is the Mistro?"

"He is in his chambers and wishes not to be disturbed."

"Where do the stairs go?"

"Somewhere you can't go" said the porter.

Jack grabs him by the throat, and drives him down stairs with him to see a bigger party than ever. Out matched, Jack tosses the porter aside to see a laundry chute and then jumps into it, it was narrow, he saw the landing coming on fast. Someone looked up and Jack made contact, the guy was knocked out, breaking Jack's fall. Jack was thinking "That was cool, nice escape plan", he looked around to realize he was on the right side of the wall this time. From the laundry room, he went out in the hall. He heard a shot, he turned and the round went towards his heart, his badge stopped it. He charged the guy that shot at him, a kick to the leg, then in the throat and the guy was down. More bullets, this time from east and west. As he stood in the middle he dove out of the way. Jack looked around the corner to see women heels being escorted the west way. As the gun fire ceased, he crawled along to the cross hall ways, then made his move, out sprang a trap door. It looked like an abyss, he held his balance and leapt over the first one, the second one opened up, and Jack was on a slide, he slid all the way down and landed on a sofa. He saw a man with a nasty smelling cigar, and said, "So here is the man who has caused some problems for me and the Mistro. What is your name? No, don't tell me, I already know. Your name is Jack Cash, International Bounty Hunter, my two trusted assistants tell me you got Helen. Unfortunate for her, she was a good fuck buddy. We'll kill her after we kill you. Toss me your handgun, then your fancy watch."

Jack sees the man's bodyguards move in with their guns pointed at him as the guy said "Mister Cash, do as I tell you or I shall put all of your secret agents in that well so that they may suffer what you endured, now the gun."

Jack pulls it out and tosses on the nicely carpeted floor, as the handler said, "One of you two pick it up and hand it to me. So far your quite clever for an International Bounty Hunter, but I want you to meet a friend of ours, and your current nemesis."

Protima walked through the door and began to shoot at Jack. All the bullets went towards his heart as he absorbed the rounds. She stopped firing, as she and the handler looked at Jack and said, "You're not dead?"

The handler said, "Let's strip him he can't be a robot".

Jack unclasped the watch and let it go. It was as if time had stopped, At that moment, two F-18 super hornets were flying a specific mission when they received, "Number one is in duress, coordinances in your computer, fire sidewinder at target, over. Away went the powerful missile, racing towards Jack at supersonic speed.

They all watched as the watch flew, but they were more interested in watching as the first guy who attempted to pick up Jack's gun. He picked it up, short circuited and then fell over dead. As the handler said, "What is going on", the missile hit. The watch landed and Jack dove behind the sofa, as the explosion rocked the estate. A massive amount of water filled the basement quickly, a rod was through the skull of the handler, as the lake was rushing in, Jack went for his gun. From under the humongus man, he found a rod on his back. Jack heard the siren go off, and all he could hear was, "Die you bastard Die".

Meanwhile the explosion turned everyone's attention to that house. The Black Ops group had no communication with Jack and didn't know what to do. Then they saw Captain Paul Clark and several others driving trucks, so they rushed the house, two men were dragging Audris along the ground, the trucks stopped, got out and helped her out as she said, "Where have you been?"

"Up there"

"The whole time, please."

Paul was on the scene, and began barking orders, "Take as many prisoners as possible, and let's search the house for Jack Cash."

Meanwhile Jack and Protima were at each other's throats as the cold lake water was subsiding. They fought each other, she was kicking as Jack was punching. He still couldn't get his weapon, he did however take one of hers, and one shot grazed her arm. Just as the door opened and men with guns were trapped as another stronger force mowed them down, finally Jack dove and kept Protima head under water while she struggled. Occasionally he would pull her head up, then in one motion, Jack zip tied her wrist's behind her back. All was quiet as Jack took a seat on the marble step to hear "All clear."

"All clear", then Paul Clark took the steps down slowly and said "Jack Cash is that you?"

"Yep, can you take that one, and call in everyone."

"What about your girls?"

"There behind that door", points Jack, as he gets up. Paul is at the door with Willis and Keller, only to feel the heat of the door."

Paul said, "Any ideas?, turning to see Jack, who had gotten up and said, "What are you carrying on your back, a parachute?"

"Yeah, it's your ticket out of here. I was to carry it everywhere I went, as told to me by Miss Curtis, until I assign someone else the responsibility."

Jack bent over and moved the dead guy, picked up his weapon and shook it out, then said "Stand back". As he holstered his weapon, and then unzipped the other side, he pulled out a strip of plastique.

"Is that what I think it is?" asked Paul.

"I guess."

"Are you alright, looks like you were blown up."

"That's what happens, when they launch a missile at you."

"No shit."

"Stand back", said Jack, as he watched Paul and the others move back, as Jack inserted the blasting caps, he stepped back aways and stopped. Jack went to remote detonator, then saw he had twelve new e-mails, he hit the button, and bam, the door blew inward. Jack was instantly at the door to see that the door took out both Susan and Amber. Jack put his phone away, he saw all of his girls were in a corner huddled around themselves. Jack looked at them and shook his head in disgust. He lifted the door off and it slammed down, he was tired, he allowed the teams in to help out. They stood waiting for the official word to move. Jack looked at Paul and said "Can you come on in here and have your team pick up the girls and get them out of here?"

"Yes Sir, come on men, come in here and lets help these girls out."

Jack leans up against the wall exhausted, he staggars out of the room, down the steps, through the water, to sit on the steps. He put his hands to his face and began to cry, in that moment he felt so alone and not loved. He doubts why he was even doing this. He felt around in his pocket and pulled out a prepackaged protein bar. He pulled off the wrapper, Jack ate it slowly, watching the girls get a ride on the men's shoulders, up next to him. As the last girl was placed down, Paul stood behind him and said, "Jack, all girls are out, what now?"

Jack thought about it, thinking "Why in the hell, can't they take the initiative?" and said, "Paul go back upstairs and divide the room upstairs. Then zip tie those that respond to you, all others are the victims."

"Yes Sir."

Jack finished the delicious protein bar. He felt refreshed and renewed. Jack got up, stepped out of the water, and worked his way up the stairs. He got up to the living room to see two groups of people, on one side was the adults and the other was young girls, once they were segregated its apparent how brain washed they actually were. Jack began to clinch his fists realizing how delusional this community was over the degradation and exploitation of these young girls. He thought "What a shame".

Jack saw Audris with the backup team and said "Can you guys go in and help the other guys and secure this place". Jack looks off to the left as Paul comes out and said, "The word is that the Mistro is at the concert hall on the other side of the lake."

"Alright, have your men locate a boat while Audris and the rest of these men take care of this group. Any signs of Dylan or her group?"

"Nah, it looks like they are separated, "said Paul, as the four of them took off one way, Jack whistled to get their attention, they stopped as Jack said, "The dock is the other way."

They ran past him as he felt Audris's hand on his arm and said "What are we going to do next?"

"We're going to go crash a party."

Jack hears his named being called, as he goes to the sound, Audris is right on his heels. He went through the gate to see steps down to a very large boat. On the boat were Paul and his men, awaiting Jack's arrival, he jumped aboard. Paul waved off Audris, then released the boat. Jack was on the controls as he should be. Jack pushed up the throttle to full, Paul and his men were on the stern. The boat did a quick ninety, as the boat came to a stop by the dock. Everyone exited, and up the ramp they went, where black tie and long evening dresses were the norm. Jack was the first to jump off the boat and was on the move. As he past the lines of beautiful women, one caught his eye, he slowed. He saw it was Debby, stunningly dressed, as she sashayed over to him she said "I was beginning to think you would never show up. A couple of the girls were worried, what happen to you?"

"Oh, just an explosion, what have you guys been up to?"

"Well after you left with that girl, an older lady came in to the shop and asked if we were new and needed a ride to the concert hall. You see were the Mistro's ladies, there are ten of us."

"Good for you." Said Jack.

"Wait, where are you going?" She held onto his arm and said, "You can't go in there like that."

Jack stopped, looked at her then heard his phone ring, he pulls it out to see who it was. He answers it and said "Yes", it was Lisa. Lisa said "Jack we have enough information to implicate the Mistro, aka Donovan Beatty, his wife Cherilyn, the Professor Allistair Richards and Preston Roberts and his wife."

"Too bad Mister Roberts is dead. I'm outside awaiting to go in to take down and apprehend the Mistro."

"Good, go ahead, but can you have someone open up the gates so we may come in?"

"How about using that rocket you fired on me?"

There was a long pause, then Lisa said "Sorry, I'll make it up to you". Jack slid his phone shut and said to Debby, "Can you go down to the boat and tell Paul to take a vehicle over to the north gate and open it up for the Calvary".

She moved closer to him and said, "Only on one condition?"

"What's that", said a worn and tired Jack. As she stepped forward she gave him a kiss on his mouth, she lingered it. Jack tried to break free, but it was no use, she was stronger than him and he was drained, so he gave in to her. She finally let him go, his momentum carried him down to the deck as she helped him up she said "Now that wasn't bad, was it?"

"No, I'm just a bit tired, I'd like to have lingered a bit longer," said Jack.

"Next time I will arrange It." said Debby.

"I'll be waiting" said Jack sarcastically. He entered the social gathering, as people mulled around, he heard the announcement for people to go back to their seats, the second act was about to start.

Jack went through the door with the curtain. A hand held him back, it was from a large man who said, "You're not one of them", as he points to all the girls dressed in white colored gowns, he heard, "Upstairs, for the riff raft".

Jack had enough, as the orchestra was set to play, a famed blonde haired, thick mustache and sharp goatee man took his place, and the music started. Jack and the large man began to dance holding each other's arms, till Jack used his foot and drove it into the guys inside knee. Instantly the guy let out a loud yelp. The music abruptly stopped, the Mistro turned around and yelled, "Who dare to interrupt my performance."

"I do" said Jack, walking towards him, as all were watching him, behind him the men in suits were gathering.

"This is a private place and you are trespassing."

Jack continues to walk closer to the larger than life figure and said, "No, I'm not the one who has trespassed, it is you."

"What are you a cop, where is your warrant?"

"No, I'm no cop, I'm making a citizen's arrest."

"On what proof do you have? How can you make an arrest? Looks like your outnumbered" said the confident Mistro. The audience begins to laugh at Jack, as Jack turns to see them coming at him, Jack pulls his gun and without warning shoots the first of the ten men all in the head. Jack yells "Shut up your laughing. You're all under arrest." Jack reloads his weapon. Just then all the exits were filled with his reinforcements, it was the National Guard. They were locked and loaded, it an instant it quieted down as peace was restored. Jack said "I'm looking for the following people to come with me. Will the wife of Preston Roberts stand up, thank you, take her." "Will Doctor Allistair Richards stand up, now will the real Cherilyn Beatty, stand up, a vivacious woman stood. Jack said, "Take her too" Jack circled the stage and said, "Now lastly I'm looking for the Mistro, also known as Donovan Beatty."

"That's me, on what grounds?"

"For disrespecting me." Jack zip ties that one himself, as he forcefully takes him along with him.

"What, that's bull-shit, I want my lawyer", as he jumped and Jack jumped after him. They landed on the stage below. The Mistro said to Jack "Who are you, you can't do this to me, I have connections."

"I have Helen, and she told us all about how you stole her community from her. Listen, I'm done with you", as a couple of soldiers, took him from Jack. Jack got up and holstered his weapon.

Lisa was standing by the door when the Mistro was led to her and said, "I want my lawyer."

Lisa raised up his head, and said "Sorry, you're not allowed one where you're going, you'll not need one."

"What are you saying?"

"You don't get it do you? You're getting deported out of this country and taken to one that allows enslavement, abduction and cruelty."

Jack followed him out to hear him plead his case. In the background the orchestra was playing the national anthem. Jack saw Lisa and she said, "This is huge, you have uncovered this in a matter of days, wait till we dig into the cabinet files."

"I can hardly wait" said Jack kiddingly.

"What wrong Jack?" asks Lisa.

"I'm just tired, I want to go home."

"You know I can't let you do that, you're going back to the Academy to graduate with your class on Friday."

"And why is that important?"

"Because the President, first lady and the VP's will be there to officially accept you and us in the program. They will give us the funding we need to carry on, and we couldn't have done it without you, but I gotta to go and secure our prisoners."

Jack watches her drive off. As Lisa was in the passenger seat she says to Ramon "on to the airport, we're going to Quantico."

Just then some guy gets out of a car, walks over to Jack, pulls a watch out, and a fixates it to his wrist. He pulls the pin out, closes the box, doesn't say a word, turns and gets back in the car he came from.

Lisa turns in her seat to face the two women and said "You're lucky."

"How's that, we haven't done anything wrong."

"Well for starters, you met Jack, and well, you see Jack works directly for the President of the our United States. He has the power in trusted in him from 75 countries around the world to kill who he wants for no apparent reason or rhyme, so I'd say you're lucky, now sit back and shut your traps.

Lisa turned around in her seat with a smile on her face to think, "Yes, were on to something, and I like it, yes I do."

Jack walked over to see Audris in a jeep, she said "Hey mister get in, where do you want to go?"

"Somewhere off this compound, say a motel."

"There is an Inn about a half mile off to the left" said an older woman then , "thank you sir for liberating our village of him and his kind."

"You're welcome ma'am" said Jack, as he got in next to Audris, as she drove off.

They passed a huge quantity of women and girls lining the street. As Jack passed by he waved, they waved back. Audris said, "You're their savior, you did a good thing."

Jack was really tired, as he just held on for the wild ride. The National Guard was all over the place. As Jack's car past a check point, Audris took a left, and then turned into the Inn. It was overran by troops. Jack said "Audris slow down, I want to see if I can get a room."

"For us, great" she said, as he looked back at her weirdly. He jumped out and went to the main door, inside was quiet as an older man stood the counter and said, "How are you, sir?"

"Fine, do you have a room?"

"Have a room, well of course, my place is empty, all fifteen rooms."

"What's up with all the troops?" Jack asked.

"I guess their waiting to hear what is happening in the village," said the old guy.

"What is going on there?"

"Oh you know the Mistro is holding and auctioning and all that other stuff, you know that's the best way in finding a wife, that's where I found mine."

"How much for all the rooms?"

The old man just looks at Jack and said, "Well I have fifteen rooms, at fifty each is $750."

"Alright here is "Jack was looking around his pockets of his burnt up and ripped up jacket. He remembered seeing some cash, he dug it out, and gave the guy one thousand dollars.

"Yep that will take care of it, here is the key to number five, it's the largest, it has a King size bed."

"How is the shower?"

"Good it is a handicap bathroom."

"I'll take it."

"Just sign in here."

Jack saw the page was empty and at room five, signed Jack Cash.

"Here you go Mister Cash.", Jack takes the key. He stepped outside as all the trucks and troops roll on past him, then Jack sees Audris and said "Alright, can you wait, I need a shower and get cleaned up. While I'm in there can you wash my clothes?"

"Sure I'd be honored, looks like there is a laundry mat down on the end." said Audris.

Jack places the key in and opens the door, the room was cool. As he went in he saw the bathroom, then went into the living area and began to undress, he laid out all of his stuff, wallet, phone, holster, as he looked at his badge, he noticed three castings molded to the badge itself, he unbuttoned his shirt and pulled off his t-shirt and slipped off his wet shoes and socks, then off went his pants and underwear.

Jack went into the shower. Audris came in armed with quarters and a box of soap from the main office, piled up his clothes, and went off to the laundry.

Jack finished his shower, dried off, and crawled into the bed and under the covers. Moments later Audris came back in and sat by Jack and began to rub his shoulders, the door opened and shut again, this time she was tapped on the shoulder and was asked to leave, which she went and followed Audris out, and then locked the door. She turned around and began to undress all the way, lastly popping off her bra and sliding down her panties, she turned down the lights, then pulled the covers back , and slowly got on top of him. She began to rub out Jack's aches and pains while he slept on his stomach.

The next morning was a bit different, instead of a knock, the door was wide open, as Lisa came in with Jim. They had sent Audris away for ruining Jack's clothing. Everything new was on the table, as they closed the door, Jim turned up the lights. First to wake up was Msgt Snyder. Debby got dressed, then was escorted out of the room. Jack turned to see Lisa as he opened his eyes she said,

"Ah, finally you're up."

"What do you want, my room, I still have it for another couple of hours."

"No, silly I'm here to take you back to the Academy. In a couple of days you'll graduate and then it's on to your new career. All you have to do is listen", Jim ask Trixie and Mitzi to come in.

"Just lie back, relax and it will be a brief debriefing, and probably the last, for a while."

Jack just looked up at her, then he saw the two girls, "What do you think of these two?"

"Their fine", said Jack wondering where all of this was going.

"To be part of your team." Said Lisa.

"Sure, them and Debby, where is she anyway?"

"On the plane waiting for you."

"Alright, what's next?"

"Which men stepped up enough for you to accept them to the team?" asked Lisa.

"Surely not the one who fired that rocket at me?"

"You took off your watch," yelled Jim.

"So you're the one who fired that rocket at me, come here you son of."

"Enough boys, Jack, it's not Jim, it comes on automatically, either from a ship or aircraft. It depends on your location, and that's it, no more discussion."

"That's fair, I guess none, they are all like robots."

"How so, what do you mean?" asks Lisa.

"Well they can't act or do something without being told, and I need two other Jim's, don't get me wrong you're a nice guy, but."

"Enough already, I get the point, you want to kill him. Well you can't he works for us, he is off limits", said Lisa, then added, "Then what do you suggest I do with the men?"

"Simple, divide them into two teams, one to help you and the other as support, but no women. I liked how that device you had for me worked, thanks Jim. I like Paul, but he needs to go with the commandos."

"Alright what about the girls?"

"Well I'd like Debby to join Jim's team as far as supply goes, but all others could be used elsewhere like training and recruiting others."

"What about Audris, do you want her as your personal assistant?"

"I don't think I really need one, all I could think about was having sex with her."

"Well that was the point." said Lisa.

"What you mean, they are here for support, to defend and fight," said Jack.

"Yep, that's right" said Lisa.

"Well that was a missed opportunity, said Jack a bit disappointed.

"Listen, you're my number one priority, you have the utmost power and all the money. Now I will just provide you the most beautiful women we could find."

"Nice try, I still don't think that will work," said Jack "Are we done?"

"No, one last thing, the result of you capturing Helen is still on going. Also at last count five hundred have been arrested, which means you get five hundred million dollars. How do you want it, by wire transfer, or by five hundred briefcases?"

"You keep it for the start of spy club, remember I'm still in school, besides I still have my bag. Oh do I get that car to take home?"

Lisa looked at Jim who looked back at her and said, "No, it's just for operations only."

"Alright, are we leaving?"

"Just as soon as you're ready"

"Give me five; I need to take another shower."

CH 6

"Released, Free and Graduated, Sort of"

Wake up" said Daphne, pushing on Jack's arm, Jack was savoring in the moment with both Alex and Maria, he opened his eyes to see his handler Daphne.

"You're supposed to be at class, very soon."

"I just got off a long flight."

"Three hours, I wouldn't say that was a long flight, besides, I'm the one who picked you up at the airport, remember?" said Daphne, taking a seat next to him, placing her hand on his arm. Jack looked up at her, with a smile, and said, "How may I help you."

"Knock it off, I'm not one of your field girls to lie in your bed and say, Oh Super Spy please fuck me, for I'm a helpless and defenseless girl."

"That's not what I mean, and I'm not even thinking that." said Jack honestly.

"I am", said Daphne, leaning in for a kiss, they both met to a warm and open reception. She kissed with such strong intentions that her taste was sweeter than that of Maria's. Thought Jack.

Jack took the liberty to put his hand down her dress to feel her firm breast. Daphne continued to kiss away, just as her phone continued to ring, she broke away from him to get up.

Jack looked at his hand that got a rare chance to touch her secretly covered up possessions.

"Jack let's go, they are waiting for you."

Jack rolls out of bed, placing his gun in his holster, then slipped it on. He then put on his new jacket and follows Daphne out.

The bright sunlight blinded his eyes, as he shielded them from the light, the two walked together. Jack followed Daphne into the headquarters building, many familiar faces were milling around especially that of his old team of Bennie, Raphael and Teresa. Each dressed in slick black outfits with a book or something in their hands. Jack acknowledged their presence and walked by them as Daphne led Jack into the conference room. Jack took a seat next to Allison, and seated by them was everyone from his platoon.

"Listen up, this is the last of your nine week program, were almost through and the top spot goes to the German, Jack Cash, and next is Raphael from Croatia, followed by Teresa from Honduras. This week we will focus on hand to hand combat. And for some of you professional etiquette", as the Commander looked at Jack.

"So we would like you to get up and go to the gymnasium." Everyone went their separate ways, except Allison who lingered, holding onto Jack's hand, then Jack pulls away. Jack and the others arrive at the gym. A tough looking soldier was commanding everyone to break into groups of five, beginning with the numbers one, six, eleven and sixteen. Jack looked around as if he was in a daze. Jack's platoon assembled within those numbers that were called. A guy named Julio, of Spanish descent, stood next to him and on the other side was a little Chinese girl, she said her name was Julie. Off to his left was a tough looking girl from Jersey, with long brown hair, her name was Michelle. "She was a tough looking chick", thinks Jack, as he was the only one carrying his weapon, he thought with a smile, as they exited the room.

Brian the armorer, stood at the door, holding that now familiar pearl box as Daphne appeared and said, "Jack come with me."

Daphne led Jack to the armory, Jack knew what was coming. He and Daphne got to the secured armory and they waited for him to unholstered the weapon and placed it into the open box. Jack looked at the others, and then closed the box. Daphne said, "The Commander has asked me to keep it in safe keeping while you're in training. If at any time you need it, just call and I will bring it back to you."

"Here, you might as well have this too", as Jack takes off the jacket, he hands him both his jacket and his holster. Whereas Brian promptly hands Jack his jacket. Jack and Daphne leave the armory, Daphne says, "I'm going to leave you to go do my reports, I'll see you tonight."

Jack watches her leave, and then goes back to the gym, to follow the rest of the bad people, inside the gym. Inside was five distinct areas, each with its own uniqueness. Each instructor wore a blue vest and just when a whistle blew, and all was quiet.

Captain Jon, stepped up onto the boxing apron and said," Alright one through five choose an event and the rest please follow. Each of you will compete against each other till a clear winner emerges, then in a hour we will move to the next event until we are through. This is supposed to teach each and every person, so help each other out, on my whistle; let's begin."

The shriek noise went off, Jack followed Julio over to the boxing area, Sgt Snyder the tough looking soldier, came up to them and said, "Does anyone have any experience?"

Everyone looks at everyone else then Julio says, "I can hold my own."

"Fine, put on some head gear and slip on those gloves, I will tie them down, anyone else?"

Jersey Girl steps forward and says, "I'll fight em."

Jack helps Michelle with the helmet and then the gloves.

"I thought you and I could go a couple of rounds" as she punches Jack in the chest.

Jack steps away, to watch Julie on the ring ropes as Julio squares off against Michelle. The Sergeant blew his whistle, but before he ended the screech, Michelle stormed him. She clocked him with a huge unsuspecting uppercut, which dropped him like a sack of potatoes.

"Next, said the smiling Sergeant, "Which one of you is next?" As Julie went to attend to Julio, who threw off his head gear and pulled off his glove with his teeth.

"Your next Jack, you're the only one left."

Jack looked around to see he was next, much to his dismay. This tough chick was now reminding him of another girl, who was a thorn in his side, Candace. Jack said "Let's do this."

Jack climbs through the ring ropes, he hears a loud scream. Jack turned to see a big black guy just got sliced by a sword, his name was Richard he was bleeding and holding his arm. Off to his right was Jesus, Julio's brother, who was holding the sword. He was laughing and mocking Richard. Jack turns his attention to Michelle, this viper chick was jumping up and down swinging her fists, she was ready to go. Jack picked up the head gear and placed it on. The Sergeant puts the gloves on Jack, both had their backs to Michelle. Jack was at the corner, he waited for the Sergeant to leave, and then waited for the whistle to blow, when a burning sensation affected his kidneys and his legs went numb. He felt another blow to his head and then a rapid succession. He was losing control, as his back went out, he went down. Jack felt fatigued and he fell over, he just laid there, to hear another whistle and "You're out."

Jack's eyes were glazed over, as a kind hand pulled off his gloves and his head gear, his body ached. Julie and Julio helped Jack off the canvas. Jack had his arms around both Julie and Julio, as they laid him down on to the mat. Quickly both Teresa and Raphael came to his aid.

Raphael knelt by Jack to place him into her arms and said, "Are you alright Jack, who did this to you?"

Jack looked up at her, but couldn't speak. As the pain subsided, he was able to look into her eyes to see a kindness and compassion, his strength was returning, when the Commander blew the different sounding whistle.

"What do you guys want to go to now", said Julio.

Who saw what was left, the empty mat where Jack laid. The pervert Doctor already had his hands all over Julie, as he demonstrated on her how to place the hands. Jack watch the doctor grope Julie, and the doctor said, "Now, you can touch any area."

Jack shook the cobwebs out with some smelling salts from the medic, who was now present. The young medic looked familiar, but couldn't place him.

First up was Julie and Julio. Michelle and Raphael had exchanged some words, with Raphael promising to "knock her block off". Michelle sat at the end of the bench in silence. In the background, you could hear Raphael doing some damage in the boxing ring. Jack watched as Julio was grabbing everything he could to hold on to, but much to no avail, as Julie pinned him.

Doctor Greg looked at the two and said, "Whose next?"

Jack remained still as Michelle got up and said, "I'll fight her."

Michelle lunged at Julie, who did a single leg take down flipped Michelle over into a rear naked choke hold, Michelle tapped out. Julie exacted some revenge and held onto the hold a bit longer choking her, when the Doctor pulled them apart.

"Your next Jack" said the Doctor.

Jack stood wavering a bit off balanced, staggers onto the mat only to hear "Begin."

Jack, felt Julie grab his leg, and Jack heard, "Fall on top of me."

Jack fell onto Julie, holding her arms, as his head was at her buttocks. He was spreading her legs apart, as he realized he was at the advantage, he had pinned her down and was holding that position. The doctor tapped him on the back and said, "Get up, your resting and not gaining any more position". They got up, this time Jack dove for Julie's leg, missing it and hitting the mat as Julie got on Jack's back and tried to put her arm around his neck. She was straddling him, so Jack was awakening with more strength. He got his hand free. He tied up hers and he was able to turn, he saw what was coming and couldn't do a thing about it. Her arm was twisted in a way that she held it behind his back, then she pinned him to a three count and heard "You're out." The Doctor said, "Boy, for being the next greatest thing, you're sure failing miserably. I may fail you myself if you don't snap out of it."

Jack laid onto his stomach to realize that they don't play for fun, this is real. Definitely some more practice is in order, as another whistle blew.

Jack got up and staggered, as his group went to hand to hand combat. It was led by a Japanese warrior, who arranged them in poses and doing what some call Tai Chi. This lasted some thirty minutes, until they were all proficient enough to fight. First off were the two girls, as Julie won on points, next was Julio and Jack, Jack lost on points. He then sat down to watch Julie beat Julio, the whistle blew, something different, "Lunch time", was announced.

Everyone made their way to the kitchen, through an opened double door, a waft of food could be smelled. Jack went through the line and sat down and began to eat to regain strength, he knew he missed breakfast, it showed.

Now was the time to exert the most energy and be ready. Raphael came and sat by him and said, "Have you heard?"

"Heard what?"

"They, the organizers, have decided to put on a boxing match to see who the best of the class is. Guess what will happen, everyone will fight each other in three minute rounds. Then as each round goes by, those that advance can pick anyone to help them train. If I get to the end, will you be in my corner Jack?"

"Yeah sure, why not, how about the original team."

"Great idea, I'll go talk with Teresa and you go see Bennie."

Jack finished off his meal thinking "There must be some sort of energy pill I could take".

The whistle blew again as Jack and his team went to the rubber knives. Jack picks up one, looks at it, as it shook in his hand.

"It's a synethic rubber" said Capt. Jon "Now let me show you some poses and strikes, then how to defend yourselves and attack. Alright who wants to go first?"

Julio stood with Michelle, she hacked him up, leaving some serious welts to a win. Next was Jack and Julie. Jack dodged her advances with some countermoves and won.

Then Michelle stepped onto the mat to face Jack this time. As they began, from the first strike, Michelle stabbed Jack in the side, it hurt a bit, but not like the slash Jack used as he jumped up and came down across her neck, drawing a blood trail as he went. It all stopped as she held her neck. Immediately medics were there to assist her. She was crying, cursing and saying, "Jack I'm going to kill you" in an angry tone. Jack sat down to investigate his wound, a little piercing, but not bad.

The last whistle blew, the three of them stood in front of Souza, the Samari warrior, who was posing with a rubber sword in one hand and a stick in the other.

"Sit, now listen to me very carefully, these swords are very dangerous and at all times you must have your defend stick out for protection.

"Julie come up and let's show the men how it's done."

Both Julie and Souza went back and forth, there were plenty of shots, but it was fun play and not to serious, just what Jack liked. Souza caught Julie's shoulder and gashed it open.

Everything stopped as she screamed in agony, blood was everywhere, as Medic's ascended on her.

Julie left with the medic. Next up was Julio and Jack. Jack was taking it easy, just then the blade caught Jack's wrist and Julio laughed at him and said "You better keep up your guard, ole man."

Jack continued to feel that Julio was hitting harder than he was. Jack kept up the defense, then Julio nicked Jack's wrist a second time and Jack let Julio have it by bringing the sword down on his defense stick, slicing it in half. Julio's arm came off in a clean swipe. Jack moved first to scream "Medic, we need a medic now." Julio went down. Jack pulled off his shirt and wrapped the wound, Jack stepped away to see others helping.

"Now that's a first, I've never seen that before", said the Captain and "have someone take Jack to go see the Commander", he said to his Sergeant.

The Sergeant jumped in between them and said," Now break it up and act like agents". Julio's brother was swearing avenging to killing Jack. The Sergeant assembled the rest and said, "This officially ends today's workout. All the rest of you go to the dorms. Jack you need to see the Commander, would anyone like to escort Jack there?" looking around to see the MP's holding Jesus down as Jack was sitting in a chair nearby.

"I'll help him out" said Raphael. Helping Jack up and leading him away from the crowd and the enraged brother, who was fighting to get to Jack, swearing to avow what happen to his brother.

Raphael led Jack out of the gymnasium and down the hallway to a room, a key pad on the door, first was entered by her, she then led Jack into a dark room. The lights came on as the door closed shut, he then saw Captain Jon Phillips. He said, "Please have a seat Jack, that will be all Raphael."

"How did you know he was the mole?" said the Captain.

"The tattoo on his now amputated wrist." said Jack calmly.

"Good job, sorry you had to endure all those challenges, you can go rest up and wait for the retribution to occur."

"Thanks, do I get my gun for this?"

"No, we need this to look like an accident, so that the Commander won't think were on to him and his four plants" said the Captain. He then says," Now, you must face the Commander, be on your best behavior and behave, your dismissed."

Jack gets up and leaves, Raphael re-enters. The Captain looks at her and says, "Raphael, go with Jack and watch over him."

"Yes sir."

Jack entered the room, and was led to the Commander, who shook his hand and said, "Have a seat, I want to review what happen."

"Jack take a look at this, if you ever play lame like this again, I will send you through this school again". They both reviewed the tape and the live feed. The Commander said, "I know you're suppose to be the next greatest thing to happen to the CIG, but when you're under my roof you'll play by my rules and that means controlling your anger. Now I do know what you just recently went through, so for that I will cut you some slack, why don't you go off and get some rest, we'll talk tomorrow." The Commander said, "Do you have anything you want to add?"

"I'm sorry." said Jack showing his remorsefulness.

"I'll let Jesus know, you said that, you're dismissed." Jack got up mumbling something as he made his way out of the office. Raphael was waiting for him.

Raphael led Jack, the two walked hand in arm together, only to have Jack say, "What did he mean by going through the school again?"

"Don't you remember, it has been eight months since we first came here together."

Jack walked with her, as they made it out in to the sunlight, Jack was trying to remember what she was talking about, the ring, and he looked down at his finger, no band.

She led him to his quarters, a sentry was standing outside his door. Jack opened the door for her to enter then he followed her in. He took a seat on the bed, as he watched her go over to a desk and retrieve a newspaper clipping then bring it back to him. As she handed it to him Jack read the headlines that said "Hero Jack Cash, exposes slave ring, then a Presidential assassination attempt and is awarded the Silver Star for valor. He read while Raphael was stroking his hair, he felt his watch pulsing. His eyes became blurry with trying to read the words, he reached up to get to Raphael, only to collapses to the floor, and he was out.

Raphael stood over Jack, pulling off the elastic glove that contained the suppression oils. She waited on the bed till there was a knock on the back door.

"Doors open, come on in."

In the doorway stood the splitting image of herself and a super big guy.

"Come in Serena and help me out."

"Looks like you don't need too much help, you have him under control."

"Johnny, pick him up and throw him in the car", said Raphael, who was behind Serena.

"Hey, you didn't say anything about this guy, he helped me out and why are we taking him?"

"Because Rod, he can help out our cause, his ties to Carlos will get the guns we need for our people" said Raphael.

"Do as you're told or you will be cut off." said Serena.

"Yes ma'am" said Johnny, as he picks up Jack and throws him over his shoulder only to see Jesus with a sword in hand, yelling "my brother is dead, now this fucker must die."

"Raphael I need your help", yelled Johnny, as the blade sliced across Johnny's neck, just barely missing Jack. Jack was in a dream like state. Was he really in a dream, as he hit the grass, the watch was doing the job, counterbalancing the poison. He felt his faculties returning. Jesus lunged at him with the sword out and spearing as it hit the grass, it stuck.

A shot rang out, and Jesus fell over on his sword, he came to lie next to Jack. Military police just saw what happened, and swarmed in and arrested the two girls, and attended to one of their fallen. Jack could see slightly, as coherent as he was, he was lifted on a stretcher and whisked away with Daphne at his side. She held onto his hand while he went to the hospital. Jack reached up to try to touch her breast as she pulled away and hit his arm with a hand slap.

Jack laid back into the pillow with a smile on his face. He now knew he was safe as he went to sleep.

Daphne watched as Jack was wheeled into the emergency room and went into the waiting room.

Daphne was on the phone to Lisa, who informed her to stay put and that she would send a team to her location.

Some time had passed, she turns to see what looked like the Commander coming in, setting off the metal detector. She immediately flung herself over the sofa to hid as several others joined him, and the Commander said, "Spread out I want him dead, the article has been discovered, we only have a few minutes before the teams arrive."

"Wagner, you and Henderson get into the E R." said the Commander "Where's your man?"

"You need to find out who the breech was" spoke a familiar voice.

Daphne peered up at the top of the sofa to see it was a tall black man talking.

"How would I have known she would care enough to get involved?" said the black man.

"This is your problem now, deal with it the right way, do you hear me?" yelled the Commander.

Daphne felt for her gun, pulled it out, released the safety and felt a gun to her back.

"I found her" Wagner said, "Now get up and drop your weapon."

Daphne rose, surrendered her weapon to the guy they call Wagner and stepped out to face Eddie and the Commander, Mike Johnson.

Jack awoke, to see a doctor who stood over him, and said, "You're coming out of it, good. Looks like you were poisoned with some sort of mind controlling drug to suppress your sub-conscious. We found your badge and made the call. Jack felt his holster, and touched his gun butt, instantly he sprang up.

"Whoa, you can't get up so soon."

Jack pulled his lines from his arm, and then pulled out his gun and was on the move. He hit the lobby and saw a tall black man and Commander Johnson, and it was time to end this game.

"Let her go" he screamed with his gun out and ready.

The pair turned to see Jack as they made their move, a shot rang out barely missing Jack, who spun, turned and aimed. He shot Wagner between the eyes, watching him go down, the pair released Daphne, who came after Jack. While the other two were shooting at the pair, Jack shoots again and gets the Commander in the leg.

"I'm hit, Eddie, help me out now."

The fire fight continued between Eddie and Jack, Jack checked his ammo and pulled another clip, reloaded it and then saw Eddie running to them.

Jack hit's him in the leg with one bullet, the next was in the side, as the guy turned and fell on his lower back, as he lunges at Jack and Jack fell down. Jack looks up to see the red-headed Lisa carrying a gun and yelling "Put your guns down this is the C I G and I'm in charge here, let's find Jack."

"I'm here" said Jack, holstering his weapon and coming out from behind the planter.

The S I T team came in to include Michelle and Magdalena to arrest Eddie and pick up Wagner. They strapped down the Commander and above all else you could hear Henderson screaming.

"We need to talk" said Lisa, as she leads Jack to her vehicle. They both get in as Daphne got into the back.

"This was supposed to be the week you graduated, but look at you, your finding corruption everywhere you go, how ironic, not to mention Cuba?"

"What about Cuba?" asked Jack?

"We'll all you were supposed to do was capture Carlos, but instead, you end up marry into the family."

"So I am married? I thought it was a dream."

"Yes, to the riches Princess of Cuba, Maria, and to a princess from the Dominican Republic, and one other."

"So I do remember." said Jack excitedly.

"Had you forgotten that I'm your handler" said Lisa, asking Daphne to come forward, while saying "You will take orders from me, well not really, but directions."

"O Kay, I will listen to you, you both", said Jack.

"It was a good thing you had your gun on you or they would have killed you."

"What do you mean?"

"Aside from the badge you wear, Installed in the butt of your special gun is a powerful magnet, designed to attract and deflect bullets, or any other metal objects as they get close to you. Anyone other than yourself that tries to use your gun will receive an electrical shock, strong enough to kill them. This force field protects you especially when you are sleeping at night. This weapon becomes your protector, that's why they call it a smart gun." Lisa motions for Ramon to drive the SUV off. "Thanks for saving my life" said Jack looking over at Daphne. "Wait a minute, we need to turn around, I know what their plan was." Said Jack.

"What are you saying?" said Lisa, then telling Ramon to "slow."

"During their conversation, they said something about assassinating the President."

"Which one?", said Lisa.

"What do you mean?", asked Jack, trying to remember.

"There's the outgoing one and then the incumbent, but it can't be our President, this is a re-election year". "Are you sure?" said Lisa.

"Hold on let me think" Jack concentrated for a moment, "Raphael read that headline or was it? She said it was our lady, the President."

"Oh my God, that means it is this weekend, Ramon turn us around, were going back to Washington, and I know who the target really is", said Lisa, who was on her cell phone talking to some people. As Daphne switched her seat to get closer to Jack, she rested her hand on his shoulder and said "I'm glad you were O' Kay, do you remember me coming in and holding you?"

"Yeah, I think so, how come you didn't get shocked?"

"The gun has a special imprint for those that are friendly and that those are the enemy." Said Daphne, "But that's all I know."

"They drugged you with a virus that tells your mind to search for people, good or bad, that you recognize to work against you, overall it was staged", said Lisa, then added "I know who is getting potentially assassinated, she is the new head of the nationwide union organization, she influenced her members to vote for a female president. She will be speaking here in Washington D C tomorrow and I want you to protect her".

"Alright, I'm all yours. What about the graduation?"

"Let's just hope you're finished by then,"

"That's what I like to hear" said Jack.

"Let me see your badge." asks Lisa.

Jack pulls it out of his heart pocket and gives it to her.

"How are your rounds?"

"Down on my last clip."

"Georgio, hand me those shells marked special, please."

A hand from the rear seat hands her a box, which she gives to Jack and says, "Here are your rounds, reload your current clip. Do you have your spent one?"

Jack felt around his pocket and said, "No, I must have dropped it."

"From now on everything you have is yours, inside each clip is an explosive, hold on to it all costs, if you leave it somewhere out of say 100 feet, it becomes armed. It's design is to take out that person who touches it. Georgio, call the bomb squad to go back to the hospital, and evacuate it."

Jack popped out his clip and looked at it.

"It is safe, Jack, just be careful. If you want we could fold down the back and let you sleep."

"That would be good."

Daphne spoke up and said "Or he can just rest his head in my lap." She wasn't even heard.

"Ramon stop the vehicle, let's put the seat down and pull out the bedding for Jack."

"Yes Ms. Curtis."

Jack refilled the clip with rounds, reloaded it into the weapon as the vehicle came to a stop. Only one person got out, Ramon. He instructed Daphne to climb over the seat and sit by Lisa, who moved over for her to pass. Jack watched as the two jumped seats, then watched as the Italian looking guy pulled out a pillow and a sheet then he made up and several blankets. On the sides he put up some curtains, then said "It is ready for you Mister Cash." Jack had help from Georgio, who was in the back by Daphne.

Jack crawled over the seat as Ramon closed the door. Jack grabbed the pillow and propped his head up as he laid catty corner, then covered himself up in the blankets. He listened as Daphne and Lisa talked, as he fell fast asleep.

Daphne watched as Lisa pulled out a large black box, the size of a legal pad, and opened it. Inside she pulled out two credit cards, and replaced them in Jack's badge, along with his I D card.

"How do you know the enemy didn't tamper with it?" asked Daphne.

"There is a built in tracking device in the I D card that is standard on all field agents, it becomes active as you pull it out. Do you see when I place it on this screen, the only fingerprints are that of mine."

"I'd like to be more in the field closer to him", said Daphne.

"I'll take it under consideration, but for right now your assignment is to stay close to Jack. You see my only job is to take care of Jack's welfare, he is my assignment, and you work for me. This was all last minute, but were catching up and because Jack is a rare find." said Lisa.

"What do you mean a rare find?"

"You don't know who he is?" asked Lisa.

"Yeah, he is some recruit who went to the academy and was chosen to become an agent."

"Alright I will tell you his story, usually agents must have a master's degree in political sciences and spend their first five years in special situation group, like Michelle and Magdalena, because everything is predictable. As for Jack, he was a former German Spy, trained by the East Germans for counter terrorism tactics and intelligence." said Lisa, smiling.

"Jack's reputation far exceeded that of any current past or present agent we have in the system. He does things that are out of the norm and when you think you have him figured out he surprises you. I was working as the deputy assistant to the director of the Central Intelligent Group when I was called to be Jack's handler. We still have no idea what he is capable of, or ever will. But I will tell you this, we are on a ride that will be full of action and adventure".

Lisa looks at her again and said, "Now it is your job to stay close, and that is why I want you to get closer to him. Be like his wife, take care of him, watch over him at night, protect and give yourself to him."

"Are you suggesting what I think you suggesting?" asked Daphne.

"Absolutely, if you won't I'm sure I can find a few candidates. Listen, this job isn't going to be easy, and in the end we may all die at some point. But you will always be his closet asset, so be his friend, companion and lover. I know that's hard to swallow for you but we all must pay our own dues. The greater you play, the easier it will be for you to become accepted. And listen, between you and me, don't be the aggressor, let things develop." said Lisa.

"And if I don't play along?" said Daphne.

"Then I will replace you with someone more compatible, and for your information, on this case, I have brought in just that person. I have recruited her from the DEA, her name is Devlin. She is her groups' most successful field agent, so this is yours to lose. Will you accept this challenge?"

Daphne looked over at her new boss and then back to the now snoring Jack and announced, "I'll do it" and begin to undress.

"What are you doing?" asked Lisa, surprisingly.

"You said I should play."

"No, you need to be seductive and coy, just stay with me. I'll get a protocol manual for you to read. Now I know what Jack was talking about." Said Lisa looking at her disappointingly.

"You now know I'm ready to do anything for my agent." said the ever present and unknowing Daphne.

"Only time will tell, not a single action of stupidity, go rest a bit, you're getting on my nerves. I need to make some calls" said Lisa.

They swung the SUV around to park as the plane lowered its ramp. Jim climbs out and asked Lisa "Do you want your SUV to go on the plane?"

"Yes, will it fit?"

"I don't know, let me move the car up," as Jim went back inside, then moved the car ten feet. He then allowed Brian and Debby to secure the car. Jim checked the clearance, he said,

"Brian come here and help me remove this plate,—but later!"

Jim went outside to change places with Ramon, and drove the SUV up the ramp and directly behind the car on the plane, as Brian guided him up. Jim parked it, and said "let's modify that plate."

"It's on my checklist" said Brian, to add, "Where's Jack?"

"He is in the rear, sleeping" said Lisa, "Is his room ready?"

Jim looked at her then said, "Yeah that's for him exclusively, not you."

"So who is your boss now, Jim?" said Lisa, angrily.

Brian walks over close to Lisa and Jim and says "He is sleeping in the back of your SUV, you're a colleague of ours, right?"

"Where are you coming up with all of this you two?" asked Lisa.

"Oh, don't you remember the whole rocket issue, you know he can kill me and you as well that room is off limits to everyone, remember protocol." said Jim.

"What smells so good?" says Lisa, changing the subject.

"Nothing, you're not listening to me. On this plane we're the technical support team, the three of us, and the food is off limits, it is all for Jack, if you want something we have MRE's for the crew, so sit back and enjoy the flight." Jim reiterates.

"Set the G P S to these coordinates and let the other team members know, what we are doing, I have another call coming in." said Lisa. "Yes this is Ms. Curtis, oh hi, is this Devlin, now this is my plan, I was thinking that you could pose as a wife, to be his partner."

The plane took off and was airborne instantly, as it leveled off.

"Yes, you will do that; great, when you get to those coordinance, then wait till we arrive and I will introduce your husband and what your job is." added Lisa.

She then switched over to the speaker on her phone, for all in the cabin to hear, "Yes I will have a passport and I D ready for you and a special credit card and some cash."

"O' Kay I'll see you there", said Devlin.

"Bye" said Lisa, turning it off.

Jim spoke up over the intercom and said, "We're on the approach to Andrew's Air force base and will be on the ground shortly."

"Thanks for the lift." said Lisa.

The plane landed, taxied, then pulled into an awaiting hanger and turned around. The ramp went down. Brian was already ready at the wheel of the SUV, he began to back it out while Jim was directing him down the ramp. The plane finally shut down. With the SUV ready, Lisa and Daphne got in the SUV and with Ramon now at the wheel, they took off.

"Ms. Curtis, we are close to that coordinance, it's starting to rain." said Ramon, as he was looking in his rear view mirror.

The large SUV came to a stop and Lisa slid over to allow the door to open, as a woman was standing outside.

The two smiled at each other, and Devlin got in, and said, "Here is the dossier you need." said Lisa, hands the folder to her.

Devlin begins reviewing the info when she says, "Where's my contact?" she was looking at Daphne, who sat next to her.

"Not here, he is behind you." Said Daphne, pointing to over the seat, but she was looking at Georgio, who sat by the door, only.

Devlin looks over her shoulder to see something wrapped up in his blanket, snoring and well covered up.

"Now that's classic, how in the world can he be asleep at a moment like this." said Devlin.

"That's because he is one of our best agents and a little thing like this doesn't affect him", said Lisa

"A little thing, this woman is the head of the labor union and in my opinion, is one of the strongest women today. So what's your plan?" Devlin said excitedly, after starting out in near hysterics.

"Simple, you and Jack will be a couple at this resort that we are driving to. Jack will get close to her and you will work the crowd, like you do so well. The two of you will try to uncover the plot and stop the assassination attempt." said Lisa.

"Who's she?" pointing to Daphne, who mouthed the word, "Hello." back to Devlin.

"She is Jack's personal assistant."

"I have been a spy for over five years and don't have an assistant." said Devlin.

"That's because you were with the DEA, over here we do things differently. We will try to take care of you, so are you in or what?" asked Lisa.

"Yeah, I'll try it out and see how it goes."

"Ms. Curtis we are here" said Ramon.

"Out you go Ms. Babcock, here is your I D and credit cards" said Lisa. Lisa gets up, leans over the back seat and pulls on Jack's leg.

Coming to from a dream of Sara, he sees Lisa. He put a frown on his face, and said "Yes, what is it?"

"We're here, you need to get out and here is your badge. Your wife Rachel is waiting outside, your name is Jack Babcock for this mission. Here is ten thousand cash, just like your use to getting, or at least that's what Jim informed me that you wanted."

"Yeah that is fine, so what is my mission?" asked Jack.

"I thought you would be hearing what I told Devlin."

"Yeah, bits and pieces. I get it now, find the target, protect the target, find and locate trouble and dissolve all of it with minimal action. I got it boss." said Jack. With cash in hand Jack unlatched the swing up door and slid out from the back of the SUV and shut the door. The SUV sped off.

Jack stood up, trying to get his bearings, as he was putting his cash away.

"What are we doing out here? Let's go" said Devlin, impatiently walking into the resort.

Jack walked around as Devlin looked at him. Jack stepped out onto the sidewalk as Devlin wrapped her arm around his and the pair walked into the Grand Hotel. As Jack put away his badge, the two made it to the front desk.

"Hi, how may I help you both, together, or" asked the woman at the front desk.

"I believe my husband and I are under the name of Babcock." said the smarter agent.

"Yes, I have you here as Jack and Rachel Babcock, could I please see some sort of I D and how will you be paying for this room?"

Jack pulls out his expense credit card along with his I D and hands it to the front desk clerk.

"Would you like all hotel charges on the card as well as phone, mini bar and room service?"

"Yes that is fine", said Jack. The desk clerk handed all of his cards back to him.

"Alright we are all set, your luggage arrived earlier by a courier, we will send it up to your room. Tonight is poker night in our main ballroom and the winnings go to support breast cancer awareness, can we count you in Mister Babcock?" said the desk clerk.

Jack paused to think about it, when Devlin spoke up "Come on honey, it is for charity."

"Black tie event" said the front desk clerk.

"Absolutely" said Jack kiddingly.

"It comes with a steak and lobster dinner as well." said the clerk.

"Fine put me down" said Jack. "Did she give you the key?"

"She gave us two card keys, let me show you the way. Have you ever been here before?"

"No, can't say I have, have you?" asked Jack.

As they stepped into the elevator, another couple stepped in. Devlin hit the eleventh floor and stepped back against the wall beside Jack to watch the two love birds kiss each other, so she caught Jack off guard and kissed him. Jack pulled away from the kiss and looked at her and said as the door opened to let them out "What was that for?"

"Just thinking of our time together, the future, you know, as husband and wife, interested?" Said Devlin.

"Sure, I'll play along" said Jack.

"And you were there, supposed to be protecting me, how did all that work out?" said Jack.

"I'm just playing my part, as a loving married couple." Said Devlin.

"Watch your ground, I know what you girls are all about." said Jack.

"Us girls, what do you mean by that?"

The elevator doors opened, as Devlin took the lead and seemed so excited, Jack followed, and said, "Now you're acting like a school girl."

"What, is that your fantasy now?" she said.

"Not really", said Jack in a low tone of his voice" Come here", he pulls her close.

"Listen they may have had time to install listening devices let alone a camera so watch what you say and how you act. If you want to talk let's go to the bathroom and run the shower that will be the signal to talk, you got that?"

"Yeah, I got that, you're not the only agent here, can you let go of my arm your hurting me."

Devlin inserts her key and hands Jack his, the door opens to a spacious living room with a small dinette across from a huge bathroom. The room was overlooking the pool area, being drenched with rain. In the middle of the room stood the modest queen size bed. Devlin jumped on it and announce "Look honey we can do it doggie style and I can hang onto the headboard, or you can positioning me at the end of this sleigh bed like this."

Jack pushes her head back, away from him and walked into the bathroom. He begins to wash up while Devlin begins to sing while looking out the big sliding door glass window. She sees a pair of binoculars looking at her, she eases off the bed and crawls on her hands and knees to the sliding glass door. She sees across form her, in plain sight, two men.

A knock at the door makes her jump. She gets up and yells "Alright I will get the door."

She flung the door open, it was the porter, he said "I have your luggage Ma'am, shall I bring it in?"

"No, leave it there" and hands him a crumbled up five dollar bill, she picks up the two bags and slams the door shut in his face, and says, "Honey your luggage is here."

"Yeah, put it on the bed, said Jack, coming out without a shirt on.

"Now that is what I like, you're getting ready without me." said Devlin.

"Hush", said Jack, picking up his bag right side up. He turned the hatches and put in his code, the case sprung open. She watched as all of his clothes were packed neatly, he pulled out his tux and an iron. He pulled out an ironing board to set it on and plugged in the iron. Next was his socks, underwear and t-shirt, then he lifted up a small bag and went into the bathroom and turned on the shower. Devlin was in the doorway and said, "Do you want to talk now?" coyly with him.

"Nah, I'm going to take a shower, get out."

"Can I Watch?"

"Suit yourself, Jack faced the wall as he began to undress, keeping his gun close by, as he laid it down on the toilet seat cover and turned to see her smiling, still at the door.

"Hey if we're married, I want to get a piece of that." she said.

"What are you waiting for?" said Jack, pausing in the shower to see what she was going to do."

"Alright, I'll play along" Devlin began to unbutton her sports blazer, to reveal a white blouse, which she pulled off in one motion, exposing her bare chest. Unbuttoning her skirt, she let it fall , pausing at the sink to pull off her socks, then pulled down her panties. She followed Jack into the shower. Giggling, she washed him and he washed her back side, she turned to see that he was aroused. She slapped it so hard, Jack reeled back, he went limp and grabbed it.

"Ache, that hurt, why did you do that?" Jack said in a rather mad manner.

"Were colleagues, were not fuck buddies, I don't play like that. Right now we are just getting to know one another. Maybe we'll do this tomorrow, then let's see where we are at."

Jack climbs out, still holding it, as the pain subsides and he dries off and closes the door on her.

Jack quickly dressed in his tux and attire, and left the room before Misses Babcock came out . . .

Jack was at the bar when his two favorite people arrived. First it was Trixie who said, "Jack I'm sorry for the way I treated you over Damien, I just want you to know I'm all yours. Will you forgive me?", as she kissed him. Then Mitzi, who knew she let him down as well and said "I know I took advantage of you when you were tired, but will you forgive me too, we both want to make it up to you, right Trixie."

"That's right Mitzi, so were serious, just tell us what you want to do." said Trixie.

Jack told the girls "Just be yourselves and I accept your apogee, go mingle and don't be afraid to cut in at any time."

Jack waited at the bar as he watched his two charges mingle while he waited for his suppose torturous wife to appear. Devlin walked towards him, paused and said, "I thought we would have dressed together."

"What are you doing?" asked Jack.

"Taking a seat next to my husband."

"That place is reserved." said Jack.

"Then I will sit over there" said Devlin.

"That place is also reserved."

"What do you mean, what's going on here?" asked Devlin.

Jack turns on his bar stool to face her and said," While you were being mean to me, I had to seek some sympathy elsewhere. So if you don't mind, ladies come on, this is the big bad wolf I was telling you about."

A young beautiful blonde passes Devlin by to take her place on one of Jack's arms. Then she sees an equally beautiful little older coed brunette fall in on his other arm, as Jack says, "This is Trixie and the other is Mitzi, or vice versa."

The blonde said, "I'm Trixie and she is Mitzi silly, but I will forgive you later, when you will remember my name", she said with a smile.

"Meet Rachel", said Jack.

Devlin looked pissed off and now begin to show her fury.

The blonde said "That's no way to treat your man. My friend and I will be kind and caring for him, so bug off bitch."

Devlin told Jack, "I can't believe your choosing her, or them, let alone that for me, whatever."

Devlin turned and ran into an older gentleman causing him to spill his drink. The place was filing up quickly, a young Arab descent looking man stepped forward to offer Devlin assistance and said, "I couldn't help but notice you were with that guy at the bar."

"Yeah, so what" said Devlin wiping away a tear.

"That guy ain't worth it." said the Arab.

"And you are", said Devlin raring to go.

"Listen, give me a moment, come on over and let me buy you a drink so that we can get to know each other better."

"Well I don't see what it will hurt," as she smiles and looks back at Jack who is now kissing the blonde, while the brunette is hanging all over Jack, "Lead the way."

"Who is that guy?" said Devlin, infuriated with Jack, then added "He is some John, I mean."

"My name is Ackmed."

"What is that Russian or something", said Devlin acting dumb, sitting, facing Jack and his two mistress's. The waitress comes over to them. "Could I have a vodka straight up, hold the ice?" said Devlin.

"Wow, I would like a rum and coke", Ackmed ordered, as he turned in his chair. The two watched Jack, when Ackmed says, "So how much do you charge?"

Devlin looked at him, in her evil eye way to get ready to swing at him and said, "Oh around fifteen hundred an hour", she said nonchalantly. As the two continued to watch Jack behave silly with the two young coed's. They both kissed him on the lips, the girls left again, as another woman comes up to the bar, this one a bit older, she extends her hand and said loudly, "Hi, my name is Barbara White, I couldn't help notice you and those two girls. Are they your daughters?"

"No, they are two girls who just want to have some fun, what about you, what are you seeking, can I buy you a drink?" Jack asked.

"Yes, I would love one, may I take a seat."

"Sure, sit down" said Jack turning and said, "Hey can you get this lady a drink" and, "You were saying?"

"Aren't your girls coming back?"

"Nah, they had to go off and go back to work, but I imagine I'll see them later If you know what I mean", said Jack with a wink to Devlin.

"So what is a handsome guy like you doing all alone?" said Barbara.

"I'm not, you're here now", said Jack taking a sip of his drink.

"This is true, so then why are you here?" she asked coyly.

"Just waiting for dinner to start, then later play in the game I guess", he said.

"So what do you do?" asked Barbara.

"I'm in the security business."

"That sounds exciting, you could be my security if you want" she said, jokingly.

"Why do you need security?" asked Jack.

"It's mainly my job, you see, I'm here secretly to promote my mom's annual event."

"How's that, you know what they say, when you're in the secret the lies tend to surface a lot sooner than expected and you're more likely to get into trouble." said a wise Jack.

"Is that from previous experience talking?" asked Barbara.

"Absolutely."

"So mister handsome, I don't even know your name."

"The name is Jack Babcock, let me be your special bodyguard tonight."

"Well Jack, my name is Barbara, Barbara White, and yes, I will let you be my bodyguard in exchange for a donation."

"How much do I need to give, and who does it benefit?" asked Jack.

"Most of my fundraisers target smaller donors. By the way you dress and the physical attraction you have to women, I'd say your worth more than a small donation." she leans in and says "The higher the donation, the more likely of your chances with me later tonight."

Jack pulls out his wad of cash and counts out five thousand dollars and hands it to Barbara and said, "How's this?"

""Wow, that is nice, let me write you out a receipt and can I put you on our mailing list."

"Sure, do you want to take down my address, its a PO Box, alright," asks Jack as he searches his phone for an address to use.

"Yes, sure, what is it"

"It is P O Box 1000 Washington DC 00001 and attention me."

"Here is my card" she hands him the card and lingers with her hand on his, as Jack reads it, "donation in the amount of 5,000 dollars to the Helen White Memorial fund for the advancement and research for Breast Cancer." She leaned in and gave him a kiss on the cheek and said, "You are a kind and decent man."

"So for a girl who doesn't care for that guy, you are sure staring at him, how about you and I go back to my room and have a party", asked Ackmed.

"Yeah, maybe after dinner, and if your donation is big enough then I'll consider throwing it to you." said Devlin.

"I got friends, who would sure love to spend some time with you." stated Ackmed.

"Oh yeah, what do they do?" asked Devlin, watching Jack kissing this older woman. It was getting her blood boiling and she was getting annoyed with this terrorist.

"Thanks again for that donation" said Barbara and added, "I want you to come sit with me at my table, and be my guest for the evening", as she pulls Jack along, the two walk out of the bar to the dining room.

"Alright Ackmed, it's time to go" said Devlin.

CH 7

Barbara White

The room was filling up, as Jack surveyed the surroundings, each round table had a center piece. On the right side of the room was a huge board that had a picture of Helen White and of her Daughter Barbara, under that was a list of corporate and private donors.

Jack saw he would be near the top of the private side. He stood by her side as she started to greet people, he nodded to acknowledge them when one of the patrons said "Oh you must be the husband, what do you think of our girl here?"

"She's doing a great job. I support her one hundred percent."

Barbara walked on and said, "That is a nice couple, they will donate big, thanks for what you said."

Jack continued to assist her and watch people. He saw Devlin and the terrorist coming through the line. Devlin walked up to Jack and whispers "he's a perve."

"So eliminate him and we can go home" said Jack looking at her. She looked at the terrorist and nods her head. She walked hand in hand with him. Jack continued to stand next to Barbara until the line faded out and Barbara said "Sorry about that and thanks for the support."

"No problem, it is why I'm here, to help and protect you. I'm just standing in for your husband, I'm sure he would be here if he could."

"That's nice" she kisses him on the cheek and , "You remind me of my estranged husband."

"You didn't say you were married." said Jack.

"Well technically divorced, he one day went missing and I declared him dead, enough of that, let's get to my table dear."

Jack followed her to the front. They stopped near the stage, at the number one table. Jack pulled out her chair and then let her sit, then pushed her chair in. Jack then took his seat on the left of her. As servers set out their plates, Jack ate slowly. The first course was the salad course, then next was steak and lobster, Jack ate and kept quiet. He was thinking "this whole steak and lobster thing is overrated." He kept to himself while Barbara was out spoken and very abrasive to most people. At the table across from him was Devlin and her two new bad boys and joining them was two hot girls that associated themselves with bad boys. Then came the dessert course, which Jack passed on, as Barbara said, "Not having your dessert, you can have me later" she said, as she had her hand on his leg.

Jack nods his head in acknowledgement, and then she taps his shoulder and gets up.

Barbara stands up on stage and walked to the podium and begins to speak. Several times Jack went to feel for his phone, knowing it wasn't with him, so he sat in silence as Barbara spoke about wide range of topics. As she closed, she started to give individual recognition, then asked if anyone wanted and said anything. No one volunteered, then she started talking about a compassionate man and said "I'd like for you to give a big hand for my dear friend Jack Babcock, who donated five thousand dollars today. Would you like to come up and say a word."

The audience erupted, egging him on. So Jack got up, went up to the podium and said privately, "Thanks."

Then waited till it died down, as he had a momentary flashback to a day in his prison cell, to here, now in front of hundreds. He said "First off, I'd like to give a huge thanks to all the friends, family, supporters and volunteers who have made this possible, each day millions of women and some men are diagnosed with this deadly disease and the more we find ways of discovering a potential cure, is a step for a better quality of life. So on this day, I challenge all of you to make a single large contribution, and I will match it personally."

The crowd began to clap and whistle loudly, as it died down he continued "At the end of tonight's game it will be announced all that was given prior to the games beginning. I will make that matching donation then, so other than that, thanks again for coming out and we will see you tonight".

The crowd went wild with the clapping. Jack took his seat as it died down. Barbara finished off the speech and came back to sit by Jack and said, "That was gracious of you, you didn't have to do that, it may cost you over a million dollars or more, I'll get you out of this."

"Don't bother, I want to do it, I'll pledge you a million anyway, give me an account number and I will make the transfer immediately. Do you have a private room we can go for the transaction?" said Jack.

"Yes, follow me" she said quietly to Jack, then announced, "I'll be right back."

Taking Jack's hand, she led him out of there.

They went down a hallway on the first floor, on the left was her room, as Jack said, "I thought you would be in the penthouse."

"So does everyone else, so I'm taking some precautions. I stay down here in one of the maids' quarters, seeing it's only me."

"Tell me about your real husband." said Jack.

"Not now, let's savory the moment, I'm horny." said Barbara.

"Tell me what the circumstances were, why he left. You seem like a nice, caring woman, who seems quite loyal."

Barbara stops and pins Jack up against the wall and said, "My husband cheated on me with an eighteen year old, in my own bed. Then I got a call saying he was leaving me for her and that was the last I heard from him."

She was touching him down below the belt and kissing on his face and said, "Make love to me, it will be the best money spent."

"Tell me more about your husband."

"Your ruining the moment" she pulled her hands in. She stopped, looked at him and said, "Alright, I reported him missing three months ago."

"Let's go over this again, you actually caught him putting it to her, or what?" said Jack.

"Well, come to think about it, he was kissing her."

"Like what you were doing to me?" smiled Jack.

"Yeah sort of", she began to look at Jack differently and said "He was lying on our bed, on top of her."

"Had you seen her before?" Jack asked.

"No, it was the first time and only time" she said in anger.

"How bout this, maybe it was a setup and your husband was being used to get to you." Jack places his hands on her arms and says "Listen to me, sounds to me like your husband was being held against his will and when a certain person contacted you, you surprised them and told him to probably forget about you. So in essence you killed your husband."

"Oh my God, I never realized what I did. I just assumed he was cheating on me." cried Barbara.

"Listen Barbara, if he was in fact captured, then if logic serves me right, you're the primary target, and your life is in danger. Do you have any kids?"

"No, Greg didn't want any." said Barbara.

"What is his real name?" asked Jack.

"Doctor Greg Hughes, he was a plastic surgeon, he was the rich one. He had the big house and great life before I came along."

"Yes, but you complimented him, you are probably the one who kept you guys together. I know your horny and you want sex, but think of your husband. He chose you to marry, set up a life with and make you the woman you are today."

"You're right, so do you want to fuck me now?" She said as she leads Jack into her bedroom and closes the door. Instantly Jack was hard as Barbara knelt down to her knees and began to work on Jack's massive size, getting it fully erect enough for her to slip on a condom. She stood up and bent over while pulling down her panties. Jack inserted into her, he did all the work. She just took it, till she let out a small scream, then erupted to a small orgasm. Jack continued the pace only to hear "Come on and finish up, I've got to get back, drop your load already."

Jack hesitated, then felt uncomfortable and then made a noise and faked his orgasm and pulled out. He pulled off the condom.

Barbara was ready, Jack had a hard time putting it away, then zipped up and said, "Did you have that account number?"

"Oh you were serious? For that I'll let you do me as much as you would like." said Barbara, as she hands Jack her account book.

"Can I borrow your phone? I seem to have misplaced mine." said Jack.

She hands him hers, he dials up the number. He watched her pace, then she says to him "I'd like a cigarette, can I go?"

Jack waves her on as she leaves. Jack sees her purse on the table and accidentally turns it over. He begins to look at the contents; some pills, more cigarettes, lipstick and then he saw it, a transmitter. He puts all the contents back in and walks over to the stereo speaker and hangs the purse over the speaker. He hangs up the phone, turns the stereo dial to max.

Jack leaves the room, the noise was deafening, outside he could hear the music, still loud. He saw Barbara still outside taking big drags on her cigarette, she saw him and put it out and came to him and said "What is happening? Did you turn on the stereo" as she went inside and turned it off, Jack's ears were still ringing.

"Can you tell me why you did that, you're starting to piss me off?" yelled Barbara.

Jack takes the bag off the speaker, dumps the contents and shows her why.

"What is it?" She asked.

"It's a radio transmitter, designed to listen to your every move, sound or actions. They must have figured out that you were semi-paranoid and that any such thing could set you off. I'd calm down if I were you. There are people here to try to kill you, so listen up, I want you to stay close to me tonight and I will protect you or you can go home and let your body guards do their jobs." said Jack.

"Do you think there are more?" she asked.

"What, the listening devices" asked Jack.

"Yes. Whatever" she said hysterically.

"Calm down, usually they could put them on your person, sometimes luggage or"

"Can you search me, and my stuff, please?" she begged.

"Alright come here, Jack looked around her neck, her collar, then down to a lapel pin and said, "How long had you had that?" Jack asked.

"Just recently, bought it."

"Take it off." said Jack.

"My top", she said hesitantly.

"Yeah, take off your top so I may see if your lapel pin is a wire."

Slowly she unzipped the back, and then turned to face away from him, she lowered it off her shoulders.

"Turn around, let me see." Said Jack.

"No, I'm ashamed to." she answered.

"What is going on?" said Jack moving around to see her bra holding up pair of plastic breasts, tears were streaming down her face in anguish.

She said "See I didn't want you to see, I had the same thing that killed my mother and they took off my breasts."

"I thought you said your husband was a plastic surgeon." Jack said surprisingly.

"He was a prosthetics enabler, he tried to fix them and left me grotesque. For that I will always hate him, so yes, I don't care if he is alive or dead."

Jack just stared at what the butcher did; the scars were bad, as the bra barely concealed the evidence left behind.

"I'm sorry" as he pulled out the lapel pin and said, "Yes, this is a camera."

Slowly she redressed and then took a seat to watch Jack work. He was going through her suitcase and found two more. He said "That should be all for now, you need to check everything very closely."

"I will, can I ask you something?" Barbara asked quietly.

"Sure, what is it?"

"Do you find me attractive, be honest." she said.

"Well your sexier to me than attractive, it's things you do that I like. Overall, I like you."

"I mean my body, does it get you excited?" she asked.

"Sure, but I like different things which gets me excited." said Jack.

"Like what, I'm here for you right now, tell me what you like." she said as she moves closer to him.

"Well to start with, I'm not much into smokers and how they smell or taste." he said.

"Interesting, how I taste, what do you mean?"

"Well I like for a woman to undress in front of me, naked then let me have my way with her." He said.

Barbara went into sexy mode and began to tease Jack by undoing her shirt. Then in one motion let it fall, then slowly, she undid her bra, and pulled her bra straps down to the point she could let go, finally letting it fall to expose what she had been ashamed of. Her flat chest and the two scars on both sides.

Jack smiled and said "Come to me, let me touch your chest".

Slowly she moved towards him, unbuttoning her skirt, she let it fall. She was one step away when she pulled down her last article of clothing, her panties. Now full exposed for him, she stood inches away from him, Jack still fully clothed he began to touch her chest, deep in enough to touch her rib cage, he felt her pectoral muscle as the tears were streaming down her face.

She began to tremble, goose bumps began to form as Jack continued to touch that area. He was thinking of how flat Devlin was in the shower, only exception was that Barbara had no nipples. Just skin was pulled over and sewn shut, she was a beautiful woman, even with her double mastectomy.

Jack continued to touch her chest, following the contours of the muscles below the surface, with her free hands she undid his trousers to let them fall naturally and then touch him quickly. This was getting him hard, Jack had moved down her tight firm belly to her sacred spot, which he had already claimed earlier. This time he saw what he really liked, a natural growing patch, running his fingers through it to her area of wetness, he looked into her eyes to see she had stopped crying, the tears were gone, a wanton desire now filled them as the two kissed on the lips. She was now taking long strokes with her tiny hands, she could feel the power building, as she whispered to him "Take me and this time come inside of me, I'm ready."

Jack nudges her down to the carpet where she is down on her hands and knees, as he placed on protection, then easily slid in. Then it began and this time he was in charge, she had submitted to him mind, body and soul.

Jack was the stamina king, as he directed her to hold back letting go entirely. He began to coach her in her breathing, while maintaining the stroke, still fully dressed from the waist up Jack held onto her hips as he was building up the energy. She was near panic as her breathing was more rapid, till she let out a scream and yelled "I'm coming". She let loose a wave of built up emotion, fluids and finally the action was real for the first time as wave after wave she let go with each stroke as gushes of fluids soaked Jack's belly and his shirt. It was a mess when he finally let go and dumped it inside of her, he was exhausted and still felt her convolutions as he was still inside her. She fell to the floor. He was on his knees still while her phone was buzzing around on the table. He watched her get up and answers it and said, "I got to go".

Jack watched her get dressed, as he stood still proud and rock hard again then followed her to the bathroom where she was using a washcloth to cleanup. She turned and smiled and said "Thank you for making me feel like a woman again," she was beaming "You can take a shower if you like, I'll be at the game table" she said as she reapplied her makeup and left him to cleanup. He started taking off his jacket and then his bow tie then his shirt and finally his t-shirt.

Jack stepped into the shower stall as soon as he turned on the water, the coolness, then the heat was perfect. He washed up, rinsed off, then stepped out and toweled off, he used a washcloth to clean up his clothes and then heard the door close.

A fresh looking Barbara was on a mission, her big smile and her new glow was evident as she stepped into the other ballroom where they were playing poker. One of the event organizers came up to her and said "Here are the pledge numbers, your friend was able to raise a million four."

"That's fantastic, I'll let him know, this is further exceed all my expectations."

"What have you done, you have a new Aura about you, you look alive," said the organizer.

"Thank you, I feel ten years younger" said Barbara, who worked the room as Devlin watched her transformation from this dark looking host to this new vivacious looking woman, with a bright glow about herself. Devlin knew who to thank for that as she had to keep the terrorist company and had to listen to the two bimbo's talk about their men only to have their boss reveal himself. He introduced himself as Sevo, as he whispered to his associates what had just happened to Johan, who was bleeding from both ears with two ruptured eardrums and bleeding from his nose, I guess someone said he was dead. Sevo sat next to her and put his big hairy hand on her exposed thigh. She was ready to let him have it, if he moves it up any farther. She continued to sip on her drink as the three men spoke in bad English about their friend Johan and of his family, then it went quiet as Jack arrived. They watched him make his entrance, then their true colors came to light thought Devlin. Maybe they were after Jack as there chatter became foreign, she finally exposed them for what they were worth when Sevo said to Devlin, "O' Kay we are ready, will you come with us while we go upstairs?"

"Sure, let's go." she said.

Sevo takes Devlin's arm and wildly pulls her along as Jack steps into the room.

He didn't make any grand entrance, he scans the room for Barbara, then sees Devlin leaving in a unfashionable way, so he decides to follow them, staying back, but close enough to follow. That's when Jack noticed the two event organizers together waiting for the elevator, as Devlin's group came to them, Jack came up behind them and put his hands and arms around them and said, "Hi ladies, I've been looking all over for you."

"Hi Mister Babcock "said Trixie.

Everyone got into the elevator when Jack whispered to Trixie and began to talk explicitly, as Devlin and the terrorist were standing in back of them.

"Ten please", spoke one of them, as Trixie and Mitzi began their explicit talk about what they were going to do to Jack, much to the liking of the terrorist. As the elevator stopped on the tenth floor, the doors opened and Jack and the two girls walked slowly at Jack's slow pace. The terrorist easily passed them to hear, "If you want you could party with us", said the unsuspecting Sevo.

Jack wheeled the girls around and said "Sounds like this guy is making you both an offer, fair sir did you want to party with my two girlfriends?, they're going to cost you." "I'll trade them for that one."

"Oh Jack, they look fun, let's go inside" said Mitzi.

"Can't argue with the lady", said Sevo as their door was open, Jack saw the terrorist scurry to close some doors of their slightly larger than most rooms. "Wait a minute", Jack realized it was a trap, when they all pulled guns, it was over before it started as Devlin took her free fist and hit Sevo in the throat, sending him back. Jack pulled out his gun, and fired one at each of the terrorist hands, then dropped them both with knee shots. He turned to the girls and said; "Call Lisa, I would but I don't know where my phone is?"

The two girls fled the scene as Jack said, "Let's tie them up."

"Way ahead of you," Devlin said as she pulled zip-ties from the lining of her Jacket.

Jack opened the door to the room that contained the last man, slumped over the table with blood oozing out of both his ears and nose. He saw what he was looking for on a computer screen, it showed a man being held in a room, in a chair, beat up.

Jack quickly rifled through the papers to find the whereabouts to the hidden house. Then he searched the dead guy to find a cell phone and made the call to Lisa, using an encrypted code, she answered "Jack do you have something" she said loudly.

Jack pulled it away from his ear and said "Terrorist neutralized, need further assistance."

"Confirmed dead", asked Lisa.

"None just wounded, well one, by accident", answered Jack.

"I'll send you our clean-up crew, Capt. O' Donald, they're on their way." "Bring the leader in, can you video tape the others and send to me", asked Lisa.

Jack looks up at Devlin, who hands her phone to him, he takes the phone and takes each one's picture and the sends them to Lisa. He then takes it off speaker phone, looks at Devlin who hands him the paper, as Devlin says, "The target's husband is being held at this address, Jack and I are on the move, and we need pickup."

"Speak for yourself, were through." said Jack.

"We will be waiting and I will have crews' enroute to that address" spoke Lisa loudly.

Devlin unhooks the laptop computer and picks up several flash drives, while Jack searches the dead guy, for his wallet. He finds a money clip and takes his watch, then searches the three others and pockets it all, to wait as the first responders arrived. He pulled out the two he was leaving behind, Ackmed and Rahim. Then he lifted up Sevo and pulled him along still choking, from the blow dealt from Devlin. She found a box in which to collect all of the pictures and correspondences.

Jack opened the door and then pulled his badge, as a policeman had his weapon drawn saying, "Everyone with their hands up."

Jack still held onto Sevo and said "I'm a federal agent Jack Cash and this is my partner Devlin.

"The policeman looks around, then he lowers his weapon and said, "What do we have here."

"A terrorist cell" said Devlin with the box in both arms.

"Is that evidence you're taking?"

"Leave her alone, these are my prisoners, here are there ID's, but I am taking this one, do you have a card, so that I may find those guys if need be."

The policeman hands Jack his official card as Jack gives up the two men's I D and said, "If need be Devlin and I could come down to the station to fill out paperwork."

"That won't be necessary, I work with Lisa as well, our crew will handle it from here and if there is any reward you'll get it". "You ought to go down stairs she is probably waiting for you."

Jack takes Sevo, still coughing as Devlin carried the box. Devlin says, "Oh come on, I barely hit you" as his tears had subsided.

"Don't worry my friend, she did the same thing to me", said Jack. looking at her while he hit the L button. They hit the lobby, to an open uneventful room, through a sliding door they see two black suburban's, as doors flew open, another agent takes Sevo.

Lisa steps out to face them and says, "You both work well as a team, guess what, you're passed, you're now partners, here is your phone Jack, sorry I forgot to give it to you. Jack slides it open to see "You have one hundred and twenty five new messages and two hundred text messages and thirty three picture messages. Jack closes up the phone and sees Lisa and Devlin talking.

"So Jack, what will it be, a week at your new favorite spa or"

"I'd like to go home to Mobile and see my girlfriend Sara." said Jack.

"Alright, do you want to fly?" asked Lisa.

"Nah, I'd like to wait here a bit, I need to see the client one last time. Were you able to find her husband?"

"Yes we did, he is enroute as we speak, we cleaned him up and should be here in ten minutes or so" said Lisa steering him away from Devlin, and said, "You are going to have to eventually give Sara and Mobile up and live a life of seclusion and secrecy."

"I don't think so, I'll take my chances, and I plan on marrying Sara and live in Mobile, so if you need to find me give me a call, do you need my badge?" said Jack.

"No, but I need to give you your resting credit cards and compensation money from your last job. From this point forward, I'll be paying you all in cash."

Lisa goes back to the suburban as Jack gets on his phone and makes the call, it rings and rings, then her answering machine comes on, Jack says, "Hi honey I'm through with training and I'm coming home, you have my number call me."

Jack slides the phone shut, and places it on vibrate. He sees that Lisa had returned with a brief case.

"Here you go, as we have discussed your fee is one million per person."

Lisa looked at Jack to add, "You had five, not to mention the countless others we found in that basement."

Jack takes it and says, "Thank you."

"Here is your I D, as she hands them to Jack Cash and your resting credit cards, both with unlimited credit and one has your debit card to your retirement account."

"Thanks" said Jack as Lisa leans in and kisses him on the cheek and whispers, "I'm really glad this is working out. In the future I will really take care of you, I'll give you my Suburban to take with you."

"Nah, I think I'd like to fly" said Jack.

"How about my private jet?" said Lisa.

"That sounds good to me."

"When the husband comes and when your through, I'll have you taken to the airport. And of course, let me know when you want to go back to the spa." said Lisa. She wore a huge smile.

"Oh do you have a list of the top 500 most wanted." said Jack.

"Yes, why do you want that?" asked Lisa.

"While I'm resting up in Mobile I thought I would start catching some criminals while I wait for the next big assignment."

Another black Suburban pulled up, as door opened and Doctor Hughes stepped out, Lisa said "Doctor Hughes, my name is Lisa and I'm in charge here, this is Jack the man who let us know where to find you and this is Devlin, his partner."

"Pleased to meet you, when can I see my wife?" asked the Dr.

Jack looks over at Devlin, who looks at him and says carefully "Listen I want you to follow me inside, then I will signal for you to come, do you understand?" said Jack.

"Yes, whatever." said Devlin.

Jack led Greg back inside, past the elevators to a hallway, where he had him wait, then Jack went into the game room and found Barbara, who lit up when she saw him and gave Jack a big hug and kiss.

"So lover, where have you been?" said Barbara.

"I need to talk with you." said Jack.

"Is it serious, you sound down, are you alright?"

Barbara led Jack to a private room, she closed the door part way, Jack said, "First off, I want to let you know, we have neutralized the threat against you. I also want you to have this briefcase, it contains one million dollars and this"

"Oh thank you, she kissed him and held him and said, "You have blossomed me, I feel like I can do anything now, I won't ever forget this, you can be in my life, if you would like."

"Sorry, but I got to go and save someone else, we called your security team, they should be here anytime." "For now I'm leaving my team here for you and for your protection and safety."

"Jack, this is fine, but you still owe me four hundred thousand, you raised one million four, this will be the largest single day money total ever, and all thanks to you."

"Thanks to him" said Doctor Hughes who enters the room to add, "If it weren't for you I would have never been kidnapped, subjected to a lot of torture and pain, you're right bitch, I'm leaving you, yes I did have a mistress, ha, ha." "And for you mister, whoever you are, thanks for nothing, you can have my whore of a wife."

Jack pulled his gun aimed for his knee and fired.

A searing pain went through his lower calf and dropped as he fell clutching his leg. Everyone in the game room stopped, it was dead silent, as Jack gave Barbara a kiss on the mouth and said, "Someone needed to defend your honor, I don't take to kindly to people who show no gratitude or respect."

"Thanks again Jack, you are a saint among worthless men" she said. The two walked towards the door, they stopped, Barbara knelt down and said to her husband, "We're over, I'm getting a divorce" and left with the briefcase in hand. Jack bent over, pulling one of the doctor's hands behind his back and whispered "The next time someone rescues you from very bad people, don't you think you should thank them, and show your gratitude? I asked you to stay put till I was ready for you and you disrespected me again, then you disrespected your wife. That's, three strikes and now you're out."

"But you shot me, you can't do that."

"Who says I can't, I m a International Bounty Hunter with a license to kill from our Commander-in-Chief." "If you want to press charges then take it up with the President, if I were you I'd grant Barbara her divorce, give her all your possessions and make sure she is well compensated for the rest of her life." "If I find out, you're not helping her out, I will find you again and torture you far greater than what you have been exposed to, you got that, Greg."

Jack stands up, puts his gun away to announce, "It's alright everyone go back to your games."

Barbara stood at the door with her arms open for him, as Jack walked towards her, tears again were streaming down her face. She said, "I'm going to miss you, you are truly an inspiration."

Jack hands her checkbook back, she takes it and says, "My marriage was over long ago, I knew that, so thank you for finding my husband and for giving me some closure." "Now I must move on, you're welcome to be in my life, maybe another fund raiser?"

"Possibly, that would be fun." "In addition, I wire transferred another million dollars to your account and you'll be getting a call from the best plastic surgeon on the planet." "They will be giving you your dignity back and a new set of breasts, my gift to an amazing woman." said Jack.

"I don't need them now, you gave me my dignity back." "You showed me how lovely I am, but if they can make me feel them again, I will do it."

"That's the Barbara I know and have come to love" said Jack, as the two kissed on the lips. Barbara said "Are you going to take my secret cell phone number down?"

"Excuse me," said a paramedic who split them up to help Greg.

Jack finished entering the number and said, "You're on my speed dial."

The two kissed for a last time, as Doctor Hughes was on a gurney, Barbara fell in behind and said "I should go with him to protect my investment."

Jack shook his head in disbelief. Then he saw Devlin standing by the door and Devlin said, "You're a touching and romantic guy, I said I'm sorry for what I did to you in the shower, next time I will be more tender, I owe you one, besides your worth a million dollars, all I got was my standard pay of eight hundred a day."

"That's the difference between you and I, you're all about the money, and I could care less, I'm in it for the justice and freedom we all expect to have," said Jack.

Jack then looks at her and said, "For that they choose to compensate me well, but really I'm having the time of my life, I'd do this for free if I could." "I earn more than money, with the relationships I cultivate, then all the money you could ever earn."

Jack turns to leave, as Devlin says, "We are partners now, we need to be together."

"Sorry, I guess you didn't get the memo, you're my partner, here to help me, so the mission is over, go back to your job in the DEA and if you find Candace give her my best."

Jack takes a few steps and said "bitch" to himself." "These women with their power trips and control issues" then he sees Lisa in the lobby and said, to her "I'll have that car to the airport now, I'll call you again good luck."

"That was a nice thing you did for this cause."

"Oh yes, one more thing I still owe Barbara White four hundred thousand dollars from the matching funds raised, can you take it out of my compensation, and give it to her, via a wire transfer, of another million?"

"Yes of course," said Lisa.

"Oh yeah , one more thing, if I did in fact marry that Princess, is it true, I may have all the wives I want?" Jack said.

"I'll check on that one and let you know, but that's probably right" said Lisa.

"Lastly, did you approve the building and renovations I asked Jim to take on for me?"

"Yes Jack, that too is being handled, and funded by the money owed to you."

"Then thank you", said Jack, as he went out the door. He saw a waiting limousine, as the driver held the door for him, and said, "I have all your luggage in the back, if you need anything just let me know, my name is Damien, I'm your driver."

"Thanks, nah, just get me to the airport please." said Jack.

The car sped off, as Jack rested his head back and relaxed, he went to sleep.

"We're here Mister Cash," said Damien, through an intercom speaker. Jack looked out to see the inside of a hanger, he got out, he felt his phone vibrate. He answered it as he watched two men off load his luggage and put it on the small Lear jet. "Hi Sara, how are you? Yes, I'm flying in tonight to the airport on private flight, hold on." Then he speaks up louder, "Does anyone know how long it will take to get to Mobile?"

"Is that where you want to go?" asked Damien.

He held a small bag in his hand, then , as Jack looks at him, "Now I'm your pilot, if you need anything just let me know."

Jack smiled and went back to talking to Sara, to hear Damien say, "Usually takes three hours, but if you want to go elsewhere that is totally up to you." "We'll leave when you're ready to go."

"So look, if you, oh, and your sister Kate and Debbie, sure. All can come and make it a foursome, I got to go, I love you "said Jack.

Jack closes the phone up, walks up to the door and into the jet's cabin. Then chooses a seat and sits down as the door closes. He puts on his seatbelt, leans his head back only to see a blonde haired girl turn towards him, it was Trixie.

"Hi Jack, it's me Trixie and Mitzi, we're your flight attendants. Now where were we."

Jack watches as the two come towards him.

The flight was fast from Washington D C to Mobile A L. The first hour was bumpy but the second was a nice meal and the third was a little rest. Damien woke Jack, with a notice over the speaker as the plane touched down, taxied, and parked. The door opened to a wet and rainy night, a collapsible hood was placed onto the entrance. Jack walked to the door and shook Damien's hand and said "Thanks for a safe and easy flight." As he turned, Damien handed Jack another silver case.

Jack just shakes his head, accepts it and turns to see the two girls together and said, "Thanks to you two and I look forward to working with the two of you in the future." Jack steps off the plane to a pelting rain hitting his face, he lifts the case upward to block the rain, quickly jogged to the waiting reception area. He opened the door to see Sara, in the middle was Kate and on her left was his secret sex partner Debbie. They all came at him with such force, it drives him back to the door, with Sara kissing his face and the other two girls at his side. Jack was bombarded with multiple kisses and hugs. Then Sara pulled back and began to yell at him, "Why haven't you called me in, it's been almost a month, what is going on? I thought we would be together!"

"Hold on, I told you, I love you and yes we will be together for the rest of our lives."

Jack then pulls out his badge and lets her see his accomplishment.

Sara then speaks, "I'm sorry, please forgive me."

"Of course, don't worry honey we will be together, until my next mission." he said.

"You're what and when, mission, what is that? You mean that this is only a stop, so when . . ."

"Come on", he says to her, her sister and Debbie. Jack leads them out while Sara is behind them still venting, they are the only ones in the whole building, with the exception of the operations manager, who personally carried out Jack's bags and placed them in the open trunk. The manager watched, as Jack and his three lovely girls took off.

Jack rode in the passengers front seat next to Debbie, while Sara, was behind Jack occasionally kicking his seat, while Kate was all smiles and said, "Jack, we got your blood tests back and your cholesterol is low. And how has your stomach pain been?"

"I feel fine, no major problems, can we go to the hospital buffet line?"

"No, we're taking you to our parents' house." said Sara.

"Well, I've taken the liberty to instruct Sara what to cook for you while you're here."

"He turns to look at Kate and said, "That's fine, but Sara doesn't do any of the cooking."

"I can try" said Sara, still a bit upset.

"Listen, if you need a chef I could come over and cook several meals everyday" said Debbie, as she took her free hand and placed it on his wrist, to rub it lightly.

She then put her fingers into his hand and pressed down hard, Jack pulled away and said, "Stop it"

Debbie just smiled then says, "Where do you want to go first, your boat or Sara's apartment, before we go to her parent's house?"

"Sara's apartment." said Jack.

"Good choice Jack "said Sara, and adds, "That better had been the only choice, besides, we need to discuss your boat."

"What about the boat? asked Jack, as he turned in his seat to see Kate, whose skirt was hiked up to reveal her white panties. He looked up at her eyes and down to her legs.

Jack said "What's going on."

"Well, this is a hard one, you asked me to meet up with Sam." "She is a nice girl, we hit it off right away, she is very fond of you, she said, that you saved her life." "She is out of the hospital and she set up a fishing charter service, then when we couldn't reach you." "So Guy, who I liked, took over and every weekend he and I have been going out into the Gulf of Mexico." "Oh Jack, that boat is so beautiful, a guy named Jim came down and spoke with me." "He told me that you were undercover and not to worry, he paid off your boat, and gave Guy the fishing rights and licenses." "So there, you have it, it's your boat." "It's nearly brand new, paid off, and all is taken care of and wait till you see the inside, I helped to repaint it."

"Where is the boat being kept at?" asked Jack.

"It is on a private dock that is under twenty four hour security. Sam has actually rented an apartment near there and Sam, Guy and me, we all run your charter business."

"What about Medical School?" asked Jack.

"I've decided to help you instead, so Sam and I run the business" said Sara proudly.

"Alright let's go to her apartment then" asked Jack.

The car came to a stop in the parking lot. Jack was ready to move when Debbie grabbed his face and kissed his lips.

"Come on Deb, let him go."

"Aren't we all happy that he is back" said Kate.

Jack stood up, then bent down and said," Thank you both for being there for me."

"I'd like to visit both of you later, but now I need to rest, so thanks", Jack shuts the door to see that the trunk is part way open. He hands his briefcase to Sara, while he pulls out two bags and Sara closes the trunk. Jack follows her up the stairs, onto the top floor. On his left he looked down to see a huge party was being thrown, complete with a band. As they reached her door Sara knocked, Jack watched the door open and Leslie stood nude in the doorway to greet them.

"Wow" said Jack in amazement, and said, "The surprises just keep coming."

He came in and she closed the door. Then the two of them attacked him, both ripped the tux from his body.

The two of them made Jack their play doll, right on the floor, then to the sofa, then the three ended up in the bed after several hours of play.

The three of them collapsed and fell fast asleep together.

Sunlight, blazed through the window, as Jack had a girl on both sides of him, with both hands around each of the girls. Jack stroked Sara's hair, as he had a firm grip on Leslie right breast, playing with it.

Sara woke up first, she turned to face him, propped up on to her elbows to look at him and said, "You know from the moment I first met you, I knew then, that you're the man I want to be with for the rest of my life." "Since you have been gone, I've had the chance to talk with my parents and my family." "My sister absolutely loves you, her girlfriend is obsessed with you, I guess you drive her crazy, and yes I know about you and her, she told me." "You know its O'Kay, I don't care, you're a man and you have needs." "I also know about what you did with Sam", she began to cry, tears were flowing down her cheeks." Then she added, "She is pregnant with your child, but she is dying, she is doing her best to dedicate the rest of her life to repaying you back for the gift you gave to her." "Her and I have become the best of friends, I gave her a promise that I will raise him like my own son, her and I have grown close, she is an amazing woman." "I've learned so much about life and I am ready." "So Mister Jack Cash, will you be my Husband, to love and cherish till death does it's part?"

"Wait", she said, placing a finger to his lips, then adds, "This arrangement won't lessen your passion for other women, I know that, I also know that I'm pregnant, too, it's a girl.

Jack was silent as he looked at her, to say, "That is wonderful honey."

"I want you to know that everyone supports us and that stuff at the airport was a goof, to piss off my stupid sister." "From this point forward, I want to be known as Misses Jack Cash, so go ahead and answer me, what will it be Jack yes or no, I'm waiting for an answer."

"Yes, yes, yes, we will be together for the rest of our lives, so let me sleep on it baby, and baby." as Jack touched her stomach.

"Turn off the radio" said Sara "I'm serious Jack, I love you and I will in no way get in your way while you are working." "I wanted to tell you that the charter business is booked for a solid three weeks in advance, yet we are having some cash flow issues."

"Sam wanted to put together a report to show you the company's profit and loss and where our balance is" said Sara.

"That's fine; I may have a solution to that problem" said Jack "Yes I will marry you, but I was thinking of changing my last name to yours."

"Why would you do that?" asked Sara.

"I like Sanders better than Cash." said Jack.

"Well I don't, a lady doesn't let a man change his last name for any reason, here in the south, come on man, think of your pride." "You're a manly man and Sanders is a worker's name." "We are from Germany, as well as you." "My great grandmother was raised as a worker and married a peasant boy who looked in at the royalty." "I also looked up, Cash, it too comes from Germany and means royalty."

"Fine we will keep it, so why don't we look for a place to build our next house." said Jack.

"How about on the top of the hill, I just love the overlook of the harbor and the sound of the lighthouse and Coast Guard beacon at night."

"Fine whatever you want," said Jack as he held onto her tight and the two went back to sleep.

CH 8

Dealership

Jack awoke to some commotion, he looked around to see both of his black bags on the dresser, with his silver case. A smell of cooked food filled the air, Jack rose, looked at the dresser to see that his gun and holster were in-tact, next to his badge and a wad of cash.

Jack remembered lifting off that dead guy, he got up and went to the bathroom, then came out. He walked into the well-kept living room and stopped at the closet. Jack remembered something, he opened it up and there it was, the moneybag, he pulled it out, and took it into the bedroom. Jack decided to get dressed, so he pulled on some shorts and a tank top and found a pair of slippers. He walked back into the living room to see his soon to be bride creating a masterpiece. He came up behind her and slid his hand down in her shorts and kissed on her neck. She pulled away from him, smiled at him and said, "Have a seat honey, eat what you like and I will bring you these eggs."

Jack sat down to eat. As he ate, he thought about the hospital cafeteria, finished off the plate and said, "That was good, thank you."

"What are your plans today?" asked Sara, as she sat next to him slowly eating her food.

"Oh I thought I would lay out in the sun a bit, to absorb some sun and relax." "Do you know if the door is open to the patio?" asked Jack.

"If not, I have a key, wait a minute and I will go with you."

"Fine, hurry up, when do you go into the office?, and will you see Samantha?" asked Jack.

"Whenever you're ready, she will be there."

Jack followed her to the bedroom and watched her undress and then put on a two-piece small bikini. She then slipped on an over top and a pair of shorts and said, "I'm ready."

She led him out, and down to the hotel's patio, she unlocked the patio door and the two found a super-hot spot near the street, a place the sun stayed for a while. Remnants of a massive party was evident. Two guys stopped what they were doing to watch Sara remove her top then wiggle out of her shorts, her near perfect body was tanned and unblemished in all the right ways as she took a seat by Jack. He was laid out. She watched the two workers watch her, "Can I put suntan lotion on you?"

"Of course dear", said Jack, relaxing on his back.

Jack had his eyes closed, he knew she was his lookout.

He began to listen as the two workers began to talk in thick Italian accent, something an bout a huge bank heist in Montgomery that had netted over twenty million dollars and all the mobsters were coming to Mobile to split the lion's share of the take. He heard them say that they have a mole in the federal government, they went on and said other related things but Jack was interrupted as Sara said "Turn over, you're getting fried."

Jack looked up at her as she was applying the lotion to his back when he said, "Let me do that for you", he moved in behind her and applied the lotion, from her shoulders down her back to her waist line and pulled down her thong, a bit.

"Stop, I would let you, if we were on your boat, but not here, not in front of those two perves." she said.

He handed the bottle to her and laid down face first into a towel she had brought, he made it into a rolled up U shape and placed his head firmly on it. As she applied the lotion she heard,

"Jacko and Briano what are you two idiots doing out here?" said a voice from the hotel.

"Mister Maxwell told us we had to cleanup outside." said one of the perves.

"Get back inside, leave these two love birds alone and call the cleanup crew to come in and fix this mess, I will talk with my brother about this."

"Yes father."

Jack turned his head to see the back of the man as he was leaving, he caught the bottom of his shoe to make out that of a world map. He closed his eyes to sleep some more, as quickly as it was warm, it got cool, the sun was gone. Jack and Sara got up and went upstairs into the apartment. Jack went into the bedroom, Sara pulled off her bathing suit and started a shower, Jack stripped and followed her in. The shower was hot and heavy, as they took it to the bedroom and finished with a good bang for both of them.

Jack got up and turned off the shower to see Sara get out of the bed to proudly show off her well-toned and un-shaved body. She was three month's pregnant, the little pouch showed, as Jack watched her towel off herself. She turned to look at him, a picture of pure specimen of a male. "Adonis" she smiled and said, "I may have to get you a girlfriend to keep you busy at the end of the pregnancy."

"Why do you say that, I thought you could do it right up to the birth?" asked Jack.

"True, but I know your type, you won't be happy unless your banging something." she was smiling at him, "I knew the moment I met you that you were a bad boy and bad boy's require needs, which girls like me either deal with or they choose a good guy. But you see Jack, they are just that evil as well. But they just don't show it till the very end, then they are more evil than any bad boy could ever be." She began to toy with him and his chest as she said,

"Their problem is that when they meet that single prettier girl, they become wild, possessive and controlling, hence my last great stalker." "Jack, you are different, you are just like all the bad boys, all you want to do is stick it in every girl you meet". "So what I thought I would do is recruit all my good lesbian and straight friends together"." I'd say at least four more would do it, because you already have Samantha, which at first I really hated you for, but then I realized your logic". "She is beautiful and so much more knowledgeable than I ever could be." "I now look at life through her eyes and through your lust and not keeping it a secret to me". "It means you trust me enough to introduce me to her."

"Now, let's talk about Debbie, she is the total opposite of both of us, she says you're the most inventive guy she has ever met". "If she was straight she would be with you in a heartbeat and may consider being one of your wives if she could?"

"Doubtful, but anything's possible." said Jack slightly amused with Sara over all of his conquests.

"Then my world came crashing down, when I met Kim, Red's girl, who was just like me." "She explained to me, this train of thought is that you and Red are similar, and that women are naturally drawn to you both, your both protectors." "Even though he shares her with all his friends you don't want to exploit me like that". "She also said to me, at the end of the day, you will come back and be in my bed and love me for the rest of my life." "All those other girls are merely a tool to succeed you further". "This puts it all in perspective, we are free and wandering people, so I'm fine now and forever will be." "All I ask is that you go and get a checkup and sexual screening after each encounter and try to wear a condom." "Also go see a clinical psychologist, to keep your mind intact."

"O Kay" said Jack stepping into the shower for a quick wash up. He stepped out, to hold her around the waist, his hands between her legs and said, "Who did you have in mind, you know, to go see?"

They both laughed, as Jack toweled off while Sara poured lotion all over her tight taut body, she spent extra time doing her legs so that he may watch, she turned and smiled at him.

Then the two went into the bedroom to finish getting dressed.

"I see you have a new gun" said Sara.

"Yeah it's a present from the U S Government, they want me to keep it with me at all times, now that I'm an International Bounty Hunter. My area of domain is the Southeastern States and the South Island Chains." said Jack.

"Will you ever bring me along with you?" "You know I could help", asked Sara.

"Maybe we could take a trip, but first I want to go get you a present, so let's go". Jack puts his holster on, and then a blue windbreaker from her former store, then grabs his briefcase and follows her out the door. He walked slowly to observe the courtyard, then thought to himself, "Maybe it's time to visit that hotel again."

He saw her standing by her car and said, "Do you want to drive?"

"Nah you drive, I'll be your passenger". He met her and leaned into her to kiss her, she parted his mouth and explored further and said, "Stop, we may have to do it here."

"That's O' Kay too", said Jack going to the passenger side and getting in.

She hurried to the driver's side got in and fired it up, and took off.

"So where are you taking me, Mister Cash?"

"Where would you like to go?" said Jack with a smile and adds "Or should I say what would your little heart desire."

"Now that you put it that way, first I want a huge engagement ring" proclaimed Sara.

"But you asked me, why should I buy you a ring?" asked Jack.

"No silly, what I meant was I just want a ring."

"Really, if you get a ring, where is mine?" said Jack.

"You'll wear a ring?"

"Sure why not, if you have one why can't I, especially from you, then I'll always think that you love me." said Jack.

"Most bad boys don't wear a ring; it shows sign of weakness and possession." said Sara.

"So then they must be that" and adds, "Slow down."

"Where" she said, "Do you mean that dealership? You're buying me a new car?"

"Sure", said Jack looking at the billboard of a jewelry store. Then turning his attention to all the new large, medium and small vehicles, she pulls in and parks. A swam of men and one lady stood outside on the sidewalk.

"Are you coming?" said Sara then tells Jack "Leave your briefcase, we're going to have fun."

Jack sets it down on the floorboard, gets out and closes and locks the door.

"Miss, can I help you?" said one of the salesmen.

"No but she can, seeing her brighten Jack's day. The tall red headed girl with freckles, long arms and perfectly manicured nails stood by herself.

Sara made her way to her and said,

"Hi can you help us?" The red head turned with a cigarette hanging from her mouth, pulling a drag to exhale and then stamped it out. Jack stopped in his tracks to watch as all the smoke dissipated in the air. Jack caught up with Sara, "This is my boyfriend Jack and I'm Sara."

"My name is Jo, Josephine Carter, pleased to meet both of you, so how can I help you? You know actually, my appointment has arrived", she leaves to meet a couple of guys.

"What a bitch" said Sara.

"Don't worry about it, let's follow them and see what they buy" said Jack.

Sara was a bit giggly around them, though they looked like they were good people, thought Jack; he said to Sara "Are they good guys or bad?"

"Hush up Mister", then she decides to play along by saying, "Well the driver is a pretend bad boy and the passenger is supposed to be good."

"How can you tell?" Jack questioned her.

"Watch their body actions, you see the driver, we will call him Dick and his passenger Able." "So do you see Dick trying to swarm in and get close, using his hand gestures, while Able is back a bit, looking whipped."

"Yeah, so I see what you're saying."

The two followed Dick and Able with Jo to the parking lot. Jo began to open the big sized vehicles doors and said "Is it the size or color are you looking for? What kind of features do you need?"

"You", said Dick laughing.

Jack and Sara propped themselves on the seat, Jack in the passenger side and Sara went in the back. They were in the vehicle next to them.

"Hi folks, can I help you?", said a voice from behind Sara.

They both turned to see a handsome guy. "My name is Carl Hanson, I'm one of the managers here." "Are you folks interested in this vehicle, you know it is the top of the class for Suburban, it is also a hybrid, meaning it is environmentally friendly". "Do you want to take it out for a ride?"

"Sure she can, she is the driver of the family." "Sara would you like this vehicle?" asked Jack, seeing her stare at the younger salesman.

"Sure Jack", said Sara, still watching Jo.

"What's the story on that one?" asked Jack.

"Oh she is one of the bosses' girlfriend's, so he punished her today by having her work the floor. Why do you ask?"

"No reason in particular" said Jack.

"Besides if she had upe'd you first, she would get half the credit." said Carl.

"Yeah she's our sales person, we are just actually waiting for her to help us" said Sara, climbing into the driver's seat, then said to Jack, "I like this, it's big and I could really smash the cars in front of me."

"I need to see your driver's license and a proof of insurance" Carl said as he was looking down her top. Sara sees Jack pull it out of her purse and hands it to him.

"Thanks, I'll make a copy and away we will go."

"Look Jack, feel the dash, it is leather and the wood graining, it has a sunroof and a stereo." "Oh Jack, I like this vehicle, you know we could tow your jet skis with it."

"How do you know about them?" said Jack.

"I know everything about my man, besides their on the boat." said Sara smiling.

"There you go" said Jack pointing to Carl. Carl opens the door and hand her info back to her and the key and said, "Here Miss, I'll get in back."

Sara started the new vehicle and said "Is this right, only two miles on the odometer?". "Jack, I want this car."

"It's actually a Suburban and it has anti-locking brakes", said Carl.

"Shut up" said Jack, getting annoyed with Carl.

Sara drove it around a bit and then parallel parked it, in front of a restaurant. Sara looked over at Jack to smile and say, "I'm hungry, can me and my husband go inside? As she was looking in her rear view mirror at Carl.

"Do you plan on buying it?" asked Carl.

"Maybe, just depends on how nice you are to us" said Sara, taking the lead, but still looking over at Jack who has kept quiet. She knows that look, he is bored "Come on honey, let me buy you lunch. What do you say Carl, eat in or take out?" asked Sara.

"I'd prefer take-out" said Carl.

"And I'd prefer eat in, why rush a good thing." said Sara, giggling.

Jack got out and was looking at this huge vehicle, with its 20-inch rims and folding out running boards, it was nice, he went to the back and pressed the handle and the tailgate lifted automatically, as Sara watched. She was in his world now, as she kept quiet, following him around.

"Yeah let's get something to eat" Jack knocks on the window.

Carl opens the door and said; "Don't be long, I need to get back, so I can do the paperwork."

"Would you like something to eat?" asked Jack.

"Sure could you" Jack slams the door and Sara follows him in.

Jack is at the head of the line, with Sara next to him as Carl made his way in and said, "I locked the vehicle", as he got really close to Sara.

Jack looks down at Sara who says, "Good boy."

"It figures" said Jack, who pays for all three meals.

They all sat down. Jack and Sara ate quietly while Carl began talking.

"Do you know what your credit is like?"

"I don't know, I pay all my bills on time and besides I think my husband is just going to buy it for me, aren't you dear?"

"Possibly, depends on the price of the vehicle." said Jack.

"That one is around sixty thousand, give or take."

"Is that your rock bottom price?" asked Jack.

"No, but we have to make money." said Carl laughing.

"Let's go back to the dealership and work out a price, if it sounds good to me I'll buy it, if not, then will go somewhere else" said Jack.

"Sounds fair" said Carl and adds, "Do you want to drive it back?"

"Sure, let's go for a ride" said Jack, leading the way out. Carl handed Jack the key, he hit a button and the vehicle started up, unlocked the doors. Sara got in the driver's side, as Jack held the door open for her, then she scooted over enough for Jack to get in.

"Now you have to put the key in or it will die" said Carl, sitting behind Jack.

Jack slammed it into drive one and shot off as Sara held onto the bar she slid over to the other side. Carl was tossed out of his single chair into the space between the seats. Jack said, "Hey Carl, how do you like the ride now?"

Jack continued swaying the vehicle back and forth, causing Carl to stumble and just hold on as Jack continued to act like a boy. Sara and Carl then put their seatbelts on. Jack noticed a stop sign and slammed on the brakes, sending everyone up then down as the seatbelts held onto them.

"Hey Carl how are you doing back there?" yelled Jack, with a smile as he took it easy the rest of the way back. As they returned to the dealership, Jack parked it in front, next to their car.

Jack got out and handed the key to Carl, who in turn, said "Don't hand me your key, that is unless you do not want to buy it."

"Fair enough", said Jack waiting for Sara to get out, they all walked around it a second time. Carl wrote down something and asked, "Are you trading that vehicle in?"

"What does that mean?" asked Jack.

"Well usually people bring in there unpaid vehicles to trade for something newer, is your car paid off."

"I don't know, it's my wife's car, I'm sure she will tell you."

"It's paid off, what do you think I could get for it?" asked Sara.

"I don't know, I'd have to ask my manager, come inside, do you want something to drink?"

"Sure, water would be fine" said Sara. Jack pulled his briefcase out of the car, the two followed Carl into the dealership, to see a whole array of different vehicles. Carl walked up by the tower, talking with his manager only to see Jo was back with her two friends Dick and Able.

"I don't think they are buyers" said Sara.

"Why do you say that?" said Jack looking at a sports car.

Jack was reading the sticker and looking inside, it was red with a black interior.

"What do you think of this?" said Jack.

"Looks nice I could see you in that" said Sara.

"Alright folks come on over and have a seat" Jack and Sara followed.

"Now who has the best credit?"

"She does, what are the figures?" asked Jack.

"Thanks honey" said Sara sarcastically.

"The truck is set at a price of 57,200 with dealer rebates of 4,000 dollars, and excellent credit, you can drive off in this vehicle for 525 a month for sixty months, with a down payment of 10,000 dollars, how that sounds to you?" asked Carl.

"Nah, seems a bit high, that vehicle we drove is 53,200", but was cut off in mid-sentence.

"Plus tax, dealer handling and so on and so forth" said Carl.

"You get it at 45,000 and we got a deal?" said Jack.

"I could take that in consideration, but I need for both of you to fill out a credit application, while I go talk with my manager."

Jack pushed the paper towards her and said, "Here honey, will you fill it out."

"I need your I D and SSN card." said Sara, looking at Jack.

Jack pulls the two cards out, they were stuck together. Sara filled out the documents, she said to him, "How much do you make monthly?"

"I don't know put one million down." Jack said.

"Really, I didn't know, then I guess you will be buying me something much more bigger than I could ever imagine, just kidding I'm not material in that sort of way." She X'd the box annually and continued on, while the meetings of the minds spoke up in the tower.

"Listen Carl, this guy is pulling your chain, that's way under book, cut him loose and let him go, there are people all over." Jo came up to the desk and said, "Talk about being pulled along, I got two guys all over the place."

"Why don't the two of you switch." said the manager.

"They were with you in the first place" said Carl.

"That settles it, Jo go back and get a credit appt from that couple".

"Carl, go out and see what those boys really want", He watches Carl leave and said, "Listen, after you dump that couple, how bout you and me go back in my office so we can get down to business."

"Oowe" said Jo.

"Hey Carl, where are you going Buddy?" asked Jack, watching him go out the door, to see Jo.

"I've been told to work with you, do have the credit appt filled out?" said Jo.

"Yeah sure, talk with my wife, Hey, can you add this vehicle to that list?" Jack was pointing to the sports car.

"Don't think you can afford that one?" she said in an insulting tone.

"What did she say?" asked Jack, taking a seat across from Sara.

Jo handed her boss the paperwork and her manager said to her, "If I ever hear you say that to a customer again you are fired, now granted what we do is one thing, hold on a minute," He watched the screen as Jack's credit score was 900 plus and the vehicle total went down as a result of a military and special government incentive displayed the total for that vehicle.

With a payment of 200 a month for twelve months, at zero percent interest. He printed it out and read it to himself, the note on the bottom, he was stunned. He made a call to the store's owner.

The owner said he would be up there soon. The owner made his way up to the tower and said, "What do you got?"

He hands him the paper to read, "Yeah so what, it looks like we have a car deal." said the owner.

"Look at the vehicle." said the manager.

"Oh, yeah, that can't be right, compute the numbers again, is it a lease?" asked the owner.

"No it's a purchase, the same thing comes out, I've ran it again."

"Try another car, like the Camaro." said the owner, to add,

"Call our finance company, and I will visit with the customers myself" said the owner, then adds "Jo come with me."

"Yes father." said Jo.

"Hi folks how are you today, my name is Robert Carter, but my friends call me Bob. I own this dealership, this is my daughter Josephine, I hope she had been treating you fairly."

"Well actually we were thinking of leaving", said Jack.

"Why's that?"

"I gather you don't want our business, when your daughter said that I can't afford that red car." said Jack.

"Oh, you must be mistaken, Jo go to the desk and gets those figures for this nice couple and did you say you wanted that Camaro? It has a big 6.0litter engine." said Bob.

"Can I take it out for a spin?" asked Jack.

"Absolutely, let me go get the key."

"Hey Bob, send Jo out with us, cause if she plays nice we may decide to buy them both." said Jack.

Bob made it back up to the desk and said "What do we have here?"

"I've got good news and some pretty bad news." said the manager.

"Let's have it, I don't have all day," said Bob, as he gets on the intercom and tells Steve, the lot tech, to come to the show room floor and move the Camaro out. "As you were saying?"

"I called the leasing company number and it patched me to the I R G (internal revenue group) and they connected me with our brand and they told me to sell it at this price along with any other vehicle he wants." Then they said a representative will be here in a couple of days to sort out how many vehicles he wants and the costs will be taken care of. They also said to ask for no down payment and allow them to take what they want." said the manager.

"Fine, I have nothing to hide, they could come down and audit my books for all I care. Print me out the form for the Suburban and one for the Camaro. When he gets back, I'll ask him if there is any other vehicle he wants. You don't look so good, is everything alright?" said Bob.

Bob watches the desk Manager, take off to the bathroom and said, "Weird."

The lot tech fired up the powerful car and moved the other cars to drive it out, then stepped out of the car and said, "Here you go mister, there is not much gas in it, if you like I can fill it up?"

"No don't worry, he won't be long" said Jo and adds "You better get in while it is still running Mr. Cash."

Jack steps into the clutch, then had a flash back to the days when he was a kid and they played in his father's Jeep, he let off the brake and did a full smoke burn out.

The Camaro tires began to catch the tread, and off they went.

Bob walks up to Sara and said "So Miss Sanders or should I say Mrs. Cash, here is the figures to the Suburban and one for the Camaro, all we need is your signatures, it is all been approved. May I ask you something?"

Sara looks up to see him, as Sara was drawing a picture.

"That looks good" said Bob, he was saying to her in a respectful tone.

"Thanks"

"How come you didn't go with your husband?" asked Bob.

"My job is to guard his briefcase. Let me see the forms, oh yes that looks more reasonable and for the Camaro too? I guess for that price, I will take them both. She signs her name, then says "If it was Jack's credit you pulled, shouldn't he sign too?"

"Not necessary now, all this is an intent to buy." "I need this form to fill out all the paperwork, which I will get you started on while he is gone." "If you don't mind, can you tell me what he does?"

"Sure, he is a Bounty Hunter, but on a Federal level." said Sara proudly.

"Thanks" said Bob looking back at the desk to see his manager was still not there. He grabbed a work folder, then asked the lot tech Steve to look for Jacob. Bob handed the folder to Sara and said, "Fill out all the highlighted areas and we will do the rest."

Bob asked Sara, "Did he mention any other vehicle he would be needing?"

"I don't know" as she began to fill out all the forms. She finished and took it up to the desk and handed it to Bob, while she was holding onto the briefcase.

"Thanks Miss Cash" said Bob.

"My name is Sara Sanders."

"Like in the hospital's name Sanders?" asked Bob.

"Yes, that is our family's hospital."

"Doctor Greg and I go way back, he has bought all of his vehicles from me, and now you." "Is that man your husband?"

"Soon to be, but for argument sake, you could say that." "I'll be over at my table" said Sara.

Jack was focusing on his shifts when Jo spoke up and said," You don't like me do you?"

"What is there to like about you." said Jack.

"What do you mean by that?" she asked, as she coughs.

"Just that you're unsanitary and smell, you stink."

"How dare you say that to me?" said an upset Jo.

"Are you even a salesperson?" asked Jack.

"Well sort of, I'm in training, my Dad own the business and my boyfriend runs the company."

"I'm happy for you, sounds like you're on your way", said Jack in between shifts.

"What way is that" she said sliding around in her seat.

Jack returns the car, parks it, then gets out, closes the door and walks in. He hear his and Sara's named being called. Bob is standing by a door saying, "Right in here folks, oh Mister Cash, can I ask you a favorite" and steers him away.

"What do you need Bob." asked Jack.

"Well I believe my desk manager is embezzling money from my company."

"How does that affect me?' asked Jack.

"When I hired him he said he was on parole for something."

"Wonderful for you to hire him." said a sarcastic Jack.

"That's just it, all of a sudden he's now hooked up with my daughter." "Can you get him out of here, I'll pay you, he kind of scares me."

"Alright, I'll see what I can do," said Jack, quickly on the move.

Jack knew the desk manager was still in the bathroom, ralphing his guts up so Jack checked the locked office, then yelled, "Hey Bob do you have a key for this door."

"No, he has the only key."

"Mister, do you want to get into Mister West's office?" asked the lot tech.

"It would be nice," said Jack as he watched the guy leave then came back with a sledgehammer, and said "Stand back, I'd love to do this for you."

Jack stepped back to watch as the man pulled back and took a swing, hitting the knob and blowing it in , then the guy kicked it in as a slug from a gun went off, the lot tech just dropped and yelled "I've been hit, I've been shot, he got me in the leg."

Jack swung his head around, to see and hear another shot.

The shot whiz by his head, Jack swung down and rolled, pulled his weapon, took aim and fired. It hit its mark and the shooter fell grasping his splintered shin from behind the desk as he tumbled down.

Jack charged in, as he ducked a swinging three hole punch. Jack swung back, backhanding with his fist, connecting to the red head, thus knocking her out. Jack moved in and kicked the gun away, and said, "Lie on your stomach", Jack saw a whole slew of titles and some form of cash dividends.

"Your day is done", picks up the phone and dials 9-1-1. The number is connected to Lisa, "Hi this is Jack, I got two injured, requesting assistance."

"A team is dispatched and will be there in five minutes, looks like your hard at work, good job, keep me informed, bye." said Lisa.

"Jack, it's Daphne, are you alright?" said a voice behind him with her gun drawn and ready.

"Yeah, come on in, do you have any cuffs, or I will use my zip ties?" asked Jack.

Jack saw Daphne, then smiled, to hear her say, "I can't leave you for a day without you getting in trouble." She came over to see what Jack was standing on, only to surrender her cuffs to him, she turned to see Jo was awakening. Daphne went over to her and asked Jack, "Handcuff this one?"

"Nah, I think she will be fine" said Jack and adds, "You got this under control?"

"Where are you going." asked Daphne.

"To go buy a truck."

"What?", said a puzzled Daphne.

Jack left the room as he put his gun away, he walked down the hall, and into the lobby to the room where Sara was, came in and sat down.

"Hi my name is John, the finance manager. Your girlfriend signed her paperwork and when you guys make it official, you'll have to come back to resign. Here you go sign and the two vehicles are yours."

"Congratulations on your purchase" said John, as he shook Jack's hand. Sara said, "Bye", getting away from that guy and said, "Now that guy is creepy."

"Was he a good guy or bad guy?" asked Jack.

"What do you think?" said Sara, sounding a bit upset.

"What's wrong with you" said Jack as he pulled her towards him.

She was crying, as tears were flowing down her face. Jack asked "What, why are you crying?"

"I heard the gunfire and all I thought of was you, your safety and if you were alright or not?" she said.

"That's what I do, seek out criminals and bring them to justice."
"It just so happens these bad guys were either good or bad, they don't

play nice so I have to resort to violence, I'm just sorry you had to hear it, next time I'll be quiet."

"Shut up", she pushes him away with a smile and sees Carl standing by both of their new vehicles. Carl said, "I guess after all I'm your sales guy, too bad about Jo, I really liked her."

"It's the criminals you do tend to like, that mean all of us, so Honey which do you want to drive?" asked Jack.

"Do you need anything from this old vehicle?" asked Carl.

"Yeah, were keeping it and giving it to her brother" said Jack as Sara looked into the glove box. She got all her CD's, then looked under the seats, in the trunk then closes it down and said, "I'll have my brother come by and get it, I was going to let it go, but what Jack says, Jack gets."

Sara runs to the Camaro and says, "Where to?"

"I wanna see my boat" said Jack, losing the race to her.

"Then follow me, and see if you can keep up", she said in spite.

"I filled up the two vehicles with fuel and had them both detailed earlier. Here is a coupon for another detail and the first oil change" said the lot tech. Jack pulls out a hundred dollar bill and hands it to him and says, "Thanks."

Jack took the coupon from him, then placed his briefcase in the passenger seat of the Suburban. Jack then went around to see she was ready, as she was pushing the accelerator down, she had a huge smile on her face and said, "Will you come on already."

Jack opens the door, then got in and closed the door. The lot tech said, "Your welcome."

Jack fired it up and found a satellite radio station he liked. He slowly followed Sara out, she keep a pretty good pace. They drove to the public shipyards. As day was turning to night, Jack saw the clock said 6 p m he parked next to her.

Sara got out and immediately went to wait with her keys in her hand.

Jack saw his boat, the beautiful blue and white paint job made it stand out.

Jack got out with his briefcase in hand. He was in the lead, on the left was a building with its lights on, next to the harbor master.

Sara walked to the office, to open it up and there was Samantha as cute as ever. Sara hugged and kissed her first, then Jack swooped in and hugged Samantha. He felt her breast and she kissed him and said she was sorry for telling Sara the truth.

"That's alright, everything worked out for the best, so how are you doing?" Jack asked.

"Well, I moved out of my mom's house and into this place that I run." "I call it Mobile Fish Charter service, is that alright?"

"Absolutely, that is fine, I also need to start a Bounty Hunter business."

"Come over here, let me show you the books I've arranged for you." "As you can see, I've organized all the accounts receivable, then here is the accounts payable."

Jack just stared at her, her pure and lovable beauty. She added, "I pay Guy ten percent of the take and pay Sara and myself a small salary, I live here in the back room."

"I open the doors at seven am and close at six pm". "Now over the last two in half months we have made 76,000 dollars and have expended 54,000 with a net profit as of today as 22,000 thousand dollars." "I took it upon myself to grow that money, as I have invested that money in a high performance money market account, which as of today you have made 4800 dollars, for a net sum of 26,800 dollars." "For the charter business, we also have pre-paid orders of over 50,000 dollars, ran on our credit machine which Guy said we could have, but I have yet to post it to the account." Samantha said, as she was very long winded.

She looked up at him and smiled and said, "That money is in an escrow acct, so if that party or person cancelled, I can give a refund without having it affecting our bank account."

"This all sounds great, you're doing a fabulous job." "May I ask, how much do you charge to go out?" asked Jack, looking at the figures on the paper.

"Guy suggested 100 dollars per person, per day."

"What about a weekend trip, say an over-niter?" asked Jack.

"We haven't, Guy doesn't like to be out after 6 pm, so the charter has only been on Saturday and Sundays, they will leave at 6am and return at 6pm, for twelve hours."

"I have been going with him" said Sara, jokingly, then adds "Just trying to help him out, my brother Tim wants to help out, what do you think?"

"That's fine, make it happen." said Jack.

"My parents want your exclusive approval first, and then he will be allowed."

"So let it be" said Jack, waving her away so that he may concentrate on his beloved Samantha.

"Yes, I guess they want to see their future son-in-law to be for dinner and a celebration that we missed, when you first came back." "Then we could make an official announcement of our wedding."

"That's fine" said Jack with a heavy breath of air in and then he let it out. Sam was handing him another piece of paper.

"What's this?" asked Jack.

"It's to account for the 76,000 dollars so far, I broke it down even further to show all the accounts receivable." "As of this date, we've taken 30 trips, with about twenty five guests at a time."

"What about other services, like bait, poles, and storage?" asked Jack and adds, "Is there some book out there that shows what to charge for each of those services?"

"Let me get on the Net and find such a book" said Sara. Moments later she said, "Here is one, its twelve dollars, and I'll used my visa, to pay for it."

"Great, how about surveying other fish charter companies and see what our competition is doing?"

"Great idea" said Sara "I'm on it."

"So, you seem upset, I'm sorry, I've done the best I can do with what little resources I had. I used over five thousand dollars of my saved money to start this" Sam began to cry.

"Stop it, come here" said Jack as he bent down and embraced her. As she settled down, she whispered, "Now that you have Sara as your fiancé, you and I can't be intimate any more, I wish for you to be back inside of me one more time."

"It will happen again, and again, and again, for forever." Jack said.

"Really, when?" "I'm excited, but what about Sara, she has been like a sister to me these last few months, I don't want to feel the guilt." said Sam.

"Hey Sara."

"Yes Jack?"

"Sam wants to sleep in bed with us tonight, is that O' Kay."

"Is that O' Kay, I've been trying for two month's," exclaimed Sara.

"You have, so that's what you meant, I'm sorry." said, Sam.

"Heck yeah, let's go in the back, I'm ready" said Sara.

"Listen, I'm not ready now, but let me consider it." "So thanks Jack for saving my life and for giving me a chance at life, but most importantly, thank you for getting me pregnant." "We know that it will be a boy, and I want to name him Sam Smith Cash or Jack Cash Junior, which do you approve of?"

"Whatever your wishes are." said Jack in a graceful tone.

"You see Jack, the doctors say that for me to carry full term means when the baby is born that I could lose too much blood, and become more septic and die of blood poisoning." "Wait before you say a word, I decided to keep the baby and give him as a present to you." "I already talked with Sara about this and she has assured me she will raise him like her own son."

"Absolutely, you're already one of the family, let me marry you too." said Jack.

"Don't be silly, our country forbids you to marry more than one woman at a time." said Sam.

"Well, then why don't I marry you now", said Jack, "So that you can have the wedding of your dreams, I get a son, you get a husband, and if it happens that you do pass, then I will be free to marry Sara." "How does that sound Sara, would you go along with that?"

"I don't know, this comes as bit of a surprise, what will my family think?" Sara asked.

"I think they would support a dying wish from a woman who has missed out on a good part of her life." "I've already given her a child, so let's make it official." "What's the harm?" "If she agrees to let you continue to be my girlfriend, she takes the title of Misses Cash." "Our baby is born as a Cash and if you pass, then I will marry Sara in a formal ceremony."

Both girls went opposite directions and away from him.

"What, what did I say something wrong?" said Jack with his hands in the air.

Both Sara and Samantha were talking. Jack looked down at the sheet he was holding that stated the commercial fishing licenses. Seeing that the numbers did not match up. Jack said "So, as of today, we have made 1.4 million in receivables, paid out to Guy?"

Then Jack looked at the payout sheet and that said, "A quarter of that is for the lease and for the next four years, at 350,000 dollars, now that we are left with eleven more payment to go, for Jack to say, "And the rest went where?"

"It's in an escrow account drawing 13 percent interest", said Sam.

"This is nice, who set that up."

"I did and we are not talking to you now" said Sam.

So get in your car and get away so she and I can talk this over" said Sara.

"Wait Sara, I thought you said Jim came by to pay off Guy the money for the licenses and the boat"

"Yes and I told Sam that."

"When I confirmed that with Guy, he said it took care of the remainder of the boat and those that worked on it, but he said we still owed for the licenses" said Sam. Jack was on the phone to Jim and said "This is Jack, say how much did you pay out to Guy, the boat owner?"

"As per the Government, it was 2.5 million for the licenses and 500 hundred thousand for the boat repairs, and all should be square and done." said Jim, over the phone.

"Thank you", said Jack as he slid his phone shut and said, "Alright you two have fun, sorry if I've upset either one of you."

Sam turns in her wheel chair and said, "You haven't, we just under estimated what you are capable of." "You see, we had it all planned out that I would have the baby and you would marry Sara and adopt him." "But now it makes more sense and it may work, if only I would die, what happens if I'm still alive? Will I always have Sara as my friend?"

"What if I could make that happen?" said Jack with a smile on his face.

"What do you mean, make the fact that you can marry two women?" "Then make it official, then we may consider it, but for now, we both want you out." "Oh before you leave, you better kiss us both good bye", said Sam.

"Don't you just love a demanding woman" said Jack as he looked at Sara, being her reserved self. She was an outgoing woman, beautiful in the face and gets the job done right and a woman who made all the demands, I love it, "said Jack to himself, as he moved in and gave them both a kiss and lingered with each one, then left.

CH 9

Big Red Fire Engine

Jack placed a call to his friend "Red, this is Jack, really, I can be over in a flash."

Jack slides his phone shut to see he still had over one hundred messages.

Jack chooses the suburban to drive, gets in and rolls out onto the highway.

He decides to make a short call to Guy, who answers and said, "Hey Guy, it's your old friend Jack, I just found out that a representative of mine came and paid you off for those rights for 2.5, as we agreed upon." "Really, you're charging me 4 million plus interest, really, guess what, tomorrow I will find you and take back that money he gave you, then I will cut off any more ties with you, we're done", Jack hung up.

The short trip ended as he arrived at Red's bail bonds, parks and gets out, then holds onto the remote to lock it. He stops and makes a call to Sara, she answers, and he tells her to put the contents of the briefcase into the safe, if Sam has one or two briefcases, put them in a locked closet. And that he will see them later.

Jack leaves the suburban and knocks on the door.

"Come in" yelled a voice, the door buzzed and Jack pushed his way in.

"I'm back here, my friend" said Red who had propped his big hand against the doorway, his pants were at his ankles, while Jack watched a girl work him over. They stopped and Red said "Hi Jack, this is Kim."

"Hi Kim it looks like you're having fun." said Jack.

"I am, do you want to be next?" she said to him, as he came up behind her.

"Nah, I'm good, I'd rather watch you have your fun." "So how's the married life treating you?" asked Jack.

Kim pulled off her top, to expose her two beautiful breasts. She showed them to Jack, then stood up and pulled her panties down, turned around and held the doorway while Red inserted in from behind and the two made grunting noises until he was done.

Red pulled up his pants, turned around to face Jack. Kim waved to Jack and said "Haven't you heard, Red's my old man now" and went into the back room.

"So what do you have?" asked Jack.

"First let me see that badge" said Red. Jack handed it to him, touching his sticky fingers. Jack saw a ring on his finger and said, "Should I ask?"

"Nah, it's from Kim and, Wow, do you know what this means?" said an excited Red.

"Yeah, I guess." said Jack.

"It means you have the license to do whatever you want." he paused, his mind was racing and said, "To whom you want to and still get paid for it!, I believe the going rate is one hundred thousand per capture, that is without any particular rules, this is great." said Red.

"Try one million per capture." said Jack confidently.

"My friend, you hit the jackpot." "You know what you should do is invest in some houses and in property, pay with only cash and put it into someone's name you trust." "You are also licensed to have as many wives as you like, the more you have, the greater chance of your survivability."

"What do you mean, by that?" asked Jack.

"Well, I guess there is a loop-hole in the agreement process, but you alone are a dead man, so in order for the government to continue to pay you, there must be claims." "Honestly, I knew an agent who had over one hundred women and for each wife they paid them 100,000 dollars a year, until they died." "Then half goes to each child, till they die, then a quarter and so on till four generations past your passing they will be paid government issued checks." explained Red. "You see, I was basically a chicken, what you have done is what I dreamed of." "My dad was a Hunter and I get his checks and live on 50,000 stipend a year, plus I do bail bonds and make over 100k a year and all of this is tax free." "You don't have to pay any taxes ever again, you're a representative of the President himself." "When you retire, if you make it, you'll receive a million dollars a year, plus what your kids and wife's get, all thanks to yours truly." "Did I hook you up or what?"

"You did, Thanks, now what about tonight?" asked Jack.

"This guy is a fugitive and is on the top ten most wanted." "He's armed and dangerous, lives in a parish in Florida called Pace, where he is living with a girlfriend." "Do you want to drive or shall I." asked Red.

"I'll drive." said Jack.

"His name is Chester Johnson" said Red.

Jack watches as Red dresses and puts on two gun holsters. Then Red asked Jack "Did you get a gun?"

"Yeah it's this one "Jack pulls it out to show Red.

"Oh my God, you have a signature gun, that is nice." "I imagine its digital and x-ray proof."

"They said its porcelain and something like that" said Jack.

"No worries, put it away, so let's talk about your career now." Red puts his hand on Jack's shoulder and the two walk out of Red's office as Red locks the door.

Red turns and said, "No, no, no this won't do, you have a brand new Suburban, it's shiny silver rims and black exterior, you're going to get this shot up my friend."

"What am I suppose to do, go to the dealership and ask for a slightly used and beat up one?" said Jack unlocking it with his key fob and added, "Get in, shut up and let's go."

"Yes sir.

The ride over was interesting. Red told Jack all of what to expect in the coming months, he said, "The more active you are, the sharper your senses will be".

Jack says, "Should I expect to be out almost every night? And doing work as a local Bounty Hunter, catching criminals?"

"The night time is the play time for the criminals to come out and scare people" said Red. Red continued on and talked about how family was there to protect them and what Jack needs to do. Red said, "Establish a set of rules and include a curfew for your loved ones to be in by seven pm every night and to break up their patterns." "All the wives need to go in a pack, make it a social adventure." "I can teach them all about self-defense moves and have each of them carry a Taser." "I can get them to where they are a well-oiled unit, able to encounter any obstacle and be as effective as they could be."

Jack was thinking a gun for each of them might be necessary.

Red's talking hasn't over shadowed their reason why they were there. As Jack drives, he day dreams about Maria, was she real? Was that encounter with Carlos real or was it a part of the elaborate dream he was in just three months ago? He felt confused and not understanding.

"Jack, Jack wake up, you need to turn off here" said Red, who slugged him in the arm.

Jack awoke from his day dream to steer the black Suburban off the highway, just in time for the turn down onto the lower road.

"Now, at the stop sign, turn left" said Red.

Jack wheeled the Suburban in the right direction, the dark of the night reflected how shiny everything was in this rural part of the country.

"Now I can see why Chester lives out here," said Red.

"It's a ways out here, in no man's land."

Jack proceeded at a moderate pace, the thick trees over-hung the road. As they drove, they encountered no one. They came to the town of Pace, one flashing stop light. Jack drove through it, then over a bridge, and continued till Red said, "Next road, take a right."

Jack stopped at it and said, "The dirt road?"

"I guess, heck I don't know, just proceed."

Jack turned onto the private dirt road, they passed a sign that read,

"No Trespassing, Will Shoot on Sight."

Red says, "Now to me that sign represents that there is going to be some violence tonight."

There drive was short. They came to what looked like a set of buildings which resembled a fort. The road side being to open wider, quickly Jack pulled the vehicle next to the side of the last building, parked it and killed the lights and said, "Now what?"

"Let's go serve the warrant", said Red. Red pulls out a flashlight to check the address. As he got out, he looked and the building matched his address and said, "Yep this is it, let's go Mister Bodyguard."

Jack takes up the rear. The two take the side walk up to what appears to be a main door, Red pounds on the wooden door. Jack says, "Red, they're not going to hear you." Jack presses the doorbell he heard a whiz noise and yelled "Duck."

Automatic gun fire ripped there position. Both Jack and Red were scrambling as several men came out that door, which was open now. The men laughed, as they were within hand gun range. One of them yelled, "We got you now Red, you and your friend are going to die this night."

Just as the lights went on, around the front, it lite up the area, Jack now knew he had walked into a trap. Quickly thinking, "From this day forward, I want to control my own way of capturing fugitives." he moved as more gunfire laced his last position. Jack noticed a half open window and moved with his gun out. Several bullets that were aimed at his back were deflected by the guns strong magnetic pulse. Jack slid the thick window open and jumped in, crashing down on top of a desk, then onto the floor. He was on the move, he realized he needed help. People were in the compound yelling and screaming, "We're under attack."

Five guys were outside his door, firing multiple weapons in his direction. One yelled, "We're going to kill you, you're trespassing."

Jack stopped and decided to set up a diversion. He got on his phone and dialed 9-1-1 and then put in his number to be connected to Lisa. Jack told her what was going on and that he was going to start a fire. She said the nearest relief group was an hour away. Then Lisa said,

"I will send to you a fire truck, rather than a local sheriff that would come anyway." "So sit tight." "I have a part-time agent in that region to help join in your fight." "I have just alerted a fighter out of Pensacola, they will do a fly over using your coordinates and take imagining pictures for our SITREP groups." "Hold out as long as you can." Jack slid the phone shut as the gunfire continued. His friend Red was in agony, he was screaming, "I've been shot, I've been shot, Jack can you help me out?" Red was hit again, and again.

Jack popped up in the window to see the men were advancing on Red's position. Jack fired and one of the men dropped. Inside, the firing stopped momentarily. Jack heard, "Chester, Bob's dead, that guy shot him, Bob is dead, he blew up his head." "That shot was well over 200 feet, he is in the first room off the entry." "I guess Red brought him a pro." "Call up the boys, we're going to have an old fashioned shoot out and open up the armory. We're going to kill this guy, whomever he is," said Chester.

The men disbursed, another shot was fired and Chester's friend fell at his feet. Chester said, "Oh my God, Sam, you've been hit" then he knelt down, turned his friend over, saw in his face, he was dead.

Chester used his hand to close Sam's eyelids. Chester then pulled him away from the door, Jack occupied. "Goddamn it lets get inside and get this fuck, then we're going to butcher him and eat him for breakfast." Chester turned to feel an immerse pain in his right bicep, he was unable to hold the rifle and let it fall and yelled, "I've been hit", tears were welling up and he hid his head with his arm. One of his men come closer and said "Chester, let me see it."

The guy catches up with him to see it was square on the bicep and said, "This guy is good, you won't ever use this arm again."

"Shut up Roger, just wrap me up" said Chester, in an angry voice.

"What happens if that guy finds our women?" one man said.

"They're fine, safe down in the storage bunker, under the kitchen." said Chester.

"What, instead of the fallout shelter, why?"

"Cuz they came on sudden, I guess Bob was asleep again and they drove right past him", said Chester.

"Now he is dead, who do you think they were after, the children or"

"It was me they were after." "That guy we hit was Red, my Bail Bonds man, he probably brought a hired gun."

Their discussion was interrupted by an unfamiliar sound of a large siren,

"What the fuck, it's a Fire truck, what's it doing out here?" "And where is that sheriff, Roger gives him a call, oh shit", said Chester, then adds, while pointing, "Look and the kitchen is on fire."

"Let me go, Chester, my wife's down there, she will be burned alive."

"Stay here, we will get her as soon as we get rid of the fire fighters." "We know Jim, tell him we don't need them."

"Alright, I'll go see Jim, but you need to put out that fire and get the women and children out."

Chester was angry, injured and feeling like shit. He hugged close to the wall as he made his way to the kitchen on the other side of this H shaped complex. Meanwhile, the fire truck was rambling down the road, siren's blaring away, a single guy at the wheel as the fire truck came to a stop.

The man Chester sent was at the closed gate. He saw a guy come running to him, he opened a small door to look up at the guy and said, "You're not Jim?"

A shot rang out, and the guy fell down, the firefighter backed up the truck a little distance and then went forward and rammed the fence. They drove through the barbed wire fence, seeing men scattering, the fire truck was gaining momentum, as it crossed the field towards the fire.

Jack heard voices underneath him, as he laid flat against the pantry's floor. A single light was on after the stove ignited, with the sheets he put in it. The fire spread quickly. He lifted the trap door to see a young face and yells, "Get out of there this place is on fire." Jack held his gun out as he opened the back door to the garden. First the children, then the teenagers, then lastly the mothers all fled out the door. Jack stood at the door to see the fire truck roll up, a guy jumped out and began to assemble the hose. He turned on the water and began to extinguish the flames then said, "Have them get in on top, we'll get them out of here."

Instead, all of the kids and their mothers ran off into the darkness and disappeared. Jack noticed a head appearing around the corner. Jack shot low this time, hitting the guy in the leg. Chester fell, grasping his leg, he looked up at Jack who stood over him and said "Who are you?"

"I'm an International Bounty Hunter and you're under arrest for bail jumping and shooting a friend of mine." Jack pulls out a zip tie, and says, "Chester Johnson you're under arrest."

Jack watches the firefighter put away his hose. Then sees that the cavalry is here, quickly more black Suburban's arrive. Agents swam the remaining hostiles.

Jack was talking with the fire fighter and he told Jack he was a carpenter too and when Jack decides to build, he could do the job for him. He told Jack his name was Mike Adams. The two shook hands as Lisa comes face to face with Jack and said, "Looks like you captured one alive, you just bagged number two, on the most wanted list, impressive, what is your plans now?"

"Oh I think I need to ask you a few questions" said Jack, steering her away from Mike.

"Come with me" as she led him to her Suburban.

An agent runs over to them and said, "Red will be fine he was shot in the leg, were taking him to the hospital."

Lisa nods her head and the agent leaves. Lisa said, "Get in."

Jack climbs in, as Lisa sits next to him and closes the door and asked, "What do you need?"

"First off, I want to say thank you for the response and support". "Do you want me to let you know in advance what I'm doing?"

"No, it's not necessary." "Why have us waiting to move in when you can put down the threat first and besides, our presence may blow a bigger operation." "Like in this case, it's a compound. We had no idea it existed, so now we will investigate it while you go on and live your life and get into danger yourself, how is your cash holdings?"

"I was going to buy something for Sara, like a ring." said Jack.

"If I were you, I would find a place to hid the briefcase, in case of a situation to where your credit is of no use." "The money is in all non-traceable, non-sequenced bills, use the credit cards for everything." "The ten thousand I gave you in cash, give to your friends and or family and use it for small purchases, you don't want to be traced to." "We track you based on your purchases, however, you don't ever do anything small, even at the dealership". "What's your next question?"

"Was Cuba real?" asked Jack honestly.

"Yes it was" she said.

"Is it true that I can marry as many wives as I like?" he asked.

"It's true, listen and talk with Red, he will tell you what to do and what not to do." "This is a learning process for you and us, as a Bounty hunter." "We expect you to do the unexpected, so just do it, and whenever you need extra cash, call Daphne." "She is your liaison and when you need help you need to call your partner, Devlin, she lives in Mobile now." "From now on try to get her involved, I think the best thing you could do is call her." She stops to allow him to process all of that information.

"I will tell you this, we have some agents that could assist you. This is all new to us, but do what you need to do and along the way, I will have agents for you. And thanks to you, that money you gave to us as seed has blossomed into over five hundred working agents, all being sent all over the world."

"Like Mike, the fireman." asked Jack.

"Yeah, like Mike." "If you like him, I'll promote him to your team, you have Trixie, Mitzi and Damien, their all at your disposal and are programmed in your phone." "From time to time the gadgets man Jim will show up and ask you what kinds of vehicles would you like." "We know you hit that dealership, which is fine, but I think Jim wanted to put some sophistication in at least one." "So have you considered which type of vehicle you want?"

"Just thinking about it, I liked the vehicle I used in Cuba, and maybe a large truck, not like a fire truck size but a little smaller with a ram bumper and a winch on the back."

"Like a tow truck?" she asked.

"I guess." he said.

"Any other questions?"

"Nah, not that I can think of, wait, how about a handicap ramp for a friend of mine?" Jack asked.

"It shall be done, you'll be hearing from me soon." said Lisa.

"Thanks, I'll be going now" said Jack, beginning to open the door, when Lisa said, "Wait, here you go" and hands him another briefcase, "Find someplace to hid this one and have fun?"

Jack got out and began to walk over to his Suburban. He unlocked it as people were mulling about. He got in, pulled out and took off, he pulled out his phone and called Sara. She picked up and Jack said, "Is it safe to come home now?"

Jack placed it on speakerphone, so he can keep his hands on the wheel, as he kicked it into overdrive. She said, "Yes of course darling, how was your night?"

"Fun, exciting and interesting." he said.

"What did you do?" Sara asked.

"Well I worked, made a little of money and captured another bad guy."

"I'm sorry, I didn't really want you to go, but Sam and I talked and it did make sense that you marry her and give her a taste of joy and happiness in her last few months." "Then I will marry you and adopt her boy Sam."

"Speaking of that, I talked with my supervisor and she said it's not uncommon for an International Bounty Hunter to have more than one wife."

Jack paused to wait for her to answer, still nothing he said, "Because she said that the government will support them and their family for the rest of my life, hers and the children for four more generations."

"How does that work?" asked a curious Sara.

"Well I guess, once its official, the government will start sending you out stipend checks. Just for you having to live with and being married to me, I don't know what that amount is, but I heard it is quite substantial."

"Really, then yes, let's all get married, how many wives can you have?" she said all excited.

"As many as I would like, I believe it is to protect those I really care about, not so much that I'm in love with."

"Well then I'm all in, let me know who you might be interested in and I can help with that process." "We're going to need a large house, like a mansion, so we can house everyone."

"Whoa, you're getting way too anxious about this, I only suggested marrying Samantha and you." said Jack.

"That's fine for now, but what about the future, how about Leslie or Debbie?" "If they knew about this they would go along with it, let me talk with them and get them involved."

"No, this is not a cult; this is my life we are talking about."

"Yes isn't it exciting, you know I'm excited about this." she said.

"I can tell, let's keep this our secret." asked Jack.

"Only if you promise to build me a huge house, so that in the future I may have lots of other women over."

"Fine, you got a deal." said Jack.

"You don't sound too happy about this." "I just gave you permission to sleep with and marry as many women as you would like, any guy in this world would relish a chance to do that." Said Sara confidently, to add, "So Mister, I want you to be more grateful." "How long will it be before you come back to our apartment?"

"Is that where you're at?" asked Jack.

"Yes, I'm usually home by eight pm every night."

"What, no night club scene every night?" he said.

"No, I'm just a boring housewife, wait, I mean girlfriend, waiting for her man to come home and be with her."

"Well, you're far from boring and you're not a house wife yet, so you should be living it up." Said Jack.

"Believe me, I am, but only for you, so where are you at now?"

"Just outside Mobile going out on a high speed, to race to your arms." said Jack.

"Hey honey, if both Sam and I agree to get married, can we get married together?"

"What about a big family get together for you, you know your mom and dad and relatives?" he said.

"Oh yeah, you're right, but what I was thinking was, how about we all get married together, then it will be one less thing you have to worry about." "I will keep it a secret that I'm married to you until we have a big church wedding, one that me and my mom will plan out over the next three months?"

"Yeah, sure, whenever you want it." "As for getting married sooner, I'll call my Boss and set it up for this weekend, how's that?" Jack asked.

"For Sam, I'm sure she would like that." "Fine, I love you Mister Jack Cash."

"I love you too Misses Sara Sanders." "Look, I'm outside now."

Click the phone went dead as he saw Sara running down the stairs. Jack waited as he stood by his door. Sara ran and leaped into Jack's awaiting arms, she kissed him as he walked up the stairs outside. She was kissing the back of his neck.

Jack walked back down and onto the sidewalk as he heard an argument down below. It was getting heated, it was about the loss of a son and how a new crew from New York was coming to replace them. Then he heard, "Keep your voices down."

"Me, keep my voice down, you're not the one who is getting replaced, I have the mind to call the feds."

"Shut up, my brother and listen." "In a few days we will have a meeting of the minds." "Then we will either stay here or go to Montgomery and then plan for an attack in Atlanta at the end of the month."

Jack carried Sara inside and kicked the door closed, as she said, "You smell of smoke?"

"Yeah, I was in a fire."

"Oh my God." "Let me help you out of those clothes."

Jack's mind was racing, when he said, "Stop Sara, I need to make a couple of calls." "Do you have anything to eat?"

Sara got up from her favorite position and said, "I can make you a sandwich and give you some chips."

"Fine whatever", said Jack pushing her away from him. He used his free hand to push her back onto the bed. He was on his phone to look at his hundred plus contacts, he scrolled down to see Mike's name and called him. Mike answered and said, "It's about time?"

Jack looked at his phone, and then said, "Do you know who this is?"

"Yeah, it's Jack Cash from tonight, what do you need, I'm here to serve." said Mike.

"Well, I got a case for you." "Can you meet me at the Sunrise motel tomorrow morning at 8am, here in Mobile." Jack asked.

"Yes, sir."

"Bye", said Jack.

"Later, Boss", said Mike.

Jack turns to see Sara holding a plate of food and said, "Bathroom or bedroom?"

"Neither, right here" said Jack.

Next morning Jack was up early and on the phone to Damien. He had agreed to help out on the boat. Devlin also agreed, she was flying in from Washington D C. Then there was Trixie and Mitzi, the two decoy girls, agreed to be hookers, to get into the building. They all agreed to meet at the motel Jack had rented this morning. Sara was excited about helping him out. She made muffins and fresh coffee for the crew. She took an immediate liking to Trixie and said to her, "Is that your real name?"

"No, it's my alter ego, it gives me a character that lets me be bad without reservations."

"How have you come to know my boyfriend?" asked Sara.

"Jack needed our assistance on his last Bounty." "Mitzi and I are best friends, so we are a team." explained Trixie.

"How did you get involved with all of this and do you know your dressed like a hooker?" "Is that what you want to be?" said Sara rudely.

"Listen, between you and me, stop asking questions and go with the flow." "I will tell you this, I was recruited for the adventure." "I was a model and I was part of a cover up that led to the arrest of a famous criminal." "Since then I was asked to do smaller roles."

"Then I was recruited to become a helper to a super, I mean an International Bounty Hunter." "Now I'm at the disposal of Jack and do as he sees fit, literally." "I know I'm on the side of good versus evil and that I will sacrifice myself to accomplish a mission." Said Trixie. "If you want to get involved, play the support role with Jack."

Trixie tried to move away from Sara and said, "Please stop asking questions, because in the end, he is the only one in charge and we all go along with it."

"So if he asked you to sleep with him you do it?" asked Sara.

"Without hesitation or regret." Trixie said and left Sara alone, as she eats her muffin. Trixie goes over to Mitzi and said, "She doesn't understand."

"No, she just doesn't know yet" said Mitzi.

"She grilled me earlier, until she asked me if I would sleep with Jack." said Trixie.

"What did you say?" asked Mitzi.

"I told her no, I would not sleep with him, but I'd rather have sex with him."

"Your bad, how did she take it?" said Mitzi.

"I think she rather liked that idea" said Trixie.

Jack was going over a building document Damien had laid out and said,

"Girls, over here please, here is our layout, I want Miss M and Miss T to go in the front and distract some of the guards in the lobby." "Damien and I will go in through the parking garage where Damien will set up surveillance and have the getaway van ready to pick up as many as we can that's on the America's most wanted." "Then when Devlin arrives from Washington, Sara, can you pick her up in the Suburban and drive her to your apartment." "Then on my signal, Devlin will jump the fence and work her way in". "Here are ear pieces, courtesy of Damien, you're getting to be a real gadgets guy."

"I learned from the best, Jim taught me how to support." said Damien.

Jack put his finger to his mouth, as Damien nodded in acknowledgement.

"As I was saying, M and T go ahead and leave", said Jack.

Mitzi led Trixie, both dressed in revealing outfits, left the room. Then Jack said, "Sara, go to the airport and pick up Devlin, so you won't miss her, go now."

Sara came up and gave Jack a big kiss and a loving hug, then left the room." "They heard a knock on the door, Jack opened it to see Mike, dressed in all black, with two gun holsters showing.

"Get in here and shut the door", said Jack, as he was looking over his outfit, he really stood out.

Mike saw Damien, the two hugged "Good to see you mate" said Damien.

"Alright now that is over, give Mike an ear piece, what role do you want?" asked Jack.

"To go in there and shoot the place up." said Mike.

"Sounds like you have some issues to get out" said Jack.

"Yeah, I hate the mob, their an evil root, they take peoples land and cause as much waste as possible." said Mike.

"Alright enough of that". "Damien, give Mike a set of coveralls and go inside and poise as a janitor." "Then gain intelligence along the way and report back using first letters only." "I already sent in M and T." D will be for Damien, A for you Mike and J for me, when Devlin arrives she will be R, so let's go over this again." said Jack.

Meanwhile, Trixie and Mitzi walked a short distance only to have a car slow, as a guy, was a Spanish speaking guy who said, "Hell-low ladies, I'm Marcos and my buddy in the back is Julio. How would you and your fine friend like to go back to my room at the ambassador hotel, would you both like to go to a party?" Both girls agreed to it. Trixie, the big flirt, sat in the front seat and hiked up her skirt to show off her leg.

While Mitzi, the more conservative one, sat silently in the back watching the two marks, thinking "Finally, I get a chance to be an agent and I have to do it this way, as a pretend prostitute. "Only if my mom could see me now."

"Are you girls new, I haven't seen you out on the streets before?" asked Marcos.

They both tried to answer at the same time, when Trixie said, "We're both from Atlanta."

"Oh yeah, so am I" said the guy in the back, and said, ""Where about?"

"Who cares" said a stern Mitzi, looking at Julio, in displeasure.

"Alright, don't get your panties in a bunch" said Marcos.

"I don't wear any" said Mitzi and they all laughed.

Marcos slowed the car to turn into the parking garage, finding his spot, he parked. Everyone got out at the same time. The two girls slowed the pace as the men walked faster and ahead of them, off to their right Trixie saw Damien as he made his presence known, then disappeared into the shadows. Both girls regained that air of confidence and sped up their pace. They stepped into the elevator with the two men.

Jack began to lay out his plan with Mike when he received a phone call. He answered it, it was Sara. She told him that Devlin's plane had landed, and in a matter of moments she would meet up with her. Jack looked at his watch, to see it was still early morning. He knew the last time he hit this place was a while ago but this time was with purpose and attitude. He closed up his phone, he remembered what his boss said,

"You don't need to be the hero, just get your team involved, they're there to support you in any capacity as you see fit." "So use their support." Jack looked over at Mike who was readying his weapon, as Mike looked at one of the fliers and said, "Which one are we going to pick up?"

Jack lifted up a bag of twist ties and said, "As many as we can find."

"Let's go then."

"Were waiting for my partner." said Jack.

"Who's that?" asked Mike.

"What's it matter to you" said Jack looking at him sternly.

"Nothing man, forget about it, I'm just ready to go!"

"I chose you because of your ability to improvise, so your job today is to hold on to the prisoners." "I'll catch them and bring them down to Damien, waiting in a van, under the hotel and that's it."

Jack handed a bulk of the large zip ties to Mike, who had just sat back down. Jack took a seat, as well.

Meanwhile back at the hotel Trixie led the group out of the hotel's elevator to the fifth floor.

"Hold on there, have you been here before?" asked Marcos.

"Nah, I was just walking" said Trixie with a smile. She was ready for action.

"Well it's this door here" Marcos opens the door to let Julio and Mitzi in and watches Trixie pass by him, not before placing his hand on her chest to feel her as she walked by. Marcos closes the door and sees the two girls standing by themselves and said "Let's get this underway."

"What do you want us to do?" asked Mitzi.

"I know the drill they want us to strip so they can get off, and then they will finish us off" said Trixie.

"Clever girl, unfortunately for you" said Marcos pulling his weapon and pointing it at Trixie, "So tell us who you really are?"

"Listen Mister we don't want any trouble, like I said Mitzi and I are college coed's who needed some extra cash." "This is our first time we've done this" she giggles, "well maybe second" she begins to laugh "oh our third time for me and my best friend, this is her first time."

"Well then let's start with her" Marcos was waving his gun, motioning to her to begin.

"Mitzi I think he wants you to strip" said Trixie.

"That's right girl, take it all off I want to see the goods I'll be getting" said Julio.

"Back off animal, she is a delicate flower, let her be, we got all day till the meeting happens" said Marcos, moving in for a better view.

"What meeting" asked Trixie.

"None of your business's nosy one" said Marcos still waving his gun.

"It is mine or shall I say ours if it means we're going to be a part of it" said Trixie, looking over at her friend who was going slowly.

"Here let me help you sister" said Trixie, moving over to face Mitzi, she began to help her take off her blouse.

"You and her will be long gone, oh I like that" he said watching the two of them kiss.

Trixie turns and said, "If we're undressing, why don't you guys strip too and put that gun away."

Trixie helped Mitzi out of her blouse, then lets loose her skirt, to reveal her bra and panties. Mitzi slowly popped the bra off, as Trixie continued to stand in front of her. The two girls watched Marcos set the gun down and began to strip. Julio had quickly striped to his briefs, which he still had on, as Marcos caught up with him.

"Now, you get over here next to your partner, so when I turn, I want to face you", said a very demanding Trixie.

Marcos did as he was told, while Trixie continued to face her friend. She was shielding her exposed breasts from the men, as Marcos made his way over next to his partner Julio.

"Drop your drawers" said Trixie, looking over her shoulder.

They watched as they slid them down at the same time, they stood up and with both hands covered them up.

"Now, hands to your side, do you want Mitzi and I to pleasure you both first?" asked Trixie.

Both men nodded in unisons, as Trixie watched Marcos grow, she wheeled around, still fully clothed to touch it and began to stroke it. It was getting larger by the minute. Mitzi moved up, with one hand behind her back, holding her weapon and the other reaching for his manhood. She grabbed it to feel how big and thick it was, she said, "Both of you spread your legs, I like to see your balls hang" announced Mitzi. Trixie was using a two handed method, she barely could hold it with both hands, as she noticed his gap. Trixie stood up and together with Mitzi they both pulled up there foot and smashed their balls upward, sending both men to collapse in a heap. Both men were holding onto themselves and crying, both girls used zip ties to secure their hands.

"Hey what are you doing" yelled Marcos.

"Shut up" said the topless Mitzi, who delivered a strike to Marco's head. Trixie zip tied both men, with their hands behind their backs. Then Mitzi held their mouth closed as Trixie zip locked their mouths shut tight, going under the chin to the top of their head.

Trixie dialed up Jack and said "Both DEG agents down and secure. You should see our girl here, she is topless."

"Tell him I will be bottomless, if he wants" said Mitzi.

"Did you hear that?" "I found out that they are having some meeting later tonight, Mitzi and Me are going to explore a bit and find some other poor slups to bother with." "We're on the fifth floor, alright you too, bye."

"Jack says that the third floor is the action floor, but I'm curious what's on this floor" said Trixie, watching her friend get re-dressed. Trixie picked up Marcos's gun and said "This could come in handy."

"Looked like you were getting pretty involved with him" said Mitzi to Trixie.

"Yeah, I thought we agreed we were going to do these two guys. Why does Jack have to have all the fun" said Trixie, a little disappointed.

"Change of plans, we're the first in so let's go find trouble and if I'm gonna do this, I want more than a bad DEG agent, I want the boss."

Mitzi led Trixie out into the hallway and down to the end. Replacing their guns into their concealment position, they came to the penthouse suit and Mitzi tried the door handle.

"That won't work, they are all locked" said Trixie, "Just knock on the door."

The door slowly opened to show a blonde, nude girl with a smile on her face, who says, "Who are you two?"

"We're here to see the boss." said Trixie.

"Vito is asleep; who should I say are you two." said the blonde.

"Tell him, Were the party" as Mitzi pulls out her gun, the girl begins to scream "Vito, Vito honey this hooker has a gun."

"What did you do that for" as they watched the girl slither down and began to cry. The mob boss was awake now. Trixie shuts the door and Mitzi says, "Get up, and put your hands behind your back."

"Leave her alone she's harmless" said Trixie, who turned her back and in an instance the girl sprang up and landed on Trixie, knocking her over. She saw Vito pull a gun up and fire a shot at

Mitzi, who dove out of the way. Trixie and the girl wrestled around, she was getting in some punches and yelled, "Vito, we got a couple of whacked girls out here, I could use your help."

Vito was frozen, looking at Mitzi, who had a gun on him.

Just then a door opened off to her right, she saw a big tough looking guy naked, watching the two of them wrestle. Mitzi took a shot, Vito slumped down, the door shut and in a matter of moments the outside door was being banged on and men's loud voices could be heard. Mitzi got up, went over and whacked the girl on the back of the head and she was out.

"Thanks for the help" said Trixie who zip tied the young girl. The two worked together and dragged her back behind the sofa and made a call. "Thank God, Jack, were in deep trouble, Mitzi jumped the gun and now were in the penthouse, yes, O' Kay." said Trixie.

"What did he say?"

"He said he would send Damien up to help us, in the meantime aim low and shoot to wound." said Trixie.

"Where is he at?" asked Mitzi.

"He is on his way and said after this he was going to spank you for jumping the gun." "He can do that and much more", she said, with a smile.

"Shut up." said Mitzi.

The door opened slowly as the two girls watched and then bullets began to fly everywhere as the automatic weapon sprayed the windows and the wall and the sofa. They positioned themselves in the mini kitchen. Peering around the corner, Trixie began to fire, using all of her rounds. She pulled back and said "I'm out."

"Great, I only have eight, let me down there. I'm a better shot than you, as Mitzi laid on the floor, she peered around as a bullet whiz right by, she pulled up and said "Find a kitchen knife or anything to defend ourselves with." Trixie slid over and keeping low she pulled out the top drawer first, as bullets began to fly her direction.

"This is no use, I can't get a clean shot, were doomed" said Mitzi.

"Don't worry, Damien will come to our rescue and help us" said Trixie, confidently.

"I don't care about Damien, I want Jack."

Meanwhile Damien was on the move up to the fifth floor, the elevator was moving slowly. His gun was drawn and ready. As the doors opened, he saw a girl turn and fire a quick burst his way, he dove out of the way. He aimed and shot back, his shots missed but did startled the others. He heard "Hold your fire this is the FBI."

Damien held his position against the wall. One guy passes the girl, with a smile on his face. Gunfire erupted again in the distance, a door opened as Damien fell back into the door and turned to see a half-naked black-haired girl helping him up and then close the door. Damien looked up at her with a smile, they both turned to see a fully nude tattooed man with a gun in his hand saying, "What the hell is this", and began to fire at Damien. He dove into the mini kitchen with the girl, he pulled her along as a hostage. He grabbed her breasts from behind and held her close as she pleaded, "Danny, he has got me, don't shoot."

Damien laid on his back with the girl on top of him. Danny stood in plain sight, both fired. Damien's bullet hit Danny's arm and deflected off. Damien now held the lifeless body of Dita, blood was dripping on his arm. Damien shot again, this time he hit Danny's the other arm.

Danny stood brave with a smile on his face, aimed and fired again, this time canoeing Dita's head. The brain matter sprayed matter all over Damien.

Damien fired again, this time the aim was lower, hitting Danny's thigh. Danny said, "My next shot is your head", that was the last thing Damien heard as the bullet went into his skull he rolled around and laid down. Damien was dead.

Jack and Devlin met up and were on the move together, Mike brought up the rear. They took the stairs, now running, Jack was in the lead, they reached the fifth floor. Jack slowly pulled the door open and heard a group of people banging on the far door, a shot whizzed by Jack's head. Jack rolled out of the elevator, into the hallway and took a shot at a girl, he hit her hand and she dropped her weapon. Then Jack shot one to her knee, she dropped and began sobbing. Two men charge at them yelling, "Were with the FBI", both men dropped, as both Devlin and Jack shot at them. Jack said to Mike "Zip tie them up." Jack and Devlin were moving closer, past the fallen agents, who kept saying, "Were with the FBI and now you're in trouble, who are you guys?"

"I'm an International Bounty Hunter, and you're all under arrest."

"The penthouse door's opened and several men came out. Jack shoots repeatedly and the men were flying all about, one cried out in a yelping manner, "I'm hit."

Jack and Devlin rushed the room, behind them the door's close. "It's locked" said Jack, trying the now locked doors. Devlin was at the other side trying to pull the door hinges, then affixing a clay like substance.

"Stand back and shield your eyes" she counted out load "3 2 1" then Boom!

The door exploded sending the men on the outside into the wall, there was blood all over the place as screams of agony were heard. One of the men had his leg injured, he was bleeding profusely.

The tall nude man had splinters all over his body. He pressed the trigger and began to spray them with bullets. A single shot to the temple, from Jack's smart gun, and the east coast untouchable boss died instantly, still holding the trigger as all the rounds were spent. The Boss had fallen down to the floor, as the other door closed. Jack said, "Tricks and Mits are you guys alright?" They both said, "yes" and both came to him and held onto him and began to kiss him only to hear, "Come on girls."

Devlin tried the next door, it was locked. A shotgun blast was heard and Devlin moved away as the bullets came through. Devlin kicked the remaining door open and fired a single shot, striking his temple the man laid on the bed dead, she checked him and confirmed his death. Then she yelled out, "Number two, most wanted Serial killer, Wylie Zenith, is dead."

"Good job, I think we also have mob boss Vito, number fifteen." Jack was still holding onto the two girls.

"You make me sick Jack, not now, girls leave him alone", said Devlin, a bit jealous.

"Yeah girls, help out that poor old man over there and lets go find Damien."

Jack led Devlin down the hall to the next door and banged on it, a nude black woman answered the door as Jack forced his way in to see a guy was sound to sleep.

"Don't worry he is out, I gave him four sleeping pills, after we had our fun." said the nude woman.

"Do you know who he is?" asked Jack.

"Yeah, his name is Vinny, he is connected to Vito, here is his wallet" she hands it to him.

"Have Mike zip tie him" only to see Devlin was already doing it, by pulling away the covers to expose his manhood fully erect.

"Do you want us to leave you alone with him?"

"Honey you're not missing much, but go ahead, I got a man" said the black woman.

Jack looks at her and said "Who's your man?"

"His name is Danny."

"Where is he at?" asked Jack.

"Across the hallway" she said, pointing to the opposite door.

Jack grabs the woman by the arm and whisks her out of the room. She says, "Hey watch it, you're hurting me."

"Get me inside and not a word of this" said Jack, gun ready.

She began to bang on the door and called out, "Danny let me in there is a killer out here, he took down Vinny."

The door opened. Jack forced his way in, tackled Danny and threw the woman aside. Jack lost control of his gun, as the two wrestled. Danny was throwing punches as Jack did the same. Jack was able to get the upper hand, and was able to bring his knee up and into Danny's groin, nothing happened as Danny kept up the throwing punches. Jack got up and Danny gave him a right cross, sending Jack back into the sofa. Danny got up and took a few steps then crashed through the plate glass window, onto the balcony, then leapt off. He sailed down five stories and into the bushes. Jack got to the railing, only to see Danny fleeing.

"Did you see that?" said Jack, eyes wide open. "Thanks for the help". Jack said to Devlin sarcastically.

"Hey it looked like you had it under control, who knew that guy was crazy enough to do that."

"You're in trouble now," said the black woman.

"Really, who says Miss" said Devlin.

"Do you know who he is?"

"Not really, but fill us in" said Jack.

"He is Danny, The Cobra, Davis from New York, he looked pissed."

"So, what does that mean, why didn't he stay and fight it out like a real man, not some coward", asked Jack.

"He is a vicious killer."

"And you're with him because?" asked Jack while searching the place. He found a briefcase.

"He is cool, and treats me nice." said the black woman.

"You mean he abuses you and shares you with his friends, zip tie this one too."

"Who are you?" she asked.

"The new law in town, I'm an International Bounty Hunter, and you think I've seen the last of this guy Danny, it is just the beginning", said Jack, "He is my next new target."

Devlin says, "Jack come on in here."

Jack walks over to see Dita lying on a body. Devlin pulls her off, to reveal Damien. Jack checks his pulse and said, "Yes he is dead", Jack closes Damien's eyes with his hand and gets up and said, "Let's call the Calvary in and lock this building down."

Devlin and Jack went floor by floor searching for people, they pulled people out and Mike zip tied their hands. On the second floor they came across a bizarre thing, as Jack opened up a door, there were several doors attached. All of a sudden, all of the doors opened up revealing a large room. The first thing they saw was a young man going at it with an older woman, whose legs were spread wide for him. Jack place his newly found gun against the young man's temple and said, "Stop what you are doing and put your hands behind your back, what is your name?"

"Tim Pewter."

"Any arrests or warrants, where are you from?"

"No, I'm from Montgomery."

"Who's the woman." Jack asked.

Mike zip ties Tim as Jack pulls him out. The woman was still panting and still had her legs spread wide, saying, "You could be next."

"Devlin, you handle this one." Jack walks to another sliding door.

Jack opens it up a bit to see a young woman tied to a bed, on all fours, crying and telling her captor to stop. The guy had mounted her from behind and was using a whip. Jack moved in and with his gun strikes the guy on the side of the head, knocking him off instantly. He rolled around till Jack put his foot on his groin to stop him. Jack pointed the gun at him and said, "The girl said No, what part of No did you not understand?"

"Get out of here, or I will, have you killed."

"Are you talking to me" said Jack, looking down at the maggot, "Is that it, kill or be killed?" asked Jack.

Jack fires into his knee, Mike moves in to zip tie him while the girl is in hysterics. Devlin steps in with the help from another. She sees that the girl is in a body harness and whispers to Jack," You know if you and I had one of these you wouldn't have to worry about me hitting back."

"It will never happen again." said Jack.

"That's too bad because I like all this sex stuff. My last job was dirty and grimy and this is all about pain, pleasure and the pursuit of happiness."

"Cut her loose, and find out who they are" said Jack.

"Well this one is the Hotel's owner, her name is Gloria, she is the wife of the guy you shot, the Mob boss Federico. As for Timmy's girlfriend, they have an arrangement, she told me watch out for this little vixen, she's dangerous." said Devlin.

"Thanks for the update, ready to hit the last few rooms" said Jack smiling back at Devlin.

Jack went across the hallway and banged on the door, it opened. A guy dressed in a suit was standing there.

"Who are you" said Jack.

"Name is Jess Marlin, of the Marlin clan."

"Zip tie this one, turnaround and hands behind your back," Jack did it himself.

Devlin was at the next door, she lightly tapped the door and slid it open to see a black man tied to the bed, as a girl in lingerie held onto a whip.

"What is this? the circus de discipline, come on, let me have a shot", said an eager Devlin.

"Go for it" said the girl, as Devlin picked up the whip and was ready to swing when she heard a familiar voice, "What are you doing?"

Devlin turned and dropped the whip and said "Nothing."

"SITREP Jack", spoke a booming voice on the phone, as he held it out and said, "We cleaned out the hotel and will wait till you arrived". Jack covered up the phone and said, "We have everyone except the last door, check it out."

"That's alright you and your team can leave, I'll have Daphne deliver your money after we get the total count." Said Lisa as her arrival, dispelled any further action.

"Oh yes, there is one more thing, Damien is down" said Jack in a somber tone.

Jack leaves the room, takes the stairs and gets out his phone. He dials up a familiar voice, and said, "Are you at home? Open the door."

Jack walks through the lobby across the courtyard and over the railing and onto the balcony to see the door open, and Jack walked in.

CH 10

Three Idiots & a Naughty Carpenter

A couple of weeks had passed, they moved the Parthian Stranger, the boat, from the private dock to the public dock right behind the crab shack. The building had an upstairs. When Jack bought the building outright; they installed an elevator for Samantha as she lives there. It was business as usual at the office, Samantha was up and dressed before Jack and Sara had walked through the door in the mornings. Jack turned the open sign outward, to tell everyone they were open and strolled up to the desk. He saw Sam. He bent over and gave her a kiss on the lips. She stroked his face with her left hand, that had the new sizable rock of a diamond on her finger.

There was excitement in the air as they were down to the final week for the wedding preparations. It was Sara that had been doing everything for her newest dear friend, for her wedding.

Sara received a call on her cell phone, she answered it and said, "Hi sweetie, how are you, fine, when will you get into town?" "Really, have I got some news for you, first off he can marry whomever and how ever many." "Yes, well at first I was like, yeah, whatever, but listen, she is a very good friend now, I love her, like you will." "She is wheel chair bound, but she has some sensation in her legs." Sara paused to listen, then said, "The wedding ceremony will be this weekend, up on the hill overlooking the bay, I agreed to be the maid of honor, even helped picked out her dress she will wear." "It will be private and personal, we even invited her mother."

"Well listen, I need to go, I'll see you soon, bye."

Jack overheard the conversation and said, "Why don't you go and pick up your friend or allow the local agents to do that?"

"That's just it, we have no support." "You say that there is support coming, I haven't seen it, have you Sam?" "So Super spy, where is it at?", said a disappointed Sara.

"I don't know, they just show up, so had either one of you received word on if Sam's mother will attend the ceremony?", asked Jack.

"No, not yet said Sam.

Sara steps in and said, "They're still not talking, even that money you gave her wasn't enough, she thought of you as some big time drug dealer."

"Well she is wrong."

"We know that, but she doesn't." said Sara. "Everything is all about perception, and she perceives you as a drug dealer." Sara turns her chair around to face both of them to add, "When Daphne came and visited you, you have to admit, Jack with those twelve briefcases worth over 12 millions of dollars, it became clear, quickly that you're a very special guy."

"So says, the President of the United States", said Jack smiling.

"A funny thing happen a couple nights ago, Leslie, said that she would like to be part of our love triangle, and if it were possible she too wants to get married to you Jack." "Now she told me that in confidence of course." "If Leslie will do it, you'll be on board?"

"Sure, the more the merrier."

"Interesting, you know Jack, you're the only man she has ever been with, but all the same, when the time is right, I'll let her in on the good news."

Sam was on the phone, and Jack was looking over the scuba gear. "Come on over, we have a meeting" said Jack to the two girls.

"Coming honey" said Sara, holding a pad of paper and a pen.

Jack sat at one end of the table, Samantha in the middle and Sara came over to sit on the end opposite of Jack who said, "What progress do we have with that list I gave you Sam?"

"Well so far only twenty out of two hundred have confirmed."

"Did you send out the first class tickets?"

"No, what Sara and I decided on was we will leave them at will call, then when they plan on coming they will use them." Sam looks over at Sara for help, the two smile at one another. Sara said "Honey, if we sent those tickets to everyone, then some wouldn't show up." she paused to justify herself, by adding "And others would."

"I specifically asked you to both to send the round trip tickets to them, end of story." said Jack, somewhat upset.

"But honey, you're wasting our money?" said Sara pleading with him.

"Listen, I don't mind spending what 500 dollars or even one thousand to make one million dollars, don't you see what I'm saying?"

"Not really" said Sara.

"Sam, help me out here."

"Jack, I do understand what you want, but I think Sara and I were only thinking of your best interests, and regardless of what money is spent or what you will earn, we were just thinking of the practicality of sending those tickets. I understand now and will handle this myself, is that alright with you Sara?" said Sam.

"Yeah, whatever" said Sara.

"Now Honey" said Sam to Jack, "Here are the boat numbers and of the fishing permits, I've narrowed it down to these specific boats and the listing of what they will be fishing."

"I sat down with Guy yesterday and I want to tell you, he has been a lot more cooperative and nicer, so whatever you said to him, he sure has changed his tune. He still couldn't tell me all of them, so I researched it and this is what I came up with; Guy was right when he had four permits and twenty sub permits, shall I go over each one?"

"Nah, spare me the details" said Jack.

"Alright, I need a go ahead to confirm with each captain, a price and a surplus for us" said Sam, impressively.

"What does that mean?" asked Sara.

"Well, Jack or Us, You and I, are entitled to a percentage of the catch, usually five percent of the total, say if it is, 140,000 pounds, that roughly translate to 70,000 dollars and the surplus is how many pounds of that type of fish do we want to keep for ourselves?"

"So is that what they will pay to use our permits?" asked Sara.

Jack was busy reading the already read paper, letting the two girls talk it out.

"Yes and there is more, we have over 500,000 pounds in permits, which come out to a quarter of a million dollars, annually forever, forever that they are fished."

"Yes, but is that our best price?" asked Jack, pulling down the paper to look at her.

"No, were kind of stuck, Guy promised several boat owners that percent and were stuck on that, whereas if we were to work them ourselves, we could make four times that and much more."

"Why's that?" asked Jack.

"Well from what I gathered from the Maritime Outfitters Association, that holds the permits." "It means that these are only partial shares and if we decided to fish the gulf and the Eastern seaboard, we would get back over 2 million pounds at over a million a season, forever, that we fished."

"Let's hire a captain", said Jack.

"I second that" said Sara.

"Alright, let me see what we need to do, maybe Guy knows someone, like an old captain."

The bells on the door rang, as the door flew open, Sara got up to see, who it was.

"Hi Misses Smith" said Sara, as Samantha's mom closes the door, against a strong wind.

Jack stood, knowing this confertation was waiting about to happen and went the other way.

"Sam, it's your mother, are you going to come over and see me?"

Samantha turned her wheelchair and spun around, while smiling and as Sara positioned herself at the counter, she looked out the window to see a car pull up and three husky men got out.

"What do you want now, mother?"

"After thinking about this, I've decided I'd like to go to your wedding." "Is that drug dealer around so I may personally congratulate him myself?"

The door swung open as Sara eased back to announce "We got company" the three men towered over Sara who was backing away, while they stared at her as they walked in and said, "Where's Jack Cash?"

"Just as I expected, tough looking men want their money, this ought to be good." said Glenda as she was smiling at them.

"Look mom can we talk about this later" said Sam a bit concerned and said, "Sara, go get Jack, Now, hurry up."

"I don't know when, you're always busy and your keeping that man a secret, not to mention that bastard of a boy you're having. Fine I'll leave" said Miss Smith as she cleared a path, as the large men allowed her to pass. Sara saw to say, "she is gone now, its free to come out, besides you have company."

Jack, was walking back, when he said, "I'll handle these three, realizing he didn't have his gun on him, he walked forward, to allow them to see him.

"Hey Yuri and Vlad what's up" said Jack looking at the third to give him no recognition.

They all shook hands, and in a deep Russian accent, Yuri says, "Heard you have a fishing boat, in our native Russia, we would go out and sail and fish some, can we take a charter?"

"When do you want to go out?"

"Tomorrow morning, we heard there is an excellent place for sand sharks and stingrays."

"Sure let me check our schedule" said Jack looking down at the front table, to see the schedules. Sara stepped in and said, "We have a small party of two already booked and you three, that will be 240 dollars each please."

"Come on Jack, why don't you comp us" asked Yuri.

"Were your friends from school "said Vladimir.

"Sure, let me ask the boss."

"Ask the boss, you are the boss", said the other guy who pulled a gun out and point it at Jack and said, "You son of a bitch, we all know what you're doing with that boat of yours, now you got two passengers tomorrow and there not even going to leave the dock, cause we're going to take them in, before you have a chance at them."

Jack sensed he had no real options; he looked specifically with his eyes at Sara who too was caught off guard, and said, "Fine you can have them."

"Oh yeah, were going to take over this operation" said Yuri.

He pulled out his weapon as did his brother, all pointed at Jack. "Now pretty little thing, go over there with your boyfriend."

"Name's Sara" Sara keep her front to them as she walked past Sam, then tripped on her wheelchair, all three watched her go down as Samantha pulled out a hidden pistol, aimed and fired three quick shots, catching Yuri, who spun around and hit the wooden floor dead. His brother, reeled back against the wall and slid down to his death, still blinking. Psycho took several shots that missed his heart but still bleed from his chest as the bullet paralyzed him from the neck down and he dropped like a sack of potatoes. Jack moved to get Yuri's weapon. Seeing that Vlad looked like he was taken by surprise by Samantha's ferocious behavior.

Jack pulled Psycho over to hear him say, "Word is it that your soft, from your mob stir up, but you got a fight coming, we're all coming". these were his last words. Jack closed his eyes with his hand, collected the weapons. He saw Samantha watching over him and she said, "You know he is right, you are getting soft, for them to get the jump on you like that and for little old me to come to your rescue." "Well it was good of Daphne to give me this gun and it was my pleasure to protect you and our son's life, we will all help you and protect you, but Jack you need to start carrying your weapon, who knows who else is watching us."

Jack gets up and said, "Your right, as a bounty hunter, I need to watch over every move I make and thanks for saving our lives". Jack dials up 911 and connects to Lisa and said, "This is Jack three down at the fishing wharf" Jack folds up his phone, while he watches Samantha reload her pistol. Then she hid it back in her wheel chair and said, "The next set of rounds are for my mom."

"Here, here now, why would you say that?" said Jack comforting her, to add, "Didn't she like the money I gave her?"

"Yes, but as Sara said, she thinks you're a drug lord and that was drug money, so she won't accept it."

"It will be alright," said Jack.

"No it won't" say Sara, "If she squeals then was all doomed to another attack, like this one."

"Then tomorrow, let's install a metal detector at the door, and stock weapons under the counter and nearby" said Jack.

"Tomorrow, how about right now" said Sam, looking through the phone book for the number. She couldn't find one then went on the net to search, as Jack and Sara were in a embrace, seeing her friend crying she said, "Found one out of New Orleans, I placed an order." "Now it says it's around 5500 dollars or a complete surveillance package is over 20,000 dollars, which one?"

"the latter, and much more, let's have them place camera's everywhere." Said Jack. "Let's get someone in here to build a security box over there and a monitor up front with a secure door." "We will buzz them in as we see fit." "I'm going to place a mirrored glass up front, so we can see them and they can't see us." "I'm going to call Mike and have him come in and watch over you."

Sam nods in agreement, as she searches for a carpenter, found one and calls, as Jack is talking on his cell phone. Sara is the only one answering calls, quoting prices and looking over the schedule book to place in new names.

Jack folds up the phone and said, "Mike will be here in a flash, he was in Mobile for the day."

Jack went back to the table and said, "Can we finish our meeting now?"

Both girls just let the phone ring while sitting at the table with Jack they listened to his wants and demands, keeping quiet and smiling. "Now for the bit of information", Sara stood up and said "I have purchased a parcel of land overlooking the harbor, as soon as we can find a builder, we need to get started."

"Also from now on Sara, I want you to stay with Sam at night, until this surveillance mess is taken care of", said Jack.

"Fine, where will you be at?"

"Between the two of you."

"Good answer" said Sam "And It's about time I get some love from the two of you."

Sara walks over and hugs her and the two begin to kiss.

"Enough of that girls" said Jack.

"That's right, we are your girls, old man" said Sara laughing as Sam joins in. They hear a knock at the side door, people with blue plastic from head to toe and a smoky visor came in without saying a word and picked up the dead men, several others washed the floor and sanitized.

"I hope that isn't what will happen to us when we die?" asked Sam solemnly.

The blue team left and a single person appeared. Jack saw her and went to her. It was Lisa, the very pretty Red headed woman, she said "This is the reason why you need to stay on the down low."

"If you really think it is necessary" said Jack.

Jack placed his hands on her arms and said "Is this the time for me to go to the spa?"

"Maybe, or maybe I could assign a few more agents to watch over you."

"About that, we have decided to add some surveillance in and around the place and we are in the process of building a home overlooking the harbor."

"How may I be of some assistance to you?" asked Lisa, with a concern look on her face.

"Well for starters, give us more agents in and around us."

"Fine, what else?"

"Well, nothing really, I guess that was about it."

"Let's see where this goes and play it by ear, as for the spa, just say the word and it will all be yours" said Lisa.

"Oh by the way, I have assigned a new driver for you, he is actually someone you could use during your down time, his name is Mark Reynolds and he is actually a boat captain by day and a undercover spy at night, seeing you have a boat and your former Captain retired, I thought a young buck could help you out."

"Yeah that would be nice; we actually talked about going full time fishing." said Jack.

"Is that after you wipe out half the list I gave to you?"

"Yep, and continue the charter business in between, we have new engines and a refurbished hull you ought to come out for a weekend fish trip."

"Maybe I will when all of this settles down" said Lisa as she leans in and gives Jack a kiss on the cheek, and said, "Goodbye."

Lisa leaves as Mike passes her, who actually opens the door for her, then enters, he waves to Sara as he says" Hi" to Jack, he goes over to see Samantha and said "Hi" and hands her a bouquet of flowers he had behind his back.

"Thanks Mike, for the flowers" she takes out the old ones and places the new ones in, as the phones kept ringing, "Can you help me out and answer the phone" asked Sam.

Mike answers the phone and said "It's some guy on the phone who said he is a carpenter, do you guys need a carpenter?"

"Hey Mike, Sara and I need to go, will you be alright?" said Jack. he collects her and the two wave their goodbyes to Sam and leave through the side back door.

"What did you say Mike, sorry I couldn't concentrate", said Sam.

"I said, there is a guy who said you called, a carpenter, what do you need built? I know a discreet general contractor who is a nice guy that can send us someone over and build it lower than any other and plus I'm a good contractor."

"Then tell that guy the job is filled, you got it", said Sam.

Mike puts down the receiver and said "What is the job you need done?"

"I didn't say to hang up on the guy, you should of told him the position was filled."

"Oops, sorry" said Mike.

Sam wheels around and says, "Follow me over here, Jack wants a room built to hold several monitors. We contacted a company in Louisiana to install some surveillance cameras in here."

"Don't fear, my General Contractor and I will take care all your needs." says a confident Mike, to include "I will come here and do all of the surveillance at cost and I will take care of all of it."

"Go ahead, oh by the way, Jack also is looking for someone to build a house for us."

"I'll take care of that for you too."

Sam went back to answering the phones and compiling a list of most wanted for these weekends' trips for Saturday and Sunday.

Meanwhile, Mike took it to heart to help Jack using all of his contacts and calling his friend, who was based out of Mobile, but was in Michigan on a major bridge project. He said he would send over his best new carpenter and a load of timber and supplies. Then he agreed to build Jack's house and come in on Monday to meet with the owners. "Thanks" he said and hung up then said to Sam, "It's all been taken care of, a guy will be by here shortly." "I'm going out to walk the perimeter and swing by the crab shack do you want something?"

"The usually please, or just surprise me."

"Will do Sam", he said with a smile, and walked to the side door. He looked out then walked out into the cold, off to his left was the Parthian Stranger. "What a cool name, that best sums up Jack", then Mike walks around the building and over to the crab shack to order.

Sara pulled the large Suburban into the hospital parking lot and into a place reserved for herself, next to her sister's car and Debbie's sleek new black convertible, which Jack bought for her. She parked and said, "Do you need to visit Debbie today."

"Nah, let's go to the cafeteria" said Jack as he was out the door and was on the move.

Behind him was Sara trying to catch up, she was running with her purse dangling between her boobs. She caught up with him, and hung onto his arm and pulled him in to the hospital.

"Cafeteria is that way" said Jack.

"You don't have time for that, you're already late, come on" said Sara. She led Jack to a door on the first floor, a newly painted sign read Dr. Annie Herndon, Sara knocked. Jack was muttering something like

"What about the cafeteria?"

"Hush up" said Sara and said, "You can go after this appointment."

As the door open, there standing was yet another beauty a short blonde-haired woman with long fingernails, heavy makeup and gold wrap around strapless dress and high heels.

"You should do fine here" said Sara.

"You must be Jack, I'm Annie come on in, your late, are you his wife?"

"No, just fiancé." said Sara.

"You'll have to wait outside, while the session is on."

"How long will it last?" asked Sara.

"Depends on the individual, but usually the first session takes 2-4 hours, depending on what info is being shared. So Jack come on in" said Annie in the most sinister way, with her eyes and her smile.

"Well honey, give me a kiss", Jack turned to face Sara then placed both of his hands on her face and the two kissed in the hallway, Sara broke away first laughing and said, "Stop it Jack, I know what you're doing" says Sara leaving him and said, "When you're done I'll be with my sis in the cafeteria."

"What, come on, what did I do?" he said innocently.

She turns to face him while walking backwards and said "I know your little games you play like to play", as she runs into a doctor.

"Who's laughing now?" said Jack.

"Jack are you coming in?" said a stern Annie, in a demanding tone.

Jack enters and closes the door, then walks to the middle of the room, whereas a large black chair, with a head rest.

"Have a seat, let's talk", says Annie who led Jack to the sofa.

Jack sits by Annie on the sofa, then she moved to the chair. Her dress was somewhat hiked up, as Jack made it obvious that he was staring at her panty line.

"So Jack, looks like your fiancé filled out your questionnaire and info, so how long have you and Sara been together?"

"Oh about six months now." said Jack.

"What are your plans with her?"

"Get married and have five kids." said Jack.

"Is she aware of this?" asked Annie.

"Yeah."

"How would you rate your relationship with her?"

"A perfect ten" said Jack, still looking down to see that her dress had risen up some more.

"Interesting, she said the same thing, she also put that you're both sexually open to see other people, is that true and who's decision was that?"

"Hers, she was a lesbian when we first met, then I held her captive for three days and she fell in love." said Jack proudly.

"Interesting, do you find me attractive?" asked Annie.

"Of course."

"Well Jack, for this to work we must be able to trust one another, actually sexual chemistry is the best way, what I have found is that if you're comfortable with me you'll be more likely to become easily more aroused and thus you will reveal better more complex answers." "Do you want to begin?"

"Sure." said Jack.

"Well stand up and begin to undress, take everything off."

Jack stands, slips out of his shoes and said," What about you?"

"In time, let me see what stimulates you first, I noticed you staring at my panty line, does that excite you Jack?" said Annie.

"Yeah, who wouldn't," as he was striping at an alarming rate.

"Well you'd be surprised, like some men can't get it up at a sight of an exposed pair of panties, let alone a woman's naked body." "It's only a body, right?"

"Right", said Jack, who was positioned at half-mast, standing in front of her.

"Your turn", said Jack. He was really ready to go.

"Be patient, in time you can see it all or do you want something else," she said with a smile, looking down to see he was at full mast.

"It doesn't take you long to get stimulated, good that is why I have been so successful."

She continued to talk, as Jack was listening to her, as she said, "You see Jack, it is the immediate stimuli that triggers deep emotions to produce successful results." "Now go over and sit in my chair, but before you do, think about a worse moment for you, lock on it then turn around and face me, you see, what you're going to tell me is only half the story." "It's the physical response that's connected by an emotional response which will connect to your mind for the whole answer." she watched as Jack took a few steps, then turned to face her.

"Good job, I can see that worked." "Can you tell me what that was?" said Annie.

"Being held as a prisoner", answered Jack slowly and methodically.

"Good, so you don't like being held down?" asked Annie.

"Nah, just the knowing I can't go anywhere, you know like a jail cell."

"Interesting, so now sit down, I want to test your visual responses." "Then after each time I will say one word and you think of being held prisoner, then as the session goes on you will hear that word and respond." "When we're finished, I'll use a safe word, like"

"Sophia" said Jack.

"Why did you say that name?"

"I don't know, maybe it's someone I once knew." said Jack.

"Alright Sophia it is, let's begin our session. Do you like me?"

"Yes" said Jack staring at her, as she gets up to face him and said, "Now concentrate on me and at no time will you touch yourself. Place your hands and arms in the side rest, let's begin." She teased him by pulling up her dress slowly to see a response, she got to her panty line, to see he was still unaffected, and said, "I thought you were aroused earlier when I did this."

"Back then it was forbidden, so yeah that's a turn on, but now I'm waiting for it all to come off." said Jack.

"Really, so if I were to sit in my chair, and hike up my dress, you would get aroused." asked Annie.

"Probably, probably not, I'm not into much teasing, either you do it or not." said Jack.

Then Jack said, "I see where this is heading, if you want I can think of Sara to produce the same results."

"It won't be the same results because you have emotional ties to her. As for me, I'm simply an object to look at, like a muse for a painter." "But if I turn you on, I will get an immediate response" said Doctor Annie.

"So strip already and I will give you a response" said Jack with a smile.

Annie stood, then in a slow and calculating move she pulled up and off her shirt, to expose her bra. Jack held flaccid, she waited for a response, she knew Jack was testing her, so she undid her skirt and let it fall, still no activity. Then she said, "Are you concentrating on me?"

"Yep, it has a mind of its own" said Jack with a solid smile. In an instant she knew she had to go all the way, which she resigned herself to that realization. She unhooked her bra from behind, then pulled it off quickly. Jack made a good response to that, he answered her questions as she asked them. He looked at her small perky breasts and knew there was more coming attractions to follow, so he paced himself. He heard her say, "Is that all you're going to give me?"

"Yep, let's see it" said Jack, now in charge. She hooked both her thumbs under the thin line of her panties and started to pull them down when Jack said "Slowly, I want to savor this moment."

She listened and slowly revealed that her carpet did not match her drapes, then Jack said, "Hey you're a brunette."

"I know and from what I can see that doesn't matter much" she said, to add, "Let me make sure, you won't have any issue when your concentrating." She walks over, kneels down and with one hand begins to stroke it, easily Jack is fully aroused for her and he said, "How about this?"

She lowers her head and opens her mouth, to feel the throbbing increase, she continued this motion till she felt the vibration stop. He was where she wanted him and released her grip on him. She stood up and said, "Now we're ready, lie back and put your head in the rest and now close your eyes and I will place a set of headphones on you." "I will ask you a series of questions, then we'll see what happens, let's begin." She came around to him and whispered "Prison".

He could smell her, and then thought elsewhere, to reveal his response.

"Good Jack, now tell me about the earliest memory you have of a woman, ... now."

Jack thought of Annie then Sara, then Debbie, then Maria, then he went deep and said, "Her name is Melissa, Melissa was my partner" his physical response was steady and firm.

"She and I were working together, I think it was undercover, literally, she like to be naked all the time, she is what they call a nymphomaniac, so anything would set it off." "She was assigned to me because I was the opposite, I was cold calculating", his physical response showed.

"Go on, tell me about Melissa." asked Annie.

"She would always tell me to touch her breasts, when she had the desire to strip and it would turn her on, so that was my cue." "It actually didn't do anything for me", as evident to his physical response. "So I went along with it, she and I were investigating a lead about a warehouse, we went down there, we entered to see it was some sort of sex play ground."

"I remember Melissa saying we should discard our weapons because we were going to get naked, so we pulled off our weapons and badges and placed them in a hiding spot." "I turned to see she was gone, I followed slowly to see she had made contact with a large guy, she pulled her top off and before I knew it she was naked and doing something to his lower naked body." "There were people all over, doing the same thing, when all of a sudden the dim lights were turned on." "Everyone stopped to see Melissa still going at it with this guy in the middle, as others watched him get pleasure from behind another guy." "They quickly tied her hands behind her back, which she let happen and the next thing you knew, there was a line on both sides forming, each taking their turn with her." "After that I was turned on incredibly, she fell to the floor, probably from exhaustion or something. Then the lights went out, then a door opened, and there was my mom Sophia."

Jack opened his eyes, he saw the Doctor fully clothed; he looked down to see he was dressed as well and said, "Was all of this a dream?"

"Yes actually, as soon as you hit that chair you were out, I believe the session went well."

Jack stood up a bit wobbly, he rested on the edge, and said, "what did I say, I can't remember a thing."

"That's because you were in a trance and I suppressed your beta brain waves so that your Delta may surface." said Annie.

"And what about us." asked Jack.

"What about us, do you want to know?" she said with a smile, "We will keep that as our little secret."

"Did you and I have sex?" asked Jack.

"Did we, or did we not, that is why you're coming to see me, to straighten out your issues." she came closer and whispered, "You were the best I ever had." Then turned away with a pair of panties she whirled around her finger. She went behind the desk to put the panties back on.

Jack tried to watch, but the desk was too large.

"See you soon, how about on Monday, maybe then you will remember the time we had." said Annie.

Jack got his bearings and cleared his head, his mind was still spinning, he had no recollection on just what happen. He shrugged his shoulders and walked out, and thinking of who Sophia is.

Meanwhile back at the office, Samantha and Mike just finished lunch and Sam set all the booking for the next Saturday. Mike said, "Who is all going and do you know what Jack's plan is?"

"No, he hasn't told me, why, did you want to go out?" said Sam.

"Maybe, I was just thinking of him and all these criminals, his idea to lure them all on a fishing trip is brilliant."

"That's why he will be my husband" said Sam proudly.

Mike was a firm supporter of Sam and her impact on Jack, he knew his job was to protect her and whatever Jack wanted he got, no questions asked or answered he knew his place, and said, "I think our carpenter is here."

Sam looked up out through the large front glass to see a huge truck pull up and a couple of guys get out, Mike was out the front door, to meet them, he was directing them to the side door, then he went out of sight, next moment she heard voices, she turned to see Mike and this man, handsome of sorts, extend his hand and said, "Hi I'm Kevin, the carpenter, you're quite beautiful."

"Thank you, my . . ."

"Her name is Samantha, and she would like you to build a room over here." Mike showed him where.

"Are you her boyfriend?" asked Kevin.

"No, she is engaged to the owner", I only work for him, answered Mike.

"Is he around?"

"Why do you ask?"

"I need approval to do this", as he winked at Sam who turned in her chair to shake her head. In disbelief.

"Listen friend, I'm the one who is in charge, so leave the lady alone and build us that room, Bradley is only a phone call away." said Mike.

"Yeah, I got you man, you don't need to threaten me with knowing my boss, I'm a sub-contractor and I am my own boss." "I just do jobs for Mister Hughes." said Kevin.

Mike didn't answer him, then went back over to Sam and sat down by her, while Kevin and his crew began work. From time to time Kevin would ask Mike for modifications like a window to view the desk. Then Kevin asked what the room was for. Mike said "a new security system." Kevin said, "I could install some cable feeds, for a quarter of the cost that other companies will charge."

Mike O'kayed the work with hesitation, while Kevin worked on and continued building the safe room, his other guys installed the cable lines, and went out to buy some monitors and cameras.

The crew came back with boxes and were unpacking them, then led the wireless feed to a bank of monitors. From time to time Kevin would look over at Sam just to stare at her pretty face and her striking features.

Mike was at the desk when he saw another car pull up, it was a limousine, jet black, a guy with a black hat and a suit got out. Mike stood to wait, his hair on the back of his neck stood on end, waiting, then the guy just stood there lit a cigarette and leaned up against the car. Mike said, "Sam, I'm going outside to check out this Joker." Mike exited the desk area and left out the front door. Samantha looked out to see Mike and the driver talking and then heard, "So

Sam, you have a fiancé, you ought to leave him for a guy like me, I know I can make you very happy", said Kevin directly behind her.

"You're too late, my fiancé is nice and I'm not really looking for anything else, but thanks for the offer, don't you have some more work to do?" said Sam, with a smile on her face.

Mike outside, was talking with Jack's new driver, Mark.

Mike was looking through the window to see Kevin directly behind Sam and said, "Look I got to go, but you know now to park that limo up on the upper lot, then come on down here."

"You got it boss", said Mark.

Mike hurriedly went inside, after closing the door he saw Kevin touching her hair. Mike said, "Step away from Sam", sounding a bit more angrily. Mike went up to Kevin to get into his face, then led him to the back by the arm and said, "I warned you to stay away from her, she is another man's property, from the way I see it you have two choices, take all your tools and get off this work site or stay and focus on the job and finish it."

"That's it," said Kevin comedic to Mike.

"Let me have at him" said a commanding voice, both Mike and Kevin turned around to see Mark.

Behind him spoke a softer more daintier voice, "Enough boys, Mike leave Kevin alone, he is harmless, besides if he knew my fiancé he wouldn't act that way, just let Kevin finish his job." said Sam.

Mike released Kevin with a sneer, Mark stood by ready for action.

"I like your style" said Mike to Mark.

"That's what a limo drivers got to do." said Mark.

Mike had to restrain Mark from getting to him.

"Everyone get back to work, Jack and Sara are back."

"Is that Jack Smith, your fiancé?" asked Kevin.

"No idiot that is Jack Cash, the Bounty Hunter" said Mike.

"No I believe his title is International Bounty Hunter, with a license to kill anyone he dislikes" said Mark, looking at Kevin.

Kevin said solemnly, "Oh him, that guy is famous" said Kevin, as he grabbed his tool belt and exited the building.

Jack was looking over the truck with all the lumber and sheets of plywood. Jack turned to see Kevin and said, "Are you the builder?"

"Yeah, who are you?" said a cocky Kevin.

"The name is Jack and my friend Sara, how are you making out?" as Jack looked at the guy.

Kevin looked nervous as he looked back at Jack, in that instance, they both knew where it was going and Kevin dropped his tool belt and ran towards the dock.

Jack yelled stop or I will shoot" Jack put out his weapon only to see a flash of a man in a tux run across his path, easily catching up to the man and jumped on him from behind. He was sending down a rain of kidney punches and then a final blow to the head.

Jack and Mike caught up with him and said, "Get up off him and who are you?"

"Name is Mark Reynolds, ready to serve."

"Excellent, did Lisa send you?" asked Jack.

"Yes, I was drafted out of a pool of agents in training, my background is Special Forces and Black Ops." "I'm a Ranger through and through, I'll be your driver." "Where the other men let you down, you can count on me, I have an extensive background in weapons, explosives and can be your sniper, I'm a certified diver and a boat captain." "Last year I was fishing in Alaska and am now a certified pilot as well, I can fly anything with wings and a propeller." said Mark proudly.

"Enough, let's get this guy up, he is familiar, I believe he is on the list of two hundred" said Jack, pulling out a sheet of paper from his pocket and said "There he is, his name is Steppe Danover, professional thief, and wanted by Atlanta, so let's zip tie his hands and get him into the suburban." "Mike you stay with Samantha while I get to know this new guy, Mark." Then added, "And take Sara with you."

Jack calls 9-1-1 enters his code and connects to Lisa, and said, "I got another one for pick up."

Slides his phone closed and said, "Let's get him inside, I hope this doesn't set us back building."

"Don't worry I will finish it till they send someone new" said Mike.

"I guess your friend, the general contractor, is the one to thank for him", pointing to Kevin.

"Need not to worry Jack, I'll let Brad know he had a thief working for him, he'll owe me big time" said Mike.

Another Suburban pulls up, a team of men in black suits get out and there in a yellow dress stood another beauty who had all the power. Jack's boss Lisa. She said, "You're at it again, a couple in the morning and now this one, what is it for you that attracts criminals to you, you're a magnet."

"Just doing my job, well, this was a team effort." says Jack.

"And doing it in a fine manner I must say, when do you want to go to the spa?"

"I don't know, this weekend I'm getting married, and the next I have a couple of criminals I'm taking out and do you want to go?" he said.

"Maybe, of course if I apprehend any one of them, I get to keep the million." said Lisa.

"I don't care, you can have them all."

"No, that's not our deal, that's what I like about you Jack, you're not money driven, just a humanitarian at heart." "So how is your team?" Do you need anyone else and how is Mark working out for you." "You know I picked him specifically to pilot your boat and of course he is an expert in San Soo, the art of offensive combat." "From this point forward you'll only get well trained agents, and we got a whole new program that were launching, to specially support you and Ben Hiltz."

The two walked together as others watched.

"I'm fine, your compensation is very rewarding and your support is great, I'll just go on doing what I'm doing." "You know, the offer still stands, you and your entourage can come onto the boat and enjoy yourself." "Fish a bit and enjoy the Gulf of Mexico while staying in my Captain's cabin." said Jack.

"That's a tempting offer, but I'm going to have to pass." "A girl has a girl's work that never ends." said Lisa, smiling at Jack.

"The offer is always open" said Jack.

"That's nice, let me get your bag, we ran out of briefcases."

"Do you want them back?" asked Jack as the two-walked back to her Suburban.

"If they're empty, you can have Mike or Mark drop them by when they pick up their checks."

Lisa instructs someone to bring the bag and then says to Jack, "There is a meeting of the minds for the mob in Montgomery on Monday if you're interested, maybe you want to show up?"

"Is that an invitation?"

"Yeah, possibly, you could hit that, then spend the rest of the week at the spa." said Lisa.

"Is that a request or an order?" asked Jack receiving the large duffle bag of cash.

"Neither, just a little info passed on from one colleagues to another."

Jack watches Lisa get into the Suburban and it drives off, as two more vehicles follow it. Jack turns and goes into the side door to see Mike and Mark working as a team. Jack sets the duffle bag down on the table to see Sara and Samantha answering calls, confirming flights and then he sat down.

"Hey honey, what do you want to do for dinner?" asked Sara.

"Nothing, I'm still full from the cafeteria, but, you could do me a favor?"

"What's that honey?" said Sara, climbing onto Jacks legs and sitting down.

"Take Mark and you too, go to the store and stock up for this fishing trip." said Jack.

"We'll he know what to get?" asked Sara.

"He was a ship's boat captain, I'm sure he does."

"Can I go with you tomorrow?" asked Sara.

"What will you do?"

"Be with you, and I guess I could cook in the galley." "Guy let me go a few times and I'm beginning to become a better cook, allow me to show you", as she pledged with him.

Jack finally let his guard down and said, "Alright you can come, but if you do, so will Sam."

"Did you call my name out, Jack?" asked Sam.

"Yes I did and you're coming along", said Jack. He got up to set Sara aside and goes over to Sam, slides out her wheel chair and in one fatal swoop he picks her up, she grabs a hold of his neck as he swings her along, then says, "You seem lighter, shouldn't you be gaining weight?"

"I don't know" she said, and began to cry.

Jack yelled over her and said, "Everyone out please." Both Mike and Mark herded the workers out into the now wet parking lot, as Jack put her back down into her chair and said, "Have you been eating, exercising and resting?"

"No, I haven't been" she said as she wept "I'm sorry Jack."

"It will be alright" said Jack as he kissed her on her wet lips, she held his head.

Jack broke away from her to see Sara who was equally crying as she saw her friend in despair.

"Look, you need to help Samantha, make sure she is eating, exercising and taking a mid-afternoon nap" said Jack.

"How do you suppose I do that, I can't lift her up." said Sara.

"Hire someone to help out, what about your brother, what's he doing nowadays that he's got probation and community service." said Jack.

"Nothing I guess, he could help us out, I'll give him a call." Said Sara.

"Can you tell everyone they can come back in" asked Jack.

Jack took a seat next to his real love interest, the beautiful Samantha and said, "Listen Sam, you need to eat, sleep and exercise and now Sara will stay with you at night."

"I think she is going to have Timmy help you out, I stocked the upstairs with all that workout equipment, but you're going to have to work out." "I will see if I can get someone from the hospital to come and see you". "We have the whole upstairs to work with, I'd like to convert that to a master bedroom, bathroom and workout area." "Please use the elevator, I want to make you as comfortable as possible."

She rests her head against his and whispers, "Jack, I love you and thanks for my new life, I just wish we could all grow old together." "Sometimes it saddens me to think that when I go, what Sam junior will be like, I just wish there was a way that I could see him grow up."

Jack just held her and he himself was being emotional when he let out a teardrop and said, "I too love you Miss Samantha Cash."

"Shut up" she said as the two laughed and cried together as the crews went back to work.

"Promise me this one thing, can you make sure the men in blue suits don't take me away when I past on, only you, my love."

"Yes, I promise, I will be the one who carries you to the morgue."

"Now you shut up Mister," she said jokingly.

CH 11

The Wedding; to Samantha

This Saturday was that of Samantha's, the planned out two-day event that covered Saturday and Sunday, the reception and a honeymoon to the Virgin Islands, for a five-day stay.

The next morning everyone was up. It was Sam, Sara and Jack all in one bed upstairs in the boat shack. The excitement was building for Sam, who was helped up by Jack. He hoisted her up and the two went to the shower together. Meanwhile, Sara was in the makeshift kitchen making breakfast. Bacon, hash browns and eggs to order, for Jack she knew it was eggs poached hard. She set and laid all the food on each plate, as she heard they were done in the shower. Jack finished drying her off, as she sat on the cushioned bench. He pulled up her panties and she said," I'd never thought I'd ever see you do that."

"Do what?" asked Jack, looking up at her.

"You know, pull my panties up. A guy like you always wants them down" she smiled at him, as she wiggled the rest of the way up, he hands her a matching bra.

He dressed in front of her. Then he found a dress and placed it over her head and then lifted her up by the arms and her dress fell to cover her body.

Jack then picked her up and carried her over to the table to an awaiting chair, the room was filled with fresh smells. The three ate in relative silence, when finished, Sara cleaned up the dishes and Jack wheeled Sam into the elevator. They went down a flight, the door opened and they went past the new room, it was nearly complete on the right side. Jack and Sam was looking at the two big front windows that were now covered in a reflective sheet. Jack said to himself," I like that, I can look out, but I Imagine you can't look in?"

Jack took his usual seat, across from Sara at the table, who smiled back at him and said, "Just think, we could be doing this for the rest of our lives", Sara looks at Sam and said, "Oh dear, I'm sorry, I keep forgetting."

She was strong, and said," I know I've come to terms, that my body is shutting down, as it's a host for my baby." she looked over at Jack, who was busy reading the paper.

A knock at the side door, Sara looked up to see it was 8 o'clock and said, "It must be Guy, we have a fishing party this morning going out." "Do you think, you'll go out Jack?"

"Nah, what for?"

"Well, so you can get familiarized with your boat and all of its features."

"I'd like to go out," said Samantha.

They both said in unison," No."

"Maybe?" to add, "What about when you said you wanted me to go out."

"Changed my mind", said Jack.

"That's why you need to go out", said Sara.

"Alright, I'll go" said Jack. He saw that Sara had let in Guy, and the rest of the construction crew were waiting. Quickly men were in their place, as Sam was at the long front desk, to yell back, "Here comes our customers."

Guy went to the front door, unlocked it and pulled it open and said, "Howdy Ma'am", in walked a girl with hair pulled back, blonde, she had attitude, as she said, "I had a reservation for Roger Snider and I'm Genie Dahl, who do I give this to?", showing her credit card.

Sam wheeled over to accept it and said, "That will be two hundred and forty dollars, would you like to add a tip?"

Genie looked at her, then at her boy-friend and said, "Can I wait to see how the service is?"

"Yeah sure, all this is, is a deposit of two hundred and forty, in the event you forget to come by afterwards, that's all, Sam hands her the card back and said, "Guy, this guy is your captain, he will show you the way."

Jack looks up from his paper to see them leave with Guy, he was thinking, "Yeah, him and I, we need to talk."

Jack went outside to see Mike was helping the construction crew carrying in a huge monitor, while his new driver was propped up on the limousine, smoking a cigarette. Jack walked up to him and said, "Enough already?"

"What" said Mark looking at him.

"You're way over dressed, drop the suit and that hat and change into some working clothes. From this day forward, stop smoking, it stinks and lastly, get rid of that car."

"What shall I drive?"

"Look up there, I got a Camaro, or that Suburban, you choose." said Jack.

"Alright" he said with a smile.

"While you're out, can you and Sara go shopping, make something for lunch, we're going out on my boat."

Jack stood in line to grab something from the truck to take in, he carried a couple of small monitors and went in.

Mark moved the limousine up to the upper parking lot and then ran to the front entrance. He saw a very pretty girl with two guys pass by, then went in.

He stood at the railing and said "Sara are you ready, he was looking at Sam and talking to her.

"Not me, it's her." said Sam, showing him she was in a wheelchair.

He looked at her with a frown and said," Sorry." Mark saw another very beautiful girl come towards him. She said "I'm Sara, and you are?"

"I'm Mark, Mark Reynolds, I'm mister Cash's new driver."

"That's nice, she is Samantha, she will be Jack's wife on Saturday."

"Oh, Okay, yeah, they told me about that, congratulations."

"Thank you" said Sam with a smile.

"Listen, Jack wanted me to get you and we would go shopping for lunch."

"Sure, are you ready, you look like a chauffeur."

"Well I am, well was, I ready don't have any clothes to change into."

Sara looks him over, smiles and says, "I think I know a store I can take you to."

"Great, let's go, wait, are you going on the boat this morning?"

"Yes, I guess."

"Then let's go, we don't have very long, you're leaving in an hour."

Sara pushes him out the door with herself, grabbing her purse on the way out.

Jack was in the back room in his new office, a desk in the middle with windows all around, on the desk was a stack of documents to go over. He sat down and began to open each one, first was a letter, addressed to him, sent to Washington D.C., that read "Dear Jack Cash, thank you for the rescue of my daughter, we are forever in your debt." "You're truly an amazing man, for the life you lead and how you care about others." "We wanted to give you something." A cashier's check falls out in the amount of 25, 000, he saw it and set it down. The check had his name on it, he looked at it. It read "Pay to the order of; Jack Cash." then he said to himself, "That's my name on that check, Wow" then realized "How do I cash it, do I go to the bank?"

Jack folded up the check and stuffed it in his wallet. Mark and Sara were having fun together, she got him into a tight pair of jeans, a nice shirt and a leather jacket. He paid, and even made the statement that while she was with him, He would be paying. She agreed and she led the way. They were playful together, down every aisle, in a mad dash to get to the register, they cashed out and loaded it up. Then they went back across the street to see the boat was still there, Mark swung the suburban up next to the boat, they both got out, joking as they were carrying the groceries. Mike was on the stern, he went over and said, "Hand them to me, I'll take them into the galley. Mike saw Mark and gave him a dirty look, then went in.

Sara got on as Guy was finishing the tour, showing them how to use the fishing lines.

Mike was unloading when he saw Sara and said," That guy is sure long winded, do they even need to see the whole boat?"

"I don't know, he does his thing and I stay out of it" said Sara.

"There is sure a lot of food here, are we going out for a couple of days?" asked Mike.

"Why, do you have a date? Mark suggested we get over stocked than under stocked, just in case." Mike finished what he was doing to hear, "Besides, I'm going to cook a hearty vegetable stew."

"Nice." said the man behind her, she turned and kissed Jack as he held her in his arms, instantly she whispered "You're carrying."

"Yep, better safe than sorry", he sees Mike and said," Hey can you do me a favor?"

"Sure."

"I received a check in the mail, can you cash it?"

He releases Sara who was trying to take it away from Jack, he was playing around with her as she was trying to grab it. Mike finally took it and said "This isn't a check, it's a cashier's draft, you can go anywhere, well, the amount is quite substantial" He tries to give it back, Jack said, "Keep it and just get it done, when you can." "Are we all set?"

Mike said to Sara, "Yeah, can I talk with you?" as he was looking at Jack. Sara looked at them and said "Yeah, I know what that means" she said leaving. Mike said "No, No, it's not like that, you can stay.

"Whatever," she waved.

Mike led Jack up to the wheel house and said, "What is the deal with the old timer, why can't we shove off and go already?"

"Well I think it's this rule that says you have a certain window of time to leave port, I read about it." "Is that the port authority that has to know when you leave and how long we will be gone? Asked Mike.

"It's similar to an air traffic controller and the planes leaving, port authority needs to know how many is on a particular vessel and its intentions." said Jack. "Those that don't comply, well they won't send a search team for them and on this boat, we try to follow the rules."

"He is right" said Guy, behind him. Guy says "Jack, here are the two that have chartered your boat, Mister Snider and Miss Dahl."

She looks Jack over and said, "Yes, he is very nice, you can call me Genie."

Jack nods and him and Mike leave out the captain's door to the platform. Mike said, "You won't believe what is under that tarp?"

"Try me", said Jack.

"It's a jet boat, then there are Jet skis, there are some mighty fine toys aboard this boat."

"Mister Adams, will you go secure the lines" spoke Guy, intentionally interrupting them.

Mike used the rail and hopped down to the stairs to see his new found friend Mark getting on board and said, "Dude, what are you wearing, Jeans, really."

"What, Sara liked them" he said Joking.

"Sara is your boss." his happiness turned to frowning, realizing the reality, that Sara was Jack's girl. Mike said, "You better watch it or you'll be swimming with the fishes."

"I hear you man, your right, I got to get my head in the game."

Jack saw Mark, who was coming towards them and said, "Mark, I want you to pilot the boat, leave exactly at nine and follow procedures". Jack looked at Mark weirdly over his clothing change and thought, "He should of kept that uniform on really."

Mark went in to see all the state of the art cockpit, he sat in the most comfortable chair he had ever sat on and adjusted it. The monitors were on some on swing arms, so he could push them all the way forward. He was on a pedestal. In front of him, through the window his view was that the water was flat. Then he saw the lounge chairs, he had flash backs to a sunbather, quickly he erased that memory only to see Sara smiling and she put her hands on his neck and said, "You're not joking anymore, what's wrong?"

"Your Jack's girl."

"Yeah, so what, you were hitting on me, remember you were saying how you were restraining yourself, well how is that going now?"

"Alright."

"Fine, play it that way, I thought you were cool, just because we're having a little fun, doesn't mean I'll sleep with you." "You better have a stronger backbone than that, especially if you're suppose to be my man's driver and bodyguard, cause right now, you're doing a shitty job of it." Sara left after giving Mark a neck rub down. He sat in silence, looking at the radios, stereo and sound system. He swung around to see a door that read Captain's quarters. He slid the two doors open, to reveal a huge bed, smartly made up, with pillows.

"That's Jack's room" said Guy behind him, "It's off limits, your bunk is in the front hold." "Ever piloted a vessel before?" asked Guy condescendingly to Mark.

"Yes", Mark steps back, then sees Guy slide the doors closed and inserts a key to lock it.

Mark backs up to the chair and was a bit clumsy. Guy just looked at him. Mark gets on the chair, he was waiting and Guy moved in his space and turned on the intercom and said, "Listen up, were leaving now, find a place to sit & relax till we get there, it takes about thirty minutes." "We will fish for three hours and then come back by one."

"See Roger, I told you we would be back in early." She turned to see Jack was on the platform, his deckhand Mike had cast off the lines, the boat roared to life and moved with power. It was jerky at first, but Mark got the hang of it. Mike was checking everything. Genie said, "You guys sure have a nice boat."

"Yeah", said Mike not really looking at her, as he was pulling bait. She was behind him, and said, "Do you think anyone would mind if I sun bathed?"

"Nah, there is a place up front, the lounge chairs are secured, and just put your stuff underneath" said Mike.

"Thanks you're sure helpful" she said with a smile.

"You're welcome". He said respectfully.

She led Roger along the starboard side, and said, "He could surely make one."

"Really, why do you say that?", Roger asked.

"Oh you just can tell, he has bad boy written all over him", as they passed under the pilot and up the stairs to the Bow, she looked back to see Mark, who saw her, but didn't acknowledge her, he was too busy getting a lecture from Guy, who stood right by him.

"Listen why don't you go and mingle, I'm going to get some sun." she looked back at her man as he left. She looked up at Mark, still not her type and then the old man . . . Ooh, then there he was, Jack, she said, "Now that is a man I need to show off to."

Jack took the other seat, as a confertation was looming, but for the moment, everyone's attention was on Genie, who was striping her clothes off, even Sara said," What is she doing, it's cold out there. Oh my God, she just didn't do that", Genie had turned to show the boys her bottom, as she pulled down her panties and stepped out of them and picked up her clothes. The wind showed just how cold she really was. Sara said, "That girl is crazy."

"Yeah, crazy cold," said Jack smiling.

Then instantly Jack had an idea and said, "Hey Guy, now that we're out of port, can we trawl?"

"No, but, you can take out the jet ski's and launch a boat, or take out that jet boat that the Government people sent down to you. A guy named Jim said for you to take it out and really open it up?"

"Did you try it yet?" asked Jack.

"No, he said it was off limits to everyone except you, they say it goes over two hundred miles an hour."

"What that means is that I could get to Cuba in that?" said Jack, going to the door of his room, trying it and said "It's locked, who has the key?"

"I do, it's to keep people out." said Guy, unlocking it. Jack looked at him, and said, "Anyone can use this room, even you Guy, maybe", Jack opens the two doors, to instantly getting that flashback of Samantha, but that was then and this is now. What a difference, there was actually a place to walk around to the rear windows and it was hot in there. Guy said, "Here on the wall is a climate control heat or cool, whatever you like?"

"You ever sleep in here, or do anything else?", said Jack with a sneer.

"Look at me, I'm an old timer, you're the young buck, I couldn't do anything if my life depended on it, besides I have the Misses."

Jack shakes his head thinking the confertation was over, "He knows he has had his best interests at heart, he was really trying and it showed. Money is just money. Guy had backed away respectfully and that showed too, especially when Guy said, "Shall I close the doors?"

"Nah, I may just do that."

"Do what now?", said Sara overhearing them.

"Take the boat out" said Jack in the form of a statement.

"Great, I'll get it set up" said Guy, interested in helping out.

"No, have Mark come see me and you take the wheel."

"Yes sir?" said Guy. Instantly Mark shows up to hear, "I need you and Mike to un-secure the jet boat."

Mark leaves, while Jack see the two helpers doing as they are told. Jack leaves his resting spot, goes out to see Guy and said, "You got this?"

"Oh yeah, it's fine."

Jack goes down to the galley, to see Sara hard at work chopping. Jack said, "Whoa, look at you go?"

"I've improved greatly?"

"Sounds like you need to go to culinary school?"

"Sure, I'd try that, do you know where a school is at?" Sara asked.

"I don't know, maybe New Orleans?" said Jack checking his phone for the answer.

"That would be fun, will you be there?"

"Perhaps, sure, why not, it will be fun won't it?"

She came to him embraced him, leaving the knife behind, and said, "Sorry, I keep forgetting your work is so much more important to you, I didn't mean that, Sorry."

They held one and another, then they kissed, as the boat slowed to a stop, Jack broke away and went out through the back to the deck, where Roger was watching as the sleek prototype, that was set down on a frame, it was solid black. Mark scampered onto the lower deck and the two worked together to mount the rear wing, fitting it and tightened it down. The cockpit slid back, to see only one seat, Mark said, "That looks like a formula one car, that thing is small", he exclaimed.

Mike was on the phone with Jim, who was telling him the procedure and the details, to include that, "The drivers' capsule is a one unit piece, if there is a crash, the pod will float to the surface and it can be plucked from the water." Then lastly, Jim said, "There is only one that can test this, it's Jack, any others need to follow in a safety swift boat, or we get the Navy or Coast Guard involved."

"Will do", said Mike, as Jack came over to see it. Mark escorted Roger into the cabin.

Jack looked at Mike, who looked at him. They saw it was a reach. Mike said, "Let me get you a set of stairs" he goes and retrieves them and sets them down for Jack, who walks right up, steps in, slides down, so he is lying on his back, but slightly elevated. Mike hands him a helmet and a head neck support and said, "The visor is your guide, the solid capsule will seal and lock into place when you get in the water, you hit start, that will initiate a sequence, then hit go and off you go.

The capsule went down and locked into place, the visor was up but Jack could see nothing but total darkness. Then the swaying of being lifted, as soon as he closed the helmets visor he saw everything, it was amazing. It was as if he were there, it was like it was a simulator, but real. Then he heard a woman's voice" Hi Jack, its Jim, this prototype, is for you to try, it has unlimited range capability. Because you're on a nuclear reactor, it's top speed, we don't know yet, we had it at two hundred. Anyway, look at the steering wheel, all of those buttons represent something and we will go over each one."

The boat was idling forward, while all of that was going on, a Curios Genie got up and got dressed to look out on the starboard side. She saw the black jet boat and said "Cool," and went down to follow it back, only to see Mark, who ushered her into the cabin. She said "Did you guys build that, that is cool?"

Instantly it fired up and the magnet released, as the boat hit the water it waited. As Jack applied the throttle, the boat began to move ever so slightly. The boat was still in stall mode as the engine began its warm up sequence, then the fins extended outward, at an angle. Jack checked the rudder and the wing, he was ready and just like that, a shot, there was a boom, and that jet boat launched itself, forward, skimming the surface, and rocketing up to one hundred, then two hundred. It was solid and at half power, it rode like a tank, as it sat in the water so well. It was coming close to land Jack saw it was Mexico and slowly turned the wheel, the boat was a bit choppy, but once he straightened it out, and opened back up, it was clear for miles in front of him. He let it out, two hundred, three hundred, four hundred, it was going way too fast. As the tracker was accumulating all the data, he buzzed the Virgin Islands and then hit the Atlantic. Then it was a different story, as he slowed, the ripples were now waves. As he turned around and slowed he was being tossed around, he made his turn and throttled it back up, only to see it showed he was halfway to south Africa. Then he was off, at about a hundred he buzzed the Virgin Islands again and then picked up speed in the Gulf of Mexico. He was at this for some time, just staying in the gulf. He saw it was around twelve noon and thought he needed to get back, he slowed to a hundred and punched in the boats coordinates. He set it to autopilot.

With the boat on its own, it set the speed and how it was to perform, the data was saved. It cruised at half pace but still accomplished what it needed, it was back in a flash, as it was shutting down, but still alive, as the boat was in sight. Jack saw the two guests were on the stern fishing, as the boat came to a stop from the bow to the starboard side. Mike was ready for hook up, once the magnet hit the capsule, the engine shut down and the fins retracted. The jet boat was hoisted up and all the way to the platform, where Mark was guiding into place and into the rack, on its side. Mark and Mike to quickly threw the safety tarp over it, leaving the engine to cool down. Mike turned a knob to release the capsule and slid it back, while Mark undid the harness and helped Jack out. Sitting down, Jack pulled off the helmet and gave it to Mark to secure.

The two went back to fishing, they were alongside Guy, who was reeling them in, he was up to three, to their two fish caught. Genie said "How did you know that this place was filled with big eye tuna?"

"Oh, it's a trade secret."

"So what's up with those guys and that rocket boat?"

"I don't know?" said Guy fibbing.

"Is he some scientist or something?" she asked.

"Nah, just some guy who likes to build things."

"He sure has a nice looking bunch of guys working for him."

Jack scrambled off the platform, down a flight of stairs and into the galley to see and smell something amazing and said, "Wow, that smells so good, is it ready?"

"About a minute or two, I got fresh cornbread, shall I plate and bowl you up?" asked Sara.

"Sure, thanks" said Jack, getting his plate and going up to the wheelhouse to sit. Sara called all the rest to eat. Jack finished and went back down to deposit his plate and saw a very satisfied Sara, happy with her work. Then Jack went outside to see Guy had five presents laid out. Guy said "These three are yours, and the other are theirs."

"You can keep them" said Jack.

"They're like worth twenty grand?" said Guy.

"So you have them, I'm fine, did you get some of that stew?"

"Not yet, you don't mind?" Guy said.

"Hell No, you're just like family, go on in there and get some chow." Jack said.

Jack continued to fill the fish with crushed ice and heard, "So you're quite a remarkable man, so what do you do?"

Jack turned to face her and said, "Oh, nothing I'm just a guy."

"That was a mighty nice boat you had, can I see it?", asked Genie.

"Nah."

"Why not?"

"You know its new and all that," said Jack trying to be quiet.

She said, "I know some people who would pay good money for a boat like that, or like this, that is if you ever wanted to sell it."

"Nah, I'm fine." Jack tried to move away as she caught his arm, to wheel him around to face her and said, "Listen, I know you're a shy guy, but you and I could have a night you'll never forget."

"What about your boyfriend he seems tough." said Jack.

"What Roger, he is a pushover, besides I'd dump him for a guy like you, what do you say, you and I hooking up?"

"I'd have to consider that one, this isn't the place nor the time to talk about it?" said Jack.

"Oh, I get cha, the girl, she's your girl, do you have a number I can reach you at?" asked Genie.

Jack pulls up his phone and scrolls down his phone numbers to isolate a specific one and says, "Alright, here is my number, but call me exactly at ten in the morning, then we can meet up for a drink?"

"Oh no, it won't be a drink, it will be more like sex, intercourse, do you get my drift." she said.

"I think I do" said Jack as the boat surges forward. Jack leaves her to go inside, he reached his cabin, slid the doors open, then shut and pulled up her picture, he ran it through everything, it came up clear and a perfect credit score of 900, well, in general terms, 900 means something is wrong. He made a call to Daphne and said, "I need a tail on one Genie Dahl, Mobile Alabama."

"Yes, Sir."

Jack thought, "So she has someone interested in the prototype? Let's find out who those sharks really are."

The boat got back a little after one o'clock and there was a welcoming committee, a Coast Guard Cutter was at the dock, as the crew was all on stern. Guy parked it behind the Cutter, the two passengers saw the Cutter and all the service men and waved then scurried off the boat. Mike said "Miss you're forgetting your fish."

"They left in a hurry, what now?" looking over at Mark who said, "Like anything, aren't they Jack's?"

"True, you're right, let's get this deck cleared off."

"Permission to board" spoke a Coast Guard officer.

Mike looked at him and said, "You're the Coast Guard, enter?"

"Alright, it doesn't work like that, but alright, is Jack Cash available, I'd like a word."

"Sure, let me get him." said Mike. "Or better yet, If the Commander would please, he can come up to the wheelhouse, he will be waiting."

Mike knocked, and Jack slid the doors open and said, "What do you have?"

"A commander, from the Cutter?"

"Alright, help Sara off, and take that stuff into the shack, for Sam."

The Commander entered and said, "Sir, do I have your permission to enter?"

"Yes, come on in, how can I be of some assistance?" asked Jack.

"Well, not so much for us, per say, but if you had the time, would you care to come to our base and speak to the seaman."

"Seaman you say, not troops?" said Jack, as they both laughed.

"Well, I wanted to give you a heads up, that test has some pretty interested parties, we got several locations that had been tracking your whereabouts." "As we speak, were going after all those positions." said the commander.

"How may I help you specifically?", asked Jack.

"I've been ordered, at your disposal, for you to do as you see fit."

Jack looked at him, and said, "As a back up, I don't follow what you're asking?"

"What I understood from that order, was bring the boat here and wait."

"And how does that help me?"

"I don't follow?" said the Commander.

"Look at it, it's magnificent and all that, but it's a beacon. As for trying to be secret, the cats out of the bag now."

"Oh, I see, Sorry, Yeah, I guess I didn't interpreted that message correctly and I can see how you're exposed."

"Listen, take the ship back to wherever you come from, when I need you I'll call you, how is that, actually it would be nice if I had that helicopter." said Jack.

"To tell you the truth, you actually have the whole base at your disposal, from C-130's to ships."

"Really, and you're the Commander of all those assets?"

"Yep, Commander Bernie Abeyta, at your service."

"I will give you a call when I'm ready, but for now, a lesser presence would be best."

"Yes sir." said the commander.

Jack watched the Commander leave. He was trying to decide what to do, he went off the bridge, down the stairs and off the boat in time to see the huge Cutter leave, and take all the Seamen with them.

Jack was heading to his office when a call came in, it was from Maria, he answered it, and said, "Hi Honey how are you?"

"Fine, Mister Cash, when do we come and stay with you?"

"Soon, I'll send a plane to pick up all three of you, it will be soon I promise."

"I love you" said Maria sincerely.

Jack paused and said, "I love you too", he then slides the phone shut and goes into his office.

Jack walks in, to see a very enthusiastic Sam, who wheeled around and said, "That women gave you a forty dollar tip, isn't that lovely?"

"Swell", said Jack "Why don't you keep it."

Thursday and Friday had come and gone, they locked up. Jack had placed Sam in the back seat, folded up the wheel chair and placed it in the furthest back and got in the passenger seat. Sara drove, got on the freeway and took the 4th exit, got off and came to a cul-de-sac and off on the left, was a newly paved road. Up the hill they went to the right, then up the hill to a clearing, then right, to see the field, then, another right, then a left where a huge garage stood. Sara hit the door switch, the door went up and in she drove and parked.

The door went down, and the lights came on, Sara got out, Jack was helping out Sam. Sara went to the double wide mobile home, unlocked the door and turned on the lights, as Jack wheeled Sam up the ramp on the south side to the sliding glass door, Sam rolled in. Jack slid the door shut. He turned out the inside garage lights, turned on the TV, looked at the list and turned on some music. Then he went over to the Pool table and set up the balls. Sam was in the kitchen with Sara, the two made dinner, a quick spaghetti, with a sweet meat sauce and a crusty garlic bread from a baguette that was in the refrigerator.

They sat down and ate in silence, Sara cleaned up the dishes. Jack ran a bath for Sam, he undressed her, then took her from the bed to the tub and gently set her in and turned off the water. He left the room through the bedroom, this was her time to soak. Sara was ready as Jack grabbed the pool stick and broke the balls, a stripe went in, Jack took careful shots and the ball went in. he moved his position around, as he had the advantage, that was until Sara began to cheat. She began to undress, first was her top, revealing her bra. Sara said,

"Look Jack."

Jack missed, she missed, he lined it up and she popped off her bra, it hit the table and stopped the ball, she said "Oops, sorry."

She was then on a roll and took the lead, till she barely missed. He was next up, took a shot and missed because she was pulling her pants down to show off her butt. She finished Jack off by ending the game and scratched on the eight ball, then announce," I guess you won again, now take me to bed and go get our girl and meet me in there." Undressing the rest of the way, Jack was nude as he hit the bedroom and then rescued Samantha from the tub.

The day broke to the sound of the construction crew building the platform outside. It was wedding day, from Sara's estimates, there would be over a hundred people attending the event, with one particular person in attendance was Samantha's mother, Glenda, she was a bitter, condescending bitch. She was extremely objective to the fact that Jack and Sam hooked up in the first place, let alone it was Jack that help to discover her daughter's internal bleeding, this wasn't what was supposed to happen. That's what Glenda says to all of them, every time she comes and visits, especially after Sam left her mother, to live on her own. I guess you could say, she felt like her daughter abandoned her for some drug dealer.

Jack awoke and as always, he loved to stroke each girls face. Jack always loved being in the middle, so that he could spoon either one, as both were naked all the time or whenever he wanted. It was also available for him, but he didn't take advantage as he used to, he realized it wears him out.

Getting up was Sara's job, she was up and moving around, starting breakfast of eggs, freshly grated potatoes, making hash browns, but adding peppers and onions. A couple strips of bacon and the bread of the day, usually a jalapeno cheese bread, sliced, with peanut butter and strawberry jam. Jack was next up, he put Sam in a robe, he wore one too. He carried Sam into the kitchen, then Jack went and did his business, came out and sat down to a lovely meal.

Afterwards, Jack cleaned up the dishes and Sara cleaned up Sam. Jack finished the dishes and he went and showered. Sara dressed Sam and went into the living room in her wheel chair. Sara came in and saw Jack finishing up, and said, "Darn I missed all of that?"

"There really wasn't much to miss, but maybe later we could go a round or two?"

"Just name the time and place and I'll be there." said Sara.

Jack finished, stepped towards her, as he turned out the lights. He kissed her on the lips, they embraced, then Jack broke away and said, "Gotta go, I'm suppose to meet the builder this morning."

"So go then, and miss out on all of this", she said as she flashed him her open robe. Jack, while smiling said, "Now that is something to consider".

Jack hit the garage door opener, the door goes up and in front of him was a sea of workers, a super tent was already raised, at least fifteen feet tall. On the right side, by the cliff, was the huge portable crane and there was the guy barking out the orders the man saw Jack and came to him and said," Hi mister Cash, my name is Rob Bradley, the general contractor.", the two shook hands, for Jack just to nod. Rob said, "Allow me to show you what we're doing." Rob leads Jack past the platform, to the north side and to a set of scaffolding and said, "From the plans, were sinking a dual hundred and fifty foot high speed elevator, reaching the bay of Mobile, and then the other is for the six floors, forty six rooms, two story above ground house, and four below facing north. We'll use glass panels.

Jack points over to his right and said, "That building on the right, what is that?"

"That was a makeshift, to house the round the clock workers and feed station."

"Well I like it, it might even be nice to have a solid wall that ties that around to the back to the garage."

"Whatever you want, sure that's fine, let me show you", as he led Jack over to the other side of the building, to the west. They see a foundation that was already poured. Rob said, "See that area, it will be the atrium, a thick glassed, twenty foot building, with doors on both ends. An archway Segway's into the courtyard, a formal kitchen garden will be planted by the fame Country gardener, Jack Thompson, and finally a wall, will run over to the entrance, on the other side." "That is where Sam said she wants her plot, after checking with the city, they will allow it, just as long as the city has access from time to time to inspect it and maintain it."

"Sure, that's fine" said Jack.

Jack stood at the plan that Sam had drawn out for the formal gardens, when he heard a few familiar voices. He turned around to see the two of them, Sara pushing Sam over to him. Jack said "Isn't it bad luck to see the bride on the day of the wedding?"

"No, not in our case, both of us already feel like were married to you" said Sara.

"What do you think?" asked Sam.

"It looks good, I like it", said Jack.

A car pulls up and parks, a stunning long haired blonde girl gets out and Sara shrieks and runs over, the two embrace. Arm in arm they walk up to Jack, Sara said" This is my friend Tabby, from Iowa, isn't she lovely?"

"Yes, indeed she is" said Jack, seeing her bend down to introduce herself to the bride.

Jack leaves to see all the progress on the rest of the house in the last hour, especially the main frame. Jack sees the precision and accuracy on which the team worked. Jack went into the other building, where the workers were, it was quite nice, well built, gorgeous views of the city. He walked down to the end bunks, to see a door, he went through it to a fenced outer perimeter line, to hear. "We're going to finish with a six foot wall, tying in this building to the garage, so your little ones won't decide to fall off the cliff." Jack looked over the four foot fence easily and said, "Yeah it's a bit of a drop."

"Yes it is, have you had some time to think about the pasture on the west side of the property?"

"Like what?" asks Jack, looking at Rob, he looked at him and said, "I don't know, not really, that's up to Sam, I'm just looking around."

"Fair enough, anything . . . ." Rob started to say.

Jack walked off, away from Rob and back into his garage and into the mobile home. Morning turned into noon, then late afternoon, it was now time for the wedding.

All the invited guests were taking their seats. Jack in his Tux and positioned, off to the right, the music started up, a single pianist playing a few recognizable songs. Security was tight, provided by Spy club and the secret service, an agent was close to Jack, he made himself known as Sam's new bodyguard, his name is JJ, or Joe Javier. Off to Jack's right was Mark Reynolds and Mike Adams, Sam's side was empty, then you could hear a commotion off to the east. Going to the west, as rain began to fall, right on time. The rain was increasing, drowning out the sound of the piano, as it pelted the huge tent. To Jack's left the construction crews had heavily tarped the openings and made sure everything was secure.

The rain died down and the music started a rendition of "Here comes the bride". All stood as the bride rolled in, Jack saw her, she was dressed in all white, with a veil, it was Sara that walked with her. Sara actually pushed Sam, as she held onto a bouquet of fresh roses.

The music stopped, as Sam was wheeled up a ramp to Jack, who took a seat on a chair alongside of Sam. They faced an equally seated Pastor Wayne who began, "Dearly beloved, invited guests and associates, we are gathered here on this wet and wonderful day, to witness the bond of two lovely people." "We have our man Jack, the tireless civil servant, who puts his life on the line every day for those that need him the most and of his love, Samantha, who carries their son, let us all pray." "We ask of you lord, to look after their union and make it one that will last forever, either here in the mortal, or in the future years in the spirit." "We ask that you be the beacon of light to guide, direct and inspire both of them while they're on this journey, we ask in your name, Amen."

"Amen", said Jack, holding Sam's hand and looking into her eyes.

"Now I usually read a scripture here, but I've been asked to withhold it." "So that the bride can make a statement."

Sam turned in her wheel chair and said, "Let me begin by acknowledging my friends, Sara and Jack, why just the two of them, because everyone else had abandoned me, including my mother." "She was the one who imprisoned me in my room, I had no one around to help me, finally after I begged my mother for a wheelchair, she gave me a cheap old one, it was clumsily to move." "My disability checks I did get, she spent on herself." "Instantly Glenda lost her smile, to feel handcuffs, as police stood by her as Sam continued to proclaim the abuse and torture. "This is why I'm getting married, to my protector, so take away my mother, she's a bitch."

Sam's request was fulfilled, as her mother was skirted off to a black SUV and into the back seat. She sat to see Lisa turn around and say, "So you're the famous Glenda, you know when I first heard of the abuse Sam went through, I was ready then to take you in."

Glenda looked at Lisa in defiance and said, "On what grounds?"

Lisa responds, "Well really I don't need one, I would be doing a favor to Jack."

"Jack, that drug dealer." said Glenda.

"Where did that come from, you think the man that is marrying your daughter is a drug dealer?" asked Lisa.

"Yes, he offered me cold hard cash, who does that, especially here in Mobile and in the area of the docks." "Look at him, he is always dirty, no rich man would be down here."

"Well you got a point about that, however; he is a working man and no, he isn't a drug dealer." "He is what you call an operator, he goes in and extracts people who are held by a captor and he frees them. If anything, I'd call him a humanitarian."

Glenda looked at Lisa, she saw her badge that flashed out, then the radio said, "The FBI will be there in two minutes for a pick-up, as requested" Lisa said, "That's right you're going away for a while, till either Jack or Samantha has you released."

"Wait, why, I did what any parent would do", said a somber Glenda.

"No, not any parent, you're a parent that doesn't even care and for your information, Jack is a federal and international special agent." "You're lucky, if he wanted, you'd be dead now, so count your blessings.", Lisa stepped out, to hear, Sam had continued to explain the abuse and then how Jack had noticed her. "Yes I know he is twice my age, but he had shown me attention, where I had none." "The countless days of being ignored, shunned and accused of causing the accident, do you think I like being confined to this chair, to now, where this man and this woman, Sara, have taken me in and made me feel loved." "For this I honor them on my day." Sam looks over to the pastor, who was looking at his watch, and said, "In closing, I just want to say, I love you both."

"Now who has the ring?" said the pastor. Jack presents it to her, and slips it on, the Pastor said, "With the powers vested in me, I now pronounce you Mister and Misses Jack and Samantha Cash, so kiss each other." They embrace as Sam says, "Here you go my man, she slides his ring on his left ring finger and said," I love you Jack Cash, my hero, protector and provider."

Jack swooped her up, as she wrapped her arms around his neck and he carried her slowly to the music, down the aisle, down the steps, through the light rain, to the garage, where the reception started up. On the left was the head table, in front of the mobile home, which had a white tarp over it and a banner that read, "Congratulations Mister and Misses Jack and Samantha Cash, best wishes."

Another piano played as all the guests filed in for celebration and food catered by the hospital's buffet line. Jack showed Sam all the choices, she was tired as she whispered, "I'm tired, can you put me down?"

Jack nodded, as he pushed her around to the back of the mobile home. They see a guard who opened the door for them, they went in to the bedroom and he laid her down. Then he gave her an energy pill, with some water. She closed her eyes and was fast asleep.

Sara had Tabby on her hip as she said, "Whatever Jack says or does, I know I am on board."

"Why don't you try it, you know on a trial run?"

"Really he'd do that?" asked Tabby.

"The attraction's there, isn't it?"

"Yes, but I don't know about all these wives things", let alone have sex with an older man."

"All you have to do is sign up, you don't even know him, but once I ask, he will go for it." "But listen Tabby, Jack isn't like any other guy, he is much older, even for me, at first I was unsure, but now more than ever, I know, deep in my heart, it was meant to be." "To be with this man and to have as many children as he wants, at first, I was devastated, then relieved, then worried, then with the realization came a price, and that was what really love is like." "Look what it did for Sam, her whole being has changed, and so could yours." said Sara.

"I don't know, really, maybe, it would be nice to have a protector and waiting for the right time, that will never come?"

Sara embraced her friend and said," Besides if I can get you with us, well then, we will see." "You're going to stay at my old apartment, Jack and I will stay either on his boat or here at the house when it gets finished, but I really like the dock."

"Who is that? Asked Tabby.

"Oh, that is Jack's secret mistress, Miss Debbie, I know Jack goes and sees her at almost every lunch hour, she is at the hospital, he just loves that hospital buffet line." "I guess she strips and he watches, something like that, she too has the offer on the table, as she points out Kate and adds, "So does my sister, who had an immediate crush on him." But because of the rift, her and I had Jack has stay away from her, and rightly so, she is a bitch". She continues by saying, "I pretty much just let Jack do as he pleases and see who he pleases but in the end at night he is with me." "Oh I almost forgot to tell you, I'm just heartbroken over the fact that he spent eighteen years in prison for something he didn't even do and now you know what his motives are for and why he is the person he is today." said Sara.

"Look at you you're getting bigger" said Tabby, looking at Sara's stomach.

"Yes, I too am pregnant, with a girl, tentative names we have selected are; Chelsea, Naomi and Sophia, Jack says that last name is somewhat familiar with him." "Also, I've arranged for Jack to see someone who is a new Psychologist, who is a friend of my dad's partner from St Louis". said Sara. "I mention to my Dad that Jack was having some issues and he asked her to come visit a bit, so she is staying with my Dad and Mom, we're going to see her later."

"Sara who are you talking to?" said Jack looking at her.

"Just a friend" she said looking around seeing Tabby was at the buffet line. Jack said, "You better stock up, I know I will."

Daphne was present, alongside of Joe, as Sam made her entrance after a nap. She was now dressed in a tighter version of her wedding dress, she was able to move in her chair better. She wheeled next to Jack, where a sampler plate was set up for her by the hostess. Jack's liaison officer made her presence known, as she came to the front of the table and said, "From this this day forward here are two credit cards with your name on them, the blue one is a per diem card, it has about 500 dollars renewed every day and the other is a savings/checking debit card to make purchases." "And finally, each year a check in this amount or greater will be presented to you." "The amount is usually around 120,000 dollars." Sam had tears flowing from her eyes. Daphne continued, "This is all tax free and with this, the title of Mrs. Samantha Cash, you'll have a special bodyguard to assist you and watch over you and be your driver." as her phone rang, she answered it, then handed it to Sam who took it and said, "This is Samantha Cash,"

"Hi, this is the President of the United States, George White, I want to be the first to congratulate you on this very special day, I have a very special present for Jack and you at the airport, Daphne will drive you, oh I mean, you Have Joe there now for you, hope you have fun, bye." "Sam hands the phone back to Daphne and said,

"Thank you, as she hands the check to Jack, who looks at it, then folds it up. He motions for Mike to come up to him, he stops eating and makes a bee line to Jack. Jack hands him the check and said, "Cash that out for her, and do you have mine?"

Mike pulls out twenty five one thousand dollar bills and hands them to Jack. Jack sways them back and forth and said, "What do I do with these?", I need them broken down to hundreds, please."

Sam grabs them from Jack and said, "I'd like them, is that a gift or a down payment . . . for something?"

"Nah, it's just cash."

"You mean Jack Cash," said Lisa behind him with a briefcase, and said, "This isn't yours, Jack it's hers", and sees Sam turn to see Lisa. Lisa sets the case on Sam's lap, and bends in to whisper, "This is a secret between you and I, but don't tell the others, open it up, then I will take the case, that is your gift from the President." "I wanted you to see it, as Jack was on one side and Ramon was shielding on the other. Sam opens it up and sees what looks like a million dollars, the sign read. She closed the case and hears, "That amount is loaded on your credit card, so enjoy that, as you see fit." Tears were still flowing, as Lisa hands Jack the case and said, "We have four more in the van, what do you want us to do with them?"

"Have Mike secure them, please." said Jack.

They broke up their meeting, as Sara was helping Sam out with her make up, it was running and messy. They returned to the meal. Next up was the dancing and the celebration. It just kept on coming, then was the cutting of the cake. It was the replica of the Aircraft carrier the Nimitz, from its detail to the crew, it was a picture, placed on a huge flat cake. It was marble style with chocolate and vanilla pudding in the middle and a butter cream frosting. On the ends were the roses, that Sam loved so much, especially red, which there were in seven clusters, her favorite number. They were cut off, at the ends, so all four pieces went to the head table and then divided among their guests.

Jack wheeled Sam out to the dance floor and over to the cake. He cut a piece for Sam and then one for himself, each fed the other so slow and sensual, it was steaming it up.

Next was the garter toss, Jack bent down, slowly reached up, it was high, then pulled it down, and off. He stood up and twirled the garter around on his finger, as Sam was reaching for it, he handed it to Sam. The D J began the count off, 3 2 1 and she threw it off to the side and Sara caught it, over Tabby's head, who was stepping up her game, and said, "I'm next, let me have it."

"Girls enough already, there is plenty of me to go around." said Jack, who went in for a group hug and said, "So we have a plane, do you want to go to help out?"

"I don't know, if Sam wants me to?" said Sara.

"Can I come?" asked Tabby.

Jack looks her over, to see that she was built for sex, but sure seemed naïve. Then Jack backed away from her. He saw a lot of Alba in her, and told Sam he just wasn't much into Tabby.

Sam was excited and said "Yes, Jack, I want Sara to come with us, and if she wants to bring her friend, I don't see why not, when were busy, Sara will have someone to do things with."

Jack nods his head, and said, "Shall we dance the night away?"

"Yes, big handsome man pick me up and carry me to the dance floor."

CH 12

The Virgin . . . . Islands!

The next morning was the same as the last, the consummation ritual lasted the whole week, as they camped out in that mobile home and mostly by themselves. Jack missed the meeting of the mob in Montgomery on Monday, but got the report that he was their number one target.

Sara kept her distance, JJ the handler for Sam, took a position outside in a shack made up by the construction people. The construction was going at a fervor pace, the crane was in use every day. The main house was being completed, meanwhile, on that particular day, a long tube was delivered, picked up by the crane, swung around, and set into its position behind the garage, lengthwise into the ground. Workers used a skidster to deposit earth and dirt, rocks around the semi formed hole, while Jack watched from the window looking out of the mobile home. Initially it was dug out from the natural water runoff, that formed a natural hole in the ground, inside the cliff. After the cylinder went in the hole, it was set in place with two by fours and secured. People worked to fill in around the cylinder, all the way up to the top, using water to settle the earth. They used a stamper, to make a flat solid level. Next they connected the drain lines, from the garage and the main and secondary houses, lastly, the ground surface of the compound, was swept in the landscape to divert the surface water so that it would flow to a collection box, then a layer of concrete was poured in and around the cylinder. Next up was the stonewall, six foot tall, from the secondary building around the water cistern, to behind the garage and that was done. Everyone left, Jack and Samantha were alone now.

Jack was on his phone. He reached Jim who said, "Yes, how may we help you?"

"Lisa said something about flying can you help me with that?"

"Yes, I have you a plane that is all for you and where do you want to fly?" asked Jim.

"I talked with my wife, and she wants to go to the Virgin Islands, is that possible?"

"Yes, when do you want to leave?" said Jim.

"Can we go today, is that too late of notice?" said Jack.

"No, there is never too late a notice, have JJ drive you here and off we will go."

"Thank you, I'll do that." said Jack enthusiastically.

"One more thing, Jack, will Sam need a doctor?", asked Jim respectfully.

"I don't follow, why?"

"Well in case she needs special help?"

"I don't know, what will it cost me?" asked Jack.

"Nothing, they're at your disposal." said Jim.

"Sure, alright, we will see you soon." said Jack.

Jim slides his phone shut and announces "Folks we're on, the spy is coming to us, were finally on the move." Brian stood behind the secure door from his armory box. Brian said, "Who is all going?"

"Well you and me?"

"What about Mark, Mike , Mitzi and Trixie?" asked Brian.

"I have no idea?" said Jim, scratching his head, as he placed a call to Lisa, who answered, and said, "Yes, Jim what is it?"

"Jack is ready to fly out?"

"Fine, where to?"

"Virgin Islands."

"British or American?"

Jim pauses, then says, "I don't really know."

"Well that is what we're paying you for, here is what you need to do. First call Mitzi, then talk with Trixie, state what he wants to do, they will handle the rest, but for now, I'll activate ground support on the US side, and Trixie will tell you where to land, the more information you know the more we will know to support him, remember, like when you were the spy, ask questions and be firm with Jack."

"Should I call him back?" asked Jim.

"I don't know, if I were you, I'd call Mitzi, she is his ground support person." said Lisa.

"Then I should call Trixie" said Jim.

"That's a start, just keep our boy safe."

"Yes, Ma'am." the line went dead as Jim was already dialing up Mitzi, who answered enthusiastically. Jim said, "Is now not the right time to call you?"

"No, I was just getting in some exercise, Olympic style." said Mitzi.

"Is that what they call that now a days."

"For young girls they do, what do you need?"

"Jack is on the move, he wants to go to Virgin Islands."

"I already know, what do you need?" asked Mitzi.

"What, wait, how did you know?" asked a surprised Jim.

"Well what Jack doesn't know is that all outgoing calls he places, go directly to my line, I will screen them, monitor them, record if necessary, then I check it off, it went directly to you and I heard all that was said. "Trixie and I are already, charting his destination and flight plans, and then I was just about to call you when you called me."

"Alright, who is all going?"

"Whomever wants to go, who do you have in mind?"

"Well, there is Debby, and Brian, what of Mike and Mark.?"

"There none of your business Jim, Mike is on assignment and Mark is close by Jack, both, if needed, will find their way down there, all I want from you is to fly the plane and take care of ground support." said Mitzi.

"Will do." said Jim, he slid the phone shut, looking over the brand new Mercedes, shiny silver, Brian helped him with the tarp to place over it and then the two secured it down. Jim looks up to see two very attractive girls on the ramp, as one says, "May we come aboard Captain?"

"Yes, you may", said Jim. The Chinese looking girl was short small and compact, while the other one was tall, who said, "I'm Magdalena, and this is Michelle, were with the SIT team, how may we help you?"

"Can you go to the galley and set it up?"

I'll do that", spoke a commanding voice, for them to see it was Mitzi, the brunette, and with her was the blonde, Trixie, who said, "Stow your gear, you'll both be bodyguards." "We're waiting for Devlin and Daphne to get here, Jack is in route as we speak, so let's get going, Mitz's you're in the Galley, I'll be at the flight controls."

A black SUV pulled up, Jack was out, at the back another agent popped out, with the wheelchair in hand, expanded it. Jack was pulling Sam out of the back seat. Jack carefully placed her down, and pushed her as two men stood by at the ramp. In one motion, each man took a side of the wheelchair and hoisted it up and carried Sam up the ramp and then set her chair down on the floor. The ramp went up as they went with Jack to his custom room, Michelle held the door open, as Jack went in. Jack then lifted Sam up, and carried her over the high threshold, into his room and over to the giant bed, he laid her down on the pillows to hear, "On your right is, drawers with all of your stuff, her stuff is on the far right in that stand up closet, on the left is refrigerated cabinets filled with all types of beverages, on the very far left is the bathroom." "I will tell you this, this structure is waterproof and can float in case the plane crashes over the ocean." "In addition, there is enough rations in here to last you one year, this unit is self-contained, all the water and wastes are recycled any questions?" asked Mitzi, then adds, "If you need some hot food, I'm just a call away."

Jack just looks at her and nods, and said, "So what you're saying, this is my room?"

"Well yes, this whole plane is yours, and everyone on board." they both saw Samantha was fast asleep, Mitzi went over to the cabinet and pulled out a blanket, then spread it over her, as Jack watched. Mitzi said, "Do you want to talk?"

"Sure, what do you have?" said Jack sitting down next to Mitzi as she began, "As you already know, from your last adventure, we're all here to support you, from time to time, you'll add people and you'll subtract people, It's all up to you." she then paused and said, "Jim was a former agent who knows a thing or two about what you should do, but realistically, it is all up to you on what you do and how you do it." "Now and then the President of our United States may request that you do something for him, which you will have to do, but you'll do it your way." "No one will tell you what to do, or how to do it, or how to use your support team."

Jack just looked at her as she continued, "Everything is for you, about you and it's our mission to try to keep you safe and this plane is for you to do as you see fit, any questions?"

"What about this honeymoon, is it a mission or just a trip?"

"It depends on you, everywhere you go, you find trouble, so if you find the trouble, well then we will be here to support you and if not, then it will be a peaceful stay."

"You mention something about a hot meal, does this flight serve food?"

"Indeed, but just for you, and of course, your newest wife."

"Newest wife, I have others?" questioned Jack.

"Yes, three to be exact."

"So that wasn't a dream?" Jack said.

"No, it was very real" she said. Jim announced the last two passengers were on the plane and they were cleared for takeoff, then said, "The flight time is three hours so sit back and relax." Mitzi gets up and said, "You should try to get some rest, we will talk more, bye."

Jack hopped on the bed and moved in closer to his wife, closed his eyes and fell fast asleep.

A radio signal was reached by Jim as he steered the small cargo plane to an island south of St Thomas, he came in low and landed on a make shift field, he came to a bumpy landing. The plane taxied and went into the side of a large hill, as the hanger door opened, he went in, the door closed. Jim turned the plane around and parked. Rick and Paul were first out, securing the plane, followed by the SIT"s team. The first person they saw was a tall European gentleman, Mitzi was there to meet him and said, "Hi my name is Mitzi, we will stay here on the plane, our agent is the guest."

"Non-sense, My name is Ferdinand, I insist everyone come stay, take a room and relax, I'll have the plane under wraps, besides the 7th fleet has just pulled into Puerto Rico, so the terrorism should be at an all-time low, who can I say is our guest of honor?"

"His name is Jack Cash, International Bounty Hunter." exclaimed Mitzi.

"Really, is it the same guy, who did all that damage up in Cuba?"

"One in the same."

"Wow a bonafide bad guy, but no I mean he has quite a reputation down here, all right I will keep his secret safe with me, can I show you to your rooms now?" asked Ferdinand.

"Sure, lead the way." said Mitzi.

Everyone exited the aircraft except Jack and Samantha who were left alone. Daphne and Devlin were given a room and then the pairing began, everyone had a room and a full banquet service. Each support agent was living it up, they all hit the beach, the women wearing bikinis and the men in long swim shorts. Some of the older women wore a one piece and played in the shallow waters. They heard and saw a boat coming closer to them. A guy that looked tough, who had large muscles ran the boat, as the two SIT's girls hopped in from a swim and heard "Where too? There is a cove, up around the bend, wanna go?"

"Sure, why not", said Michelle. The boat steamed off.

Mitzi and Trixie were swimming with Jim and Brian. Debby was the only one concerned about Jack. She watched them have fun, then decided to go back to the plane to see what Jack and Samantha was up to. Her phone rang, she looked at the number, it read "Restricted", she decided to answer it and said, "Yes, who is this?" cautiously.

"It's Lisa, are you guys having a party down there or what, I've trying to get a hold of my two SIT girls, are they around?" Debby goes to her window, looks out and said, "No, I think they went scuba diving."

"What about Jack, he too isn't answering?" asked Lisa.

"Well I can check on him". said Debby, watching everyone have fun, and said, "Listen I'll call you back later." she hung up on Lisa to go back to the plane. Inside the hangar was quiet, she made it to the plane, undid the latch and went inside. It was dark, she made it to Jack's room and tried the arm on the wheel, with some force it broke free, she wheeled it around and opened it up. She stepped inside and said, "Jack it's Debby, she saw nothing moving and went to the bed, pulled the cover back and saw the two were sound asleep. Debby began to stir up Jack by pulling him towards her, he awoke and went for her breasts, she took the brunt of his advances and held his weight as he came too. Then he said, "I must have been dreaming, sorry."

"That's alright, I kind of liked it, Lisa's calling you, she says, "You're not picking up."

Instantly Debby froze as another voice spoke from behind her, "Get away from him, Brother how are you," said Carlos, gun out and pointing it at Jack and said, "You don't call, you don't write, I'm beginning to get worried you never answer your phone."

"It is true, I don't, and why, because you're a ruthless killer" as he puts Debby behind him and steps closer to him. The two embrace and have a laugh. Then they both step out and Jack closes the door, Carlos said, "There is a hit out on you, ordered by a one Doctor Lester Graham of Brussels Belgium, the price is ten million dollars, you can come with me and stay in Cuba, look how easy it was for me to get in here, you have no security."

"It doesn't matter, so they come and I get killed, who cares?" said Jack.

"I do" said a voice behind them, a woman stepped out of the shadows. It was Devlin, gun out and at the ready, seriousness was written all over her face. Then she adds, "I know why your here Carlos, rest assured Jack is in good hands, there is two of us on duty, step out Daphne", she showed herself, gun out and ready as well.

"Alright, you have been warned, I gotta get back tonight anyway, looks like you are in good hands" Carlos slipped away, the girls put away their guns and Devlin said, "Are you packing, partner?"

"Nah, I was resting."

"Jack you can't be doing this, being unarmed, especially now that we're out of the country. Devlin moved in for an embrace, but Jack put up his hand, he held her back and said, "Don't worry about Carlos, he is my brother and he is just looking out for my best interests." Jack went back in and picked up Sam, carried her out past Devlin. Jack took her out of the plane, and outside, and carried her to the room assigned to them, Daphne was ahead of him pushing Sam's wheelchair the whole way. They arrived in the master suite where Jack placed her into the wheelchair and let her sit. Her level of weakness was evident now, even eating was a chore. Devlin and Daphne were Jack's helpers, they were doing most of the work. Devlin was keeping her distance as it was evident Jack wasn't having her advances.

Daphne volunteered to stay with Sam so that Jack could get out and relax. After a bath was drawn by Daphne, Jack carried the nude Sam into the master bathroom and set her down in the tub. She smiled as Jack was kneeling down, soaping up her body. Daphne was at the water controls and said, "How is that? Too hot, do we need a bit cooler?"

Jack looks at her, and said, "I think it's fine, you can go if you want to?"

"I can stay and help if you don't mind?" she said with a smile.

He smiles and says, "Only if your naked too?"

"Wait, how does that help?" she said walking towards him, the sexual tension was building when Jack said, "Well that is what Sara and I do, she is usually is in the tub, to help stabilize her and I work the front and she has her back."

"Well, alright I guess" said Daphne, beginning to undress. She started undoing her blouse, she allowed that to fall off to expose her bra, which she undid and pulled that off, next was her pants, un done and she wiggled out of it, to finally what was left was her panties, for which she said, "These too?"

"It's up to you, they will get wet."

"I know silly, oh what the", and dropped them, to expose a solid patch of black hairs Jack said, "I never knew."

"Yeah me neither, oh, I see what you're talking about, yeah, so I let it go, where to you want me?"

"Come here, get behind her and slide down, she sometimes tips over." said Jack, helping Daphne up, by holding her hand and then into the tub, she slid down on the outside of Sam. Jack gave her the soap, and said, "I did her front, can you get her back, while I'll hold her."

Daphne helped out, as Jack had a firm grip on his wife. With the bath over, Jack used a hose to rinse Sam off, while Daphne held her up. Once finished Jack took Sam from Daphne, he hoisted her up, he paused to get a second look at Daphne who said, "I knew there would have been a way for you to get me naked."

"I was just admiring the view" said Jack, as he went over to the bed, where two towels were waiting, he then dried her off. Daphne stood naked and said, "Jack I will change her bag if you like?"

"What happen to being modest?"

"Why bother, really, it doesn't matter to me, you've seen it all and besides, it was for a greater cause other than yourself, so I commend you on that." said Daphne who was proud of Jack, as she removed the bag and went to clean it out. Daphne was back, after she flushed it, Jack had Sam dressed.

Jack shrugs his shoulder and said, "It was up to you, all I know is how we did this in our house."

"I was just kidding with you, besides your reputation was that you like to see girls naked so I was already prepared for that."

"Are you all done talking, let's see some work from you" he said, in an annoying way.

"Yes sir."

Jack had her in sleepwear, Daphne put the bag back on.

Jack picked up Sam, as Daphne had the covers back and Jack laid her down, then covered her up, the room was a cool 68 degrees. Daphne said, "Why don't you go outside and enjoy the weather, sand and fun, I'll stay here with her."

Jack looked her up and down, and said, "Alright, don't you need help now" said Jack, seeing Daphne was ever so much more confident being naked that she said, "I need to finish my bath, care to help me out?"

"Nah, It's tempting, but I'm not going to do it in front of my wife."

She was motioning for him to come to her playfully, as she went back in the tub, sat down and finished bathing, and said, "I'd like a hand up, can you do that?"

"Sure', said Jack ready to lend a hand, as she popped the cork, the water was going down fast, she turned on the water, adjusted it and began to rinse off, she said, "Thank you Jack for being such a gentleman, you can leave now."

Jack went into the other room, undressed and slipped into some swimming shorts and flip-flops. He turned to see Daphne was drying off, until she closed the door. He grabbed his sunglasses and went out, the sun was fading with the afternoon, Mitzi and Trixie were playing with a ball, Brian and Jim were on the jet skis. Jack took in a deep breath, then sat down in the fading sun, a gentle breeze blew, his team was having fun. Across over to the main island, ships were convening, loads of sailors were all about. Off to his right, six people were starting to play volleyball on the other beach, over on the next closest island. From a distance it looked like three girls to three guys as one said to the other, "Do you think he knows, were watching him."

"If only I had a rifle" said another.

"Shut up, you and what Army," said the smart and intelligent one.

"Just because you like him doesn't mean I won't kill him, he is a bounty hunter, and as you know we kill them, or had you forgotten. Danica, which is better, working for the CIG or the WTN?"

"Well the WTN, they pay more and allow us to do what we want, so if I wanna get naked and go for a swim, I will."

Another girl came closer and said, "I bet he doesn't know we even exist?"

"Why should he, look at who he surrounds himself with, said another.

"If it were that easy, I'd join him in a heartbeat", said the stunning Latin American beauty, named Alexandra.

"Shall we do this or what?" said Danica, ready to shred her bikini top, when all of a sudden a power boat came into view, did a left turn in front of them and then the wave took out all three. Infuriated, they began to scream at the well buffed driver, he stopped and beached it, the two SIT girls looked over at the competition, who wasn't happy. Magdalena said, "You wanna go over there and kick their asses?"

"Nah, there not much of a challenge, let's see what Jack is up too" said Michelle.

They both jumped onto the beach and up to Jack who was getting some sun, but not enough as the two blocked his view. "Do you mind, your blocking the view" said Jack, admiring the tall Latin American looking girl, who was now nude in the knee deep water heading his way, followed by two equally hot girls, both nude as well. Seeing that, the two SIT girls stormed off.

The three reached Jack to form a semi-circle around him and said, "Mister, do you mind joining us for a game of volleyball, over on our beach?"

Jack looked up to see that they all three had a lot to offer. and said, "Just me or do you any one else?"

"Nah, we prefer you, if that's alright with you?"

"Sure, I don't mind" said Jack, getting up and following them to the inlet channel, where they all put their swimsuits back on. Jack said "You don't have to do that on my behalf, I like you the way you are."

The three girls just smiled, as they walked ahead of him.

Both Mitzi and Trixie stopped playing with the ball, to see Jack going over there, then went back to do what they were doing. Jack kept pace with them to the other side and over to the volleyball court. Up on the deck by the house was the three guys, who waved back at him, they scrambled.

"Now, I get this guy, what's your name?" asked Danica.

"Name is Jack, and your is?"

I'm Danica, the blonde is Felicia and the one your staring at is Alexandra."

"Yes indeed, when do I get to be on her team?"

"Whomever wins can choose" she said, as they paired off long enough to see two boys come down to enjoy in the festivities. Danica said, "Jack, this is Louis Carter and the nuisance one is Bradley," who had some evil looking eyes for Felicia and said," Where's Chester?"

"Oh he went to the store to get some ground beef and hot dogs."

"Jack do you wanna stay and have dinner with us?" asked Danica, as Alexandra moved closer and said, "Now, I'm on Jack's team, so will you stay for dinner, and whispers in his ear.

"If you stay, I'll give you whatever you want." said Alexandra.

Jack looks them over, and said, "Yeah, why not."

They all cheered, as the games went on for some time, then Jack was feeling sun burnt, rubs his neck and said, "I should go, I feel sun burnt." Danica said "How about we go inside, I have some cool cream just for that."

Jack agrees, and follows her up to the house, his team watches him go into the woods, Jack is behind her as she made her way up the stairs, into the house. She saw a friend and said, "Do you have enough there for my friend?"

"Sure, will he be spending the night?"

"That depends on him?" Jack looks at the guy with the sinister look, who sneered at Jack. Jack followed in through the door, through the living room and into her room.

Jack is looking around, he sees her motion for him to come to her, he obliges, and hears, "Come in and have a seat on the end of the bed, I'll get some crème."

Jack enters the rather small room with a huge bed, a dresser door and knick knacks all over the place. Jack thinks it's a girly girl room and takes a seat, she comes back in and said, "Here it is, relax, it will be cool at first then it will heat up." she was on the bed and knelt down behind him and squeezed the tube and rubbed it in her hands and then abruptly applied it to his upper back and shoulders and said, "What fine and strong shoulders you have." as she popped off her bikini top, to allow her assets a chance to find Jack's back. He said "That's different, do you have a helper?"

"Absolutely, did you think I was going to pass up this opportunity, as she pressed her chest to his back, and began to kiss his neck. She was working her way around Jack's side, to show him what she was working with, allowing him the opportunity to touch them, as she moved in such a way, she was in front of him, grinding into him. With her arms wrapped around him, her mouth to his and his hands on her breasts. Jack was at the ready, he was getting excited, enough so, she pushed him back, she was on top of him, as she was on fire, she was grinding him, he was playing with her breasts, while she was kissing him. Passion led to sweat and the friction was better, as she turned around and was pulling his shorts off. She had her clitoris in his face to enjoy and she was enjoying his manhood, which was now fully erect. She paused and said, "That is the biggest I've ever seen", she went down, gagging each time down. She was flowing good, it was wave after wave of emotion as she screamed out, she was in ecstasy. She turned back around and she mounted him, and she was grinding on him, screaming out, enough to draw attention. Next in the room was Alexandra, she was shredding her bikini to get on the bed, she lowered her clitoris, right on Jack's already wet mouth and the two girls were kissing each other, at the door was Felicia, who said "Wait for me I want some of that", she too shred her bikini. Size wise she was the smallest in all features and body, she was at Jack's feet, when she mounted a foot, with her clitoris, and began to work it. Jack was in ecstasy himself, as he knew it had been awhile, as Danica fell off, from sheer exhaustion, it was Felicia taking her place, as she worked her way up to see that huge thing. She tried first with her mouth, then both of her hands, finally, she tried to sit on it and it was just a breach, in frustration, she simply got off and said, "He is all yours, I can't do anything with that."

"You might not be able to, but I can, you can watch if you like," said Alexandra, who had moved down, but was taken off guard as Jack turned and now he was on top and in went his manhood, she was on all fours, he was ramming her, with each thrust she was moving up, she was in ecstasy, with her cries of pleasure and release.

Jack just kept on going, till Alexandra reached the dresser door and was bracing herself, till she could last no longer and collapsed to the floor. And with that, the dresser door crashed to the floor. Jack was drilling at an angle, while he held on to the cabinet, down below on the floor was the spilled contents to reveal a pistol, it was a glock. The more he went, the clearer was his thoughts, the more he worked, he was doing some damage on her and she just took it, exhausted, she passed out. He dumped his load into her. Jack pulled out, wiped off, found his shorts and flip flops, then bent down, picked up the glock and went to the door. He looked back at the carnage he created and stepped out into the hallway, he saw Felicia in a room nearby and that she had showered and was nude. She shrieked and dropped the towel and screamed, "Get that thing away from me, help."

Instantly Chester jumped Jack and was punching him. Jack used the glock and struck Chester's head, he went down, he was out. Then Jack heard "Chester, are you alright?", Felicia ran to his aid. Jack now held the gun, at her temple and said, "Look you got your boyfriend killed, Shut up."

She was on her knees crying and at Chester. Jack went room to room, he saw a briefcase, then in another room, one more and finally, one more. He heard voices and then an alarm went off in his mind and he went looking for the nearest window, he slid one open and he tossed out the cases, then himself onto a deck. With a hurl of each, he launched the cases, looked at them land and twirl off into the trees. He was contemplating jumping or going back in, he knew the way. He leapt down to, and went back in, the voices were louder, it was Louis Carter's voice who said, "Chester is dead, he killed Chester, you crazy bitch and then Jack heard a thud. Bradley started screaming himself, till gun shots rang out and the screaming stopped, people were running and so was Jack. With the gun out, getting to Chester, Felicia, was lying on him, bleeding from the head. It was quiet then Jack heard, "Where are you at, fuckers, the next one who tries to screw me will be dead. Jack looked into the room to see Alexandra was still upside down, legs spread. Jack was on the move, he slowed, to see in a room, three more cases. He went in, opened the window and used the first case. He sent the case out, as it took the screen with it and then the next two had no resistance. Jack was at the window to see Danica firing her pistol at the two boys, who were running from the house. He began to laugh and walked out into the living room and over to the grill, he opened it up and saw it was charred, he turned off the heat, took a hot dog and bit off a piece. He said, "Ooh hot, that burned my tongue, but it sure is tasty." Jack stood on the deck, consumed the dog and three more, as they cooled quickly. Out in the woods, two more shots went off, but they were way off. Jack closed the grill, walked down the steps to see that the Calvary had arrived. First on the beach was the boat with Willy, they said his name. then Rick and Paul had landed and were off and running towards Jack. Jack said "It's over, can you help me with these cases?" Jack picked up each one and handed them to Rick first and said "I have three more on the back side." Jack saw the SIT girls, Jack said, "Check the house, there is two dead and one severely injured and three running around in the woods."

Jack carried his case to the boat along with Rick helping and said, "Willy, can you take us around."

He nodded and allowed Jack and Rick in and piloted it around. One case was floating, Rick retrieved it and then saw Paul had the other two.

Michelle and Magdalena hit the house running, with guns drawn, room by room searching, they discovered some documents that Magdalena was collecting. While upstairs they came across the two dead people, the smell of urine and shit were evident. Michelle saw Alexandra first and said "Wow, what happened to her?"

Magdalena entered the room with her and said, "Is she dead as well?" she quickly took a pulse and said, "I got one, but barely, help me with her legs", said Magdalena to Michelle, as they both looked at the gap between her legs. Michelle said, "do you think, what I'm thinking?"

"If it is, I want no part of him?"

"Neither do I" said Michelle, as she was on one side. Together they closed Alexandra's legs and rolled her off of her head, for her to rest, Alexandra's eyes were glazed over. Magdalena said "That was some way to go, constrict the airway while he pounded her out, Wow, come on let's get out of here."

Jack was on the other side of the beach with Rick and Paul helping him out, it was Mitzi that made a call to the cleanup crew. Just like that, a helicopter landed and that little island was swarmed with all agencies. Clearly, there was one person who was in charge, he barked out orders with authority and kept saying, "Where is Jack Cash?"

Jack and his team helped him carry the cases to his cabana. Magdalena and Michelle both looked at him, then down at his crotch and said, "Here are some documents we discovered, then they both left, staring back at him. Just as the loud man had entered the room, all eyes were on him, as if they were all doing something wrong. Jack looked up at him and said, "Hello."

"Hi Jack, I'm Hans and this is my partner Jayden, stepping from behind him. She was a beauty, a blonde smart looking woman, who said, "Hi" waved and fell back into place. They heard Hans say, "Mister Cash, can we have a moment to talk in private?"

"Yeah, sure, everyone out" said Jack lining up the cases.

Hans said, "The UN has sent me to protect you and your interests, everything seized at that kill zone is yours to keep as you see fit, but allow us to open it first, in regards to those cases, as you can see, their written in German.

Hans moves in closer to the cases and said, "If there is any evidence that relates to you, we will tell you immediately, otherwise we need to confiscate it and hold it for six months." Jack pulled away, he even set down the Glock he had on him, with his hands up. Hans said,

"No, no, you can put your hands down, were just here to help you."

Jack looked at Hans, then said, "Is it alright if I go shower?"

"Sure, but Jayden needs to escort you."

Jack looked at Hans, then over at the young blonde and said, "Sure, come follow me", Jack led the way to the master bedroom, while Hans and his team removed the cases and left the room.

Jack entered the master bedroom, in the bed was Samantha asleep and Daphne by her side. Jack went into the master bathroom, dropped his shorts, Jayden followed, she stood and watched. He reached in, turned on the shower, then stepped in and closed the door. The see through glass revealed everything, especially how endowed he was, causing Jayden to look away and blush. Jack said, "It helps if you're not wearing any clothes" he said staring at her, as he soaped up. Unsure what to do, she slowly backed up and out of his view, she then went to the toilet and threw up. Jack finished up, turned off the water, stepped out, dried himself, then put on a robe and cinched it up. He stepped into the sink area and saw Jayden, on the floor, looking flush. Jack reached over and flushed the toilet and said, "Nerves, yeah, it happens to all of us, is this your first assignment?"

She nodded her head in acknowledgement, as she went back at it, Jack knelt and held her hair back and said, "Looks like you got some in your hair, maybe you should get in the shower."

She looked up at him as he flushed it again, she nodded her head but the glaze over look in her eyes meant she needed help. It was something Jack wasn't willing to wait for, so he left her, went to the door, opened it, saw Daphne and he said, "She needs help in there, will you go in?"

She was up and in she went.

Jack dressed in his usual gear, realizing the fun was over and so was the honeymoon. He heard a knock on the door, Jack opened it to see Rick Teal was at guard on the outside, he allowed Hans and his people in with the six cases. Each man came in and set them down and opened them up and left past Hans and Jack. Hans said, "What you have uncovered is what we call a sleeper cell, where a terrorist organization employs a group of inexperienced people, except for this one." he hands Jack a picture and said, "This is Danica, she is the leader, along with this one, Alexandra, who had the next most experience, next was the dead one, Chester, and his girl Felicia, who were an item." "Then there were the two workers, Bradley, who sung like a canary and told us he tried to get with Danica and she shot him and lastly Louis Carter, a local, who was there supposed

Intel guy, he is the quiet one." "It would be nice to have some guy to be an interrogator, it would sure come in handy." "Michelle and Magdalena uncovered the related documents that correspond with their affiliation to a specific contact who has since been caught." According to your terms with the UN, all property confiscated is yours, it will all be cataloged and ready in six months." "As for the briefcases, well as you probably already know, their filled with money, all in US currency, each were paid a million to use as they saw fit." "Their job was to watch, report and keep an eye out for you." "Not to make contact with you or try to kill you themselves." "So something here doesn't add up, especially them coming over and making contact, totally unheard of, in the world of terrorism." "Not to mention what you were up to either, having unprotected sex with both girls, that was dangerous to your health."

"I waved my wrist watch over them." said Jack.

"And what good did that do?" asked Hans.

"It was supposed to identify poisons, like chemicals or drugs in what I eat." he said trying to convince him. Hans said, "Yes, mister Cash, I'm well aware of what that watch does, I spent yesterday morning in a class from the watch guy, he was really weird, but for sex, those are diseases I'm talking about, not a poison." "So no, it doesn't work like that." "Its purpose is to identify potential lethal combinations for your protection, like if you had ate one of their hamburgers they had rat poison in them."

"Good thing I had a dog, well, four to be exact." said Jack.

"You have to be careful, now I'm not telling you what to do, but be careful, in those cases, there is 5.7 million or so and some loose diamonds, some sex magazines and a bunch of needles what appeared to be some steroids, did you want them?"

"I'll have to ask Jim or someone what to do with them, but no, the cash, I'll put in a duffle bag, do you have one?" asked Jack.

"Of course we're a military unit, I'll have my assistant count it out. He told someone to fetch a bag, Jack said, "If it's your assistant you sent in to accompany me, I don't think so?"

"Why not, what's wrong with her now?" Hans said.

"Been having some trouble." said Jack.

"Yeah, you know, the younger the supposed better, she's just so nervous, not knowing what's right or wrong, that type of thing to do, act or say."

"She's", Jack turns to see Daphne helping her out, to the men, "It must be the nerves." said Daphne.

Hans said, "We'll take her from you," he directs two of his men to her aid, and said, "What if I say, instead of waiting six month's on that cash, you say, we forgot any of this ever happened."

"What do you mean, are you talking about the girl, sure, I don't care, but why should you concern yourself with her?" asked Jack.

"She is actually a friend's daughter and if she went back now, well she would be disgraced, as you know, when someone fails to meet expectation."

"Fine, allow her to come back to me, but I want to see a bikini or I'll make the call myself." said Jack.

A figure stepped in, that even set the UN agent back, to see it was Lisa, who said, "You have no leverage with those cases, that is his to take with him, as for your assistant, I'll take care of her, I want those waters in and around this place secure, and at least twenty miles for that matter, do you understand that, Hans?"

"Yes, Ma'am." He gracefully leaves and takes his agents, except one came in with a duffle bag in hand. All it took was a glare by Lisa and he dropped it, and left. Jack picked it up and opened it up and began to take the tied bundles and tossed them in while Lisa watched and then said, "What is your plan for the rest of the week?"

"I don't know, thought something would be going on across the way." said Jack.

"Look around, you have many agents to do that with, take your choice."

"No, that isn't the same, there is no fun if they're just going to give in and give it up so easily." said Jack.

"So what you're saying is you want a challenge." said Lisa.

"No, that isn't it either, I don't know what I want, I'm supposed to be having a honeymoon with my wife and I realize I need help and all she wants to do is sleep, it's pretty clear to me, that this is our last go around."

"Well then tell me what you want?" said Lisa.

"I don't know, I guess separate my spy life from my family life", said Jack honestly.

"I don't know, it's something you're going to have to figure out." "I can tell you this, the Navy has sent over a Cruiser, along with Virgin Island's Coast Guard." Each Commander is at the ready and this whole place will be secure, so stay as long as you like, you're still bound to get into some trouble, I guarantee that. She watched him and said, "Alright I shall leave you."

Without turning, he said, "Yeah, see ya."

The next morning was a lot different, the sun, woke up Jack and Sam, Jack helped Sam get dressed, he wheeled her into the dining room, where a banquet of food was, half sheet trays of scrambled eggs, asparagus steamed, hash browns, bacon crisp, sausage, fresh fruit and toast was optional, whereas butter and jam awaited too. Jack served Samantha, she fed herself and ate half her plate. Whereas Jack had a hearty plate, especially that of the steamed Asparagus, with butter and garlic, "Emm, Good", he thought.

After finishing the meal, Jack said, "Let's get you ready for the ocean, how bout you and I go jet skiing?"

"Sure," she said, as she looked at him, he wheeled her into the bedroom and lifted her off the chair, to the bed, where he undressed her, exposing her bra and underwear. He reached around and undid it to feel her pull him in and he said, "Remember the bus stop?"

"How could I forget it, that was the day I fell in love with you. Said Sam.

"You fell in love with me, really, in that moment, all I can really remember is the banter we were playing and you gave up so early, you need to fight for what you want." said Jack.

"I think I did fairly well for my-self." "Well I'm not complaining, kiss me." Jack obliged, as he was lifting himself off of her, as she could no longer hold him, she let go, he got up and Sam said, "What, only one kiss, you have a lot to make up for, get back over here mister."

Jack pulled a one piece out, blue in color, and took it to her, he yanked down her panties and began to pull up the swimsuit, it went on easy, not much to her complaining, she rolled up, as he helped her out and said, "Alright I'm willing and ready to go." "That protein bar you had on my plate, sure gave me a boost of energy, I'm ready to go."

Jack lifted her, and put her in her wheelchair, then rolled her out on to the boardwalk. They went to a see a sea of people who were on the outskirts, along the opposite bank. Across from them, Jack saw two jet skis, parked at the water's edge, two gorgeous girls held them in place, one a brunette and the other a tall black haired beauty. Then off to his right was Jayden, who had recovered and was in a sports bikini. Unfortunately, she was uncomfortable wearing it, it showed, and she acted that way. She just stood aside from them and was the subject of being gawked from the troops, so he parked the wheelchair, swooped Sam up, and carried her to the water's edge. Sam took one herself, Carrie, the brunette, announced she was there to help Samantha, who waved her off, as Carrie directed her on the jet ski. Then Sam fired it up, and just like that went racing off, Jack heard his guide, Terri, she offered up something entirely different, as Jack said "No, no thanks," mounted it, and didn't even wait, he took off, as quick as that, he was already behind Sam. Troops still lined the islands, she turned near a beach and went back a different direction, he saw her, then veered off doing a big turn. Then he shot the throttle down and was racing to her, faster than she was going, but it looked more like she was going out of control. Sam was sliding back, only holding on by one hand and going quickly. Jack moved in and leapt from his to hers, catching her, as she let go. The machines did a dead stop. Jack took Sam into his arms, and tightened up his grip on her, as he made his way up, to the controls, he was trying to figure out a way of towing it back, when a boat had come to their starboard side and said, "We got this one, go ahead, have some more fun."

Jack saw Brian hop over to the other one, Jack took off into the open portion of the Gulf of Mexico. He was having flashbacks of the boat he drove just earlier, when all of a sudden he had a tail, a jet boat with some angry looking dudes on it, coming to him quicker than he was going. He was flat-out, but losing ground, when gunfire erupted, but they were still out of range. Then all of a sudden, two f-18 super hornets, flew over them and the boat shot at the aircraft. A heat seeking missile from the aircraft, hit the boat's exhaust, the boat blew up, sending everyone out as a huge explosion could be heard and felt. Jack doubled back towards the boat, only to see remenants of the boat. Jack instantly decided, "I'm getting out of here, this place is getting dangerous."

Jack stepped on it, and steered the Jet ski back to the resort. They hit shore with a reception party and Brian, who said, "Fun time is over, a band of guerrillas is heading this way."

"Then I'm suiting up, and I say, let's go get them", said Jack handing the passed out Sam to Brian to hold, as others held the jet ski, Jack got off and took Sam from Brian. He worked his way up the hill, off the beach, past the wheelchair, into his cabana. Anxious about this attack, Jack set Sam on the bed and he stripped on the spot, much to the delight of Daphne who said, "Wow what did I miss, you naked and all this?"

"Just getting ready to have some fun, you can come if you like?"

"Fun, what are you talking about?" said Daphne.

"The guerrillas have landed and are heading this way."

Daphne went into a panic mode, as Jack's new assistant who was Jayden, was crying in a corner. Jack grabbed Daphne's arm and said, "Hold on, calm down, we're not under attack, I said I was going to attack them."

"What, why would you do that?" asked Daphne, trying to console Jayden.

"Because that is what I do, save people's life", said Jack nearly done strapping on the holster and then opening the white box to extract the gun. He felt the pull and then loaded it and set the other clip in the holster, he placed on the windbreaker, he was started out the door, but said, "Can you care for her, get her on the plane."

"Are you planning to leave?" asked Daphne.

"Yes right after this, get everyone on board, I'll take Paul with me."

Jack was leaving as he heard, "You do that boy", said Daphne.

Jack was trotting over to the airfield, then back to where a helicopter sat. He was on his phone, moving the pieces around, the fun was over and Jack didn't take to kindly to the attack on him, now it was payback. First on the scene was Paul, with a sizable backpack he was wearing, followed by Rick Teal, who blended with the culture of the Virgin Islands. Jack said,

"I have ordered up two platoons of Seal teams to hit that island, get in, I'll have a pilot here shortly." Jack turned around to see it was the blonde who had an air of confidence about herself, as he looked her over and said, "Is that you Jayden, It's not true is it?" asked Jack.

"Yes, sir, I flew the helio in." said Jayden.

"I would of never have known that, alright let's load up."

"What, just the three of you." said Jayden.

"Yeah for right now, my other helpers are coming, let's go", said Jack taking the passenger seat, watching the young French woman go. They were in her element, she took to the controls like a seasoned pro, in an instant they were off, for a short jaunt, to the next island over, where as soon as she put it down, Jack was out. He charged into the forests of the jungle, gun out, after hearing a team of SEAL's to the south and one coming in from the north, he was going for the middle, a guard was at post when Jack shot him in the leg, he went down in agony. Jack went around and zip tied his wrists and ankles, then went inside a tunnel. This was now one shot one kill territory, he moved as he saw fit, as the above lights flickered, a guy stepped out, in front of him, Jack used the pistol and struck him down, he zip tied him up, and pulled him out of the way. Next he reached the command center, as a girl was screaming out the orders, "God damn it Carlos, why did you have to fire at that fighter, now Ennis and the others are dead, we lost that boat, you idiot."

The voice was now very familiar to him, as he stepped in the room and said, "Hands up Teresa, and the others, tell them or I send this bullet in your head first."

She raised her hands, as did the others, as she moved closer to Jack, for Jack to say, "Why did you fire on me?"

"What, out there?, that was you", she said honestly, inching closer to him, only to hear weapons fire and the scream of voices. It was evident, they were surrounded. Jack said, "What are you even doing here in the first place, I thought you were in Honduras?"

"I was, but a more lucrative offer came my way?" said Teresa.

"What, trying to be a pirate, good luck on that." said Jack.

"Why is that, today was suppose to be our first official day."

"I'd say it was bad timing on your behalf."

"Could be, now what?" asks Teresa.

"Now my team will take you and the rest of your men, take them" ordered Jack. He was watching a fellow student taken down to the floor, then zipped tied and escorted out. Jack was right behind them, only to hear, "Hey Jack you may want to see this?"

Jack abruptly turned around and walked into a room of vast wealth, stacks of bills, gems and a vat of diamonds, then off to the right was bricks of gold, he went over to see the markings. Then he remembers Carlos, the new brother-in-law from Cuba, visiting. Jack said,

"Box it all up, and make sure it's all accounted for. He was on the phone to Lisa when Hans came running in to announce,

"Jackpot, Jack your rich". Jack responded, "Get him out of here, Rick you and Paul handle this, I'm getting Lisa down here." said Jack, while on the phone dialing her up.

The Seal teams help diffuse the rest of the situation, and help move the remaining prisoners out, past Jack, as others arrived, a C-130 landed on the air strip. It taxied, then parked and the ramp was lowered. Lisa and her team came out to take the prisoners.

"Looks like your honeymoon has been ruined."

"Nah, just a little entertainment, as all of this, I may just sit in the sands and have some R & R."

"I may be right there beside you" said Lisa.

"Well come on let's go!" said Jack.

"Nah, looks like I'll be doing some sorting out, what's the story with Hans?"

"Sorry, just don't like him. He seems a bit over zealous." said Jack.

"And how is that a bad thing?" asked Lisa.

"It isn't really, it's just not my thing." said Jack.

The two walked into the cave, through the tunnel to the lair. People were looking it over and one said, "This is another lookout, the computer imagery, and ads; it's a back up". "It shows who it monitors and what was taken." "Shall I printout the list?"

"It won't be necessary, all of it belongs to Jack Cash now." said Lisa. "Nah, allow him to do that and then contact that country's ambassador." Jack shrugs his shoulders and says, "It is my honeymoon, so why not be generous."

"This was a bit of a reunion with Teresa, were any words minced?" asked Lisa.

"Nah, she didn't realize who she was dealing with; Me!" Jack said, laughing.

Jack says his good byes to his friends and colleagues and walks over the Helios where Jayden just smiled at him as he boarded. He closed the passenger door and Jayden said, "Where to Mister Cash?" He just smiled.

"Back to the main island, me and my bride have a honeymoon to enjoy."

"Will do sir".

Jack eased back in the seat, to relax, while the helio flew appropriately, back to the LZ, where she sat it down, Jack exited, and went back into the cabana, he saw his bride asleep on the bed, so he went in and took a long hot shower, cleaned up and dressed for the evening occasion.

CH 13

Bride in waiting-Puerto Plata

Daphne was present in the room, as the blinds closed she and several others helped Samantha to her evening gown, she was made up so pretty, as she was lifted to her wheelchair, she smiled from the attention and the help. Across from her was Jack, a beaming husband, as he smiled back at her. He led her out as Daphne took to pushing Sam, the grounds were wet from the occasional downpour, that just took place.

Jack was in the lead, as Ferdinand was speaking with Jack, as the two walked together, he said, "My friend, I have a sampling of only the finest wines and we held a celebration exclusively in your honor, thank you for cleaning up this island."

Jack walked into a lounge overlooking the sea, where a spread of all kinds of foods were laid out, easily enough to feed a hundred, but as Jack and Sam looked around, they heard, Ferdinand say," In our country, it is customary for the bride and groom to spend three days all alone, so here is plenty of food and drink, so enjoy the room, in the back is a suite made up, compliments of us, and of course your government."

Jack saw Ferdinand back away, and out the door he went as the doors closed shut.

Jack felt a relaxation sweep over him, as he saw Sam, sampling the different foods, to say, "Honey try some of this and that, Ooh, yes I like that.

Jack was on his own path, from what he thought was an exclusive ball he was attending to a shindig, he had been here before, so he took off his coat, and rolled up his sleeves and took a plate and sliced some beef, from a platter, added some horseradish cream, next was smashed potatoes, roasted carrots, slice of cranberry sauce, and lastly some dressing. Took the plate over to the awaiting table, where Sam had a plate herself of just fruit, a bowl of yogurt and some vanilla cookies.

He looked her over, for her to say, "What there here for is dipping."

"dipping?" asked Jack.

"Yeah, there is some melted cheese, or some sort of beef broth, and then finally, some big chocolate fountain, you know this was never how I had planned my wedding to go."

"What was your plan?"

"Well before the accident, I was going to go to college, and become a Marine biologist."

"And now?"

"Let me finish, you know it really wasn't the accident that even stopped me, I'd have to say, it was probably my mother, she was the one who told me that my life was over and that no college wanted me, and no man was ever going to be with me and finally, who was I going to marry, my childhood sweetheart, left me, so then I met you and then it was over."

"And now."

"Now, I met the man of my dreams, let me tell you about my man."

Jack smiled at her, as she talked, "This man isn't the average old guy at the local hangout, no, no no, this man is a bad man a serious bad man, who gets the job done, how you persuaded me to sleep with you is still beyond me, let alone my mother, who as you saw was outraged, anyway, it's happened and we have each other, let's talk about you, your kind hearted, in love with me, yet command all the other girls attention, what I'm saying when I go you're going to have to have a lot of girls replace me."

"Perhaps maybe one or two."

"Please Jack, I know the man you are, like that French woman who has been sniffing around you."

"Jayden."

"Yeah her."

"Not my type."

"What is your type Jack?"

"For now just you."

"Really, you mean to say, I have you here with me for the whole three days?"

"Yep, that's the least I could do for you, besides I have some ideas for you."

"What are you saying?" she said kind of looking around, for Jack to stand, and lead her to the suite, to show her his plans.

"Wait, what is that thing?"

"It's called a swing, according to my phone, it's a weightless position for a pregnant lady to lie back, flat, in the straps, and I will enter from the rear."

She looked it over, as she wheeled herself around, on both sides, to say, "I don't know, the doctor did say the back was open if I were on my knees, so maybe this could work, I guess I could try it, but how will you just get up there?"

"I'm sure I can manage, are you ready now?"

"Sure I'm ready whenever you are", she said softly, as Jack was on his knees, unbuttoning the side of her lovely gown, in one motion he lifted her up, leaving her gown behind, she had only a camisole on, as her bag was on a belt, she also had an insulin boost, Jack carefully unbuttoned her blouse, to allow her breasts to be exposed, he went down to her panties, he pulled them down gracefully, to expose her overgrown patch, of black hairs, he slid his hand down to part her legs, as they were unresponsive, to his touch, his finger found her wetness, she was flowing, as her hands help him where she wanted it the most, as Jack had other ideas, and went down on one knee, and went face first to her box. Jack rotated her legs apart, to allow the box to open naturally, using both his fingers and his tongue he gave her a good lashing, till she actually had an orgasm, as she calmed, he went back in for some more, till she was ready again, this time she really let loose, she gushed. Jack paused to enjoy it, then quickly stripped off his clothes, he was ready, he was at the ready, as he was rock hard, he allowed her to touch and stroke it, she took it in her mouth from the side, till he was well lubricated, he pulled out, and with his strength he lifted her up, held her long enough to slip it in as he held her, but held back for fear of the baby, turned her, and slowly set her in to the straps, her breasts fit in a strap pocket, as did her belly, and her knees, it spread her wide enough, to see a gaping hole from the rear, Jack stood up on the bed, hanging on, he easily slid in, bout half way, he was massive compared to this seemingly small waisted girl, but a simple surgery and she was easily able to handle his length and width, not to mention his girth, she was panting heavily, as Jack went in and out, each stroke was a feeling, a meaning, she was well accommodating, he and she were spinning, as Jack had his own stirrups, so they could spin locked in together. He held onto the two top straps, as his member did the bulk of the work, he was actually getting stronger, as the adrenaline coursed through his body. Before long he was in all the way, to his hilt, sharing space with his baby, as the pair were locked in, he kept the hips a moving and the stroking on pace, till it was a wave upon wave of fluid, she let loose, and the screams of passion, became cries of agony, as it was a total lockup. Everything halted, as Jack pulled out slowly, and along came the blood. Jack saw the blood, and knew it went wrong too quickly, off of her and on to his phone, he pulled up his pants, only to see Daphne and Magdalena, extracting, Sam out of the swing, and onto the bed, and in one motion, unhooked the swing and tossed it aside as a team of medical personnel, took over, as Jack watched to hear, "She is bleeding internally, let's get her on the plane."

Jack, watched as she was wheeled out, and the lead Doctor said, "Will do what we can, if the baby has to come out were taking it, Jack nodded, to see the doctor leave with the others.

"You were pretty calm with him?" said Daphne.

"Oh, yeah, he was just doing his job". said Jack, going into the bathroom, to hear, "Shall we leave you alone, or do you need a helping hand to finish up?" said Daphne, looking at Jack and down at his massive member, to say, "But for that I'm not your girl", she scurried off with her friend, who said, "I never knew he was that large, any volunteers?"

"I know of none."

"Me either."

Alone Jack showered, cleaned up, dressed in a robe, the bed had been remade, and a woman, whom was smartly dressed, with long flowing black hair, a figure to match, paused long enough to show off her perfectly manicured nails and painted a dark brown color, said, "Ferdinand sent me in, to say, "Your wife just flew out of here, and so your all alone, if you like I could keep you company."

Jack looked at the tall dark beauty, with her ravishing eyes to her curvy figure, she was primed for adventure, as he moved closer, she leaned in to whisper, "Fear not, I'm with Spy Club, you will be safe tonight, my name is Safara. She reached in, and felt something as it drew quickly, a smile on her face, as she exclaimed, "Finally a big man."

Jack led her along back to the feast, as the chosen successor, yet at the door was another, scantily clothed, in a see through number, it was hard for Jack not to keep it down, that was till a knock on the door, and the girl, opened it, and the French woman appeared, she looked sullen, with her arms crossed, she stormed in, to speak in French as fast as Jack's phone could translate what she was saying, something about, she was now assigned to him, to prove her worth, she would fill in," that is when Jack raised his hand to interrupt her, to say, "As you can see I have company who wants to be here, your free to go."

"Wait, what, no I can't leave."

"I thought you only could speak French?"

"That's when I'm angry."

"And now?"

"Now I'm calming down, you know I can't leave now."

"Then, why are you here?"

"Well to be honest with you, my sister has been taken, and the last place we tracked her was the Dominican Republic, will you help?"

Jack looked at her, then over at Safara, who smiled, for Jack to say to her, "You and a million other women are taken every day, so why should I drop everything and go to Puerto Plata."

She looked him over to say, "Wait, how did you know all of this?"

"I know all about you, that's what I do, when she was taken and why, and now, all it is the how, but I need to wait."

"What do you mean wait, while you're enjoying yourself here, she could be getting hurt."

"Doubtful, you see those that have her, took her for only one reason, and one reason alone, export to Russia, so no I'd say she needs a few days to process, as for me, I need UN approval before I go in and stir up another town, so I guess we wait till that happens.", said Jack looking over his phone, while Safara was eating, and the other still stood by the door, all looking out at the sunset, the tiki lamps were along the beach line. Safara was up and went to the sliding doors, she slid one open to allow the wind in, which blew on her flimsy dress, in one motion she pulled it off, to expose and show the others that she wore nothing else, and went onto the deck, set her plate down and took a plunge into the infinity pool.

Jack got up, and went over to see, that the pool was lit up, then by the door, the girl came over to Jack, she used her finger, to his lips to say, "You don't mind if I join my friend, and oh by the way, my name is Fatima, and yes we both share." she pulled off her lingerie, to show everything in full view, Jack turned to see Jayden, still with crossed arms, gaining confidence, with each moment, as she knew what was happening and it was now or never, she gave in, un-crossed her arms, unzipped her top, and pulled it off, undid her pants, and allowed them to drop, a flick of the wrist, she popped her bra, and pulled it off, her exposed breasts showed her super tight nipples, she pulled down her panties, to come close to him to say, "In France were naked all the time, no big deal, are you going to join us?" she reached in, to feel his manhood, as he eyes were getting wide, with each growing minute, till a smile formed on her mouth, to say, "I've never had it so large, Oh my god, she began to shake, as she let go as Jack shred the robe, she barely could hold it, it was so big, but like any good trooper, she went to her knees, opened up her jaws, and Jack slid it in nicely. She was really enjoying it and it showed, as for Fatima and Safara, both had joined in, and was playing with each other, for Jack to allow Jayden the real fun, Jack turned her around, as she was on all fours as Jack entered her with ease, she enlarged for the occasion, she was tight to feel, but it went in and Jack maintained a pace, much to her liking, soon it was just the two of them, as those that were the servers, it was their key, to leave. Jayden took as long as she could, to the point of tears, as Jack continued, till finally Jayden collapsed and fell forward, crawling to the pool, she hit the water to cool herself.

Jack turned his attention, on the noise coming from the bedroom, where Fatima was in the swing, and Safara was playing with her, till Jack got onto the bed, and inserted in, and kept the strokes alive, she took her to paradise and beyond, as she was a gusher, till she dried up and was done, that left the two remaining, as Jack entered Safara, as she laid on her back, and allowed him to do all the work.

Safara lost herself in the passion, and finally in the end Jack erupted, and hosed her down, the pair fell fast asleep in each other's arms.

The next morning broke with the sun blazing them, Jack awoke, and was up, to review the carnage, Fatima and Jayden were both on sofas, both naked, pasted out, still, after Jack carefully examined his work. He turned when he heard a noise, he saw the ever stunning Safara, at the fresh fruit counter, somewhere during the night the foods were taken out, cleaned up, and this morning replaced. Jack surveyed her, as she was still in a playful mood, his phone was buzzing on the table, he just let it go, to concentrate on Safara, then on the two other girls who were stirring about, both were drained, especially the French woman, who walked slightly favoring one leg over the other, a scowl on her face, to say, "Good morning lover, had I known it was going to be that wild, I'd have brought back-up, you know what I mean, she smiled, and began her foraging.

Jack made a plate for himself, went over and sat beside Safara, who smiled back at him, to say in accent, "What, is your plan today?"

"Oh I don't know, maybe some pool action, jet skiing, or back in the bedroom."

"That's fine with me."

"Wait you promised to go get my sister", she sneered at him, passing by to take a seat, said Jayden.

Fatima had her plate but lingered as she allowed Jack to put his finger inside of her, she smiled, while eating a grape.

Jack looked over at his phone, he picked it up, which allowed Fatima to take a seat, behind him and next to Jayden.

Jack looked over the e-mails, to see that Samantha would be fine, just a tear, inside, laser surgery took care of it, and she will be back home in two weeks, she is doing fine. Jack scrolled down, to see his approval from the UN, as Jack texted to Trixie to get the plane ready for Puerto Plata, ASAP . . . . , she responded "Five Minutes?"

Jack typed, maybe an hour, or two?"

"Sure, were ready whenever you are."

Jack looked over at Safara, to smile to say, "You ready for another round?"

"Sure", she smiled, got up, set her plate down, to receive Jack who was getting up, he turned to say, "How about it girls, another round?"

Jayden didn't look happy, nor expressed it, but said, "Sure why not, do you promise to find my sister?"

"Absolutely, come on, your first."

She smiles, knowing what was to about happen, she stood, stretched, and slid in line, Jack looked over at Fatima, who was more engrossed with her food than with him, for Jack to say, "Maybe later than?"

Jack led the two girls in, they both looked at the swing, but Jack was ready on the spot, and allowed Jayden to bend over at the bed, for the ready Jack to make an entrance, he slid in easily, as it was more comfortable for her this time, Jack held her hips, to begin the thrusting, he reached around to grab both of her breasts, and squeeze her nipples, he was in full thrust mode, meanwhile, Safara was getting herself into the swing in the reverse sitting position, her feet were in the stirrups, and swung open for both Jayden and Jack to see.

Jayden had her eyes closed, as she let loose and orgasm, quickly they were both sweating, she was well lubricated, and doing well, the fear was gone, as she showed her stamina, she too began the rocking, as the two worked together in unison, Jack was out of his mind, as he just let it all happen, wave after wave, she began to scream in ecstasy till she let off the last big scream, and collapsed, forward, onto the bed, as Jack looked at her, then up to Safara, who was waiting, he climbed up over Jayden, and stepped up to enter Safara, it went in easily, and it was well received, he drove it down to the hilt, the two swang in the swing. Jack held onto the straps, as the two swayed back and forth, much to the delight of Fatima, who watched and played with herself, below them was Jayden moaning for more, a wunderlust of emotions were flooding her senses now, as Fatima, saw her turn over, and thrust her hand in between her legs, and that was the cue for Fatima to help her out.

Jack and Safara were still in the slow mode action, except, Jack had his eye on something else, down on the beach was several girls, playing, in and around some jet skis, he kept the action happening, then the girls took off. Jack slowed his momentum, ready for a change, he slowed his progress, to the point he pulled out, and said, "Can we try another position?"

She smiled, to say "Of course, no sooner had he said that, he was down, and inserting it back into Jayden, whose legs were spread wide, and in a lip lock with Fatima. Jack continued to work, as Jayden was enjoying herself even more, Safara had worked herself out of the swing, and onto the bed, Jack saw her, for him to say, "Let's try you face down, in the swing?"

"Sure, I may need help?"

Jack stopped what he was doing, pulled out, and stepped up on the bed, to ready the swing, for Safara, to reach the straps, she steadied herself, and went in, with each breast in place, and her knees in one at a time, Jack placed her feet in the stirrups, which spread her legs apart, made it easy for him, to enter her, and all the way in, he held on as the swing swang, he continue the drive, much to Safara's satisfaction, as she pulled off an amazing orgasm, one after another, she gushed with force, as fluids, ran down and rained on the two girls below them. Jack continued the pace, till he was finally ready, he pulled out, and let loose, he sprayed her down, as he milked it out. He backed off the bed to see what he had done, and for Fatima to claim her turn, she went down on him, and cleaned him up, all the while she herself had an orgasm.

Jack hit the shower, while the girls were all sleeping, Safara was still lying in the swing, unable to get up on her own, she called out, to Jack, he heard her, and went to her aid. One foot at a time, her knees and then the rest of her body. He allowed her to collapse, onto the bed.

Jack went over to Jayden, to see she finally had a smile on her face, her natural blonde hairs were now fully exposed, as Jack ran his hand over her now swollen mound, she stirred, and then found his hand, to which she guided it between her legs, and to her box, wet to touch, she spoke something French, as Jack inserted his fore finger for another go, as she awake, to see it was him, she lunged up and hugged his arm, looking up preparing for a kiss, there was none as Jack pushed her back, he began to dress, eager she was at his legs, trying to reach up to him, begging for more.

Jack said, "It's time to go, I got a fix on Angie."

"Can I go?"

"Sure, get dressed,", Jack looked up to see that she was already moving to the shower.

"What about us?" asked Safara.

"I don't know, what can you do?"

"How about a tour guide, I know the Dominican Republic, where are you going?" she asked as she and Fatima start heading to the bathroom.

"Oh a place called Puerto Plata."

Fatima began to shake her head, in an expressive way, for Jack to say, "What's wrong with her?"

"She thinks it the Land of the Devils, where men kidnap women for sex and trade", said Safara.

"And that's why I'm going, to shut them all down."

Safara held Jack at the door, by the arm, to say, "This is a very dangerous place, are you sure you want to go and risk your life on finding her sister?"

"Sure that is what I do, rescue women" said Jack pulling on his trousers, and buttoning up his shirt, rechecking his wallet, he put on his gun and holster, secured it in place, he tucked in his shirt, sat down, put some socks on, then his shoes, he got up, and found his windbreaker, slid it on, and zipped it up, for Safara to say, "You're sure going to be warm in that."

"I'd rather be hot then dead."

Jack went to the food table, to see a whole new spread, he looked around, wondering, "When did they come in?"

Behind him, came the girls, except Fatima, whereas Safara spoke up and said," She doesn't want to come."

"How come?"

"She thinks it's too dangerous."

"Seriously, it's only a state of the mind, any place can be dangerous."

Standing at the door, stood Fatima, for which she said," It is true any place can be dangerous, but this is the Land of the Devils, simply put, means, the men are crazy, they will do everything and anything, so unpredictable."

"Alright she's out, it must be bad", said Jack consuming his food.

The other two equally was with him, to say, "Were with you, besides you're a protector, were going to ride in on your coattails."

"I'll need all the help I can get".

Jack checked his phone to confirm the flight out and added two others to join him, and announced, "Were ready for the flight, let's go."

Jack said his goodbye to Fatima, as did the girls, did the same.

Jack led, while the two girls followed. They past the helio that Jayden flew, for her to say, "Hey, what about the helio?"

"Nah, were taking a plane, afterwards, we'll come get it."

Jack held the door, to allow the two girls in, to a well-lit hanger, where a large prop plane sat, on the ramp was an older man, who said," Hi ladies welcome aboard, first cabin on the right".

Jack followed them up the ramp, for Jim to say, "All systems go, Trixie sent me the flight pattern."

"All right, let's go" said Jack. He went to his cabin, as Jim, hit the ramp door button, up went the ramp, he went up into the cockpit, hit a button, the hanger door slid open, as he started up the aircraft, he took off, as he eased it forward, turned to the right, accelerated, and nosed up, and lift off occurred.

Jack had a seat in the middle of the floor in a special made chair, while Safara raided the refrigerator of drinks, and Jayden was a changed women, the nervousness was gone, as a more confident girl sat on the edge of the bed, she touched his arm to say, "I want to thank you."

"For what?"

"For turning me into a woman."

"I think you did that yourself", said Jack looking at her.

"No, that isn't what I mean, for actually trusting me and taking me places where only others were babying me, I think you actually believe in my abilities."

"Sure, why wouldn't I, your strong, beautiful and know your job well, if I had a slot open for you."

"That's just it, I want to come work for you."

"We'll see, let's find your sister first and then we will talk about your future."

She touched his arm again to say, "You want to go another round?"

He looked her over, then down at his phone, which was showing him, the flight pattern, and the glide slope downward, to say, "Nah, we will be landing in ten minutes, but maybe afterwards?"

"How do you know you can find her?"

"I have a tracking ability with this phone, matched up with current DNA, found locally."

"So what, you just go in there and everyone surrenders."

"Something like that, actually more like, how many of them can I take down, till I find the ones who have Angie, and many others."

"Oh", said Jayden. A bump occurred and Safara found her way into Jack's arms. She fed him a drink, as he held her, she wasn't anxious to get up either.

Meanwhile in the flight cabin, Jim was told to fly off, that the Airport was under siege, for their safety, Jim countered, to say, "I carry the mediator for the UN, he wants to land, over.

"Understood, land on runway 2, park on the end a reception crew will meet your delegate, over."

"Over and out", said Jim, who hit the intercom, to say, "Jack we have a problem, the airport is under siege."

Jack stood, hit the button to say, "Land the plane I'll take care of this."

The plane turned, then made the approach, touched down, taxied, and came to a stop, Jack and Jim, were on the move as he told Jayden, to go up front and take the controls of the plane, Safara was with him, as Jim and Jack uncovered the car, unbuckled it, as Jack got in, Jim was lowering the ramp, as Safara got in, on the passenger seat, Jack inserted his phone into the dash, Sara fired up, and went back, off the ramp, turned, and sped off, Jack had his laptop out, and patched into the airports live feed, a group of terrorist had secured the airport in hopes of landing a foreign Russian general, as per their demands, Jack responded on behalf of the United Nations, and the US, and their five million dollars, by transferring the currency into an offshore account, and asking them to stand down, to drop their weapons, and come out the back and assemble along the wall. Jack and Sara the Car sped to that location, Jack got their first, no one, nothing, it was silent, Jack said to Safara, "Stay put, till I round up these guys", before she could respond he said, "Sleep", she went out instantly, Jack got out, with his phone intact, and he slipped it in, pulled his gun, and was ready, he tried the door it was locked, he then had an idea, he pulled his phone, hit the cars display, and hit the J button, out shot a pigeon, controlled by Jack it buzzed the tower for a bird's eye view with his camera, he slowed the birds flight to see men with guns, then Jack turned his sights on his aircraft and flew the bird over there, Jim and Jayden were being accosted by two men, just as Jack flew the bird, for one man's jugular, it sliced him clean and the guy went down, and it came back around for another pass, when the other guy started to shoot at the metal bird, it hit its mark, by slicing another jugular, as it flew off, and back to Jack. Jim and Jayden went back into the plane, as other groups were forming, and the bird was on it, catching unsuspecting guards, and slicing their jugulars, they went down, Jack was growing impatient with the terrorists, so he put the bird on autopilot, sweeping in a circle, while he sped up the process, he took a strip from inside his windbreaker, undid the paper, pulled it apart, set it on the door guard, put a blasting cap in it, set the radio frequency, and set a timer, while the bird was coasting, 3, 2, 1, boom, it rocked the building, the door lay open, with a dead body, just inside the door. Jack kept the bird in flight, as he raced up the tower stairs, he reached the control tower level, gun out and yelled, "Put down your weapons", instantly gunfire rained his way, he ducked, dive, and turned, his aim was knee and below shots, one shot one hit, agony could be heard as his bullets were true, his target was the knee caps, the pain was unbearable to some, one by one till finally the remaining two, spoke up and said, "Alright, alright, who are you?"

"Come out in the open, drop your weapons", Jack rose with his weapon, as one of the men, instantly shot at Jack, the bullet came and struck his badge, sending Jack back, long enough for the guy to receive his own present, one between the eyes. The guy slumped down, as the other one showed his hands, smiled to say, "It's too late, the general is going to land." and tossed the weapon, with his hands in the air,

"You forgot something, our deal."

"What deal?"

"Five million dollars, for you all to surrender."

"You know that was a ploy, you American's have no policy to negotiated with terrorist", said the man who finally turned to expose his face, for Jack to take a picture, instantly, it came back as Ahmed Casttle, number one terrorist, for Jack to say, "Interesting, Ahmed, a deal is a deal, I gave you five million of my money, I need you to come here, kneel down,"

"No, he said, to announce, "Here he comes, he said cheering, with his hands up, he was jumping up and down, for Jack to say, "And there he goes", Jack hit the G, button, immediately, a sidewinder ground to air missile shot out of the back of the car, directly at the oncoming plane, for Jack to hear, No, No, No, ...

Big explosion, as the plane became a huge ball of fire, his cheers were of anguish, and tears were streaming, down his face, as he came at Jack, whereas, Jack fired at Ahmed's knee, it hit he turned, and Jack aimed at the other, Ahmed, went down, Jack went over to him, holstered, his weapon, and zip tied, Ahmed's hands behind his back, as he did it to the four others, all crying out, as the Republics National police stormed the airport's tower, as Jack sent them a go ahead, it was all clear. Jack was long gone, as the police finally made it up to the tower, to show that they had arrived, Ahmed was screaming for a lawyer, as it fell on deft ears, there was however, a UN agent present a Miss Roberta Myers, who knelt down, and grabbed Ahmed's hair, to say, "Scum bag, number one, how does it feel to go up against our number one agent."

"What's his name I got to know."

"Jack Cash."

"Oh", and then he let out his lunch, and vomited.

Jack was driving out of the airport, as he got a wave through, by UN security force, and on to the streets, looking at his heads up display, he was empty, on the rear missile, and the bird, he lost it somewhere, but he still had one left on the E button, not to mention, the display keeps going in and out, due to the missile launch. He kept onto the streets that Angie was last seen, to a warehouse district, only to feel a hand on his arm, for which, Safara, said, "Sorry, I was out, she motioned for him to turn, Up there to the left, is a turnaround driveway, park and we can watch the action", Jack did as he was told, he drove in, under a huge tree, to the other side, he parked, the angle of the driveway, afforded them a good view of the street and the warehouse. Jack shut the car down, to see that the night was coming upon them, and so did the crazies, men and women filled the streets, warehouse doors were lifted, for Safara to say, "This is the auction, do you want to get out and participate."

"Sure, let's go.'

"Wait what about the car, she said, to add, "You know its safety."

"No worries I know the owner."

Jack whispered, "Secure". Jack led Safara down the road, to blend with the crowd, as it forced itself into a big room, like a huge platform, as they were packed in like standing room only, for an Spanish speaking announcer got up and said," I want to make an announcement, earlier today, Russian General Igor Kaminsky was killed at the airport, this is all sad news to us, but because he cannot take his share, those that were allocated to him are now open for bidding, bidding will start, in fifteen minutes, minimum bid is a thousand US dollars, just raise your hand, as Safara was translating to Jack. People were pushing him even tighter, till the Auction began, one by one, a girl came up. Bidding took place, Jack was a major player, by out bidding everyone, and through Safara's help, she translated for him. Those around him, filed out, as the new player, was taking everything, and Jack could see their was some suspicion running wild, with the handlers. Next up was coed college girls, blonde hair blue eyes. Many thoughts were going through Jack's mind, and one was it would be nice to have a force of men helping him right now. Let alone Mark or Mike, oh well, then, it was announced, a special gem, "Super model, Angie Foice, from France, a scantily clad Blonde and blue eyed beauty, who had been crying, and the bidding began, a thousand quickly went to ten thousand, to one hundred thousand, Jack raised his hands and yelled out "One million dollars, ", with gun out, above his head, someone yelled gun, and mass hysteria ensued, a single shot rang out, and Angie lay slumped down, but that wasn't all Jack was mad, and mad he was, he wasn't playing around, he used his gun by shooting for the head, of the men in his way, which they slumped down for him, through doors, over fences, down hallways, Jack was following the men, each dropping to the bullets Jack shot at them, there was a section he came to, where caged room for women was, Jack slowed, as he hit the solid door, he was outside, a car was peeling out, Jack saw him for an instant, then he sped off, Jack pulled up his display, on his phone, pointed at the target, and hit the E button, the last of the rear missiles, took off, out of the car, in an arch, and straight down, through the windshield, and exploded, a huge fireball illuminated the sky, as the carnage, and severely burned body, was evident and all the cash in the trunk. Paper money littered the streets, Jack went back inside, found a set of keys, and began to open the cells, as a girl took the keys from Jack, Jack went on, to another bay.

Safara met up with Jack to say, "Angie, is fine just a nick to her arm, local police is here, as the cleanup is beginning, the police chief has asked me to stay on and interpret, so I will see you later at some point?"

"Sure, have fun", said Jack as, he works his way back, behind him are girls assembling, to get at Jack, only for the police to hold them back, Jack made his way to the arena, to see Angie, alive and well, as a worker was bandaging her arm up, only for her to break away, and embrace Jack with a two handed hug, she kissed him on the cheek, and whisper, "You're a very dangerous man, once they found out it was you that had taken out the General, they wanted to speed up this process and cut their losses, as for me, once I found out that you were coming to get me, a total wave of emotion overcame me, and my treatment from the handlers instantly changed, when they received a call, that you were coming."

Jack shrugs his shoulder, to say," I'm here now, allow them to finish you have a reunion with your sister."

"Wait what did you say?, she said looking at him.

"Your sister is waiting, so."

"Sister, I have no sister, are you meaning the French woman?"

"Yes, perhaps why?"

"She is one of them, she was the one who recruited me."

"You don't say, said Jack on his phone, to get no response from Jim, for Jack to say, "Come on, were going."

Jack ushers Angie out, by the arm.

Meanwhile on the plane, which was allowed to taxi in, but had to park in the UN space, for neutrality purposes, Jim, was under duress, as Jayden, held a gun to his head, for her to say, "How did he survive?", she was on her phone making arrangements, Jim's arms were zipped tied to the armrests, with no way to touch any buttons, when all of a sudden the ramp starts going down, for Jim to say, "He's back,"

"Don't try anything funny, or I will come back and shoot you."

Jayden left the flight cabin, all the while Jim was trying to cut the ties on a sharp edge, while Jayden stood at the cargo bay with gun drawn, as Jack pulls the car into its place. Parks it and shuts down Sara, he opens the door, for Jayden to say, 'Now get out slowly, I didn't know how you do it, I send you into the heart of the world's worse place and you come away unscathed, I'd shoot you right now, but I've been told to hold you,

Jack stood, hands up, and said, "Now what?, what about that rain check."

"What are you talking about?"

"I thought you said we could go another round?"

"What sex, that is what you want, nah, you had your chance, that is over, and with that she fell forward, as Jim, used a bat and cracked her skull, she went down in a slump. Jim stood proudly. Jack moved in, to say, "Were going home."

"Yes boss right away."

Jack examined the fallen Jayden, her broken neck, and glazed over eyes indicated to him, she was dead, or the fact that her weak pulse, gave him hope, she was still alive, that was until, the plane backed up, and the instant jerk, finished the job, he held her limp body, she was in fact now dead. Jack sat her down, on the bench to lie and buckled her in, as the plane took off.

CH 14

Back Home

They flew into Quantico Virginia, first, and dropped off the two girls, Angie went on back to Paris, France, as for Jack, he attended Jayden's memorial, before she went back on the same flight, he was then transported back to Mobile, airport where a red Camaro was parked awaiting him, as the ramp went down, he shook hands with Jim, and went to his new car, got in and fired it up, instantly things began to look about the same as his Mercedes, so he inserted his phone in the dash, a display screen appeared, the car drove out, with the Sara back in charge. She drove him, from the airport, down the highway, Jack was thinking of lunch, so many things to do so little time to do them, and of his house, and of his boat, the Camaro cruised, to finally Jack decided on the hospital, as the car got off on that exit, construction was everywhere, as the ride was slow, till he saw the hospital, he went past it, as he took control, and around to the back, to see a handicap spot, looking at his heads up display, he saw the letter N, and his license plate, flipped to show handicap. He parked and pulled his phone, got out, and went in through the sliding door, down the stairs to the cafeteria, just as he remembered it, everything he could of ever wanted, he was lost in a sea of unfamiliar faces of that of new people, doctors, nurses and nurses' aides, young women, innocent, only to feel a hand on his back and turn to see a smile, for her to say, "So how is my sister's boyfriend?"

Jack sees her to say, "Fine, and you."

"You're looking good, you got quite a small fishing charter business going!"

"I do, I had no idea."

"Well you should know that and much more I guess."

"I can see, by looking around at all the new talent,"

"Ever since Samantha Smith has come and gone, were number one in the Mobile market and jumped up over 400 percent, and all thanks to you, can I buy you lunch?"

"I already paid, but maybe some other time?"

"Are you planning on being in town long?" asked Kate.

"Don't know, Maybe."

"Well your house on the hill, looks spectacular, Mom and me toured it, I have to tell you all those wives of yours how do you do it?"

"What do you mean?"

"You know, there is Maria the princess from Cuba, then the police chief's daughter, Alba, and lastly Alexandra, that comes to my sister Sara, when are you going to make her a honest woman."

"That's why I'm here."

"Really does she know?" said Kate excitedly.

"No not really, oh what the heck, that is why I'm here, marry her and off and then off to some exotic locale, and what about you and Debbie, as the two sat so that Jack may eat. As Kate goes off on a tirade about how Debbie and her had broken it off, then it was back on, on and off relationship, as Jack tuned it out, enough so, it allowed Kate to get up and leave. Jack finished his three plates, picked up his platter, and deposited them, and went up to explore the hospital, first door on the right was that of Doctor Annie Herndon, Jack paused to knock, but decided against it, and continued on, till he saw a very familiar face, that of Sara's mother, who gave him a great big embrace, the two hugged it out for her to say, "You're a welcome sight, Sara said that you were coming in today, so how has everything?"

"Everything is good, just doing some relax time, till I'm called back up."

"Called back up what does that mean?"

"Oh you know when the government needs my services."

"Yes, in that way."

The two locked arms and strolled the corridor hoping to meet another family member with no avail, so she escorted Jack out to his car, and waved goodbye, as Jack was eager to get away from her, he fired up the Camaro, backed up and sped out onto the highway, he was heading towards the boat docks. When he changed his mind, as Sara knew the way, he exited went underneath the over pass, and went back into the city, she was driving, as Jack watched over the huge freightliners, at the port of Mobile, she exited, at the mall he drove a short ways to the state park, he turned in, to see a sea of people, the crab shack was overloaded, lines going every which way, he slowed and again parked in handicap, checking his plates were still locked in, next to his building, he got out to see the magnificent looking boat, the Parthian Stranger, beautifully painted white with blue trim, a familiar face paused, then hopped down and came racing towards Jack, like he was going to embrace him but pulled up anxiously, to say, "Wow your back, how is everything?"

"Oh just fine, what's going on here?"

"Were swamped, every day we go out, and in the middle of the gulf, the coast guard, boards up and takes the criminals from us, and don't worry you get full credit for the captures, it is brilliant."

"How many go out at a time?"

"Oh fifty or so, but we have been running this the last two weeks, and we have netted over 700+"

"That's nice, so who has been helping you?"

"Well first off Sara's brother Tim, then there is Mike, and then a guy name Jimmy."

"What do we know about him?"

"Oh don't worry about him, he is secret service all the way, his job and only job is to keep Samantha safe, wherever she goes he is right there, as for us were here to support you and carry out whatever order you have."

"And what about Sara, who watches her?"

"Principally it is either Mike or I, but during the day, like right now, it's Jimmy."

"He in there now?"

"Yeah, but if you go in he will come out."

"What do you mean?"

"Just that, you're the number one, so he has been instructed to fall back while your present."

"Really."

"Yeah, Miss Curtis gave him explicated rules, oh and one more thing, the dock on the harbor is finished, when do you want to move over there?"

"I don't know I just got here, can I go in, is the password the same?"

"Yes and no, all you have to do is use your voice command and it will unlock."

"Will do captain, said Jack, stepping up to the side door, to say, "Open please"

"Yes mister cash, the door unlocked and opened, and Jack went in. Jack was met with waves of love, embraces high and low, the ever smiling Samantha clinged to him, and pulling him towards her, while Sara fell back to allow the couple there moment. Jimmy was trying to get by, and slipped into the surveillance room, and shut the door. Samantha held his face with her hands, a beaming smile, she said, "You saved my life again."

"Who's that?"

"Well because of who you are, the right doctors found the rupture and repaired it, you know that they have a medical ship that follows your every move?"

"No I didn't know that, really."

"Yeah it was really first class, everything they did was as if I were the first lady, and she even visited me, she looked around, to say, "I want you to meet Jimmy he is my guardian, now and for the rest of my life, hold on, all I have to do is push this button, and just like that he appeared, standing very rigid, and with a blank stare on his face, for Sam to say, "Jimmy, this is my husband Jack, Jack cash."

He nodded, and Jack said, "Thank you for protecting my wife."

"Sir, it is my honor, thank you for doing what you do."

"Alright, what have you two been up too?"

They both tried to talk at once, then Sam took the lead, to say, "As of this point we have 842, criminals caught, and the great thing is that no violence has ever been spilled, Mark will take them out into the international waters, and the Coast Guard meets with them, boards them and takes them all in custody, Mark come back with a boat load of fish and crabs, we actually supply next door with crabs every day."

"it was a permit thing, said Sara, but I made one phone call to Mitzi and all was taken care of, we can catch unlimited number of coastal crabs, and lobsters as we wish, but there not as good as those flown in from Maine."

"How do you know all of this?"

"Well John senior and junior, have given us ten pounds of lobster for every one hundred pounds of crabs we give them, and they are so good."

The doorbell rang, and in walked a couple. Laughing and giggling, as Sara went to help them, while Samantha guided Jack back to his office, whereas Jack held the door opened to her, she wheeled herself in, and Jack followed, and shut the door, while Jimmy guarded the door.

Jack knelt down on his knees as she held his hands, smiled to say,

"I have some bad news for you?"

"What is it honey?"

She began to cry, to say, in between sobs, to say, "We can no longer have sex."

"Whoa wait what, why, what do you mean?"

"well actually its intercourse, you're just so big, and you literally tear me apart."

"I'm sorry, as he held her, he said, what about other things?"

"That just it, nothing I can't do a thing, and its tearing me up inside."

"That's alright, we will manage, getting up, to leave, for her to say, "Wait where are you going?"

"Outside to see if the guys need any help?"

"We were still talking?"

"Oh right, you were saying?"

"Nothing, go outside and be with your friends."

Jack left the door open as he side swiped, past Jimmy, to hear his phone go off, Jack pulled it out to see it was from Lisa, he answered it.

"Jack I have good news for you, all of your wives will be here at the end of the week."

Jack paused. To think about it, then responded, by saying, "Sure that would be great, how will all that happen?"

"They will be flying in tomorrow, in quarantined, then driven to your new house on the hill?", is that right?"

"Yes, that will be fine." Jack thought about it then realized it was for the best, he closed up his phone, to see a happy couple, commented on how this would be fun, Jack waved them out as Mark who was the captain met them, the girl had a smug look on her face, to say, "So who will be the captain, looking around the room at Jack then to the littler Mark, then in the distance, she saw Mike.

"It's me Ma'am" said Mark.

"Alright just you, then that will be alright?"

"I could ask my partner to come along if you like?", are you needing some special needs?"

"No, just you will do, you see it's my first time fishing and I want the best you have."

"Then it's me", spoke up Jack, putting away his phone, to focus on her."

She looked him up and down, then said, "Alright you'll do, then it will be just you right?"

"Me and him, he is the Captain, and I'm the fisherman."

The girl looked at the guy she was with, then back at Jack to say, "Sure mister, you and the little guy, I'll see you both at one sharp", they left for Mark to say, "Hey since when was I the shortest?"

"Since when that girl stood easily a foot taller, don't worry about it, she is just a client, get the manifest, and let me see it."

Smiling Sara delivers it to him, to say, "Nice to see that your back, so when is the wedding everyone is dying to know?"

'In due time, looks like business is booming."

"Yeah, Mark is going, out twice a day, and we have had a few repeat customers."

Jack looked over the manifest, to announce you have three on this trip, the suppose girl, her boyfriend and her mother. Mark are you getting supplies?"

"Yes, Sara and I"

"Alright, I'll see you both later."

Jack left them to exit the side door, seeing the girl and boy get into a nice car. They waited for the very large mom, to get into the back seat, Jack watched as they drove past him, each had a sinister look on their faces, as the girl smiled, then waved, as the car sped off.

Jack went over to his boat, where two handlers were working, then entered, to see that it was really polished up, neat and tidy, a new looking crane, a pair of jet skis, a rescue boat, he went inside, through the galley, and up the stairs, he turned the corner, to see a wooden door, secured with a huge lock, and a sign painted on a plaque, that read,

"Do not try to enter this room, it's off limits to everyone."

Turning the lock up, he placed his phone next to it, a number sequence was formed, and Jack punched it in, it opened, he slid it off, and opened the two slide doors, they went inward, to expose a room, a king size bed, a thick comforter, lots of pillows, two end stands, and surround windows, lighting above, Jack took a seat on the bed, and closed the door, only to feel deja vue as he felt like he was back in his plane, except, one thing was different, the lighting came down, to show a wide range of guns and weapons, grenades and smoke devices.

Jack put it back up, to secure it, to see off to his right a cylinder, and in it was his trusty bat, and what looked like a steel bar.

For Jack to say, "That should come in handy."

He laid back on the mattress, and fell fast asleep.

The rocking of the boat, awoke Jack. He looked over to his right and then to his left, knowing the boat was moving. He sat up, got his bearings, then stood. In an instant Jack opened the doors, and went out to see Mark at the helm, who he waved to say, "Boss, what a surprise, I thought you went home."

"Nope, just here resting on my boat, so what's up?"

"Well, the three who chartered the boat turned into five."

"Did you call the harbor master?" asked Jack looking at the manifest.

"I tried, seems like the sat phone is dead".

"And your personal?"

"It's strange, it seems like its blocked", hands the phone to Jack, who, places a call, to Lisa, it failed, and hands it back to Mark, to pull out his phone, a key swipe, it was immediate hook up, to hear, "Yes Jack, we have interference on your end, were tracking the cause, do you need back up?"

The connection was lost, Jack slide the phone shut, checked his wrist watch, his gun, was intact. And said to himself, "No."

Jack went out onto the bridge, behind the cabin, to the second deck. He checked over the jet skis, then his boat, and finally, his crane to hear, "Hey old man, what are you doing, come down at once", Jack turned to see the young man already had a jump on him, a gun out stretched, pointed at him, he was motioning to Jack to get down, the boy called out, "Momma we have a stowaway."

The heavy set, chain-smoking woman said, where you been at boy?, hiding?"

"Nope, said Jack down now beside them, with his hands up.

"Momma we need to shoot this one."

"Hush up Jacob, go get your sister Gabrielle, I may have a job for her."

"Oh come on momma, how come she has all the fun?"

"Because she is older."

Jacob left only to hear, "Gaab-rielle. Momma wants you."

Jack still was with his hands up, thinking about the options, all the while looking at this heavy set girl, taking another big drag on her cigarette, and for her to move her head back and forth, till, she saw Gabrielle, was presence, to say, "Where's your brother?"

"He said he was going to show the captain, where to go, what are you doing with the fisherman?"

"He is all yours, treat him nice."

"Oh goody", she said as she grasped Jack's arm, and pulled him along, as she said to herself, "You and I are going to have lots of fun."

Jack was willing and went along with it, till she got to the door, and a horrific smell came out, and the fun and games were over, as she had pulled a little gun on him, and said, Over to the wall, inside he went to see several goats were slaughtered, and some little guy, smoking a cigarette, with long knives in his hands, to say, "Mister your next" blood was everywhere, some girl was his assistant, to say, "I have one more but she pooped on me."

Jack knew this was really weird, to say, 'Put down the knives, as he pulled out his weapon."

"Whoa mister, no one pulls a gun out on me, and comes at Jack, who in one swoop, shot and canoed the boys head, as his head exploded, and fell to a lump, only to hear, "Shoot, shoot, kill him dead", screamed the girl who was crying, Gabrielle was stunned but waved her gun, Jack turned the gun on her, to say, "Put down your weapon, or I'll canoe your head, in that instant Jack felt something, as his head absorbed the blow from a frying pan, he fell forward, dropping his weapon and went out cold, and landed onto their already dead friend.

"Come on Jacob pick up the weapon and lets finish him off."

She shot at Jack, and again, when Jacob bent over, and put his hand on Jack's gun, and in that instant pointed at Jack, only to short circuit, and falls forward as he was dead, she was mad and infuriated, she empties her gun into Jack's back. Then tosses it aside, only to see the stunned Lily just standing there, as she went over to see her brother his eyes blew out of their sockets, and one hand was burned, the attraction of the gun, drew her in, as the butt turned colors, she went in, picked it up, to show it off like a trophy, till she felt the clamp, on her right hand then in that instant, she too expired, and simply fell to the floor dead. Lily runs off.

Jack comes too, gets up, to shake out the cob webs, and for all the bullets to fall off his back, looks around and see his gun, and goes and pries it from the girls warm hand, and he is on the move, out onto the deck instantly he sees a huge cargo ship, bearing down on them, its front is split open, as Jack is up the steps into the wheelhouse, he sees Mark, to say, "Can you steer around it?"

"Nope, were being pulled in".

"Then allow it to happen, I'll be on deck, looking out at the Mama waving or doing something, and just like that the boat was swallowed up, as the massive tanker, easily took them, as darkness came upon them, there was shaking and then a voice over an intercom said, "Drop your weapons our men will board our new vessel, shut down your engines and just like that the wheel house was flooded with men.

Jack holstered, and put his hands up, as did Mark. Then came a man with a beard who said, "Fear nothing, we don't care about you, all we want is the boat."

"What do you want with the boat?"

"That's easy, we will take to the middle east and sell them for 20 million dollars."

"You're not fraid of getting caught", asked Jack.

"Nope, we have been stopped before, and where you're at is supposed to be oil."

Jack just looks at Mark, who the two, line up, as they see the mother, being consoled, as they were led out, down the stairs, to hear, "This is quite a boat, too bad you didn't have rockets on this thing, Mister Cash."

A side door opened, in the background the woman began to hysterically screaming something about revenge, just as Mark went first, he was tossed into the water, Jack looked around, to hear, "Don't try anything and even if you do find us at some later time, we have diplomatic immunity", as Jack was shoved in the back, he took the water head first, as that super tanker was really going fast, he surfaced to see the vessel was going out of sight, as he laid on his back treading water, next to Mark, who said, "Do you have any idea, where were at?"

"Calm down, conserver your energy, lie on your back."

Jack pulls out his phone, and first sees on the GPS, where they were at, and then text that position to 911, and send, he then makes a call to Lisa, she answers, to say, "Jack are you alright?"

"Yeah, were fine, Mark and I, were in the water, my boat has been taken by pirates."

"I'll have a plane drop a inflate raft, and a boat at your area in one hour, or less, any idea what or who?"

"No, it was way too fast."

"Not to worry, we have a tracking device, on it."

Just then a plane over head, dropped a package, it sailed down, as the two watched its descent.

"Jack, you O Kay?"

"Yeah", said Jack as he slide the phone shut, put it away, and swam with Mark to the floating package. Mark was on it first, went to the top, un hooked the parachutes, and threw them away with a buoy attached, and then undid the straps, as Jack was on the crate, helping he said, "If my memory serves me right, there are two, here, let's slide this one off, see right there is the handle, pull that."

Mark held the strap and then pulled the handle, instantly the boat filled and into the ocean, as it went clunk, with a splash, Jack jumped into it, while Mark held onto the rest, to say, "What about the rest?"

"Leave it, its provisions, let's go get our boat."

Mark jumped in and held the tie down rope, while, Jack was in the back, sliding the out board engine around, and turning it into the water, he clicked the handle, it came to life, and the two hundred horse power engine roared to life, as Jack was on his phone, receiving word the vessel had been captured, and was being detained, awaiting his arrival, meanwhile, the boats were being extracted, all the men captured and one woman and one jumped into the water."

Jack sent a confirmation text, and turned the handle, and off the boat went, the ride was rough, but consistent an hour later they could see a convention of huge ships, compared to them, and there was their boat, anchored off, Jack steered towards that, to come along the side, he motioned Mark, in, he jumped off, to see people in Haz Mat suits. Meanwhile Jack steered the tiny raft, towards the big cargo ship, it was open, as he drove right on in, UN people were all over the place, they steadied the raft long enough for Jack to shut it down, and hop out, he was dry compared to earlier, he also some familiar faces, Mike and Devlin, he said, "The gangs all here?"

"Nope just the ones that matter", said Lisa behind him.

Jack turned to see the red headed beauty, was in no mood she said, "He claimed diplomatic immunity, what an idiot, are you safe, doing alright, she said lovingly, while caressing his arms.

"Fine, so what's this about a tracking device, is there one on me?"

"No, why should we?"

"No."

"Then what is your worry, you have your boat back and all is safe, just one more thing I like about you, you're always finding trouble, and I'm here to rescue you."

"Miss Curtis, oh Hi mister cash, nice to see that you're alright," said the U N agent.

"Thanks Roberta, and look it's your partner Genie, what do you have."

"Information, turns out, the whole back end is filled with young girls."

"How many are you talking about?"

"Oh give or take five hundred or so."

"Why not an accurate number?" asked Lisa, walking with them.

"Because, we just found them on both sides of the engine compartments, and their telling me this on my ear piece."

Lisa led the group back, through a room past the cargo hold, that resembled a casino, cash counting machines were going off from the DEA, along with bags of white powder, Genie led the way back, to say, "The UN is giving Jack the credit, as they opened a door, to see vehicles of all shapes and sizes, even a helicopter, although mini, Jack was looking at, as the UN went to a door in the wall, opened it, other UN workers filled the room, as young girls, emerged unhappy, and some demanded revenge, for being kidnapped, all the while Jack and Lisa watched, some were angry, other extremely apologetic, and even crying, as more UN workers came to their aid.

"You know this is quite a find."

"All in a day's work" said Jack, said Jack wandering over to lend some assistance, but soon realized, he was being ignored, so he went back to being by Lisa, for her to say, "You're not cut out for the caring and compassion, so what's next for you?"

"Oh I don't know, I guess work off the top 500 most wanted criminals, and you?"

"Well from the looks of all of this, we will be here cleaning all of this up, but come with me and let's talk about how you want all this."

Lisa led Jack around, then through another door way, and they went up, for her to say, "Where do you want all this to go to?"

"First I'm fine with our deal, the rest, give to the girls being held."

"That's mighty generous of you."

"Money isn't everything, although there was some of those girls that might make good agents, nah, it was wish full thinking." said Jack.

"We just got word the captain and five of his staff escaped", said Lisa.

"That's alright I imagine our path's will cross at some point, there is my ride." said Jack making his way over to his boat, and down a side ladle, within jumping distance, he leapt and off went his boat, looking at too familiar faces, Mike and Devlin.

Lisa waved off in the distance.

Jack made it back to the dock in one piece, they shored up the lines, as Jack jumped off, it was onto the Crab shack, he thought. There was his tailor, Cassandra, who steered him, to his side entrance, as she spoke,

"You have become quite famous, since we last met, I was wondering if you could do me a favor?"

Jack looks at her, from up to down, not saying a word.

"No I don't mean that, but maybe, that is if you want that?'

"Nah, what do you have?" asked Jack being nice and polite.

Showing him a picture she says, "This is a picture of my sister, her name is Kelly Hill."

Jack pulls out his phone, and types her name in, to see that she had been reported missing two days ago, for Jack to say, "She's not on the boat, then says, do you have any leads?"

She hands him a another picture, to say, "I think its my husband, his name is Markus D'Orios, I hope you can find her, and here is 20,000 cash, she hands to him, to add, "This is a down payment, you get the rest when you locate her." She passes right by him, and then is gone. Jack walks in, the door, to see Sara and Sam, hard at work, answering the phones, for Sara to stop what she was doing to say, "So is she your newest client."

"Perhaps, depends on.

Jack stopped in mid-sentence to see the manifest sheet for tomorrow order only to hear, "It's a good thing you have your boat, maybe this time you'll keep better care of it." said Sara, comically to him.

Jack went past them to his office, and closed the door.

CH 15

Operation Criminal catch & Carly

Its Saturday morning, about zero five o'clock, Jack, Sara and Samantha were all on the boat, Jack had Mike build a special ramp over the raised surfaces of the lower deck, so Sam could come and go as she pleased, the crew consisted of Mark the designated boat skipper, he had made several runs already, one with criminals and another was with paying customers, he knew the difference like night and day, his first mate and the ship's maintenance man was Mike, then there was Trixie and Mitzi, who didn't want to miss out on all the action, were the event coordinators and hostess, Jack was the Captain, Devlin his first mate and Sara was the ship's chef, with his day fishing permits in place he could fish anything past fifty miles from shore, in the open gulf waters.

Mark did some research and discovered a place that had a field common for lobster, so they had a pot ready to drop for that, on board was also Tim, Sara's brother, Mark the skipper and Sara got re-acquainted over a run to the store where Mark bought enough for fifty, or it lasted for the weekend, of going out and coming back. Sara came back and told Jack, "that was the most food she had ever seen at one time and the bill was over five thousand dollars."

Jack reminded her for each criminal he catches he will make a million, and they have twenty four scheduled, among those are some killers, thieves and drug dealers, some were pretty untouchable like a media mogul and a hip hop artist, who is taking a day out of his concert schedule to be with them today, Jack had an early pep talk to the team, to remind them, that there are six of them, that means at least three apiece and Jack said he would get the rest, he also said don't be deceived by who they are now, as it is only a cover, and this is serious.

Both Mitzi and Trixie wore virtually nothing while they stood the railing, as cars came in all shapes and sizes. Each guest, had others as each member checked in, only the actual criminal was invited, and accepted after Samantha and Sara did some research and constant calling did they find these, some were very deceptive while others just answered the phone, some were poor, and asked for some traveling money while a third of them were rich and wanted to bring their families, Jack turned those away, but compiled a list of those new leads, of the two hundreds most wanted, Jack knew or already captured over fifty, and now he knows where fifty more is and with this twenty four, should make a serious dent in the loose criminals roaming the southeast. Lisa told Jack that there are five North American zones.

Of that, there are five international zones making up ten International Bounty Hunters and Jack is one of ten, but of them only two super class spy's, in addition, because he missed his graduation, he was receiving his award via Lisa in the coming days.

One by one criminals, would check in under their alias's, as Jack watched from the bridge, he positioned himself near the crane, sitting at the right wing skippers station, sizing up all these people, seeing their sizes, shapes and personalities, as each specially designed bus unloaded more criminals, he dubbed this Saturdays adventure Operation Criminal Catch. Jack was writing in a column when he looked up to see a gorgeous blonde-haired woman.

"That one is Carly the homemaker," said Sara, and ads, "She just answered the phone and wanted to know if we would give her traveling money."

"It's a good thing you did" said Jack getting up, he zoomed down the ladder, on to the deck, he turned to see Sara smiling, then waited till she boarded, Carly looked up to see Jack, who was dressed in a full blue outfit, as was the rest of his team, with the exception of the Mitzi and Trixie, who modified theirs, to show off more skin.

"Hi you must be the captain"

"Yes I am, Ma'am" said Jack and ads, "I'm at your service."

"That's nice, can you show me where all be staying, it's been a while since I've been on a boat."

"Come follow me," said Jack, and then ads, "We have had to do major renovation to accompany such large crowds, like installing these tables for lunch and dinner, the berthing compartments, has now thirty bunks," as they made their way down to that level, to say, "In the front part is the berthing cabins, bathrooms are here in the middle, three on each side, if you want to take a shower, turn the water on to coat your body, then turn it off, soap up, using a wash cloth and one of those buckets, then rinse off, if the water is on more than one minute you'll be seeing me, behind us is the scuba section, the back opens up to allow the divers a chance to snorkel, some of the best fishing grounds has some of the most exquisite viewing centers in the world, so any questions?"

"No, not that I can think of, maybe, I will take a shower, can you help me out, what did you say I had to do?"

"Take only the clothes you're going to change into, then pick up a small plastic bag for dirty clothes, also I do have a laundry facility on board as well, you'll have to check on those hours, then pick up a white bucket, from inside this closet, and on this shelf is a wash cloth, there are boxes of fresh soap, if you use one put it in a plastic bag and write your name on it, the shampoo and other stuff is shared, so when you use it, please put it back, any questions?"

"I'm sorry; can you tell me how to use this shower?"

"Don't worry about it, don't be sorry, it's pretty easy, once you first do it", said Jack as he opened a door up to show her a toilet, across from that a sink and mirror, and then a clear sheet shower curtain, with this single dial, turn it to the left, and down quickly, stand under the lukewarm, water, till you coat yourself with water, and then fill up your small bucket with water, then turn it off, wash up then rinse off using the wash rag."

"Do you wanna stay, to help me?"

"You'll be fine," said Jack, stepping out and then closing the door, he waited a moment, to hear the toilet flush, then the shower turned on; he tempted a look in, but heard she turned it off, and then he left.

Jack reached the deck to see it was overloaded with all kinds of people and one unexpected reality, the Hip-hop mogul had an entourage of ten with him, as Jack met up with the crew for a confertation, to say, "Only you, I'm afraid."

"No, no, no that ain't working homey; where I go my crew goes with 'em."

"Well not on this trip" said Jack.

"Come on homey, I ain't flown five hundred miles to leave my boys hanging like that your know dog."

"We have no bunks for them; they'd have to sleep on the deck."

"That's cool man, we be chillin over here."

Jack watched as the two large bodyguards flanked Jazzy J while the others from tall to short, went over to one of the eight tables of six and commandeered one, sending others away, Jack took note of that, to size up his crew, he motioned to Mitzi, Sara was at the rail to come over.

"Yes Jack" she said in a professional manner.

"Looks like Jazzy J has brought his posse with him, can you get their real names, use their I D's and then cross reference them with Samantha's computer, to see if they are worth saving or throwing over board" said Jack.

"You're a bad, bad man but I like it, oh by the way, Mark says that the water from the shower is running, can you check on it, and maybe your homemaker is waiting for her man to rescue her."

"I'll go see what she is up to."

"Be careful she is only a lonely homemaker," said Sara with a smile.

Jack laughs, then hurriedly goes down stairs, into the berthing area only to hear huffing and panting sounds, Jack open the door to see Carly under the shower and some guy drilling her from behind, through the clear shower curtain to say, "Please turn off the water."

"Get out of here man!" said the guy.

Jack didn't take to kindly to been disrespected, so he went forward, slid the curtain open, turned the water off, first, then grabbed the guy's long hair, and pulled the guy off of her, and out the door to hear, "But he is my husband."

"What is your name boy?" said Jack.

"Mister you're hurting me, my name is Jamie, Jamie Curtis, I got a ticket in the mail too, hold on."

Jack stopped at the stairs, to turn to look at the nude couple, to say, "What did you say?"

"Listen man, I got a call from some girl, and told me about this trip, so when I received a ticket in the mail, well I just came, then I saw my ex-wife, just between you and me, she is some lonely chick who invited me in."

"I don't care about that, all I care about is the water running."

"Sorry man, it won't happen again."

"I guess it's a big misunderstanding then, let me introduce myself I'm the Captain of the here boat, and you may stay with your wife, in the girls designed cabin, with her" said Jack, then ads, "If you ever dis-respect me again I'll throw you overboard, and quit using all the fresh water" said Jack, thinking it would have been nice to view her body regardless if she is crazy or not."

Jack gets to the deck to see the ever flirtatious Trixie, report all passengers accounted for plus thirteen extras."

"Fine lets cast off, can you help Sara, bring out breakfast?"

The horn sounded twice, as Mark powered up the twin two thousand horsepower engines, a whiney noise went off as the bilge pumps began to work pumping out semi fresh water, from its hull, along with waste water after it went through a carbon treatment, Jack stood at the rail to watch the sun break behind him leaving his shadow, past the inlet he jet skied, through the breakwaters, and into the open harbor, where individual breakfast was served, in the wheel house Mark piloted the boat across from him was Samantha, taking her first boat ride since the accident, and on the computer, checking all the manifest names and E-mailing them to Lisa, as directed by Jack to confirm each one.

Sara, Mitzi and Trixie served all thirty seven passengers, Sara even made a special plate for Jack, who she presented to him personally.

"Here Mister Captain, try my home cooking."

"Thanks, you made this all yourself?"

"Yep, I have been visiting my grandmother, and she has taught me."

"I didn't know you had the time to visit her, I'm learning something new about you every day." said Jack.

"Well Mister busy man, if you stay in the city longer than two weeks, I'll take you up to meet her."

"Promises promises." said Jack.

Sara left to assist others while Jack ate, quickly finishing off his plate, Jack watched those who would get sea sick and those who would have their legs under them, then he saw the Curtis couple, emerging up from below, refreshed, Jack threw away his plate in a trash bag receptacle and climbed the stairs to the auxiliary deck, where the two fixed boats lie with a set of jet skis, and a newly black Navy Seal's raft was. Jack stood above the patrons, to say, "Listen up, could I get everyone's attention please, thank you, I'm the Captain of this boat, now I make the rules and expect each and every one of you to obey them, failure to do so, and I will put you under cabin arrest for the duration of this trip, first off I want to mention the crew, in the wheel house is the skipper, name Mark, at no time while on this boat, will you go in or up on any of the third and fourth decks, you will mainly be on this deck, the lounge, where there is TV / satellite, books, magazines to read, the galley, only if asked to help the cook is Sara, right over there, then you have the two hostess who can never stay in uniform, the blonde is Trixie and the brunette is Mitzi, the first mate is Devlin she is positioned on the bow.

"Which for some of you is the front of the boat, and most of you will be fishing along the stern or rear of the boat, down below one level is the berthing compartments, there are six rooms with six bunks each for a total of 36 beds, and six bathrooms, there is two front cabins, one is the crews, on your level and on the galley level is the captain's quarters, in the stern is the engines and scuba room, which are both off limits, that is where you will find the maintenance man name Mike, then there is one other boy on board he is the purser, if you need something, just ask him and his name is Tim, just a few rules to go over", as Jack continued to talk, Mobile was getting smaller by the minute, Jack talk of respecting others, and of the shower and water consumption, and of seasickness and personal behavior, some expectations and instead of a single day, it would be stretch out till Sunday, much to everyone's happiness, but Jack told them of a migrating school of marlin off the starboard side, which everyone went and saw, an event that they would not ever forget. He finished and went into the wheelhouse to see Mark.

"Were on that heading, if you want to take the wheel you need to steer into the wind so that we can drop those four lobster and crab pots, I'll go get Mike and Tim and Devlin said she would help."

"Fine, put it on autopilot for the moment" said Jack, who went over to see a cheery eyed Samantha, who had tears dried to her face, Jack hands her a Kleenex.

"Thanks" she said and smiles at him.

"How's the view."

"I just love it, thanks for building a special seat here for me; I was thinking shall we tell Sara about the mattress and in there, that's where we will be sleeping tonight, right?"

"Yeah the three of us," said Jack.

"I feel like, I need to say something," said Sam.

"If you must then do so, but I don't think she cares, besides I think see knows, how I saved your life and how you are having our child."

"Yes your right, this is so beautiful, can we do this more often, I just love the ocean, you know I was thinking, when I die, can you cremate my body and put me out to sea, will you do that for me?"

"Is it in your will" asked Jack "and besides let's not talk about this now", said Jack to hear a noise behind him, he turned to see, a hot brunette, say, "Jack the kids are getting crazy, they want to fish." Mitzi, smiled at Jack waiting an answer, for Jack to say; "Tell them that were launching a few lobster and crab pots, have them go up onto the rail line and watch," said Jack who bent over to kiss Sam on the cheek whereas she turned her head and the two kissed on the lips, he broke apart to hear her say, "Wait till tonight, Sara and I have something special planned for you."

"I can hardly wait," said Jack.

Jack went to the wheel of the boat, took it off autopilot, and while watching the monitor, Jack turned into the wind, and watched as the first pot went in followed by the boats red marking buoy, as with the three others, another monitor showed the passengers cheering, once all four were dropped a good four miles had passed, Jack straighten out the boat, to hear, "I'd like to try that," asked Samantha.

"Sure let me help you out" said Jack as he reset the autopilot and went to her, picked her up and easily carried her to the skippers seat, he placed her feet in the resting pegs, while she adjusted her seat position with her two hands.

"Now this is our planned heading, the auto pilot will get us there, all you need to do is watch for other boats and any large debris, watch this" he said, as he turned the wheel to the right, to steer the boat, then ads, "let go of the wheel and the boat will automatically reposition itself to the heading we programmed it for, you can use all of these monitors to see the starboard, which is the right side and port which is the left, bow is the front and stern is the rear, over here is the throttle control, you have to manually move it to the position noted on this screen, lastly this is an intercom switch, click it to this position to page any one of us."

"This seem easy to do."

"Great, you feel that way, it takes years of knowledge and experience to be a skipper, so sit back relax, and observe the calm seas, and have fun, any problems, call me."

"Wait, are you leaving?"

"You'll do fine; I need to check on the crew and the passengers."

Jack took a few steps back to observe her.

Jack noticed that she was apprehensive at first, but then began to adjust the monitors, and she even slid the side window open a bit, she turned to look for him, only to see he was gone.

Jack moved through the Galley to see Sara, cleaning up the pots and pans, to say, "Hey you, that was an incredible meal."

"Thanks to you, wait, there will be more for the rest of your life, so what is my Captain up to, who's piloting the boat?"

"Sam is."

"She is, how did she get that job?"

"She asked, and you can join her, if you like?"

"Like, I'd love to."

"Then when you're finished, go on up and I will have Mark teach you."

"Yeah whatever, I was hoping the Captain would personally instruct me if you know what I mean?"

"Maybe, I will later," said Jack as the two stood a distance apart from one another, to hear, "Am I interrupting something," said a young woman's voice.

Jack turned to face her, to say, "You're not interrupting us, she is just the cook, and what can I do for you?"

"Well it's kind of private, can we go somewhere we can talk."

"Sure, follow me I'll take you to my quarters."

Jack leads her past the stairs up into a large room, and holds the door open while she passes him by to take a seat on the bed, Jack closes and locks the door, to say, "The room is sound proof, what would you like to say."

"Listen first off, I want to say I'm sorry, I had no idea my ex was going to be on this boat, come on what's the chances, he lives on the east coast and I'm on the west, if I knew he was going to be here I would have never accepted the offer as tempting as it was, do you know how they choose people?"

"Not really I'm just the boat's owner, and they charter from me, but imagine they use a new person's list for that area, I don't know, why?" asked Jack.

"Never mind that, that is why I asked you to stay, when I was going to take a shower, I thought I recognized him, but wasn't sure, until he was came in and assaulted me, you see I just melt in his arms, so I allowed him to take me, you gotta help me, and I feel like jumping off this boat."

"Don't do that, let me talk with him."

"Talking will do no good, he is a criminal, he will lie, cheat and steal to get what he wants, you gotta believe me, and look I'll even be your personal sex slave, that's all I have to offer."

Jack looked at her up and down, thinking he has been here before with Sara, her desperation and distrust, to say, "You won't owe me anything I will personally handle your problem."

She rushed him and held on to him feeling for his manhood, she began to stroke it.

"Enough already," said Jack pulling her away, to say, "Let's go, get out on board and do some fishing, I'll take care of your husband."

"Ex-husband, thank you, you won't regret it I will still live up to my deal," said Carly.

Jack followed Carly out, Jack went by her and went up to the galley, to see Sara beginning with Lunch, for her to say, "Looks like you're busy."

"Oh yaw, that's an understatement, if I weren't doing this who would?" asked Jack.

"I believe that would be Trixie and Mitzi's department" said Sara. Jack left her to walk out onto the deck, to see a line of men all with poles in their hands, some were sitting in fixed chairs and others were up on the railing, the boat had slowed to allow this to occur, but Jack noticed that there were some men missing, so Jack went forward, up to the second deck and walked around the starboard side, to come out in the front or bow of the boat, some bare feet was dangling above his head, he continued forward, to where the front anchors were, to stand on their box, turned backwards to see what all the fuss was, four girls laid out nude and well exposed, Jack himself was looking at the four girls who were all criminals of some kind, then Carly showed up, she too showed no shame and stripped down to nothing, while Jack watched.

She smiled at him, then waved for him to come over to them.

Jack stepped off the box, to walk back down the narrow plank, to a side entrance into the Galley, there he saw who he was looking for, Devlin.

She was munching on a cookie, while talking with the three other agents, to say, "Do you have a moment, to talk?"

"Yeah sure" as she followed Jack, into his cabin.

Jack let her in ,then closed the door and began to say," Which's one on your radar?"

"Well I'm getting close to Jazzy J, Hector and Nick, also it's a toss up for Myles."

"Well can you pay extra attention to Jamie Curtis."

"Who's that, don't really know who that one is, we got a lot on the boat already.

"He's the one who is attached to . . . ."

"Oh, you mean her, why don't you handle her, she seems to like you."

"Not the girl, Jaime is a guy, a little smaller than Timmy, he has been hanging out with that former football player, and I think his name is Marco."

"Oh that guy, yeah sure, I'll do it."

"You're going to have to keep him away from her" said Jack as he noticed Devlin getting closer, to say "What are you doing?"

"Coming on to my boss, is that alright with you?"

"Not really, did you forget what you did to me in the shower."

"Oh come on, that was just having some fun, I promise I will make it up to you."

"At who's expense" said Jack as he pushed her back, onto the bed she fell, then onto the floor, she began to laugh, Jack hesitated then moved forward and used his foot, kicked her in the face, she sprawled down onto her back knocked out, Jack stood over her to say, "You don't mess with me bitch."

Jack turned and left the room, to go up onto the bridge, to see Sam was still piloting the boat and Mark was directly behind her, teaching her all about piloting, to say, "How are we doing?"

"Fine, Mark has been showing me how to do this, and it is fun."

"She's a quick learner."

"Alright, I'll leave you too alone."

"No, you don't have to, I'd like you to be here" said Sam pleading with Jack, who says, "Not now, I'm looking for our two hostess's seen them?"

"No," they both said, as Jack flew down the stairs, past the Galley where you could smell fresh baked breads, and he saw Sara bent over, the stove, he continued on. Jack was back out onto the lower deck where all the tables were at, he continued to the stern, seeing all the men with those rods, in their hands, casting into the water, Jack himself, picked up a rod, only to see Timmy and Mike were the helpers, making sure everyone was having a good time, Jack looked up to wheelhouse, the door was open, to see Mark decided to let Sam continue at the wheel, while he took over operating the crane, in an instant someone yelled, "I got one."

Jack turned to see a guy was on the deck, straining hard, the rod was bent over, and he was slowly turning in the line, while Mike stood behind him to support him, it was like everyone was watching him, as minutes past, he continued on, until finally, Mike saw he was less straining and went to the rail with a grappling hook, and in one swinging motion, Mike stabbed the Marlin in the side, of the mouth and in one motion he waved and Mark raised the crane and Mike placed the hook on the line, and up came a fish, who was trashing around, as it came out of the water, onto the deck. Mike used a club and strikes it on top of the head, several times to put it out of its misery, then it was raised up, and the hunter posed with the hung fish, as Timmy took the picture.

Mike swung the fish to a holding place, where he said to Marco the former football player, "Save it or eat it?"

"Eat it I guess."

Mike gut it and cleaned it up, took it off the hook, cleaned and carved up and carried it to, an awaiting box full of ice, and slid it in, only to hear,

"Are we having it for lunch?" asked Marco.

"Sure, I don't know for sure," said Mike.

"Yeah that sounds good, is that for everyone?" asked Jack.

"Sure I'll share it with everyone."

With that Mike pulled it out and laid it on a fish cutting table and cut it into seventy one inch pieces, to form steaks, as Timmy holds a huge platter, Mike places, it half and half on the plate, to say,

"Take it over and place it on ice, in the walk in, and tell Sara what's for lunch."

Just as that occurred a frenzy of activity at the rail was happening.

One by one, guys were catching fish all kinds were being brought on board, even a sand shark, medium size, but was let go as it was a soon to be a mother, Jack himself went to the rail with pole in hand, and threw out the line with a herring attached, he let out the line for a few minutes, then decided to stop the roll out, and pulled back on the rod and took a seat, and placed the end of the rod into the metal hole on the seat, and sat back to hear;

"Jaime, Jaime is that you" said Devlin

Jack looked over to see the guy was fishing on the end, when Devlin made her presence known, other guys cleared out to let the beauty in between Jack and Jaime, to say "I'd been looking all over for you, what have you been up too?"

"What do you want?" he said.

"Well I'm here to tell you to stay away from your ex-wife."

"By who's authority."

"Mine," said Jack looking over at him.

"Well then who will fulfill, my every need then?"

Before Devlin could answer, Jack said, "You can have Devlin, to do that."

"Jack" she said.

"Think of it as a service, to this boat and to our community."

"Jack."

"Alright, I'll accept that only in one condition, you please me now," said Jaime looking at her then Jack, for Jack to say, "I guess your customer is waiting."

"Shut up," she said to Jack and paused to see Jaime leave the rail to say, "I'll be waiting in my cabin."

She watched as he walked backwards waving to her, only for her to turn to Jack to say, "Why are you doing this to me?" she said quietly to Jack.

"Why are you doing this, I thought I taught you a lesson, in the cabin."

"What do you mean, I fell of the bed, and was knocked out."

"Well what I meant was, stick to you targets, give'm what they want, and let's see how all this goes, then I'll decide if we can make up."

"Are you doing this because of what I did to you in the shower."

"You're getting warmer."

"Come on let me make it up to you," she said reaching for his manhood.

"Too late for me, but maybe for Jaime, he seems like a nice guy."

"Shut up," said Devlin with a smug on her face. And ads,

"What will this prove."

"That you can take an order, without first thinking about it."

"Then what do I have to do, fuck him" she said adamantly.

"Nothing, it's up to you, to do what you want to that guy", he pulls her in close to say, "If it were me, I'd hit him on the head and zip tie him up, but there is a slight problem with that."

"What's that?" she said.

"The whole bathroom thing, so you need to deal with him for a least today, and confront your fears, and just go in there and keep an eye on him, play like it's me."

She moved in close to him, as he saw that and moved away to see she was ready to kiss him to say, "Stop that , I know what you're are thinking and I won't be any part of it, just get going" said Jack.

Devlin slowly left him, realizing her charms use to work on powerful men, was now fading her, and now that he has called her out, she was obligated to go through with it, regardless if she liked that person or not, she knows she owed him, and at some point she will pay him back" she thought as she made her way inside, and down the stairs to catch a quick glimpse of Carly and Jaime talking, to briefly hear, "Listen, get close to Jack, use your charms whatever, then put this gun on him, we will then take over the boat, she heard him say to her, "Don't worry about me, Jack has assigned a real beauty to watch me, as a matter of-factly she should be coming down her, now, so scatter along, my dear," Devlin watched as the two kissed passionately as Devlin hid under the stair well, thinking, "I'll let Jack, find out the hard way" thinks Devlin as she watched as Carly climbed the stairs and Jaime to close the door, Devlin made her move, went up to the door and knocked.

The door opened to a nude man to say, "Yes, it's about time, what took you so long" as he backed up to let her in, she held the door knob in one hand as she faced him, to say, "You're not ready for me."

"Don't flatter yourself toots, I've had better, you're somewhat a bitch."

"How do you figure."

"Well let's see, you work for the Captain, and he asked you to keep me happy, and all you could do was wine about it, and second you need to start undressing or I will."

"Will do what."

"Start screaming, that you have a gun and is trying to kill me."

"Dream on, punk."

He started to scream, and yelling and saying all kinds of bad words at her.

"Hush up, alright" said Devlin, as she closed the door.

"Good begin to strip, I'm waiting.

Devlin delivered a right cross of a heavy punch that connected under Jaime's chin, sending him into the wall, thus knocking him out, she shook out her hand as it still stung, she turned to open the door, when an arm came from behind and started to choke her and a voice say, "Is that all you got bitch, my Grandma hits harder than that."

She squirmed around as she was trying to force his arm off her neck, but as the oxygen was decreasing as was her will and just like that she was out.

Meanwhile on the deck, Jack was practicing casting and reeling when a hand touched his, he looked over at her, it was Carly, wearing a blue jumpsuit, with a white tank top and no bra, as her breasts were literally busting out, for Jack to say, "In a minute or two, you're going to be exposed."

"Oh that, she moves her shirt to flash Jack, to say, "Do you like?"

"I've seen them before."

"We haven't," said a crowd of guys who were forming around Jack, egging her on to remove the rest, finally after a minute or so she unbuttoned the straps and lifted her shirt up to show them both, as several men rushed her when a loud voice said, "Leave my wife alone."

The others and Jack turned to see a naked man standing on the second deck waving a gun.

Carly, pulled her shirt down and pulled her gun out, to point it at Jack.

"Now I want you all to undress, or I will shoot you."

"BANG" off went the sound of a pistol.

The guy fell on to the deck, holding his thigh, where he got shot, Jack watched as Jazzy J put his gun away, and tell his bodyguards to carry him off the deck.

"Can you put him into my cabin, and handcuff him behind his back" said Jack as he felt a tug on his chair, he whipped around suddenly, brushing up against Carly, causing her to lose her grip on the gun, and out of her hand it went, hit the rail and into the ocean, Jack got on the rod and began to wheel it in, Carly leaned up against the rail and watched Jack reel in a small Marlin.

Jack looked over at her with a smile as she had a frown on her face, and her hands at her chest.

"Don't fear, Jaime is down and you have nothing to worry about, that was your gun, sorry about that."

"I'm sure you are," she said, as she stormed off.

"What's up with her?" asked Mike.

"She wanted sex, and I refused her."

"Really, that piece of ass wanted you."

"Yeah, also she is has a deadly side, she likes to play with guns."

"So do I, so I helped the two body guards with Jaime, he is secure in your cabin, I put plastic down, over the bed and floors, are we starting to assemble the pieces" asked Mike.

"Yeah, sure go ahead, I wanted to wait till tomorrow afternoon, after fishing, but I don't see why you can't put her to bed, listen that one is very dangerous, and be careful."

"Don't worry boss" said Mike as he went after Carly.

Jack took his small marlin, over to the sink, he cleaned his fish, cut it into steaks and placed it on a platter, then went inside, to pass them off to Sara, cooking away, then down the stairs, to the girls cabin to see a door part way open, Jack entered to see Devlin asleep on the bed, decided to move on, up the stairs to the wheel house, he sneaks up on Sam only to turn her to see Mark.

"Where's Sam?

"She wanted to lie down, so I put her into the bridge's cabin, as to see that your Captain's cabin is filling up with unwanted guests," said Mark.

"What's your plan now?" asked Jack.

"Whatever you want, we could turnaround and pick up those lobster and crab pots."

"Yeah let's do that and let's have a big celebration, and tomorrow morning let's start the capture."

"What capture," said a voice behind him.

"The capture of fish, of course," said Jack turning to see a huge guy, "Didn't you know that the best time to fish is early morning, were going to post an early morning call, and for those who want to sleep in, then we who want to fish will cast out some red herring bait, and wait for the fun to begin."

"Sounds good, you can count me in, hey I was going to ask you Captain, who's the hottie cook, what's her story, is she single and available?"

Jack looked him over up and down to say simply, "You're not her type", then walked past the guy and down to the galley, to see Sara, to say, "You have another secret admirer."

"What's this one like?"

"He is the football player, his name is Marco's"

"Ooh he is cute," she said sarcastically, hoping to get Jack jealous.

"I'm cute," said Marco's.

Jack looks at the pair, then shakes his head and heads out to find Mike, while Sara and Marco talk, as Sara says, "What do you have in mind, big boy."

"Well I thought you and I could hookup."

"That might be a possibility, however I'm a lesbian, and men don't interest me that much, but I am open to something new, do you think you could help me out, and I will ask my friend if she wants to join us later tonight."

"Sure, which one is her."

"The tall blonde, her name is Devlin, as my name is Sara."

"Alright Sara, my name is Marco, and I'm at your service."

"First off I need the grills taken out and all scraped clean, you know how to do that?"

"Yeah, we used to tailgate all the time."

"Then next, pull out the coolers, set up the ice, and arrange . . . ."

"Whoa, way too much information, too quickly" said Marco.

"Listen mister, if you think you're going to bed me, you're going to have to work at it, and it begins with taking orders, write it down if you have to," said a stern Sara.

"Good now, take the bags of charcoal out and spread it into one grill make a pyramid of coals, use some lighter fluid and get them going, then come get me, and I will show you how to cook."

"Can I get a kiss first, to show you're even willing to play."

"We don't kiss men, first and second if you don't trust my word, then it is up to you, I told you I would consider it, if you help me with my job, I will feel some obligation to fulfill your needs, now go along, the celebration is near."

Jack posted a clipboard, with a sign-up sheet, to say, "Listen up, anyone who wishes to fish in the early morning, write your name down, all others we will let sleep, we need you all to stop fishing, were going to turn the boat around, and pick up the pots we dropped, if anyone wants to help out with the cooking, see Sara, in the galley."

Jack made his way to the rail, to see the last fisherman reel in, to say, "How has been your luck?"

Most said, "We ain't caught a thing."

"That's why they call it fishing," said Jack rounding everyone up, as he saw Mark outside on the flying bridge, signaling to turn as Jack went to the rail, when Mike and a brightly smiling Timmy joined, Jack looked at him to say, "What have you been up to?"

"Oh just hanging around."

"How's Rosie?" said Mike with a smile.

"Enough, you two," said Jack who saw the buoy as the boat came to a stop, threw out the line, captured the buoy line and pulled it to a line wheel that did the job and pulled up the pot, to a hook which, Jack attached to the boom crane, and out came the pot, loaded with treasures, they opened it up on a portable table, using a measure device, they kept the males large enough and threw back the females and smaller males, several fish were in that pot, they did the same thing through the rest of the four pots, assembling a feast fit for a king, other men helped with the cleaning and washing, Marco was steady as the grill supervisor, four large pots were placed on the grills parts of fish and other crustaceans were added.

All the fishes were cut into fish steaks and seasoned, Sara and five others were at work, both Mitzi and Trixie, set up the portable tables, with plates, silverware, and napkins, all plastic of course, and then for each table, they put a container of juice, milk or tea.

Jack went and brought back a case of champagne, the party was in full swing, as the champagne was served, the team each had a place to sit, except Samantha who manned the wheel to take first watch, Jack sat by Carly, who escaped Mike, earlier, on one side, Sara on the other, Marco, Timmy, his new friend Rosie, said she was a model, meanwhile Devlin awoke from her unconscious nap, to begin taking pictures of the partiers, both Mark and Mike had their specific groups as did Trixie and Mitzi.

Jack loved the seafood stew, with the rich tomato broth, the crab legs were small but tasty when dipped in butter, also new to him was this thing called an artichoke, which Sara showed him how to eat, by pulling off the leaves and dipping them in butter, she said it was a family tradition, some placed ketchup in the butter, other mayonnaise, they also had corn on the cob, smeared with peanut butter and small red potatoes, but the treat was these loaves of brown bread, Jack took three pieces it was so good, freshly warm and with butter, the dinner died down, as some helped with the cleanup, music was turned up so some could continue to party and dance, Jack informed the crew to begin assembling and capture their marks, based on those who wanted to sleep in, and those who wanted to fish tomorrow morning, as the plan was to get in around six in the morning, we will let them fish for the two hours till we get back, as the night wore on, the girls did their jobs and rounded up the late night partiers mostly men, by zip tying their hands behind their backs and using duct tape to their mouth's, as the night turned into morning, Jack and Mike worked together to take out the major threats leaving the biggest one alone, and letting them fish, that was Jazzy J, with part of his crew down, only four remained, to include him and the guy who wanted to D J the night away, his name was Jerome, and the firefighter Nicky, and the real mean one Myles, they left the girls alone, as they all slept, Mitzi and Trixie were on Myles, Sara and Devlin were with Marco, Mark was with Sam in the wheel house. Timmy watched out in the Captain's quarters as eighteen or so lay on the plastic on the floor, with the door open, so if he needed help, Mark could come.

The boat sped forward, as the three fished, catching some huge fish, both Jack and Mike helped them with their fish.

Meanwhile, Marco was all over Sara, and Devlin, who led him back to the empty crews cabin and the big bed in the middle, Devlin was hot over this guy, who was hot for Sara, who was, off to the side just watching.

"What's her problem?" said Marco, in-between kisses from Devlin.

"She likes to tie people up, then she knows it's safe to play," said Devlin.

"I'm cool with that," said Marco.

"Sara, he said he is cool with you tying him up."

Sara moved towards them with a zip tie harness, as Devlin continued to kiss Marco , Sara secured both wrists behind his back, and then cranked them down hard, and in one motion pulled him off the bed, and wrapped duct tape around his head, then tossed him to the floor, the two walked out, to find another victim.

Mike went around to sweep the bow of the boat, finding no one, the day's early light was beginning to lighten up the deck, he watched as Jack was conversing with Jazzy J , while Trixie was able to led Mister Myles away, by exposing her one breast, Sara and Devlin were getting chummy with each other as they lead the firefighter away from the rail, all was quiet on the deck, as Jazzy J caught another fish, he reeled it in to have both Jack and Mike help him, he knew something was up, and pulled out his gun and pointed it at Jack to say, "What's going on here, where is my boys at?"

"What is going on here" as he slumps forward, letting his gun go and collapsing on to the deck.

Jack looks at the body to see a tranquilizer dart on the side of his neck, looking up he sees, Mark, holding the gun, to say, "I thought you could use some help."

"Boy, you sure do take some risks," said Mike.

"Life is full of risks, if you don't have fun while you're doing it, why do it at all, that's why I put on these big shows, so the criminals, can have fun, then there arrested, instead of using brute force, like him" said Jack pointing up to the D J now slumped over the disc machine fast asleep.

"I guess he did it to himself, why don't you zip tie him and get him to the front, I'll get this fish on ice" said Jack to Mike.

Jack felt a little at ease as he scooped some ice on the table to keep the fish cool, he packed it inside, and out, looking up he saw, all four girls, reporting,

"All criminals are safe and sound," said Trixie.

"That was fun, I really like that Jack" said Sara with a smile.

Both Devlin and Mitzi agreed, to say, "It was fun and safe."

"Alright, thank you girls, if you could help me, let's cleanup before we get there, in Mobile, then according to my text, we have another mission, so as soon as we hit the dock, we are taking a small trip to Montgomery, I guess the mob we hit, earlier is now assembling and Lisa wants us to defuse it, so get your stuff ready."

He watches as the three girls leave, then faces Sara to say, "And you have a wedding to plan."

The two kissed passionately, only to break up when Mike said, "Were three miles out and Lisa and her men are awaiting the arrival, also."

Sara leaves them to go into the Galley.

"Lisa called to say the FBI is under fire and need our help ASAP she said she has two helicopters available to us, who and what do you need" asked Mark at the wheelhouse door.

"I'll go talk with her, round up your stuff," said Jack heading up to the wheelhouse, to see that the boat was into the harbor, a mass of police and secret agents with lights on their cars and siren is off, as the boat, eased in its speed. Jack was on the phone to Lisa to tell her that they had an emergency; with Samantha, as she lied on the Bridge deck's bed to say, "I want to put you into the hospital, you're not doing well", with that Jack was on the phone to the hospital, dispatcher, who said it would be there before the boat landed.

"O, Kay" she said, sadly as the two kissed

Loud voices, engulfed the boat as it docked, then agents swarmed the vessel, Jack helped her get dressed, then lifted her up, and carried her down the stairs through the galley, past the four girls when one of them said, "I wish that were me."

The others said, "Hush."

Jack walked over the flat bridge onto the dock, past some agents to the awaiting ambulance, he laid her down onto the gurney, when an agent came up to say, "We will take good care of her and your baby" Jack recognized his face it was Brian the armorer.

"I've been promoted thanks to you."

Jack watched as the doors closed and the ambulance tore out, Jack went back to the dock to supervise the individual arrests, while his team assembled on the dock, Lisa said, "Your next mission is in Montgomery, on the outskirts, is a big family get together, where numerous agents are being killed, at the airport I've secured two Blackhawk's, also your ground team is on one and the other is for your crew, who are you taking?"

"All of them if they want."

Five unanimous "yeses" were said.

"Take my SUV to the airport," she said.

CH 16

The Governor & Supermodel

J ack slid in the front passenger seat across from Ramon, and off they went, to the airport, where the ride was quiet, they entered a special gate called classified, and down a street to where two Blackhawk helicopters awaiting on a landing pad, guarded by a security force, the sight of their vehicle sent them to assembly, as Ramon, the driver came to a halt, Jack and the team got out.

A captain greeted Jack with his hand out, the two-shook hands to say, "General, Jack cash, my name is Larson, or Lars for short, I'm up from Biloxi and I'm at your command, I have rockets and a 20 mm gun on the front, however you want to go."

"What about my team," asked Jack.

"There on the other gunship, you can sit up front with me to direct how you want them employed, are you ready to go Sir", said Lars.

"Yes" said Jack, watching the black SUV sped off, and seeing his team climb aboard the other chopper, as he slid into his seat next to the pilot, and buckled up as the pilot hands him a helmet, to put on, then inserts the phone jack in, to hear, "Can you hear me now, you can use this switch to talk with those in the back, and hit this switch to communicate with the other Helios, ready to go, Sir?"

"Yes", said Jack.

They quickly lifted off, and climbed even more quickly than that, Jack could feel the pull it was having on him, as the black hawk easily covered ground quickly.

"Sir, we should be there in about forty five minutes or so, and I will take you to the house under siege as instructed, and then fly off to a undisclosed location till I get your call.

"In front of you is a sat-com phone, already set to my frequency, in the event of an emergency turn it to thirty one, I will monitor both frequencies, my call sign is Victor one, your Victor two, and so forth, the other helicopter is whiskey one, so if you need close air support, you can call either one of us.", instead of that Jack took out his phone, to show the pilot, and dialed up his frequency, on his phone, to say, "Can you hear me now?"

"Yes", said the pilot.

"Do you know anything about this incident?", asked Jack.

"Nah, Sir, they didn't tell me only thing it was similar to Waco, and they want to send you in to negotiate the release of the Governor of our state."

"You don't say, the Governor is being held, what about the National Guard?"

"Not, when the best is available, your their answer for this situation, Sir."

Looking back over at his team, then made a decision to say, "Listen up team, I want Mark and Mike as one group and Mitzi and Trixie as another, I'll take Devlin with me", said Jack as he motioned to his other members as he spoke, into the intercom, then turned his attention to the front as the helicopter way on the path down, to the empty field. They landed and Jack hopped out. Jack walked together towards a group of tractor-trailers where a single lone figure stood, with a phone in his hand, literally yelling at the top of his lungs.

Jack stopped to wait for the rest of his team, waiting to see if the person sees them, as the team exit is the helicopter, and caught up with Jack to see the guy approach them to say, "Are you, Lisa's finest?"

Jack looked around, and then looked at the guy to say, "Who fucked this up? Yeah were here to clean up this mess, who are you?"

"The names Richard, I'm the secret service agent."

"Who let this happen, what is your role in all of this?" asked Jack.

"What's that?" said Richard looking down at Jack's watch.

"Do you have somewhere you have to be?" asked Jack.

"No" said Richard looking around anxiously.

"Did they express any demands?"

"Yes, but that time has passed."

"How long ago" asked Jack.

"Oh about a five minutes ago, said Richard looking dejected.

"Cheer up, were here to help you out, Mitt's and Trick's, check out the trailer and see what is going on, Mike and Mark check out the perimeter and if there is a way in, if there is one take it, remember shoot to wound, Devlin find a sniper weapon, and find a high spot for some cover." Jack turns to Richard, to say, "Earlier I asked you what is your current situation, like how many agents are already inside?"

"Well as of right now, four, I mean three, one police officer and two F B I agents."

"Great who else?"

"Well the captors took the Governor and his girlfriend and another girl is inside who happens to be a super model."

"How do you know she is a super model?"

"She is the one, I was suppose to be with, when the mob stormed the resort, and I was out back waiting for her to be with her, when, gun fire rang out, then it became quiet."

"So you're the only secret service person here for her?"

"Yeah as far as they know."

"Are you saying you're here and they don't know it?"

"That's about right."

Jack steps back to shake his head, to say, "Where is the Governor's support people?"

"That's just it, there all dead."

Jack looks around then says, "I get it now, you're here to support the governor, but your real purpose is for you to be with the model."

"Yes, alright, your right, if you can get me out of this situation."

"Don't bother, I'll go in and rescue them and give you a call when it is over, so don't send in any one else". "You got that," said Jack as he began to walk the dirt non-paved road, as he passed the berm to show a huge house with a sign that read "Welcome to the Country bed & breakfast."

Shots rang out as where he stood shots peppered his position.

Jack was on the move towards the house as the shots were getting louder and with more intensity. Jack hugged the wall, feeling the lead fly past, out of the corner of his eye he saw Devlin climbing up a tree, a big Staley oak, she climbed with the rifle slung on her back as she got up to about twenty feet or so, then set in a position and began to lay suppressive fire for Jack, who moved swiftly to the front door., weapon out, he pushed the door open, dove, rolled and hit a guy in the leg, which in turn dropped his weapon, in his ear he heard from Mark, who said, "Jack we found a way in through the garage, and into the basement, were taking heavy fire" a bunch of crackling noises, Jack was on the move, he pulled a girl free, as he drove his foot into a guy's mouth, who held onto her hand.

"Find something to tie this one up," then remembering on his jacket he had some zip ties, which he pulled on two zipped both wrists together behind his back and slid him into a closet, only to see the girl return with a long cord.

"Will this do?"

"Yeah, why don't you go hid in that closet till it is all over?"

"No I'm not mister, I'm staying with you" said the girl.

"Suit yourself, stay close."

She moved in, close to him, as he handed her the cord back, the two came to stairs going up and going down.

"Over here is an elevator."

"Get over here, do you want to get yourself killed."

"Why," said the girl.

"Because once it opens, everyone will be firing at you."

"Do you want to know a secret?"

"What's that?"

"Between the basement and this floor is a secret room."

"Really how do you know that?"

"That's where me and my lover would go, you know to have sex, it . . . ."

"Enough, can you show me this room?"

"Yeah, sure follow me," said the girl.

All the gunfire was down stairs as it seemed, Jack followed the girl, down the hallway, to a chute she pulled open, then went in, Jack hesitated for a moment, but knew all about the secret passages of the laundry chute, then pulled down the chute, he put his gun away and slowly inched in only to hear gunfire behind him so he dove in, thinking he would be on top of her he was falling, only to catch himself on a ladder step, he propped his falling body up, he rested, his legs on the wall, as he used his hands to walk down as a hand was shone from a lighted area, he made his way down, and actually had to reach in to a huge room, the girl helped him reach a bar, in which to pull himself up in as his back scrapped the edge of the opening, as he pulled himself in, the girl slid the panel shut and locked it down, as Jack, released and stepped down on a crate, immediately Jack knew where he was.

"What do you think?"

"Nice for a secure room."

"It's there, the armory" said the girl.

"I can see that, what it really was, is a panic room," said Jack.

"What do you mean by that?"

"Well your right we are safe, you see that door, is sealed shut, so like when the power was cut off, it sealed it shut, the only way out, looks like the way we came in, Jack looked around, on a far wall was several smoked filled glass doors, he tried the first one.

"We use these as our playrooms."

"Who's we and what do you do here?" Jack looked in to see behind a glass wall, laid a nude woman.

"I've never seen her before," said the girl.

"What are you doing here anyway?"

"I and my friend, Monica are the houses maids, sex slaves you name it."

"I get the point," said Jack, as he went to the next room, he opened the door to see a nude blonde woman tied up.

"That's Monica, let's open up the door."

Jack was pushed in, lost his balance, hit the mat as the other girl landed on him as the door shut. She was on top of him, for Jack to say, "If I knew you wanted to be on top of me, I'd like to know your name."

"She slid over on her side to say, "My names Jen, and you are?"

"Jack , Jack Cash", as she rolled up to say, "Can you untie my girlfriend, while I get the key."

Jen stepped aside to retrieve a key from inside the wall and unlock the thick glass door.

A wave of perfumy scent was released, Jack was untying the girl. Jen helped Monica down, then went past Jack, only to collapse onto a thick mat, as Jack stared at the two of them.

"Will you go find her a blanket, or some clothes, or some food?"

Jack moved to check the next room, it was empty, then a door, he opened it, it led to a set of stairs, before Jack went down he called back, "Hey, do you know where this goes to?"

From behind Jack could feel a push, the walls were slick and he lost control and did everything to brace for the fall, but hit head first and for the first time in his life, he was dreaming, or so it seemed, he could feel his body on top of his head, as he wanted to open up his eyes, he couldn't see anything, his eyes were glassed over, as the door he was leaning up against, opened, instantly a group of people surrounded him, he could hear one say, "Is he the one who was in that room next to yours, look he has a gun I bet he is with the governor, let's help him up, Jack could see them, his head hurt, he was shaking out the cob webs.

"You're bleeding from your ear," said one.

"We are trapped in here, it seems like it is a safe room", said an older gentleman.

"The door is so heavy," said another.

Jack walked around a bit, he was trying to get his bearings, trapped in a room with twelve or so people, mostly couples, from young to old, Jack tried the door, from which he fell down to, and went back up, he tried the door, it opened to see the girls were gone, but the trap panel was open, Jack went up to the grab bar only to see a guy, he then yanked him in and down hard onto the concrete floor, as all the others stormed the room.

"Look guns."

"Hold it, be careful, stay here and when I get the door open, I'll let you out" said Jack as this time he went feet first inside the chute, barely fitting, he turned to face the rungs and worked his way down, to the next panel, which was secure, Jack climbed back up and then used his foot to kick it, it did not budge. A sound of heavy gunfire, went through the panel as Jack pulled up his foot, to hear, "We got a mouse in the laundry chute."

"Go get em."

Jack didn't wait around he quickly went all the way up past the first place to a bright light.

Jack, poked his head out to see the two girls he left behind and into a maids room."

"What took you so long?"

"You're the one who pushed me remember?"

"It wasn't me."

"It was me," said a voice, from behind Monica.

A little man emerged with a gun in hand to say, "Climb out of there and drop your weapon."

"You want me to climb out or drop my weapon."

"Toss your weapon over to me."

"Alright if you insist."

Jack pulls his weapon, tosses it at the little guy who see the bright white pearl base, the little guy bends down, and tries to pick it up only to lock on to it, then collapse and expire on the gun.

A trail of smoke emitted from him.

"Is he dead?" said one of the girls.

"I'm afraid so", said Jack retrieving his weapon, he looked down at a small weapon, to fit the little guys hand, he picked it up, then begin to laugh, he tossed it down, stepped on it and said, "A toy gun, clever", "Stay here girls."

Jack went to room to room to find no one, also he had discovered that the back house was divided by the wall that the chute was on, and that it was open and roomy, unlike the small rooms on the other side, he concluded that all the action was at the bed and breakfast, and not this house, so he called Devlin and Mitzi and Trixie in, through the back door, to devise a plan, with both maids help, Mitzi told Jack that there was a young girl named Cody undercover and two FBI agents named Elliott and Bramwell.

Monica agreed to lead the three girls to the basement while the other girl, Jen was going to help, she was going with Jack, back into the laundry chute, as both Mike and Mark reported that the Gov. is being held in the basement, by at least ten Mafia guys, and that they have a hostage themselves the wife of the top dog, his name is Rico, that named sounded familiar to Jack, Jack was on the move with the girl named Jen. She was leading the way, back up to their room and the laundry chute. Jack watched as Jen went first, showing him how it was done, Jack waited for a moment then did the same.

Jack went in feet first, holding onto the metal rungs and made his way down, only to hear voices, it sounded like they were coming up, just as Jen made it back into that secret room, Jack looked down to see a bald man with a gun, in an instant Jack used his foot, to kick the man in the head, sending him and the gun down, where he collected up another man to fall a bit further, till Jack heard a thump. Jack continued past Jen down to the very end, to see the chute had stopped, Jack estimated the drop to be another ten feet, he looked down below him to see the two criminals, laid out, with visible blood, pools for each, carefully Jack made it to the last rung, he saw he had a short drop and let go, he landed safely, a quick glance he saw a free standing ladder in the corner, if he wanted to go back up, he checked both bodies to confirm they were dead, he was on the move, the door was open, as he went through, down a hallway, where there were rooms, Jack tried the first room, the door was locked, he looked inside to see a man and a woman, Jack went the other direction to try another door, which led to a parking garage, along the north wall was a wood pile,

"Where there is wood there must be an axe," said Jack to himself.

Jack did a quick search, to finally find what he was looking for. A tool kit which he choose a doubled headed sledgehammer, went back inside, and swung down with all of his mite, to strike a blow, driving that knob off, then he turned and swung at the door, to hear a thud sound, opening up the door, a slight bit, enough to hear.

"Are we rescued," said the woman as Jack pushes the door open to say, "Who do we have here?"

"My name is Hallie and this is our Governor, Mister Spencer."

"Come on let's go" said Jack leading them to the laundry room, where Jack pulls up the ladder and says, "Now climb up the rungs to an opening, and you will see a girl named Jen, get in, and close the hatch, any more people I find, I will send them to you, to know who they are, they those that I send to you will knock four times then pause then once then five times, you got that?"

"Yeah, but what about you, they will kill you", said the Governor.

"Nah, don't worry about me, I'm here to save everyone" said Jack.

"What is your name son?"

"Name is Jack Cash sir," said Jack.

"Now get going, up the ladder", said Jack holding it so that first the girl then the Governor, as he made it off the ladder, Jack, picked up his sledgehammer and went back to work, this time to another room opposite, the smashed door and did the same thing, as the door opened stood a half-naked girl, a topless red head, as Jack said, "Come on let's go, I don't have all day."

She walked past him walking proudly, as Jack said, "Climb up the ladder, about twenty rungs up knock on the panel with four knocks, pause and then only once then five more, now go", said Jack. Jack was pointing with his hammer outstretched, he moved to the next room, tried the door, it to was locked , he took a swing , then a side swing then the door opened a bit, he pushed it open to see a nude blonde woman on the bed, with her arms and feet tied apart, Jack moved in to assist her, pulling out a knife, Jack cut her loose, first her ankles then to her wrists, she awoke, throwing punches and kicking Jack as he sat on the edge of the bed, she was crying, as Jack fended himself with his arm to say, "I'm not here to hurt you, I'm here to set you free."

She calmed down, but continued to cry, so Jack went in, to sit by her, she leaned into him and put her arm around him as he did her, and said, "No one will ever hurt you ever again."

She spoke in broken and hurt full felt language to say, "I was raped by almost everyone."

She kept repeating that repeatedly, as Jack heard voices, to say, "What the hell."

A younger man stood at the door, looking in, with a gun drawn on Jack. So Jack pulled his weapon and fired, he fell forward dead before he hit the ground, next at the door was an older looking man, who was trying to find his weapon, only to feel nothing as he fell back as Jack canoed his forehead.

Jack leapt up and began to strip the younger man and tossed the clothing to the girl one piece at a time, she was messed up, really bad, Jack dragged the bodies into the room, and closed the door, then he helped her get dressed, first the shirt, then the lower part of her body showed signs that she had been bleeding, so Jack pulled off the young man's white underwear, and helped her put them on, they were loose, then he put on the pants for her, then a pair of socks, looking at her feet it looked like they would fit, so he tried young man's shoes on they were loose but did somewhat fit, Jack led her, out of the room, and down into the laundry room.

Jack then motioned for her, to say, "I want you to climb this ladder and up a ways to a panel."

She was still crying and talking incoherently, realizing this , Jack helped her up the ladder, by being right behind her, then up the rungs, they barely fit the two of them together, as Jack took it one step at a time, the sounds had died down, only her crying could be heard, Jack made it up to the panel, did the secret knock, the panel slid open, to see the Gov., helping out, Jack guided her in as the Gov. helped her out, inside. The Gov. looked around to see that Jack, was already gone. Jack was on the move, thinking, "This all ends now."

Jack flew down the rungs, pulling out his weapon, Jack dropped down to see a long haired freak and a bearded man, both dropped, as Jack shot each of the both of them, and decided to see what all the action was, he turned the corner, to see a longhaired person so Jack fired and that person went down, two short haired men turned as Jack fired, hitting one in the gut, one in the head, and other behind them in the temple, to yell, "Cease fire", "Cease fire" said

Jack, looking over the barricade to see Mark and Mike and two other men, taking a seat to relax as Jack said, "It is over, all clear, let's get the cleanup crews, in here."

Jack walked around to see all the lead in the walls and the bodies of the total dead.

Both F B I agents introduced themselves as Bramwell and Elliott, they said that they had a undercover operative named Cody West."

Jack tells them that they are all safe, upstairs, and walks out of the parking garage, to the waiting cavalry, Lisa emerges with Richard, for Jack to say, "Our work is done here you can send everyone in."

"What about you", asked Lisa, talking with Jack.

"It's time for a little vacation."

"Did you want to go to the spa?"

"Yeah, me and the whole team, and anyone else that likes to go, too", said Jack.

"Come walk with me, I need to tell you that Samantha is stable now, but she has contracted a dangerous disease, so we have her in an isolation chamber, until the infectious disease has been isolated, as soon as we can we will bring her to the spa if you would like."

"I'd really like to see her."

"I'm afraid that is out of the question, just let us do our job, rest and relax, rest assured she will be taken care of," said Lisa patting him on the back.

Lisa then says, "About the other issue, your other wives are safe, at Guantanamo Bay, as with their family, but Carlos is missing and believed to be switching sides", said Lisa.

Jack looked around to see that his team was assembling outside all was accounted for, as Mark said, "What now boss."

"It's down time, we will be off for a couple of weeks," said Jack.

"What about us?" asked Mike?

"You can go home or go to the spa."

"If it's all the same to you, I'd like to go home," said Devlin.

"Fine whatever you want."

"As do I "said Mike, Mark says "Is it alright if I go with Mike?"

"We will go with you Boss, "said both Trixie and Mitzi. "As will I "said Jen, who was followed by Monica, to say, "Whatever."

Bramwell shows up to say, "She got away?"

"Who", said Jack?

"Her name is Angelica, she is Rico's daughter, is was the worse one, also while she is still loose Cody is in danger, so can you take her to your spa and keep an eye out for her?"

"Sure keep me informed", said Jack, watching as Cody had regained her feet, and was walking on her own, Jack turns to Lisa to say, "Can you have Sara brought up, if she wants to meet me."

"Sure Jack, it has been awhile since I've updated your cards, so at the spa, I'll bring you what we owe you and your new credit cards, by the look of it looks like your gonna have some fun, with five girls how do you do it?"

Lisa watched as both Jen and Monica wrapped their arms around Jack as the three walked followed by three girls, Mitzi and Trixie helping Cody along, into the chopper they all went, it started up and off it went.

Lisa continued to direct the cleanup, the weapons find and the cash vault, Richard came up to Lisa to say, "Where is Jack, I wanted to thank him for saving my girlfriend."

"Secure this man, and put him under arrest," said Lisa.

Lisa then ads, "He is gone, he did what you couldn't do", said Lisa with a smile, "Yes Jack I'll see you at the spa."

The End.